Love at First Flight

Love at First Flight

Love is in the Air Romance

Janine Amesta

TULE
PUBLISHING

Dedication

To my dad
Some of us need a Captain Picard in our lives and you were mine

Author Note

About two months before the release of my first book, my dad passed away. Love at First Flight is a book that allowed me to not only write through my continued grief but also celebrate a special relationship that can happen between a daughter and stepfather. While this process has been helpful for me personally, I understand if the topic can be difficult for others. Take care, as this book does deal with the sudden, unexpected loss of a parent due to a brain aneurysm and the grief that follows. There's also mention of parental abandonment and neglect, sisterly strife, injured animals, a wild crow acting out, and social media posts gone wrong. This book does have some adult language and open-door love scenes. Even though grief can put my characters in a dark spot at times, there will be moments of sunshine along the way. Rest assured, happiness is waiting for them in the end.

Prologue

FATE SOMETIMES HAD terrible timing.

In her twenty-nine years, Selah Moreno had found this to be true more times than not. How unfair it all was when Robert, her stepdad, used to tell her about how he'd dreamed of nothing more than becoming a commercial airline pilot, only to work his family's farm for most of his life instead. Sure, he could have run off, joined the Air Force, found any way to make it happen, but that wasn't the kind of man he was.

"A military way of life just wasn't for me, and besides, then I met you and your mom," he'd told her one time. A younger Selah decided then and there that a military life wasn't for her either. It wasn't until she was older did she realize Robert meeting her and her mom was one of those fated roadblocks keeping him from his dream, even if he'd never stated this directly. This roadblock was followed by more, first with the death of his father, which was soon followed by the death of his mother, resulting in Robert inheriting the Central Oregon alfalfa farm.

Despite having two of his own biological daughters with Selah's mother after marriage, he'd always made special time for her. Perhaps because, like her, he was also adopted and raised by a father who wasn't his biological one. They'd often take short car rides to the next town over to watch planes land and take off at the small Redmond airport. Sitting on the car hood while drinking blue raspberry slushies from 7-11, he'd wrap a big arm around her small, bony shoulders and blow her young mind with things he'd learn about the weather or flying. Such as when the sun warms the Earth's surface, it can create strong, unpredictable winds, so the best time to fly is early morning, at sunrise. This was what he considered to be the best, most peaceful time of the day, the golden hour.

He was a collector of weather gadgets, put-together model planes, was obsessed with shows like *Star Trek*, and would tell her about his plans to take aviation lessons. And because Selah loved the man so much, she'd come to love any topic he was interested in.

As a kid, she realized there were people who *should* have loved her but didn't. Her biological father, for example. Then there were people like Robert, who came into her and her mom's life when she was five years old and didn't have to love her, but he did, anyway. Selah was lucky because she'd been chosen when he didn't have to pick. And while they didn't share genes or physical similarities—she had a tanner complexion due to her Mexican-American heritage for one—she'd always felt included. Robert was her dad, and she was his daughter in every respect of the word. She was a Moreno.

Robert and Selah's shared love of the sky was something that connected them together. When he watched his favorite movie, *Galaxy Quest*, or episodes of *Star Trek*, there was Selah right beside him, resting her head on the worn arm of her mother's floral sofa, sharing a bowl of microwaved movie theater popcorn with him.

Finally, the day came when, after years and years of planning, Robert was going to take flight lessons at a small private airport in Prineville, a town not too far from their farm in Terrebonne. Selah had been ten at the time and was never more excited or proud. Her dad was doing it—he was going after his dream. He promised her when he'd put in enough flight hours, he'd take her on a special ride.

"You'll be my Number One," he told her.

"Like Commander Riker?"

"Yup, that's right."

Selah started teasingly referring to him as Captain Picard, referring to the famous officer from *Star Trek: The Next Generation*, which soon became Captain for short, much to the annoyance of her younger sisters. They didn't always understand their bond. They didn't know Selah had already planned on being a captain, too, just like their dad.

Except the special flight never happened because, as fate would have it, soon after completing his flight certification, he got a detached retina in his right eye. He had a medical procedure, so the vision returned in that eye, but not well enough to make being a commercial pilot a viable option anymore. So his piloting dreams floated out of reach once again.

"It'll be okay, Number One," he'd tell her. "We'll figure it out. We're going on that special flight together someday."

Amazingly, Robert did figure it out. He got certified, bought a secondhand hot-air balloon setup, and started High Desert Tours right on the farm. Her mother, Elena, bought him a leather bomber jacket. He wore it and a blue baseball hat with *Captain* embroidered across the front almost every day. "She's called *The Blue Wonder*. Hot-air balloons are like ships of the sky. It's good luck to name them," he'd proudly told his family.

When he'd go on a flight, he'd point to the sky and dorkily say in his best fake Captain Picard impression, "Engage." This elicited eye rolls from her sisters, but never failed to generate a chuckle from Selah. She found it especially funny since the balloon would gracefully float upwards at a rate not even close to warp speed.

Being a captain of a hot-air balloon may not have been what some people considered to be a "real pilot," but Robert and Selah knew differently. She was right there by his side to help and be his Number One. Eventually, Selah had saved enough from years of working at a local grocery store and attended the same aviation school as he had.

"Permission to come aboard, Captain," she said one morning after being part of the chase crew, helping to tether the basket, technically known as the gondola, upon landing and assisting passengers as they disembarked.

Her dad gave her his usual crooked smile, the one showing a chipped front tooth he'd never bothered getting fixed, the result of an old boyhood accident. "Permission granted, Number One."

She saddled the edge of the gondola while retrieving an email on her phone, displaying her final license acceptance. Selah then excitedly told him about a job interview with a transport airline company that promised to continue training her. She hoped to make enough money from this to eventually pay for commercial pilot flight school. It was a unique opportunity that had been brought to her attention by one of her flight instructors. There was a sparkle of tears in his eyes at this news, but then he grabbed her, pulling her into the basket, and wrapped her in a rough hug.

"Did you tell your mother?" The question was muffled, with his face pressed into her hair.

"Not yet. I'll talk to her after the interview. You know she's not going to be happy if I tell her I might be moving to Portland."

"Yeah, well, I don't blame her. I don't want you to leave either. But I'm proud of you, kid. I'm going to miss having my Number One around."

"You're going to be okay . . . you know, with the business?" Selah had always tried to help and learn about the business as much as she could between school and work. It helped that her father mostly booked flights early in the morning, the best time, after all. Still, she worried about her parents, with them growing older. Her sisters didn't necessarily pitch in as much as they should. Naomi was better than Hailey. The latter seemed to have gotten into a frame of mind that she was the designated princess of the family and didn't need to be responsible for anything.

"Sure. You know I can handle it. Besides, you're going to be a big-shot pilot soon. When they see how good you are, you'll be in the captain's chair before you know it."

Despite her initial excitement, she sniffled, because the reality of the situation was sinking in. She was possibly leaving, striking off on her own to create a different future, to be away from her family. Part of her wondered why she was doing it, and thought maybe she didn't want to leave. Unlike Hailey, she didn't have the confidence of thinking of herself as the greatest thing ever. Propping herself up alone was a little scary.

She resigned herself to the single sniffle while pressing her face into his strong shoulder, and allowed no other emotions to escape because pilots weren't supposed to cry.

"You're going to take me on that special flight soon, right?"

"Yeah, of course, Dad. I'm going to take you on *all* the special flights."

He gently patted her back. "Good. Did I tell you I'm getting a new envelope?" The envelope was the balloon portion of a hot-air balloon setup.

"What's wrong with *The Blue Wonder*?"

"Nothing. It's just time for a change, and it's blue."

"I thought you liked blue."

"I do, but during the summer, it doesn't really stand out when the sky is the same shade. This one is more colorful. You'll like it. You can help me name it. With this new envelope, I think business will pick up even more. We'll do even better than Soaring Over Oregon." His rivalry with the other hot-air balloon company had always been entertaining. It was fun to play along, as though there was a long and deep hatred for this other company located near Bend. All families should have an imaginary Hatfield and McCoy situation. It kept things interesting.

"They have nothing on you, Captain Picard," she said, giving him a lazy salute. "What's the new envelope look like?"

"Nope. Nice try. You're not going to get it out of me. You'll just have to wait and see when it comes." He then peppered her with advice in preparation for her Portland trip, such as getting her tire pressure checked and making sure her phone was fully charged and looking up weather conditions before traveling through the Mount Hood region. "You want to give yourself plenty of time to get there. No opportunity is worth rushing and risking your safety."

"I know," she said, already planning to get up early because, in their family, minus Hailey, it was already a habit to do so.

When the morning of her trip arrived, she'd gotten a little later start than she had hoped, but was more than halfway to Portland when her phone rang.

"Hello?" she answered on speaker phone.

"Selah, it's Elena." Her mother using her own name when calling her daughter should have been a sign something wasn't right. It struck Selah as odd, but before she could make a joke, her mother gasped a choked sob. "He's gone, mija," and then she rambled more sentences, a mixture of both Spanish and English.

"What? What do you mean?" There was a brief moment of panic, where her heart ascended into her throat, before Selah switched off each emotion. She shifted into calm piloting mode in order to understand what turbulent problem she was about to find herself flying through. "Mom? Mom. I need you to calm down. Take a breath and then tell me what's going on." Selah found a road turnout to pull onto.

Taking a long shuddering breath, Elena said, "He's gone.

7

Your dad died. I tried to wake him, but he wouldn't wake up. I don't know—What are we going to do now?" The question ended on a wail as sobs overtook her mother once again.

As close as Selah was with Robert, despite finding herself now entirely captainless, she didn't fall apart like her mother. Maybe something broke inside her. The sting of tears never crept past the barrier of her eyes, and she quickly blinked those away. "Okay, I'm coming over there. It's going to be a little bit because I'm currently on the road—"

"Where are you? I don't want you to get into an accident. Ay, mi roca. I can't take it if something happens to you too."

"I'm fine. I'm going to turn around. Did you call an ambulance this morning?" She asked while driving her car onto the opposite side of the highway once it was safe.

"Yes."

"Okay, good. That's good. Are Naomi and Hailey with you?"

"Yes."

"Okay, ask Naomi if she can call Aunt Becky." Her large extended family lived an hour away, but they were closer in distance than Selah at the moment. Both her Aunt Becky and Uncle José had calming spirits and could provide the strength her mother needed right now. "I think you would feel better if your sister and tío José were there while you waited for me. When I get there, we can all figure out what we need to do together. Okay?"

"Okay, but please be careful, mija. You'll be strong and steady like a rock, right?"

"I'm going to be careful. I'm coming, okay?"

"Okay."

Selah wouldn't go to her interview or any other interview after that. She realized her world had completely shifted then. A tear finally broke free and she angrily dashed it away with the sleeve of her shirt, feeling horrible and selfish to be angry at the universe for snatching away her and her dad's dream once again.

But she knew there wasn't any point to her anger.

It was just fate sometimes had terrible timing.

Chapter One

A year and a half later

"WHY MUST I lose everything?" Elena cried when Selah had confronted her in the High Desert Tours office trailer regarding the family budget.

Selah tapped a pen impatiently on her desk as she tried to keep the conversation from going off the rails, since her mother had been kind enough to bring her an iced coffee midway through her workday. "I'm not asking you to give up everything, Mom. I'm just asking you to not renew a magazine subscription that no one reads. This is about being practical, that's all."

"But it was your father's favorite!"

"I understand, but if he could say something right now, he'd probably tell us to not waste money renewing a subscription for *Pacific Northwest Fisherman.*"

This response elicited a gasp from Elena, as if Selah spoke sacrilege instead of the truth. While her father had enjoyed the sport and been an avid subscriber to the small magazine for as long as she could remember, he'd become more obsessed with ballooning than fishing after starting the business. It was beside the point, anyway, because they needed to cut money from wherever they could these days, and this was one of the easier decisions.

"Where the hell is Hailey?" Selah asked when the business line interrupted their conversation, ringing at the next desk over, the same one her youngest sister was supposed to occupy.

She'd swear to God, out of all the sisters, Hailey had the easiest job to maintain for their business, and yet she struggled the most. All she had to do was answer phones, book tours, and keep an eye on reservation requests sprinkling in from the upgraded website their dad had paid someone way too much for. The job wasn't hard, especially for a twenty-three-year-old who still lived at home and didn't have any other responsibilities to worry about, like rent money, enjoying a free ride, courtesy of their mother.

"Mija, don't be mean. Your sister had a rough night. She didn't go to bed until late. And she said she doesn't like to answer in case it's another call from Soaring Over Oregon."

Selah gritted her molars together due to her mother continuing to make excuses for Hailey. Knowing her sister, she was probably up too late doing something on Loop, a video-based social media app, which always took priority over everything else, even while the rest of the family pulled together to keep their father's business afloat. Hailey, when not goofing off, was either sleeping, posting video content on Loop, or being in a dark mood because she was mad Elena kept Robert's urn beneath clutter on her bedroom dresser. While Selah could understand this complaint, she had enough on her plate. It was hard enough trying to get her mother to drop a useless magazine subscription, and Selah didn't need anything more.

The second part of Hailey's excuse, about not wanting to deal with Soaring Over Oregon calls . . . Well, Selah didn't really blame her sister in this.

The first few months after Robert went to bed with a horrible headache, only to never wake again due to an undetected rupturing cerebral aneurysm, were some of the hardest for the Moreno family. It was the same as walking through a chaotic tornado of information and emotions.

God bless him, Robert was amazing in a lot of ways, but Selah quickly learned how unorganized and messy he was in the financial part of his life and how much she truly hadn't known the extent of it.

Her mother, while she could pull herself up and be strong in some aspects, completely fell apart when it came to shouldering the responsibilities Robert normally took care of, like the business and household finances. Instead, she'd rather pour herself into cooking, baking, and spoiling her family, ignoring the harder stuff. Selah spent the first month trying to hack into accounts under his name, so things like the internet bill could continue under her mom's name. Depending on her mom to help with things like missing passwords and making decisions became "too hard," which would only produce tears from Elena.

Paying bills was one thing. Taking over her father's business was another thing entirely. As the Moreno family emerged from the chaotic, engulfing grief that arose from an unexpected death, to move forward instead of just trying to survive the day, they were faced with the question—What should they do with High Desert Tours? There hadn't been any flights, since all tours had been canceled after Robert's death.

In digging through her father's finances, Selah saw a new picture emerge, one that made her stomach churn with queasiness. The new envelope, the one replacing *The Blue Wonder*, was the tip of the money iceberg her dad had poured into the business shortly before he died. It was the balloon, a larger gondola, the office trailer, the website, the new top-of-the-line laptop, and weather gadgets. It was like her dad had woken one day and decided the business needed to be bigger, more polished, better.

The problem was, there wasn't a lot of cash to invest in the company. Getting High Desert Tours running in the first place had already put him in the hole, as he'd loaned against their land and home. The original business, the alfalfa crop, had been "let out to pasture," so to speak, many years before, as her father no longer saw himself as a farmer. Now they were all stuck. When Selah had found out, she'd excused herself from her mother's kitchen table, locked herself inside a bathroom and spent several private minutes being mad at him, an emotion she'd rarely experienced before and then felt guilty about it.

She was almost grateful when the calls from David Selene at Soaring Over Oregon came, regarding buying the business and removing them as their biggest competition in the area. It made everything easy, and it made sense. High Desert Tours didn't have a captain, and Selah could never replace Robert. She wasn't sure she could shoulder that kind of pressure—to climb out of the same hole her dad couldn't climb out of. What else were they going to do? They needed the money. The temptation to say yes and walk away from the whole operation was right there on the tip of her tongue, except the decision wasn't entirely hers.

"You can fly *The Blue Wonder*!" Hailey had insisted through tears. "How hard could it be? You already have your piloting license. Why wouldn't you want to be the captain? Why would you destroy dad's dream like that?" Her youngest sister had taken the matter personally, growing strangely stubborn and insistent, especially after being the one to answer Soaring Over Oregon's latest call, now coming from David's son, Ryland. She freely referred to them as a family of vultures. "I would rather starve to death than give them the business. I hate every one of them."

Naomi jumped in, also hating the idea of selling the hot-air balloon business. The friendly rivalry and faux hate with Soaring Over Oregon had turned into the real thing, as though their father's honor was on the line. They didn't understand that this wasn't Robert's ultimate dream. It was something he'd settled on. When their mother started crying, too, Selah hadn't the energy to fight against them.

She promised the family two years. Two years, she'd help get the business back on its feet, two years to find its real captain. She wasn't staying, because between her and her dad, one of them was going to be a pilot of a real aircraft with an engine and, with him gone, it only left her. This roadblock wasn't going to stop her. Fate wasn't going to win.

The office phone rang again, reminding her that if the business was going to continue, it would seem she'd have to do it all herself. "Oh, for God's sake. I'm not putting up with this. You need to tell Hailey that if she really wants Dad's business to keep going, she needs to start pulling her weight. I can't do everything, and you need to stop babying her."

"Don't talk about your sister like that. We're all trying. I just want you to love one another."

Her mother's tolerance at handling family strife, including small disagreements between siblings, was low since Robert's death, as if this was a sign the whole family was falling apart. It was better if Selah dropped the matter before her mother started sobbing again. Muttering a half-hearted apology, she rolled her office chair to the other desk, snatching the phone receiver up.

"High Desert Tours," Selah answered on the fifth ring. She watched as her mom moved toward her work laptop. "Don't touch that. It's going to crash. Remember?" Her mother pulled her hand away as though the laptop was a live wire.

It was questionable whether the laptop would actually crash simply from her mother using it, but Elena had a habit of treating it like her personal Facebook-checking device. With her mother's gullibility for clicking on random links, Selah didn't want to take any chances. Robert's laptop was set up exactly how she liked it and, as one of her most valuable piloting tools, she didn't want anyone to mess with it. Selah found that if she told her mom touching it could crash it, her mother's natural fear of electronics kept her away—if only she didn't have to be constantly reminded.

"Oh, God. Is this a direct line to the hot-air balloon? I'm so sorry. Don't worry about me. Just keep flying . . . floating . . . whatever. I'll call back later," a male voice said on the other end of the phone line.

"I'm sorry?" Selah responded to the caller, completely confused.

"It's okay. It wasn't that important. I don't want you to crash your hot-air balloon." The words stumbled out in a nervous ramble.

Understanding this person mistook the words said to her mother, Selah found the situation hilarious, and a laugh sprung out, her first lighthearted moment in forever. It was strange and, yet, somehow freeing to express some other emotion besides grief, responsibility, or obligation. The man had sounded genuinely worried for her. "Oh my God. No, I'm sorry. I didn't . . . I'm not, um, currently in the air."

There was a short pause before he replied, "Are you sure?"

Selah watched as her mother left the trailer before turning her attention to the call. "I'm a professional pilot, sir. I'm pretty sure they'd revoke my license if I couldn't distinguish between when I'm on the ground and when I'm in the air."

"You're the pilot? I can't believe that." His tone was friendly, but her own posture straightened, expecting some form of misogyny to spring into the conversation. It wouldn't be the first time since she'd started on her path toward becoming a pilot.

"And why is that, sir?" Her attitude shifted to cool professionalism, expecting a demand of her qualifications, certifications, and number of flight hours.

"Oh, I didn't mean . . ." He took a beat before continuing, "I just mean that you have a lovely, clear voice, one that doesn't sound at all like this . . ." Over the phone line, he mimicked the sound of static, his voice switching to an even lower octave and becoming muffled, as if he was partially covering his mouth. "Uhhhhh, good afternoon, ladies and gentlemen . . . this is your captain speaking. We're at a comfortable, uh, cruising altitude of ten million feet. Sit back, relax, and ignore the gremlin on the wing of the plane."

If, at that moment, she'd been drinking the coffee Elena had brought her, the walls of the office trailer would have been painted with it as the result of a spit take. This man had the stereotypical, smooth piloting cadence down pat, even to the point of extending the length of his *uh's*—and not only did he make her laugh, but he'd said she had a lovely voice. Selah never had a call like this, especially one which was supposed to be all business. Her insides were warm and light instead of knotted and stressed, a nice change of pace for once.

"That's because pilots only use the piloting voice when they're piloting. Passengers find it very calming. I can't be wearing it out when I'm off duty. I'm currently using my, uh, phone voice." For some reason, she thought it necessary to say *phone voice* in a breathless, sultry tone, as though it was the sexier version. Her cheeks warmed at the implication, and she smothered a giggle because professional pilots weren't supposed to blush or giggle.

"Really?" He sounded intrigued. It was as though, through the phone, they were able to move closer together, turning this into an intimate conversation—something it most definitely was not. It was a regular business call. Period.

"I think I might need to hear an example of this," he said in a way that made her heart flutter within her chest.

"O-of my piloting voice?"

"Of course. How else am I going to know I'm booking with a legit pilot? I'm surprised everyone isn't asking you for your piloting voice before they book. Didn't you do a whole course of this in flight school or something?"

Selah bit back another grin, leaning forward onto Hailey's desk and nibbling on the edge of one of her nails. Why was this office suddenly so warm? At this point, she was glad her younger sister was late. In fact, she hoped Hailey slept the whole day away. "You think you can handle my piloting voice?"

"Well, now I have to hear it."

Sliding a glance to the other side of the office, she confirmed there weren't any witnesses. Talking to a potential customer about her piloting voice wasn't at the top of the list of what she'd consider to be inappropriate behavior. And, yet, something about it did feel this way. If this conversation were recorded on some hidden black box and re-played in one of her aviation courses, as an example of pilot and client interactions, she'd go straight to skydiving without a parachute in shame. Luckily, no one was here but her and this funny mystery man on the other side of the line.

Cupping a hand over her mouth, she made her own static-like noises before deepening her voice as much as she could. "Uhhhhhhhhh . . ." The monosyllable sound vibrated from her much longer than his, like she was trying to break a record. "This is your pilot, Selah Moreno, speaking, and we're at a cruising, uh, floating altitude of two thousand feet. If you look north, you can see Smith Rock, and just below us, you can see two alpacas getting it on. Nothing like a little nature to inspire your day."

The whole thing was quite goofy, but she was rewarded with a deep laugh, making it all worth it. The sound filled her insides with giddy bubbles. "Selah." He said her name as if he was saving it in his memory. She liked the way he said it, as though it was the name of someone important, someone he shouldn't forget. Both syllables were pronounced the way she liked it, something she appreciated. She knew her name was unusual for the area, even more for someone of Latina descent, and she was used to spelling and pronouncing it for people.

Her mother had named her Selah because she'd heard it meant rock. She'd been told the name had other meanings, but her mom stuck with rock because she liked telling her daughter, *Always be strong and steady like a rock, mija.* And that's exactly how Selah strived to be. She felt like she needed to, especially now.

She was equally curious about the name of this man, wondering how she could slyly pry it out of him without having to turn the conversation weird or make it into a boring business inquiry, hoping he'd volunteer it without asking.

"With that demonstration, I'm convinced you're an excellent pilot—and you also have a very nice phone voice."

Her skin flushed at having pleased him, but she kept her voice casual, not wanting to reveal too much emotion, doing her best to tamp it down. "Thank you, sir. That's such a relief to hear."

"I work there, you know."

"Where? Here at the farm?" As soon as she said it, Selah

realized how ridiculous it was. It'd been a while since her parents had hired extra farm help ... unless her mom had hired someone without telling her because she knew Selah would be mad since there was no money for it.

Besides her family, there was only Boone, who was part of the balloon chase crew, along with her middle sister, Naomi. While Boone was inarguably good-looking, he wasn't really her type, and imagining having a flirty conversation—not that she was flirting, but someone might construe it that way—Anyway, whatever this was, she didn't want it with Boone. This man's voice was quite different, though: warm and comfortably deep, a little scratchy, unlike Boone's voice, which always seemed overly confident and smooth.

The man laughed easily. "No. Smith Rock. I'm a park ranger here."

Her relief was immediate. "Oh!" she exclaimed too brightly, as if this was the most amazing news in the world. "That's really ... cool." *Cool* being the single adjective she could squeeze from her brain, making her sound very uncool. "I love going there. What's your name?" She asked as though she were familiar with all the park rangers. A cynical person would never fall for such an easy, obvious ploy.

Fortunately, he didn't act suspicious at her attempt to pry his name from him. "Dex," he replied. "Dex Westerly. I'm originally from the Bay Area, but I moved to Central Oregon about two years ago."

Stretching, Selah pulled the work laptop from her desk to Hailey's, and quickly typed *Smith Rock* and *Dex Westerly*. This wasn't internet stalking, she told herself. Instead, it was curiosity, as she wanted to put a face to the voice. One of the first results was a *Welcome Ranger Dexter Westerly* article on the official Smith Rock website. His picture was posted at the top. It wasn't the work of a professional glamor shot, but it was a nice photo all the same.

In the image, he leaned against a wooden split rail fence. Behind him was the jagged, majestic view of the Smith Rock landscape with the large, orangish-yellow crags and mountain-sized rocks jutting skyward. A lush creek snaked around the giant, rocky formation, surrounded by dried brush and juniper trees. It was a familiar landscape, as Selah had visited the area many times, both on the ground and from the air.

Dex looked like the kind of guy who'd been a skinny geek in high school and had morphed into a taller, handsomer version of a geek into adulthood. In the photo, he held a tan ball cap in one hand that rested on the fence. His other hand was partially stuffed into the pocket of his mountain-green hiking pants. He wore the short-sleeved park ranger uniform on top, but this was partially covered by a fleece vest. He wasn't looking directly at the camera, but down and to the side, with a slight grin on his face as though the camera person said something he found amusing. Dex was somewhat on the lanky side with light-brown, neatly trimmed hair. Selah was disappointed he was clean-shaven, as she preferred a little scruff, but he still had a nice face.

She had to admit, the guy was cute. Cuter than Boone, for sure. For the first time in her life, she investigated whether there was a wedding ring on his finger. She figured he would be married, as he had a friendly husband-next-door vibe, one married to a woman named Ashleigh, who would post pictures of autumn, scarfs, and pumpkin spice lattes on her social media . . . someone Selah definitely was not. In a miracle of all miracles, the left hand had no wedding band visible. Her heart lifted with good fortune.

It was a silly exercise, though, because there was no way she'd get involved with someone—not at this point in her life. She remained partially wounded from her last relationship, regretting getting involved with a guy she met at the airport where she had attended flight school, someone who'd recently split with his wife. She'd mistaken a real relationship for a rebound one and had been cast aside after a few months. Never again.

Despite this, she wouldn't mind talking to Dex some more because he seemed nice and someone who could distract her from her current worries of keeping her family from sinking into bankruptcy and losing her father's only legacy. Simple, uncomplicated stuff like that.

"Hello?" Dex said, snapping her from her unserious speculation.

"Yes. I'm sorry . . . I was just . . . sorry." She stumbled at not being able to tell him where her thoughts had turned.

"I was just wondering if it was more appropriate to refer to you as Captain Moreno. I'm not sure what the proper protocol is here."

"Oh, yes! Sorry," she replied, flustered. "You can just call me Selah—I don't really care." On one hand, she'd already decided he could call her anything he wanted. The bigger truth was, she hadn't adopted the title vacated by her dad. She was a pilot, but he was the captain, not her. She was still Number One, holding the spot open until a real captain could take it.

"Well, Selah, as much as I enjoyed talking to you, my lunch break is coming to an end, and I think I better book my hot-air balloon excursion. I'm planning on proposing to my girlfriend, so I wanted to see what you had available and how the process works . . ."

Well, crap.

She'd never been so disappointed to discover that what was happening on the phone wasn't a flirty conversation after all. Dex had merely been friendly, and she'd read way more into the situation. She was ashamed and embarrassed because, of course, this was for an engagement. Something about hot air and altitude inspired love and romance and . . . wow, she was such a clown. He wasn't married, but it was close enough.

Dex Westerly wasn't for her.

Chapter Two

CENTRAL OREGON HAD, on average, about three hundred days of sunshine a year.

This particular unsubstantiated claim was something repeated by realtors, weather reporters, and by your everyday, friendly state park ranger, like Dex Westerly. He was even willing to say it on days like today, where he was basically nature's janitor, emptying the park's trash receptacles.

It was one of those feel-good, optimistic statements that was generally accepted and rarely fact-checked, as though life in the High Desert was on par with living in San Diego. In reality, it was used to differentiate between what people imagined to be typical Pacific Northwest weather and what they found here. Foggy, overcast, and rainy more accurately described Portland's weather, not Terrebonne. When he said it to people from those areas, it sounded more like bragging.

Except the statement was also deceptive because, while there may be many days of sunshine, this wasn't the same thing as three hundred days of perfect weather. A sunny day could be blistering hot or freezing cold with snow on the ground, depending on the season. If the sun was out, it counted. In Central Oregon, perfect seventy-degree days weren't rare, but it could usually only be expected for two weeks in spring and two weeks in fall. The rest of the year was a crapshoot in terms of temperature.

After two years living here, Dex was getting used to it and, in fact, loved the area. It truly was an outdoorsman's paradise, with lots of wide-open space, filled with the natural beauty of mountains, caverns, lava tubes, and waterfalls, all thanks to high volcanic activity millions of years ago. Yes, it was a desert, but being at such a high elevation, it was different and more unique than the stereotypical sandy ones and was pretty in its own right. He liked that about it. Plus, if he ever wanted the lusher, greener part of the state, he only needed to jump in a car and head west for an hour.

People came from all over the country to visit this particular state park. Dex was lucky enough that part of his job was informing people about neat and educational facts about local wildlife and plants. Way cooler stuff than *Central Oregon gets three hundred sunny days a year.* Such as, "Hey, see those big red ants scurrying on that rock by your feet. Those are edible and taste slightly of citrus. If you ever find yourself foraging in the middle of nowhere, you can eat those, but you'll have to eat quite a lot to ruin your appetite." Those types of facts excited and impressed kids more than adults.

To be honest, he preferred dealing with kids more than adults at his job. Kids weren't boring. Most kids, even those acting up, respected the uniform enough to listen. If he said, "Please stay on the path," most kids corrected themselves. They were simply curious and exploring. It gave him hope that some of them were able to break away from their electronic devices long enough to see the world around them.

Adults, for the most part, didn't get excited about weird facts about local cuisine involving ants. Or how white sagebrush could be used as nature's deodorant in a pinch, if a person rubbed it over their skin. He really thought that latter fact would strike people as interesting. Also, adults *could* read park signs, but assumed none of the information or rules applied to them. The number of times he had to tell adults to stay on the path was too high. The only information they wanted to know was if there was a "real" toilet around instead of the composting restroom. He'd just smile and point toward the visitor center located at the top of a steep and inconvenient hill.

Sure, his job wasn't all fun facts, but it was all right. Dex wouldn't give it up for anything. He felt he was doing pretty well in life, considering.

So well, in fact, he should keep things moving by settling down at thirty-two and ask his girlfriend the biggest question of all.

"I'm thinking of getting married," he told his coworker, Jon Takala, as they lifted black, plastic bags of trash, transferring them to the back of a state park white pickup truck.

"Married? To who?" the taller, older man asked while brushing a dark strand of hair away with a hand.

Dex gave Jon a confused look. "What do you mean 'to who?'"

"You can't mean Ava."

"Yes, Ava. Who else am I going to marry?" Dex had been seeing the vivacious personal trainer and fitness influencer for over a year now.

They had met at Smith Rock when Ava had been there

doing a meditation video for her YouTube channel, and Dex had inadvertently walked between her and the camera. She'd yelled at him, but then they got to chatting, and she asked him if he wanted to get together later. At the time, Dex had been going through a rough patch in his life, ever since Rachel, his previous girlfriend, had packed her things without warning, preferring life in California more than she preferred him. His response to Ava's question had been, *Yeah, sure, why not?* She was gorgeous, there was no way he was going to turn her down. His gut had told him, at the time, this was the best thing to get over his current bad luck, and it seemed to be exactly what he needed.

"Why do you suddenly want to get married?" Jon asked as he lifted the truck's tailgate, snapping it into place. He took the driver's side while Dex was relegated to the passenger seat. The question surprised him. The older park ranger had been married for at least ten years, had two young kids, and always seemed satisfied with his situation. Why wouldn't he want the same for Dex?

"Are you kidding? Who wouldn't want to be married to Ava? She's great and beautiful and really active." In his mind, it was a match made in heaven, or at least a version of heaven, where he'd managed to hit a home run and got someone who'd always felt somewhat out of his league. "And I'd really like to share a home with someone else, so I'm not alone all the time."

"You're not alone. You have your pet crow." Jon chuckled at this, as though Dex's accidental animal situation was amusing fodder to a larger joke about his lifestyle.

"Harper is not a pet." Dex had found the young, injured

crow with a broken wing near the backside of the tall rock spire called Monkey Face, during one of his work shifts seven months prior. With no other resources available, because local wildlife rehabilitation places didn't have room for crows, Dex had let the bird convalesce at his place. He had given her the name Harper, thinking if he treated the bird like a friend, it would quicken the healing process. It sounded nicer than Ava's preferred nickname, which was Harpy, even though they could both agree the name suited the crow's personality more.

The good news was Harper did recover, although she wasn't the best flier yet. The bad news was crows, like most wild animals, made for horrible pets. Dex considered Harper more like an intelligent, feathered ally, as the animal was free to come and go as she pleased. As such, Harper maintained her own life, but frequently stopped by to visit Dex, usually by cawing next to his bedroom window early on his days off until she was granted access through an open window.

Harper showed her appreciation by bringing him gifts like twigs and metal soda can tabs. He imagined these were valuable currency in the crow world. In exchange, Harper would steal any food she was able to sneak from his cabinets.

Dex found crows to be interesting animals and thought it would be great if other people could discover this too. He often wondered if it would ever be possible to have an animal wildlife rehabilitation and education center at the park, but felt ridiculous to even mention it to Jon, let alone his boss, Chris, since he still felt fairly new to the park. And also because, again, most people didn't care about crows.

"And?" Jon said, prompting him with a hand gesture as

though he should continue with the obvious direction of the conversation.

Unfortunately, the direction wasn't obvious to Dex. It felt more like a trap. He narrowed his eyes at his fellow ranger, remembering this was supposed to be about his girlfriend, not Harper. "And what? I already said Ava was beautiful."

Jon scoffed at what was obviously the wrong answer. "Of everything you said, you didn't even mention love. Do you love her?"

Dex's cheeks grew warm at his obvious oversight, but there was a perfectly reasonable explanation. Expressing lovey-dovey sentiment made him uncomfortable. He was an only child to two parents who didn't seem to enjoy kids. He'd been treated more like a small adult rather than a child for most of his time growing up. His parents were fine, but he wasn't close with them, mostly seeing them during the holidays.

His father was a marketing consultant in the automotive industry and was away a lot. His mother was a senior editor for a major home and style magazine, and their house looked the part. Impressions and appearances were very important in the Westerly household. He grew up homeschooled by someone his parents hired, owned a limited amount of aesthetically pleasing toys so as not to cause any clutter, and wasn't allowed to touch the walls or mess with the pillows on the couch.

Dex thought all this was quite normal until his dad was laid off, and his mom kicked him from the house to go play outside and find a friend. It was then he realized how strange and out of touch he was. Luckily, he made friends with a neighbor kid, Lincoln, who took him to his own chaotic, loud home. Dex got a taste of something different, and it was wonderful. He ate junk food, played video games, and joined Lincoln's family when they went camping in the great outdoors. It was a messy, wild world out there, and Dex found himself chasing that dream ever since, hoping he'd find something similar with Ava.

His head rested against his seat as he brought the bill of his baseball hat lower and crossed his arms. "Okay, well, obviously, I . . . love her. I wouldn't be asking her to marry me if I didn't love her." See? He could talk about feelings. Progress.

"You two said that you love each other?" It was a skeptical question from a skeptical man.

Dex opened his mouth to reply before stopping. Jon had him there. "Maybe Ava and I are in a relationship where things just work and words aren't necessary." Or they didn't have any words. They spent a lot of time together doing things rather than having long, deep conversations.

"So . . . she hasn't told you she loved you?"

"No," he answered grudgingly, becoming defensive on behalf of both him and his girlfriend. "Ava isn't really like that. This is why we're really good together. What are you? My therapist?" Dex was beginning to feel annoyed and he already had a therapist—Well, not really, but he did talk to Harper a lot. It kind of counted. "Besides, we've only been dating for a year."

It was when Jon laughed did he realize the irony of his last statement.

"Just forget the whole thing. I don't want to talk about it," he replied grumpily. He had woken that morning feeling set in his decision and optimistic about the direction of his life, but now it was ruined. Dex had mistakenly thought Jon would be happy for him.

He knew not every relationship looked like Jon's, one that was loving and affectionate. His parents were more like roommates, but it worked for them, and they'd been together for almost forty years. It had to be somewhat good for his parents to stick it out for so long, even if, from the outside, their relationship was like their perfectly designed house—it never looked entirely lived in.

"Have you told Ava you wanna get married?"

"No."

"Don't you think you should at least bring it up?"

While his brain told him Jon's words were reasonable, he didn't know how to go about it. Wouldn't bringing up marriage sort of be a proposal in itself? "Ava says that I need to work on being more spontaneous. For once, I want to do something unexpected, take her by surprise. She likes things like that." See? He knew her.

At one point, Dex had considered getting Harper involved with a big proposal, or maybe a part in the wedding itself, but he doubted his ability to train the independent bird. Also, Ava wouldn't appreciate the effort as she hated Harper, and the feeling must have been mutual. She had never been the recipient of a valuable metal soda tab. Also, there was a high probability Harper would see a sparkling diamond ring, think Dex was finally returning the trinket favor, and fly off like a bandit to live like a queen among the other crows.

Besides, proposing with a crow didn't seem like something a normal person would do, and Dex was striving to be normal. While he'd spent a good deal of his adulthood catching up on movies, TV, and general pop culture, there were days he still felt as if he was trying to fit in with the rest of his generation.

Ava was always eager to try a new club in Bend, go to concerts, eat at new restaurants. He tried for her sake, but there were some days he'd rather stay home with Harper, work on a jigsaw puzzle, or go on a hike to a pretty area. He worried this was all part of his old past creeping in on him and maybe he was destined to be as boring as his parents. It didn't help when she'd scrutinize him and say, *When did you turn into a sixty-year-old man, Dexy?*

"Ava may love excitement, but this doesn't mean she's going to love a surprise marriage proposal," Jon said, much to Dex's dismay.

Except Dex had come up with a marriage proposal that would no doubt impress someone like Ava. "I booked us a hot-air balloon ride. That's when I'm going to ask her. I think she'll love it. Why are you being so weird about this? Is there a reason you think she'd say no?"

Jon had only interacted with her a handful of times, and Dex had never had the impression they didn't get along. If his friend knew something about his girlfriend, he should tell him, right? Especially if he was going to marry her and live with her and have kids with her—Oh God, when he put it like that, it did feel like a lot. He sat up, raising the bill of his hat to ask more specific questions.

Before he could say anything more, Jon said, "Hey," giving him a pat on his chest. "I'm sorry. I'm sure it'll be fine."

"So, you think she'll say yes?" The words were more hope than a question.

Jon teetered his head from side to side as though considering it before replying, "Well, if that's what you want, then I hope she does."

Dex tried to shift the doubts away. He'd already booked the flight, bought the ring, and made plans. Everything in his life was going well. There was no reason to believe Ava wouldn't marry him. Why would she continue dating him if she didn't see a future with him? This was the next logical step forward.

Besides, in Central Oregon, there was a good chance any day was going to be a sunny one.

Chapter Three

S ELAH YAWNED WHILE getting out of her truck, grabbing her hot coffee because May mornings were still sometimes frosty. She zipped her fleece jacket and adjusted the baseball hat on her head, keeping her hair from getting into her face. The ground crunched beneath her feet as she made her way across the field to the launch spot, a more remote area on the Moreno farmland. The rose gold hue of the morning sky kissed what remained of the night away. It was a little later than she liked to start flight days, but her mom had texted, informing her the passengers were running late this morning.

Her sister, twenty-five-year-old Naomi, called a greeting, her caramel-brown hair loosely pulled into a clip. She, like Hailey, had ended up with the taller, more willowy genes of the family, unlike Selah, who had hoarded all the short, curvier ones. If her sisters were sleek, elegant show horses, Selah was a solid workhorse in comparison, her body more practical and compact. But it served her well.

"Mom said you're doing a proposal flight today?" her sister asked with simmering excitement from where she stood in another truck bed as she pushed a large black nylon bag to the lowered tailgate. One of their father's upgrades was outfitting his truck with a tailgate that worked as a lift and made it easier to transport the gondola and the enormous envelope bag to the ground.

"Yeah." This was all Selah wanted to say about it to the great disappointment of her sister, the romantic member of the family. "How's the set up going?"

"You know, half fine and half annoying." Naomi jerked her head toward Boone, who casually sat on the already unloaded gondola that was resting on its side on the ground. For some reason, he wasn't cold like the rest of them, sporting a gray T-shirt with his arms casually crossed and his long legs stretched out before him as he squinted into the horizon. The morning sun's rays highlighted the tan he got from spending a lot of time outdoors, his brown hair feathering on a breeze. He always looked like he was about to appear in a men's cologne commercial and had always seemed a little too smooth for both Selah and Naomi—but he was also dependable, which was all Selah cared about.

"Come on, love, don't be like that. I was just trying to be friendly-like and have a pleasant conversation with you," he said in a thick English accent, which was odd, because the guy was from Bakersfield and, most of the time, had an accent to match. It also was not so unusual because it was Boone, and there was something about him that always hinted at mischief maker.

While Selah could see why someone like Boone would aggravate her normally easygoing, genuinely honest middle sister, it didn't bother her as much as it did Naomi, who had taken some personal offense over it. As long as Boone continued showing up, did the work, and didn't complain much, Selah didn't care about him or how he liked to rile her sister up. Of course, she'd never admit this to Naomi, nor confess how much she found their antagonistic relationship funny.

"Go on then. Tell your sister what a good match this will be between Miss Featherweight and Lord Muttonchop Dicklespot the Fourth. Do you think there's already talk among the ton?" Boone continued.

"Oh my God. Will you shut up?" Naomi hollered over her shoulder before turning back to Selah. "I *hate* that man. We need to fire him. I'm willing to donate whatever share I get from the business to hire anyone else, someone who won't ruin my love of historical romances."

Ah, okay, so Boone had found out about that, which explained the weird accent—not that Naomi's love of swoony period movies and books was much of a secret. But the guy had a knack for finding out about everything, especially where Naomi was concerned, like it was his second job.

"Yeah, well, that's going to be really hard, since your share of the business is still the same as mine, which is barely enough to live on."

"Whatever," Naomi said as she lowered the lift. As Boone got up and dragged the black envelope bag across the ground, her sister went to retrieve a few items from the truck cab. "Here." She handed Selah a helium balloon and a small white gift bag.

Selah took a quick peek into the bag before giving her sister a pointed look. "Are you kidding me? Rose petals?"

"Tell your sister your other romantic ideas, love."

The women ignored Boone. Selah also studied the balloon her sister handed her. The latex surface was printed with an embarrassing amount of hearts. "Seriously? No one is going to see this balloon. Just buy a regular one. And I don't need rose petals when mulch from the farm is free. Stop being extra." Extra was a great way to describe Naomi.

"Yeah, but see, I was thinking. How many times did Dad get a proposal flight? Lots, right? And we should be doing more to be playing that up . . . make it a whole experience. Bring in champagne and roses and candles—"

"Candles? On a hot-air balloon?" Selah asked flatly.

"Okay, well, maybe not candles, but I was doing the math, and if we offered a special rate for these kinds of flights instead of the normal standard ones—"

"Look, Naomi, can we talk about this later? I really need to get this done before the passengers show up." It's not that Naomi didn't have good ideas, but it was hard to discuss doing things differently when Selah was trying to get a handle on doing things the standard, boring way.

She slipped the small gift bag containing the petals under one arm and released the balloon, acting as her pi-ball, into the air. Selah studied its ascent, how it interacted with the wind, while sipping her coffee. It was something she'd done many times with her dad before on launch mornings. Back then, she had so much confidence, more than she realized. It wasn't that she didn't know what she was doing. She did. Flying a hot-air balloon was a lot less technical than flying a plane, but without having her captain as a backup, to confirm her observations and flight plans, for all judgment to be on her alone, it left her less secure.

She was so absorbed in the study of the pi-ball, she almost jumped in surprise when discovering a man standing beside her. He also peered upward with his hands on his hips, as though observing the sky with her.

"Holy mother of God," she said, barely managing to keep her coffee in hand. "Where'd you come from?"

The man jerked a thumb behind him to where her mother was gathering her things and getting out of the company van used to meet passengers at the farm and drive them to the launch area. It was supposed to be Hailey's job, but once again, her mother was covering for her sister.

"Hey," the man said. "We're the passengers for this morning's flight. Sorry we're late. I'm Dex. Captain Selah, I hope?" He offered her a hand and a warm smile. He was taller than she had expected. Smile lines fanned from the corners of his eyes, giving the impression of an easy manner about him, like he had a good disposition.

He was left to awkwardly hold his hand out as she stared at him like a starstruck goof, leaving him hanging. "Oh, yes! It's just Selah," she managed to say, realizing that the appropriate hand to shake his with still held a cup of coffee. Instead of switching the cup to the other hand, she placed her left hand over the top of his as though she was a high society lady in one of Naomi's stories and expected him to pay his respects by kissing her knuckles. Rather than coming off as elegant or professional, the whole thing was clumsy. She was flustered and embarrassed and worried she'd come across as some weird, nervous person instead of a calm, competent pilot.

He, at least, didn't act as if this introduction was any-thing out of the ordinary as he continued smiling and lightly shook her fingertips, his grip warming her chilled skin, doing a better job than the hot coffee ever could. His gaze remained steady, giving her the desire to dive right into the hazel depths of his eyes.

"Selah," Dex said. "It's nice to finally meet you." He then caught himself holding onto her hand longer than intended, and dropped it quickly, as though snapping himself back to reality. Switching to a crossed-arm stance, he cleared his throat and returned his focus to the pi-ball. "What's with the balloon?"

With this question, Selah flipped into professional pilot and educator mode. "Before launch, we release a pi-ball to get things like wind speed and direction. We get this from weather reports as well, but this allows me to gauge in real time not only speed but at what elevation. Hot-air balloons don't have any kind of motor or navigation. The burners merely allow us to get airborne and provide upward mobility."

"So how do you control where we go, or do you not have any control?"

"Well, that's why I study the pi-ball. I noticed at one thousand feet up, the balloon shifts directions, the wind going north, northwest. But look at it now." She pointed toward the pi-ball as if it was clear. "At fifteen hundred feet, it's now going south. By taking the hot-air balloon up and down to catch these different streams, I can better control the direction. When you've been doing it awhile, you start to get a feel of the wind, letting it work with you. Flying a hot-air balloon is both science and art."

"Yeah, it sounds like it," he replied, his eyes reflecting

amazement and admiration. She blushed but took a quick drink from her coffee to hide it.

"Dex? What the hell? Am I allowed to open my eyes yet?" The annoyed voice came from the open door of the van, snapping them from their current conversation.

Dex shuffled away as though he'd forgotten something important. "God! Sorry, yes!"

The other passenger poked her head from the vehicle as she looked around with an expectant expression on her face, bracing her hands against the sides of the van opening, as though anticipating something amazing before her.

Dex spread his arms, as if making a big reveal. "Surprise!"

Her expression fell to befuddlement with a hint of disappointment, her lips twisting in a slight frown. "You brought me out to . . . a field?"

Selah exchanged a look with her sister while taking another busy sip of her coffee. To be fair, they *were* in the middle of a field and with only the gondola, and the fuel tanks for the burners visible at this point, it didn't appear to be much. But, on the other hand, it was a big goddamn basket, enough to fit at least six people, and should have given some kind of hint.

Dex didn't appear to be discouraged as he took the woman by the hand, drawing her out of the van. "Come here. I want you to meet someone." He brought her over to Selah, and she was struck by the woman's appearance. She looked like she could be a flamenco dancer, simply based on her sharp, striking facial features and graceful height.

Selah could understand why someone like Dex, or anyone, would want to marry this woman. It was silly of her to even consider she'd have a shot's chance in hell at pulling anyone's attention when this woman existed in the world . . . that was *if* she was trying to capture anyone's attention, which she wasn't, because she was a professional.

"Ava, this is Selah, our pilot. She's going to take us on a hot-air balloon ride this morning."

To the woman's credit, the disappointment evaporated from her face, replaced with a happier expression. "What? Really? You're taking me on a hot-air balloon ride? Aw, Dexy." Ava curled into him, her voice purring.

With that, everything was well again, and Selah went through the process of explaining safety rules for passengers before they pulled *The Blue Wonder* from the black nylon bag to set things up.

Their two passengers willingly got involved in getting the balloon ready, stretching it out across the surface of the ground in front of the gondola. Although Dex was more into it than Ava. She treated it like a task and with efficiency. Dex asked a lot of questions, wanting to understand everything. Selah may have caught Ava rolling her eyes once or twice, but Selah found his curiosity entertaining. She liked that he took an interest in everything.

Selah distracted herself from thinking about it too much by dragging out a giant fan that would partially inflate the envelope while it was on the ground and the chase crew hooked up the burners inside the basket. Taking people up in a floating device made of fabric, wicker, and metal, with a couple of fuel tanks and the wind to make the whole thing work, was something any pilot took seriously, especially since people were putting their lives in her hands. She needed to get in a pilot frame of mind, and this meant forgetting about Dex and how cute it was when his eyes crinkled with pleasure.

When everything was hooked up, she fitted herself into the gondola, which still rested on its side, and turned on the main burner. As the envelope filled with the heated air, the gondola lifted upright. This was when she felt the coolest, when she let the burner blaze, feeling like the flame-throwing guitar player in the movie *Mad Max: Fury Road*, as she got the basket in position for loading.

Time to get serious.

He was no different from any other passenger.

He was getting married, and she didn't need the distraction anyway.

"Uh, and there's Crescent Moon Farms. You can see all the alpacas are already grazing." Selah made sure to switch to the secondary or whisper burner as she did a burst, creating more hot air pressure within the envelope. It wasn't as powerful as her main burner, but it was quieter, so as not to scare the animals below.

Even those who grew up in Central Oregon were excited to see things from an entirely new perspective. Except this was one of the few times where Selah struggled to keep things interesting. She was the opening act to something better, trying to keep the audience's attention until the main act (the proposal) came along. So far, the audience (Ava) was a tough crowd. The woman wasn't rude, but Selah had the impression that riding in a hot-air balloon wasn't meeting her usual level of excitement. After making Dex take a dozen photos and videos of her for social media accounts, Ava became resigned to watching the landscape lazily slide by while sighing every so often.

There was a reason High Desert Tours no longer allowed children under twelve on their flights. After the initial excitement in launching up into the air, traveling in a hot-air balloon was a very chill experience. Kids would get bored after about ten minutes, and it made for a long hour-and-a-half flight when they'd start to fuss. Ava wasn't a child, and she didn't fuss, but it was clear that she was growing bored as she leaned forward, resting her elbow on the edge of the basket with her chin propped on her hand. Dex didn't notice her lack of excitement as he pointed out surrounding land-marks, offering regional nature facts like in-flight snacks. If it weren't for Ava, Selah would have enjoyed this tour im-mensely. She liked Dex's enthusiasm. Plus, all she had to do was pilot and leave the tour guide part to him.

"Do you guys ever offer bungee jumping off the bal-loons?" Ava asked her, interrupting Dex.

"Oh, uh, no." Her sister, Naomi, may come up with some unique ideas for the business, but even she would never come up with something that wild. Imagining how it would increase their insurance rates, more than they already were, gave Selah sweaty palms.

She pretended to be busy as she checked her tablet and brought out a small handful of the petals her sister packed in the paper bag. She'd much rather have used bark or, even better, a bag of chips because then she'd also have a snack, but the flower petals worked well too. Dropping them off the side of the basket, she watched the petals flutter downward before they were swept away by a strong breeze about two hundred feet below them. This was the stream she planned to take on the return trip.

Ugh, what was taking Dex so long? For some unknown reason, Selah wanted the whole proposal to be done so everyone could move on with their lives. She looked over, catching him watch the petals float away, his hand going to the pocket on the right side of his chest.

God. Was the ring loose inside his pocket at two thousand feet in the air? She didn't notice any jewelry box outline or anything. When her gaze lifted, it caught his. It was a pair of eyes she wanted to look right back and see her.

Of course, this wouldn't happen because he was already taken . . . and also because she was wearing a pair of aviators and a hat, giving her protection from the weather and any unwanted scrutiny. Dex blinked, his attention shifting away as he cleared his throat and nervously ran a hand through recently trimmed hair, as though trying to make himself more presentable as he positioned himself closer to Ava.

"Hey, is that an eagle over there?" Dex asked, pointing in a direction for his girlfriend to follow.

"Where?" she asked, shading her eyes with a hand.

There wasn't any eagle. Dex's hand went into the pocket of his flannel shirt while he knelt on the floor of the gondola, producing a small ring glittering between two pinched fingers.

"Dex, are you sure you saw an eagle? I don't see anything." Ava was oblivious to the kneeling man behind her, as she continued searching the sky for something eagle-like. It started to feel uncomfortably long as seconds ticked by and the woman wasn't turning around.

"I . . . uh, thought I saw it flying around to the other side. Maybe look over there," he said.

"No, wait, I do think I see an eagle. Or is that a hawk? You're usually pretty good with birds. Are you sure you didn't mistake an eagle for a hawk, Dexy? Wait until your fellow rangers hear about this. At this rate, this is the only good story you're going to give me about this trip."

"Except the eagle just landed on the basket behind you!"

"What? Where?" Ava finally turned, her expression shifting to confusion when she only found Selah.

Selah gave a small finger wave before pointing downward, so Ava wouldn't miss the proposal. It was clear when the moment clicked for the woman as she gave a sharp gasp, one hand covering her mouth. "What? No! Are you being for real right now?"

With his face tilting toward her, Dex continued kneeling and holding up the ring. "Ava Vasco, the moment I saw you, I thought you were the most beautiful woman I have ever known. Will you please continue making me the luckiest guy by becoming my wife?"

Maybe it was Selah's bitter jealousy because, while the proposal was nice, it wasn't the best one she'd ever witnessed. In fact, the previous fall, there'd been a man who could barely get a word out because he couldn't stop weeping about how much he loved his partner. Then the boyfriend started crying and they'd clung to each other, mixing tears and snot bubbles. Selah was pretty sure sharing snot bubbles was a sign of true love.

She didn't know what Ava was thinking, but Selah was disappointed Dex's words had sounded . . . well, practiced and composed, and not very unique. There was little sign of weeping or snot bubbles forthcoming. He did look happy, hopeful, and this was a typical Hallmark picture proposal, except Selah felt nothing. Not that it mattered, because she wasn't the one being proposed to. Also, it could be because most of her emotions remained boxed up, stored in her emotional attic, since Robert passed away. Why drag them out for this?

To muster something extra, Selah tossed a few of the rose petals toward the couple. Naomi would have been proud of that, at least. The action, though, was half-hearted and lackluster since she tossed them at their feet in order to avoid the burners. She wouldn't want to risk bringing the whole balloon down just for romance.

Ava had what appeared to be a million emotions passing through her. Bringing her hand down revealed a large smile. "Oh, Dexy." Her hand reached out, taking the ring between her fingers to study it closer. "Oh, Dexy," she repeated.

The first time Ava said this, Selah thought the woman had been so overwhelmed with happiness and shock she was having trouble reacting. When she repeated herself a second time, Selah had an inkling of doubt drop into her stomach. The smile appeared strained, not reaching Ava's eyes.

As much as she wasn't into this particular proposal, Selah did not want this to turn into a bad news day. For one thing, as long as *The Blue Wonder* had been in service with her dad, their marriage proposals had a one hundred percent "yes" rate. She didn't want it to get around that there was a bad proposal connected to the business under her piloting, especially when things were already hard enough. What if this gave Soaring Over Oregon the edge they needed to put the Moreno women out of business?

And, secondly, she liked Dex. He seemed like a genuinely nice guy, and she could set her inconvenient crush aside. If he loved Ava, then she wanted to see the woman fling herself into his arms and provide the couple with a happy ending they should have.

Dex remained kneeled on the basket floor, his smile blissfully unaware, oblivious to Selah's growing concerns for him. When Ava tore her gaze from the ring to Dex, the smile became more strained.

Oh shit. Selah was stuck on a hot-air balloon, with no way to escape, and about to witness a situation turn horribly awkward.

Chapter Four

"**I** CAN'T." AVA offered the ring back to Dex. "I'm sorry."

It took a moment for her words to penetrate his brain. He was sure he'd misheard her. "You . . . what?" He hadn't expected this outcome and wasn't sure what his next move was supposed to be. "Is it too soon?"

Ava tucked her lower lip between her teeth, looking pained. "No. I don't . . . I don't even know if I want to get married. I mean, you're a nice guy and all, and we've had a lot of fun, but—this wasn't supposed to happen."

He managed to return to his feet, feeling foolish and blindsided. Dex was almost tempted to fling the ring from the basket, as if this would make his proposal disappear from everyone's memory, before thinking better of it and stuffing it back in his pocket. He threw a glance at Selah, as though she'd be able to help him with this situation. Her aviator sunglasses made her hard to read, but her lips were stretched in a line. She looked as if she wanted to disappear into the wind, and he didn't blame her, as the basket felt much too small for three people to occupy.

He steeled himself for this next part, not wanting to give up easily. Maybe the whole thing was salvageable if he said the right words. "I . . . love you."

She looked at him as though an alien had appeared before her instead of a man professing his love. "Stop. You do not love me."

"So, you don't love me?"

Ava sighed. "Dex. You're very sweet and I'm very fond of you. And I know you're very fond of me, but—We shouldn't get married. We're too different. I want different things. And I thought we agreed this was just for fun." Ava turned to Selah, asking, "He's a great guy, right?"

If she wanted to make Dex feel better, this had the opposite effect. He wanted to float away into nothingness, like one of the pink rose petals Selah dropped from the side of the basket. It was even worse when their pilot answered, "Yup," thereby cementing this to be the worst, most humiliating experience of his life.

Dex leaned against one of the basket walls, turning his back to Ava and staring into the landscape, but his mind was spinning. "So now what?"

"I don't know," she responded. "I'm really sorry, Dex."

He shook his head as he squinted into the glaring sun that was beginning to feel unrelenting. "God. I feel like a— Why were you even with me?"

Ava gave him an annoyed glance. His question clearly perturbed her. "I told you when we first started going out that I wasn't looking for that. I wasn't lying. I haven't changed. I don't want the typical marriage and kids. I don't want to do that. I want to be free."

"Yeah," was all he could say, because maybe he *had* read too much into things, and this was what Jon had been trying to warn him against. "Okay. Well, I get it now."

Selah's two-way radio came to life, a static break in the awkwardness. "Sorry," she said. He wasn't even sure what she was apologizing for, as she had a job to continue doing. She chatted with the person on the other end, and it was clear it was getting close to the end of the ride. It couldn't come soon enough for Dex.

Without the sound of a flame as they lowered, it became uncomfortably quiet. He was grateful when Selah at least described what she was doing and the process of landing. Before, he would have been asking a bunch of questions because he couldn't help but be curious about it. But now he was depressed and could barely focus on her words. His whole world felt hollow, empty, and dark.

Dex was so absorbed in his thoughts, he barely noticed the basket bumping against the ground as it landed. He was snapped into the present when a sudden gust caught the deflating balloon, pulling and tipping the basket, with them in it, on its side.

Before he could react, Dex landed on his back with something soft landing on top of him with an *Oof. He squeezed his eyes* shut on instinct, waiting for everything to stop moving, wrapping his arms around the person who'd landed on his chest. At first, he thought it was Ava, which might explain why he'd naturally wrap protective arms around her. Sure, he was completely wrong, and she didn't love him, but despite this, he didn't want her to be injured. He was heartbroken, not heartless.

Except this person felt different—smaller, softer, and she had a bright sage and citrus scent. When everything stilled, he cracked an eye open. Most of his vision was encompassed in a blue glow because of the balloon fabric enveloping them. To his right was Ava, who was swearing up a storm, but otherwise was fine. He turned his attention downward and saw his arms wrapped around Selah. Dex slowly released her as she began to move, bracing her hands on either side of his body as she rose over him, her sunglasses slightly askew and a few dark curls escaping the edge of her hat.

Her own shock and embarrassment was evident as her skin flushed pink, her mouth popping open. Dex knew he was about to hear another apology, even though he didn't need one. He understood these types of things happened with hot-air balloons, and it wasn't necessarily her fault.

To his surprise, Selah covered her mouth, doing a short imitation of a static sound before saying, "Uh, ladies and gentlemen, this is your pilot speaking. We've experienced a slight bout of turbulence upon landing. Please take care when getting up and be aware that your overhead pilot may have shifted during landing and could be on top of you."

There was a brief moment of him doing nothing more than staring at her in disbelief until it hit him that this particular joke at this particular time was the most hilarious thing he'd never expected. Honest-to-goodness laughter rumbled out of him, making it difficult to think about anything else. He continued laughing and wiping away tears when the rest of the hot-air balloon ground crew pulled the blue fabric of the balloon away and was able to help them to their feet.

Ava glared at him. "What the hell is so funny? I hope you get your money back for this shit service." This had him chuckling all over again. She'd never understand, and he had no desire to share it with her. It was something between him and Selah, a person he was kind of regretting he'd never see again.

Of course, there was a round of apologies from both the captain and crew, but Dex brushed all of these aside, because the only thing hurting was his ego, and this couldn't be blamed on High Desert Tours. Instead, he watched as Ava snatched the offered bottle of champagne from one of the other women before announcing she'd definitely need it and was ready to go home and make a reel about this.

The day started with him in a relationship, thinking he was about to be engaged, and he was leaving with his relationship broken. The woman beside him in the High Desert Tour van was now his ex.

Life was weird.

He leaned against an armrest and stared out the van window as it pulled away from the landing spot. The people left behind, Selah being one of them, were wrestling with the deflated balloon. What an unusual woman.

She glanced up from her task and they made eye contact through the window. Selah lifted her hand in a farewell, and he returned it out of habit.

The older woman who drove the van glanced at them through the rearview mirror. "Did you kids have a nice flight? My daughter, Selah, is a really good pilot, just like her dad, you know. He was an excellent man, the love of my life." She rubbed the corner of her eye before brightening with a smile. "Sometimes things like baskets falling over happen, but you have to look at the positives. You picked a nice day for a flight, at least. Beautiful. You know, Oregon gets about three hundred days of sunshine a year."

A strained laugh vibrated through him as he shook his head at the irony of it all. "Yeah, I've heard." He was feeling ridiculous for all those times he'd spouted the same thing. He should start keeping track.

Dex wasn't sure he believed that claim anymore.

Chapter Five

Three months later

H AVING TO GO on a silly date tonight was all Daniel Radcliffe's fault.

For the most part, Selah enjoyed his movies, even the weird, quirky ones, but this wouldn't be enough to save him from her decision to boycott all his future releases. Of course, Daniel Radcliffe would never know this, nor would he care. It also wasn't his fault as much as it was her sisters'.

This was actually all her sisters' fault.

It started earlier that week, while she'd been on hold for an hour, waiting to talk to a customer service rep because her mother had "forgotten" to pay another bill. Selah overheard her sisters talking about some movie they wanted to see together and had asked, "Oh, is that the new movie with Daniel Radcliffe? I really like his movies."

Hailey gave her a funny look and said, "It's not Daniel Radcliffe. It's Elijah Wood."

This turned into a bigger argument where Selah was so confident the main actor was Daniel Radcliffe, she willingly took a bet, only to be proven, regrettably, very wrong. So, yeah, Selah losing a ridiculous bet to her sisters and having to go on a pointless date they set up through some app was also

Elijah Wood's fault.

Basically, everyone was at fault, and this was the reason Selah was jogging while crabby on a dusty river trail around Smith Rock today, not wanting to think about overdue bills, dates, or her sisters.

She expected this kind of thing from Hailey, but Naomi ganging up on her, too, the sister who was nice enough to share her townhome in Redmond, felt like a betrayal. Naomi's romantic side overwrote the nice sister side, and she was more than eager to boost Selah's lack of a social life. Any excuses given about her current priorities, lack of energy, her plan for not sticking around for the long term, or even bringing up how dating in general sucked balls in the modern world, did nothing to discourage her sisters' glee.

Even worse, it gave their mother some kind of hope. So much so, she broke away from her all-consuming baking to give opinions and get giggly as her sisters flicked through potential dating options on an app. It was the happiest Selah had seen their mother in a while, which was why she ultimately relented, even while being annoyed.

While jogging on the Smith Rock trailhead, Selah half listened to a true crime podcast in hopes of getting inspiration on how she could fake her own disappearance before her date tonight or how to commit the perfect crime when doing away with one's sisters. Either situation was on the table.

Listening was made more difficult by her left earbud stubbornly refusing to remain lodged in her ear. She'd already stopped twice to rescue it from wiggling out completely. It was extra aggravation on top of an already aggravating day. Plus, it was continuing to get hotter, so on top of it all, she was overheated, sweaty and her curls were refusing to stay in a ponytail—

Another woman with two energetic dogs bounded around one tight corner, almost colliding with her. "Oh, excuse me," Selah said, doing a quick sidestep to the left to avoid them. The woman offered dirty looks as though Selah should have known she was coming. Unfortunately, bouncing unexpectedly to the side brought her foot onto a small jagged rock, making her nearly lose her balance, and she barely managed to keep herself upright. She may have saved herself, but the same couldn't be said about her left earbud as it flew through the air, landing somewhere in the off-trail brush.

"Dammit," Selah said. "I lost my earbud."

If she had any hopes the woman with the two dogs would take this as a request for help, she would have been disappointed. The woman continued on the path without another word, leaving Selah by herself.

"So much for Oregon nice," she said under her breath grumpily before wading through the tall, dried out, early August brush. Using a hand to sweep aside the wild grass, she bent over as the true crime podcaster continued droning in her right ear.

The earbuds weren't expensive. She supposed she could get by with a single one or buy herself a new pair. Except it was the last birthday gift given to her by her dad, and he'd been excited about it, wrapping it himself in some old red bandana of his. It was too bad he'd purchased a standard black pair instead of something more eye-catching, like purple or pink. But that was Robert, always the practical guy.

"Ma'am, I'm going to need you to return to the designated path," said a voice behind her.

"What?" She turned her head, peering over her shoulder while bent over at the ass. Did he just call her *ma'am*? Did her ass in joggers look like a *ma'am* to him? This guy had better watch himself because she was already not in a good mood.

The man in the park ranger uniform had one hand on a hip. The other hand did an impatient flick with his fingers, motioning her to approach.

As she straightened, Selah recognized Dex immediately. Even at his place of work, she never expected to run into him again. She'd visited Smith Rock many times and never noticed any park rangers on the trails. She assumed, like chameleons, they were good at blending in with the environment. Of course, she'd run into one now and it would be him.

It wasn't that she hadn't thought about him. There'd been many times during quiet hot-air balloon tours when she'd wondered how he was. She'd been terribly embarrassed about how that particular flight had ended.

The problem with hot-air balloons—they didn't always cooperate a hundred percent of the time. Some things were completely out of Selah's control, like people who arrived late for launch days and missed the golden hour. Case in point, landing. While ninety-seven percent of the time, the whole ride from takeoff to landing went without a hitch, there was always a small chance something could happen. This was why she liked to warn people ahead of time to prepare them.

Hot-air balloons, like fate, also had terrible timing. Of all the days she needed the basket to land smoothly so everyone could go on their awkward way, she didn't get her wish. She had fallen right smack on top of Dex, and as she suspected, his arms were warm and protective as they had wrapped around her. When she should have sprung away from him and apologized, she didn't.

She *knew* it was wrong. It wasn't an appropriate way to treat a passenger, but she couldn't help it. Maybe she needed more hugs these days because, since Robert died, there was one less person in her life giving them. Getting an accidental one from Dex seemed like a good substitute at that moment.

She got the impression she wasn't going to get a repeat hug today. In fact, Dex stood on the trail, looking different from the last time they'd met. His features were sterner, his eyes duller, and he sported a few days' scruff. Although, even with the grumpy expression, the scruff and longer hair made the guy more attractive, not less. This wasn't good for her determination to forget about him.

"Oh, hi!" she replied cheerfully as she scrambled to pause the podcast. "It's good to see you." In spite of everything, it was nice to see his familiar face and perhaps he'd help her locate the missing earbud.

"Are you going to come out of the brush, ma'am?" he said.

He didn't recognize her. This was both disappointing and also put her in a bit of a quandary. The first part because, while she didn't think she was as eye-catchingly gorgeous as her younger sisters, she also didn't think she was average enough to be forgettable. Although, in her current disheveled state, with half her curls springing from the captivity of the hair tie, perhaps this was a good thing. And, to be fair, when she'd met him at the balloon launch, she'd been wearing large aviators and a hat.

Selah wasn't sure she wanted to remind him of that day or how to go about it. *Hey there, remember when your girlfriend rejected your marriage proposal? Yeah, funny story. I was there too.* It was awkward, to say the least, and perhaps him forgetting her face was for the best.

"I'm not going to ask you again," he said flatly.

"I'm sorry, I can't."

He must not have been expecting any pushback, as a brief expression of confusion passed across his features before switching to a sterner look. "Ma'am—"

"I lost my earbud and it's here somewhere. Maybe you can help me find it?"

"You can go up to the visitors center and file a note with a ranger up there. If it ends up in the Lost and Found box, someone will reach out to you."

She peered to the top of the steep hill, which was always a bear to climb since it must have been close to a forty-five degree angle to get to the visitor center yurt. "No one is going to find it and bring it to the lost and found. It's around here somewhere. Just give me five minutes. It looks just like this." She pulled the second earbud from her right ear to prove its existence.

"No. Come out of the brush now." His response was hard and unyielding.

Whatever positive thoughts she had for the man based on their past interactions flew out the window at this point.

Dex wasn't as nice of a guy as she had originally thought. Sure, he had a job to do, but—Why was he being so stubborn? Her heartbeat increased, indicating a possible internal freakout, at the knowledge she was about to lose her earbud from Robert, which now felt like a precious family heirloom.

In a move she knew was childish and demanding, Selah crossed her arms. "No. I'm going to find my earbud, Dex. If you want me out of the brush faster, then you can help me. I'm not leaving this spot until I find it, so go ahead and try to drag me out. See what happens."

As much as she didn't want to cry or rage over something as silly as an earbud, the frustration welled up inside her chest. She did her best to tamp it down because it would only make her look more ridiculous since no one but her would understand the significance of the item.

He opened his mouth, most likely to yell at her, but then stopped as he tilted his head. "Do we know each other?"

Shit. She'd said his name, hadn't she? Her gaze darted across his shirt in hopes of blaming her apparent knowledge on an obvious name tag or something, but there wasn't anything visible except his last name. Her brain scrambled. "Oh, uh, nope. I just call every random guy Dex. It's a general guy's name—like 'buddy.' Like *How's it going, buddy?* Only I use Dex instead of buddy. It's a new thing people are doing . . . on the internet."

He studied her with more intent as he rubbed one of his earlobes. "How do I know you?"

"Uh . . . I don't know." She cringed because if she wanted to remain a mystery, she shouldn't do something obvious like drawing out her *uh's* but, of course, this thought came after the fact. Time to switch gears. "Look, I understand I'm not supposed to be over here, but, as I said, my earbud popped out accidentally. And I know it sounds like a silly thing to make a big deal of, but I'm going to feel bad if I don't find it. I *need* to find it. I'll promise to be careful with the habitat. Just, please, give me five minutes."

Thankfully, his expression softened, along with his stance. "Okay, fine," he said, approaching closer.

"What are you doing?"

"Do you want my help or not?"

"Oh! Yes. Thank you. I really appreciate this."

He bent near her as she also returned to the search. With both of them looking, maybe they'd find the earbud quickly and she could escape any further scrutiny from those beautiful hazel eyes. She felt his gaze sliding over her again.

"Are you looking?" she asked, hoping to get his focus off of her and onto the real mission.

"Sorry, it's just that you do seem really familiar."

"I think I just have one of those faces."

"Is this earbud expensive or something?"

"No, it was a gift from someone who was really important to me," she replied, shifting to a new spot.

"It's too bad Harper isn't here. She'd find it quickly."

"Is that your girlfriend?" Did he have a new one *already*? She shouldn't care, but it didn't improve her mood.

"Oh, no, she's a crow. You know crows are very smart and are good at finding and picking out unusual things in their environment—"

"Found it!" In her haste at grabbing the missing earbud and jerking upright, she leaned too far forward and the bottom of her head collided with Dex's jawline with a jarring smack.

Chapter Six

"**O**W! *SHIT!*"

"Oh my God! I'm so sorry."

Dex rubbed his throbbing jawline as he jerked to his full height to avoid any further collisions with the petite woman. Truly, no good deed ever went unpunished. This didn't help with his already grumpy mood, a mood that had been consistently bad for three straight months at this point.

It was scorchingly hot today, and he didn't want to deal with the public, especially when the public was stubborn, didn't follow basic directions, and had dark curly strands that kept brushing against her pinkening cheeks.

"I didn't crack any of your teeth, did I?" She looked at him with such genuine concern he felt bad about getting annoyed with her earlier . . . but she shouldn't have been off trail.

"Are they all still there?" He revealed his teeth in a wide grimace and was pleased to see the corners of her eyes squint in amusement as she stepped closer to inspect.

"Good news. You still have a full set."

At this distance, he couldn't help surveying her features to take in the details. There *was* something familiar about her. He couldn't quite place it, and it was driving him kind of wild not knowing.

Her hair was nearly black, except for some warm brown strands mixed in, giving it added depth. Her hair also wasn't long, based on the curly strands escaping her hair tie. Maybe it was chin length? Her shoulders were exposed, her skin a light brown glow. The center of her hairline came to a subtle V-shape at the top of her forehead, giving her face a heart-shaped impression, especially with a delicate, narrow chin.

Her mouth was mesmerizing, the top lip nearly as full and lush as the bottom. Dark-brown eyes were framed by gorgeous long lashes and paired with strong, striking eyebrows. While her left ear had a single small earring, the right one had at least three silver studs. He also noticed, while they were searching, there was a simple tattoo on the inside of her right wrist, three small circles lined in a row.

A scent of spicy sage and citrus hit his nose, a smell he felt he'd been missing since . . . it was there on the tip of his brain. "Selah?"

She froze, a pink blush sweeping across her skin.

"Oh my God. Captain Selah?" It was her. Sure, she'd look different from the last time he'd seen her. With her face and hair completely uncovered, he could see she was . . . well, she was cute and, also, definitely cooler than him.

"You can just call me Selah," she responded quietly.

He had a moment of absolute satisfaction at solving the mystery but, with this knowledge came the rush of memories from his failed proposal. Because he couldn't remember Selah without also being reminded of the absolute rejection he'd experienced in her presence. The humiliation was a constant stab to his gut. And it wasn't because he was pining over Ava. It was more that he'd been foolish for getting so wrapped up in the idea of marriage and had made the biggest blunder of his life and—

Selah had known.

She had recognized him because, despite her weak attempt at an explanation, she'd called him by name. Maybe his first humiliation she'd witnessed was happenstance and not her fault, but she couldn't say the same about this time around. She'd let him stand there, looking foolish, pretending he was mistaken in his impression that there was a familiarity between them and—

He was done. He wasn't doing this again, not with someone who'd continue letting him believe in something that wasn't true at all, as though he needed to be protected or gaslighted. He wasn't living in that type of world anymore.

"How's, um, everything going with you?" Her brow lifted sympathetically, and it made him feel worse. Did she feel sorry for him? His heartbreak probably made for a diverting story to tell passengers on her other trips.

"No. We're not doing this."

Her lips stretched into a frown. "But I wasn't . . . I'm sorry."

"Your five minutes are up. Get out of the brush." He strode away determinedly, returning to the path and away from her. Logically, he knew his aggravation and anger were misdirected, but he'd been holding it all in. He hadn't had any other place to direct it.

When the van had returned to the farmhouse parking area after the failed proposal, Ava had gotten in her car and disappeared like a ghost. She hadn't even responded when he called to remind her they had driven together and she had abandoned him without any transportation. He was about to call some kind of car service when Selah's mom had been nice enough to give him a ride to Smith Rock, where he could bum a ride from one of his coworkers to take him home. He'd never felt so low and humiliated in his life and, for some reason, this moment with Selah was a close second. He couldn't escape her fast enough.

"ARE YOU BROODING?" Jon asked later that afternoon.

"No," Dex lied, because he *was* brooding as he leaned against a post, staring at nothing in particular and rubbing his jawline. It didn't hurt anymore, but it was more of a phantom feeling from some past connection. He'd never understood brooding before, but it turned out he was a natural at it.

"There's a new brewery that opened up in Redmond. Let's go check it out after work." His coworker gave him an encouraging slap on the back as though this would snap him from his funk.

"Thanks, but I think I'm just going to go home." Dex wasn't in the mood to socialize. Between going out and staying home to brood, the latter one was the more appealing choice.

Except Jon didn't listen and dragged him out to Bottle-cap Brewery, anyway.

"You always rush home. What's so special about today?" Dex asked as Jon ordered another house IPA.

Dex had never been much of a drinker and when he did drink, it was usually a single beer, but they were in Redmond, near his home. Turns out, brooding and booze went well together. He'd ordered a rum and Coke, drank it quickly, and then ordered another. If he had to socialize, this was the only way he was going to get there. He'd worry about getting home in an Uber later.

"Nothing's special. One of Steph's cousins just had an operation, so she went up to Warm Springs to help her, and she took the kids with her."

"So, you're living it up while the wife is away?" Dex asked, then took a huge gulp from his glass.

"No. I just don't like going home to an empty house. It's lonely and . . . Hey, man, I'm sorry." Jon raised his hands, apparently realizing he'd treaded onto a sensitive subject with that statement.

It was reminiscent of their wedding conversation many months before, except it was Dex who had been complaining about an empty house and being lonely. He finished the rest of his drink and ordered another.

"You doing okay?" his friend asked, eyeing the empty glasses in front of Dex.

"Yeah, fine. Why?" There was a short pause before he rambled with, "Do you know I've never broken up with a girl?"

"What? Never?"

"Nope, all four of them broke up with me, and I never saw it coming. Not one time. What do you think—" He was about to discuss this further when a glance at the door had him reacting by placing his glass in front of his face, like this was going to provide some type of concealing coverage. His brain, already getting fuzzy from the alcohol, slowly realized this wasn't going to hide him, and he then made a half-hearted attempt to turn his shoulder as a way to shield his body. "Shit. Did she see me?"

Jon gave him a funny look before turning toward the brewery entrance. "Who? Ava?"

"What? Ava's here too?" Dex couldn't think of anything worse than to be confronted with his ex-girlfriend as well as Selah. It's as if the universe wanted a sequel to the worst moment of his life by bringing back all the previous players.

"Too? Who are we talking about?"

Dex did a quick scan and didn't see any sign of Ava. At least, there was one bit of good news. He turned to Jon and mouthed *Selah*.

His friend laughed. "Who?"

He leaned closer and whispered, "Selah."

"Dex, I don't know who you're talking about, man."

For some reason, his brain found this surprising. "What? You don't know Selah? How could you not have seen her?"

Dex noticed her as though she walked into the crowded brewery with her own personal spotlight. Her dark curly hair glistened, one side swept up in a sparkly clip. Those mesmerizing full lips were glossy and pink. She wore some kind of dressy emerald-green top and curve-hugging black jeans. Selah, once again, appeared completely different from the previous times he'd seen her, but this time he recognized her straight away. Was she a shapeshifter? A kaleidoscope? Dex wasn't sure what to make of it. It was almost as though his lack of perception earlier in the day had heightened his senses to such a degree she could have walked into the establishment in a red wig, sunglasses, and trench coat, and he would have known it was her.

He was so focused on Selah, it took him a while to notice the smirking man following behind her, eyes laser-focused on her ass, before seating her at a nearby table. Oh God, was she out on a date? With that guy? Dex's asshole alarms went off, and she didn't look thrilled either. Her closed-lip smile, while nice, didn't appear genuine. Even though she was with someone else, and there was no reason for them to interact, Dex wanted to avoid her. It didn't seem fair they crossed paths whenever he was at his lowest and, with an empty glass in his hand, this situation was not ideal either.

"I don't want her to see me."

Jon motioned with his fingers toward his face. "Psst. Come here. I want to tell you something."

"Yeah?" Dex leaned closer to the man. Jon was, after all, his very best friend in the world. He wasn't sure if he knew that. He should really tell him tonight. Jon had always looked out for him and was perfectly right in his advice about Ava.

"If you're talking about the cute girl in the green shirt, you should probably stop staring at her. Just a hint." Jon's dark eyes glittered with humor.

"I'm not staring. I would never stare. Everyone knows that's rude."

"Yeah, but see, your head is turned one way, but your eyes keep darting in that direction."

"They do?" This couldn't be right. He was sure his very best friend in the whole world was wrong in this particular instance. "Look, you were right about Ava, but I think you're very wrong here. Let's both distract ourselves from staring at Selah and get another drink."

Just as Dex managed to turn toward the bar, determined not to think about Selah anymore, her date stood in the space on the other side of him, ordering two drinks from the bartender. While staring at Selah was definitely off the table, there was no reason he couldn't give her asshole date a good look. The man had close-cropped hair and wore a black T-shirt reading, *Bend over and I'll show you*. This man had a date with someone as pretty as Selah and this was the best thing in his closet he could come up with? It didn't seem right at all. It was the first time Dex wished that park rangers also had jurisdiction on fashion crimes.

While the man waited for his drinks from the busy bartender, he slid out his phone. There was a text, *Hey! Where you at, Big Daddy Sasquatch?* 🫣 to which the man responded, *Job going late. I'll be home later and give you all the beast you can handle, baby*. He then switched to some dating app, quickly swiped right on a few profiles, and sent a message to someone that included an attached dick pic. He then slipped the phone into his back pocket to grab the drinks from the bartender and return to his table with Selah.

This confirmed it. The man was a shitbag of the highest degree and potentially had Selah in his clutches. As annoyed as Dex was about his current situation, deep down, he knew she didn't deserve any of his aggravation. She had been an innocent bystander in the whole failed proposal thing, and maybe she'd felt awkward about their accidental meeting earlier in the day. He had noticed her cheeks flushing but attributed it more to being out on the trail on a hot day. She'd looked pretty. Not that he was in the habit of noticing the attractiveness of park visitors.

Either way, someone pretty like Selah, someone who was able to make him laugh on the worst day of his life, didn't deserve an asshole date.

Except it wasn't any of his business and he wasn't going to stare, and he wasn't going to notice her anymore, green tops, red wigs, or whatever. It didn't matter because he wasn't going to do anything. His best friend in the whole world, Jon, gave him the best advice, and Dex was definitely going to listen this time.

Chapter Seven

I T TOOK SELAH two minutes to realize being a person of her word and paying her debts to a bet wasn't worth it. This punishment was cruel and unusual for someone who sometimes confused Elijah Wood and Daniel Radcliffe. Her mom would have to depend on her other two daughters to bring her a bit of happiness. That's all there was to it.

While Kevin, the man who eventually showed up in the Bottlecap Brewery parking lot wasn't unattractive, he looked ten years older than his picture and dressed ten years younger. He'd instantly given her a hug, started chatting her ear off, removing any opportunity for her to cut in and say, "Never mind." Instead, she'd have to go through with it while hoping to make a short night of it so she could get a hot fudge sundae from the McDonald's drive-thru on the way home, which was sure to be the highlight of her evening.

She hadn't had high hopes to begin with, but it would have been nice if her date had been someone like Dex. Of course, it wasn't fair to compare Kevin with Dex. In fact, it wasn't even fair to compare Dex with Dex, considering how he'd been completely different at the park today. It made her doubt her first impression. Maybe he was a jerk after all. But it would have been nice if her date could have been similar to

"Phone Dex."

Kevin, though, wasn't close. Having to pleasantly smile at whatever he was talking about was becoming tiresome as he bragged about having his own mechanic's shop and how he gave special discounts to ladies if she ever needed "her transmission flushed." Selah would have admired his non-stop ability to take ordinary things and make them sound as aggressively suggestive as possible, if she wasn't too busy throwing up in her mouth.

"You know," he said with a creepy glint in his eye, his arm around her shoulder tightening possessively, no matter how much she tried to pull away. "It's a little crowded and hard to hear in here. How 'bout we go out into the parking lot to talk? My Element has seats that fold all the way down . . . like a bed. Anything goes because afterwards I can just hose it out." He said the last part as a whisper into her ear, his breath hot and humid on her skin, making her bones want to crawl out of her body.

The suggestion was tempting, but not in the way Kevin was thinking. She had no interest in seeing his car transform into a cheap motel room, but the closer she got to the parking lot, the easier she had access to her own vehicle. She could make her escape and get that hot fudge sundae.

Selah made another attempt to extract herself from Kevin's grasp, thinking half an hour was long enough for the bet to be counted as paid in full. Except the guy had a grip like a boa constrictor—the more she pulled, the tighter he held, until she all but jerked herself away from him. She made a show of looking at her phone. "Oh goodness. Look at the time. Well, it's been . . . well, not exactly nice, but—"

"Come on, baby, that doesn't work on me. Besides, you haven't touched your drink." His chair scooted closer, his hand, below the table, going to her knee and latching on. "I was just thinking we could—"

"Oh my God! Selah?" The booming voice was followed by a man nearly crashing into their table. "It is you! God! It's been forever! How've you been?"

"Dex?" It took her a second, but the disheveled man with a red flushed face, who was definitely not sober, was the familiar park ranger. His hazel eyes were glassy, his smile a little too bright. Him looking at her as though she was a long-lost friend wasn't an unpleasant experience, even while knowing it wasn't true. Being on a date with a man who was becoming more lecherous made Dex a welcoming sight.

"Hey, I'm Dex. State. Park. Ranger." He pointed to a spot over his chest before glancing down and realizing he wore street clothes and not his uniform. It didn't seem to bother him, though, as he awkwardly lowered his finger and addressed Kevin again while taking the extra seat at the table. "Anyway, did you know this is Captain Selah? *The* Captain Selah, world's greatest balloonist in the world," he said to Kevin.

Her date looked confused. "Like balloon animals?"

Before Selah could correct him, Dex jumped in. "No, you dump truck. Hot-air balloons. In the sky. She pilots them. So smooth you'd think you were floating on a cloud or a balloon . . . or a balloon made of clouds."

If Kevin was impressed by this, his expression revealed nothing. Plus, he probably didn't appreciate the nickname of *dump truck,* even if she agreed the name suited him well.

"Look, pal, we're on a date and we don't need any extra company, so if it's all the same to you, fuck off."

As though Kevin didn't exist anymore, Dex focused on Selah, taking a few attempts to prop his head on a palm as he leaned on the tabletop. "What's the world's greatest balloonist doing with a dump truck like that? He doesn't deserve to hear your pilot voice."

Selah held back an embarrassing giggle because she didn't want Dex getting into trouble. Her date's annoyance was clear, his blue eyes growing hard and menacing. She was inexperienced at having two men fight for her attention. This had never happened before. Not that Kevin cared about her. She was merely a lady body that was, in his mind, available to him.

Selah was also under no illusions Dex wanted her either, based on their conversation earlier on the trail. His motivation in all of this was unknown. Where had he even come from? But his interruption was a silent prayer answered, and it was fun to pretend they were sparring for her.

Regardless, she didn't want Dex to get in a real physical fight over whatever this was, because the whole situation wasn't worth it. *She* wasn't worth it. "Dex," she said calmly, "are you here with some friends?"

"Oh yeah. That's Jon, my best friend in the world and also a park ranger—so, just so you know, I'm not here alone, *pal.*" This last part was directed at Kevin. Dex pointed over his shoulder to a man sitting at the bar who was watching this whole thing, his shoulders shaking in silent laughter.

"Then why don't you go back to your friend and leave us the fuck alone? I'll be happy to escort you—"

"Oh my God, I completely forgot to tell you," Dex interrupted Kevin, doing a soft smack alongside his forehead with the palm of one hand. "You know that earbud you lost? Guess what? I found it!"

Selah was confused because, obviously, the earbud was no longer missing, but she replied, "Oh, yeah?"

"Yup. And then I just happen to run into you. What kind of a lucky break is that? I put it in a safe spot for you and everything. It's in my glove compartment. Do you want it?"

It finally clicked. He was risking getting punched by a dump truck, doing this friendly drunk thing, all in the hopes of giving her an out, an escape. She'd never been so touched in her life. "Oh! Yes! Thank you. I do want it back. Can we get it right now?"

Kevin again wrapped an arm around her shoulder, trying to lock her into place. "Come on, baby. Can't you get it later? It's just an earbud. Fuck off, man." He shoved a rough hand against Dex's shoulder.

"No, you don't understand. This is a very important earbud," she said, attempting to stand.

"It was given to her by someone special," Dex added, standing as well.

Kevin looked torn between wanting to punch Dex in the jaw and not wanting to let go and risk losing her. "Ok, well, maybe I should go too—"

On a dime, Dex's drunk goofball routine switched off, his face transforming into something serious and sober. It made her wonder if he deserved an Academy Award for his previous performance. He rested a palm against the table and leaned toward Kevin, lording over him. "No. *We're* going to the parking lot. You're staying here. There's probably someone else waiting for you, Big Daddy Sasquatch."

Dex turned his attention to Selah, an easy grin slipping into place. "Captain Selah." His hand swept toward the exit to let her lead them away.

The whole thing caught her off guard. What was happening here? On the trail today, he'd been in no-nonsense park ranger mode, clearly irritated with her, but this dark sternness was something else entirely, and it was directed at some loser on her behalf. Selah had never been so turned on by a state park employee before . . . or anyone else, for that matter.

Whatever Dex was doing, it worked because Kevin's expression dropped along with his arms, releasing her. He looked confused and startled. She wasn't sure why he'd give up over a bizarre name like *Big Daddy Sasquatch* when *dump truck* made him appear as if he wanted to punch a wall. Maybe this was some magical park ranger thing used to subdue angry bears and assholes. Regardless, she wasn't going to question it, quickly joining Dex on the other side of the table and proceeding out the door of the brewery.

Safely outside, they stopped at the edge of the parking lot. Selah was free to say anything, but was at a loss for words, especially since she wasn't sure if Dex remained aggravated with her and this whole thing was an act. "Thank you," she said simply, but she never meant the phrase more than she had at any point in her life.

"Is everything okay?" Over Dex's shoulder, his friend, Jon, appeared. She was relieved Kevin hadn't followed them.

"Yeah, everything is okay," Dex replied, his lids heavy as he gave his friend a playful salute. He leaned nearer to her, a scent of rum enveloping her, and in a loud stage whisper said, "He was afraid that guy was going to fight me and then he'd have to jump in and save me."

Selah had no doubt this was the plan because Jon was taller, broader, and appeared to be the sober one between the two of them.

"You weren't worried about that?" She wasn't able to keep the humor from her tone.

"Nope," Dex replied, swaying a bit. "I had to do something. That guy was a shitbag. And I also had a little bit to drink. I don't know if you noticed."

"Alright, buddy, it's been fun watching you get into trouble, but Steph just texted me that Marie forgot her stuffie at home, so I need to make an emergency trip to Warm Springs tonight. Do you still want to get an Uber or come with me?"

Dex said he'd be fine and waved his friend off. After Jon departed, Selah stood there awkwardly. She should get going as well, but instead watched Dex as he leaned against the brick wall of the brewery with a heavy sigh.

"You doing okay there?"

"Oh, yeah. Great. I—I think it's time to go home."

"You okay getting your ride?" she asked.

"Yeah. I've got an app." He had trouble pulling the phone from his pocket and it tumbled to the ground.

She had no obligation to the guy but, considering how the evening could have gone, she did feel one. "Come on. I'll be your Uber and give you a lift." It was only fair.

He stubbornly continued attempting to work his phone. "You're also an Uber driver? Is your Uber voice similar to your piloting one?"

She laughed. "No. I'm just a"—*friend* was too presumptuous and, yet, she wanted some word to describe their relationship more than *a person you've met a few times*. Unable to come up with anything, she finished the sentence with—"a person who wants to make sure you get home okay since you came to my rescue tonight."

"You shouldn't do that." His gaze narrowed in her direction, as if she was in trouble, and he might need to get stern again. Her breath caught in excitement.

"Do what? Return a favor?"

"You shouldn't give a stranger you met in a bar a ride home. It isn't safe. There are all kinds of weird people in the world."

"But I'm not giving a stranger a ride. I'm giving *you* a ride, and I didn't meet you in a bar. Remember?" What he said was true but, regardless of their complicated history, there was something about Dex that felt safe. She couldn't explain it, even to herself.

"I don't know how to argue any further," he replied.

"Good." She took him by the arm, leading him to her truck. "Come on, then."

"And I want you to know that we're even now. You witnessed my embarrassing moment and now I've witnessed one of yours."

"Fine, we're even." Although, truth be told, she hadn't been embarrassed. If there was anyone who should have felt shame, it was dump truck Kevin for being a creep. But if it made him feel better, so be it.

Dex did well enough giving her directions to his house on the western outskirts of Redmond, heading toward the town of Sisters. It was an older home, surrounded by a grove of juniper trees and sage brush. "Here you go. Are you going to be okay getting in?"

"Yeah. Thanks for the ride . . . and for not tipping the car over at the end of it."

"Ha. Ha. Funny. I guess your opinion that I'm the world's greatest balloonist was a lie. Now I know what you really think."

"You're still the best one I've flown with."

"That's very sweet but—" She was about to finish with, *but you've never flown with my dad* and caught herself in time. As far as she knew, Robert had never tipped the basket and landed on top of a client. He was a real professional.

Dex didn't make a move to exit the vehicle. He stared at her as though trying to commit her face to memory. "Goodbye, Selah."

It did feel like a true goodbye, like their paths were never to converge again. It made her sad. "Goodbye."

There was an instant when his focus dropped to her lips, and her heart skipped a beat. He wasn't her date . . . at least not the date she started the evening with. She knew he wasn't going to try anything, but there was a part of her wanting him to try, anyway, to close the gap between them and give her some of the same dark fire and tenacity she'd witnessed earlier at the brewery. The idea of it made her insides want to fizzle with anticipation.

Disappointingly, he snapped from his trance, opening

the door to the truck and promptly fell out, landing in a heap on the ground with an *Oof.* "I'm okay," came a muffled reply, but he didn't make any effort to get up as though the ground was as good of a place as anywhere to spend the night.

"God." Selah put the truck into park, shutting it off before getting out of the vehicle to help him, where he was a pile on the ground. "Are you okay?"

"Yeah, I'm okay. You didn't see that, did you? I don't want us to be uneven again in embarrassing moments."

"I didn't see anything. Here, let's get you inside." She helped untangle his limbs, getting him upright and offering support to him as they walked toward his house.

"This isn't smart. You shouldn't help weird men to their houses. You hardly know me."

"Why do you think you're a weird man?" she asked.

"I don't know. No reason. You're not afraid of crows, are you?"

"No, why—" A loud *caw-caw* cut through the air near her and she yelped, hugging her body closer to Dex's. The source of the sound was a crow perched on the railing surrounding the covered porch. She never considered herself afraid of birds, but it was unsettling that this one wasn't afraid of being near people and didn't fly away.

"That's Harper," he said, while trying and failing to get his key into the lock.

Selah did her best to ignore the bird, taking his key and unlocking the door. As soon as it swung open, the crow jumped from the railing, skittering inside. "Um, a crow just walked into your house."

"It's okay. She does that all the time." As if to prove the point, the bird did a flap hop onto the arm of a couch, walking along the back of it. From this point, it did a short awkward flight to the kitchen table as though looking for some remnants of food, but only found a stack of mail and, in some kind of protest, knocked the envelopes onto the ground.

"You have a pet crow?"

"Harper's *not* a pet. She's a wild animal." Dex fell into a pale-blue recliner, leaning back with his eyes closed. In order to not prove his statement, Harper bounce-hopped to the top of the recliner and began to pick through the strands of Dex's hair, rearranging them in a move that was very motherly for a crow.

"She doesn't seem very wild. How long has she been your roommate for?" Before considering how inappropriate it was, Selah took out her phone and snapped a picture. She wasn't planning on sharing the photo with anyone other than Naomi. She needed some kind of record, because who would ever believe this? And it was kind of cute.

Dex gently swatted Harper away. "Stop that." He squinted at his shoes before leaning forward to untie one, looking like he might tumble to the ground again.

Selah sat on the couch, setting her phone on the coffee table, making sure something wasn't going to happen to him.

"What'd you ask again?"

"Oh, I wanted to know how Harper became your roommate." She found herself working on the half-finished jigsaw puzzle on his coffee table. It was a landscape picture of some colorful scenery with wildflowers at a lake.

Dex chuckled. "She isn't the worst roommate I've ever had."

Selah wondered if Ava had been a roommate of his. If that was the case, there wasn't any feminine trace remaining. The house, at least the parts of it she could see, were quite masculine and utilitarian in its setup. Not that her bedroom was much better, as she hadn't cared about putting in any effort to decorate when she'd eventually be leaving, anyway.

"I found Harper at work when she had a broken wing. The only wildlife rehabilitation in the area wouldn't take her because of limited resources and she's a crow. People aren't generally interested in crows, but I couldn't leave her there so I just . . ." He shrugged while managing to get one shoe off.

"There's not a rehabilitation thing at the park?"

"No."

She found a piece of the lake to fit, and the pieces snapped together. This part made for a better evening than eating a hot fudge sundae in the McDonald's parking lot, all things considered. "Well, it looks like you did a good job with this one, so maybe there should be."

"I'm not an expert."

"But you seem to be knowledgeable about crows, at least from what you were telling me in the park earlier today. Maybe people should see them in a different light."

"Yeah," he replied, "but having a crow roommate makes me strange. You should know better than to hang out at some strange man's house. What if Harper was a cougar instead of a bird? You just never know, and you're too pretty to be mauled by a cougar."

Selah wasn't paying much attention to his drunken ramble until he called her pretty. That caught her attention because it wasn't a compliment she received often. If Dex thought anything more about this, she wasn't going to know because he was again leaning back against the recliner, one shoe off, his hair mussed from Harper picking through it. His eyes were closed with his mouth slightly open, and he was now emitting soft snores.

Selah got up, grabbing the blanket from the back of the sofa, and tiptoed toward him, bringing her finger to her lips for Harper. She wasn't sure the crow knew the sign for silence, but the bird cocked her head and remained silent. Selah gently laid the blanket over him before quietly backing away.

"Goodbye, Dex and Harper," she said before letting herself out and heading home.

Chapter Eight

G OD, HIS THROAT was dry as rocks. It felt like he had swallowed a bucket of salt mixed with a bucket of sand the night before.

It took monumental effort to crack his eyes, and when he did, he regretted everything. Darkness was his new friend. Batman had been on to something when he embraced the dark. But Batman probably didn't wake up with a massive headache and . . . Did superheroes ever take pain relievers? They had to, right? It didn't matter how rich he was or whatever gadgets he owned, Batman probably had to take medication, just like everyone else. Getting up and finding those pain relievers was going to take a superhero effort, especially without the aid of Alfred. All Dex had was Harper.

"Harp, get me some aspirin."

This was answered with an impatient caw rather than obedience because Harper had never buttled in her life and wasn't about to start.

"Shhhhhh," he implored the bird, bringing his hand to his pounding head, only to be met by something gross. "Son of a—Seriously, Harper?" In protest at not being let out at a reasonable hour, Harper had taken a big crow-size shit in his hair. It was a good thing he didn't have to go to work today.

The day was getting worse and that was before the memories from the previous night flooded into his mind.

Oh God.

If he didn't want to crawl into a hole and disappear before, he certainly did now. It was funny how the lack of alcohol in his system made his once heroic actions now seem downright silly and embarrassing. And—

His eyes shot open, expecting to see Selah sitting on his couch, both wanting and dreading it at the same time.

Thank God. She'd left him to his misery and— Goddamn, his neck hurt. Between his head and his neck, and from spending the whole night in the recliner, he wasn't sure if his body was permanently gnarled and would never be able to function the same again. Ava was right. He'd transform into a sixty-year-old man. The thought of going up and down on the path at work made him want to puke his guts out. Dex regretted it all. Everything. He was never doing this to himself ever again.

Harper squawked impatiently, giving him another warning to get up. Not wanting to experience more crow shit, Dex found his motivation to inch out of the recliner at the speed of a sloth and shuffle his way to the door—

Why was he wearing only one shoe?

After releasing the bird, he surveyed his home, seeing how bad it must have appeared to Selah's eyes. It wasn't dirty, but there was a blanket on the ground, his mail somehow got knocked to the floor, and some of his cabinet doors were open, revealing the clutter behind them. His mom would have a panic attack at the state of his home, and it had him second-guessing if his place was fit for company.

Both of his exes felt it wasn't, and he could only assume Selah would too.

He hadn't been expecting someone like Selah to enter his life at all, let alone his house. Dex hoped she was alright and had gotten home okay. Should he check on her? How should he go about it? He could call the High Desert Tours phone line. She might even answer.

Dex pulled his phone from his pocket. Dead. The battery life in his three-year-old phone didn't hold a good charge these days. Maybe this was a good thing, as he'd embarrassed himself enough in front of Selah. It was becoming a bad habit at this point.

The jigsaw puzzle on his coffee table was further along than he remembered. Did he puzzle while drunk last night? No wonder Ava thought he wasn't exciting enough for her.

The phone on the coffee table also brought confusion.

He glanced at the smartphone in his hand to make sure it hadn't teleported to the table without him noticing. The coffee table phone had an oval white sticker with *AV8R on it.* Definitely not his.

Picking it up, he flipped it over. The locked screen appeared. The background image was a picture of Selah and some older man wearing a blue baseball hat with the word *Captain* on the front. With the sun beaming down on them, Selah had never looked happier, her smile electric, her eyes bright. It was one more version of her Dex got a glimpse of, one he had yet to experience in person—wait, there was no "yet" about it because he wasn't going to see her again.

Except she'd forgotten her phone. He had to get it back to her. Phones were important to people, especially these days. They were almost as important as a person's wallet. Selah might need it for her business. Or perhaps this phone was important to her, like her earbuds were. Plus, she gave him a ride home and he had the day off. He owed her.

Dex made the decision to drive to High Desert Tours. After he cleaned up and took some pain relief, of course. No reason to go over there with bird shit on his head.

When he arrived at the farm parking area, the same one he and Ava used the first time, his was the only car there, besides a white company van. He assumed it meant that there weren't any flights today or they were already finished. Dex rubbed nervous palms across his pants, unsure of himself. He probably should have called first. Should he knock on the door of the farmhouse? He felt awkward as hell and one look in a mirror confirmed he looked about as good as he felt, which was terrible.

He wasn't entirely sure why any of this mattered. All he planned to do was knock on the door, drop off the phone, and then be on his way home, where he could take a couch nap while some mindless action movie he'd already seen a dozen times streamed on the TV in the background.

He cleared his throat and ran a hand over his hair before climbing the porch steps to the farmhouse door. Taking a calming breath, he knocked.

The older woman, the one he recognized as Selah's mom, answered the door while on the phone. What looked like a bit of flour was streaked across one cheek. At seeing him standing there, her features dropped, looking worried. Dex must have really looked a fright for that kind of unexpected reaction.

"Becky, I need to call you back," she said before hanging up, her brow creasing with concern. "Oh my goodness. Did you have a tour today? I'm so sorry. Ever since . . . well, my mind has been so forgetful. I really try to be better at keeping track of things." She fumbled with collecting a worn, folded piece of paper from her pocket which might have served as her makeshift schedule. "I'm really sorry about this. I don't want to ruin things."

She appeared on the verge of getting flustered, and Dex had to jump in. "No, it's fine. I'm actually not here for a tour. I'm . . . uh . . . I'm actually looking for Selah." The tips of his ears grew hot, but he did his best not to react any more than this.

"But it's not for a tour?"

"No. Just to . . . talk." Perhaps he should have explained and handed Selah's phone over to her mother and be done with it. Although maybe her mom would wonder why a strange man had her daughter's phone, and he didn't want to invite scrutiny, even if it was warranted. Her mother might agree with him that Selah shouldn't have gone out of her way to give him a ride home when she hardly knew him.

Her mom's expression flipped from relief to actual happiness. "Oh! That's great! I'm so glad you're here to see Selah. I think she's in the office. It's right on the side of the house over there," she said, pointing in a direction. "Did you want something to drink? Some tea or coffee?"

"Uh, no, ma'am. I'm good, thanks. I'm just going to talk with her real fast and then I'll be going," Dex reassured her before taking his leave.

He'd just climbed the steps to a temporary office trailer

when the door swung open. In front of him was a different woman, not Selah, but she hadn't noticed him as she was looking somewhere inside the trailer. "I don't understand why you can't just look at my ideas. You want the company to make money? Well, that's exactly what I'm trying to do too."

Selah's voice came from within the trailer. "I'm not trying to be an asshole, Naomi. I already have enough on my plate getting some of Dad's loans refinanced. I'm up to my eyes in numbers and I don't want to see any more right now. Besides, why would I want to start up a bunch of things and then expect whoever ends up being the new pilot to take over all of that? It's probably going to be hard enough to find someone. If you still want to do it after I leave, you can take it up with them. Things are already overwhelming enough."

"Whatever. You're just being stubborn and—Oh, my goodness. Where did you come from?" Naomi's hand went to her chest as soon as she turned, noticing Dex on the steps below her.

"Hi. I'm looking for Selah." He glanced over his shoulder to see Selah's mom leaning on the outside corner of the farmhouse, watching the whole exchange.

"Are you now? Well, that's interesting." Naomi's smile grew brighter. "Sister dearest, you have a gentleman caller." She stood back, opening the door wider to allow him access.

"Who?" Selah asked.

It took a moment for his eyes to adjust once he entered. Selah was leaning back in an office chair with her laptop on her lap and her legs propped up on a desk, eating a bagel. She was wearing her no-nonsense flight uniform of navy pants and a tight black T-shirt. Her aviators rested at the top of her hairline, holding her dark curls away from her face. In short, she looked like a badass.

Her eyes widened in surprise, her feet quickly landing on the floor as she sat up. "Dex? What are you doing here?" She moved her laptop to the desk along with the bagel, dusting the crumbs from her shirt.

"I, uh, just wanted to make sure you got back okay last night." His nerves hit him full force.

"Oh. Well, as you can see, yeah, I managed to get back okay."

"Great. That's good. Glad to see it." Also, duh, because nothing was more obvious. He wanted to sink into the floor at his apparent awkwardness, and would have, if he didn't have an audience. It didn't help that Naomi continued to stand and watch as he stumbled through the conversation.

"How are you feeling? Do you want some water to drink or something?" Selah asked.

"I'm fine. Actually, the real reason I stopped by was be-cause—"

Suddenly, the door crashed open and another young woman with long, curly hair burst through. "Oh, hi! Did I miss anything yet?"

"Now you show up? And what do you mean, did you miss anything? What is there to miss besides you doing your job? In that case, yeah, you've missed a whole lot," Selah said flatly.

"I'm not listening to you right now. Mom just said there might be something interesting to see around here finally." The younger woman grinned at him, while sweeping an assessing gaze along the length of his body. He had another urge to brush his hand across his hair to make sure it was truly clean and neat.

"Oh my God," Selah huffed in an impatient breath. "Mom? Mom!"

"What?" came the muffled response outside the closed office door.

"Why is everyone being weird right now?" Selah shouted, probably to make sure her mother heard the question as well. She turned her attention to Dex again. "Sorry. I don't get a lot of, uh, visitors to the office. Obviously. Those two are my younger sisters, Naomi and Hailey. The woman spying through the door is my mom, Elena."

"I'm not spying," her mother said from outside the trailer.

"Oh. Sorry. Should I not have come? You don't like visitors?"

"Oh, no, I'm okay with you visiting. Wait, are you visiting? Or did you need something?"

"I just wanted to give you this. You forgot it at my place." He removed her cell phone from his back pocket and handed it over.

She opened her mouth to reply, but before she could say anything, her mother jumped in to say, "What? What is it?!"

"It's a phone," Hailey answered. "Wait just a minute." She swooped over, took Selah's hand so she could rotate it and look at the other side. "It's Selah's phone!"

Naomi released a squeal. "Oh my God, is this the guy you went on a date with last night? So you weren't lying? You actually did it? And you went back to his place?

Selaaaahh!"

"They're dating?!" her mother asked. "Ask him if he wants to join us for a family dinner someday."

Dex's cheeks burned at the misplaced attention, but truth be told, he'd never experienced this kind of excited reception before. Meeting his previous girlfriends' parents hadn't been bad, but they were never at this level of enthusiasm. Selah's family appeared ready to declare him a member of the family. It was similar to when he was a kid, going to Lincoln's home. After a few months of feeling rejected, this was nice, even while knowing the situation wasn't what they thought.

Selah rolled her eyes. "Okay, everyone needs to calm down. Mom, why don't you just come in instead of snooping through the door?"

"I'm not snooping. I'm giving you your privacy, just like you asked." To prove this, she remained outside the office trailer.

"Okay, first of all, you all are jumping the gun. All I did was give Dex a ride home last night."

Boiling down their whole experience to giving him "a ride home" was somewhat deflating, even if it was true.

"I accidentally left my phone there. That's it. Thank you, by the way, for returning it. I was freaking out this morning when I couldn't find it and was about to pull up the Find My Phone app to locate it. I tried to call it. Why didn't you answer?"

"Oh, you must have called when I was in the shower." He wasn't ready to admit he spent a good twenty minutes of his shower standing under the hot stream in an attempt to feel human again.

"So you lied and you didn't go on a date last night?" Naomi asked, giving her sister a light smack on the arm.

"No, I didn't lie. I went on that date last night. Just not with him. Right, Dex?"

"Uh, that's right." Dex remembered the asshole, too.

"Well, now I'm totally confused," Hailey said.

"Anyway, it was horrible and I'm not doing any more bets with either of you ever again. Besides, there's no point in me going on dates because who knows where I'll be living whenever I get a different piloting job." Dex wasn't sure how he looked, but her sisters—and probably their mother—looked disappointed with Selah's speech. "Plus," she continued, "Dex just got out of a serious relationship, so you know, nothing is going to happen there. And I doubt he appreciates all of this when he only stopped by to give me my phone back. As usual, you're all making things really awkward for a lot of nothing."

"And I don't want to date a pilot," he heard himself say. Dex didn't know why he said it. Maybe because he was tired of being the rejected one. It didn't matter that neither one of them had approached the subject of dating. Regardless of the truth of her statements, it remained a blow to his ego that whatever was between him and Selah was a whole "lot of nothing," even though yesterday, there were times it felt like something.

He only blurted the words because her dating him sounded like such a no-go, it might as well been a brick wall. He wanted to assure her . . . or him . . . that, yeah, he agreed and wasn't interested either. Anyway, if she could eat a bagel while looking like a badass, it probably meant that, at some point, she'd outgrow him, and he'd be blindsided again.

"Right," Selah responded, throwing him an odd look, but her mouth kicked up on one side as if she wanted to laugh. He liked to think she'd worn this same expression during that first phone call they had. "Totally understandable. No one ever wants to get with a pilot. And, I"—she pointed to herself—"am not looking to be anyone's rebound."

"She's too short," Dex added because he couldn't help himself. Turned out, he liked amusing and befuddling her.

"Did he say my Selah is too short?" Elena asked from the other side of the door, the tone so indignant he half expected her to rescind the previous dinner invitation.

"It doesn't matter, Mom, because I find him too tall."

"And she's too cool." Okay, maybe he'd taken it too far with that one.

"Yes, okay, so there you have it," Selah said, throwing up a hand before standing. "Dex and I will never be together. It's impossible and there will never be anything between us. Let me walk you out." With that declaration, the matter appeared to be settled, and everyone grumbled while going on their own way. Selah led him from the office, and they settled into a casual walk toward his car.

"Sorry. I'm sure you weren't expecting all that just for returning my phone. Thank you, by the way."

"Yeah, you're welcome. Thanks for the lift. I wasn't too much, was I?"

"No. It was fine. And I liked meeting Harper."

"She wasn't a jerk to you?"

Selah laughed. "No. She was fine."

They arrived at his car, but he wasn't eager to leave. He liked talking to her, but finding an excuse was getting harder.

"I hope dropping off my phone wasn't too much out of your way."

Even though this was his only purpose for the drive, that and to make sure she got home okay, he didn't want to reveal this to her. "No, I . . . was heading to the park today, anyway," Dex lied.

"You're working today? You're not even wearing your park uniform."

Dammit. "No, I'm not working but . . . I was thinking about what we were talking about last night—"

"You remember what we talked about?" She appeared skeptical.

He leaned against the side of his car, crossing his arms. "Yes, I remember. I wasn't that bad."

"Okay, so what were we talking about?" Her lips pulled into a smile as she tilted her chin upward. Her cuteness would distract him to no end.

"Well, about Harper and a wildlife rehabilitation re-source and—" Like a bolt of inspiring lightning, it struck him. Maybe if she thought his idea about the wildlife education and rehabilitation was a good one, it actually was. And since she ran her own business, Selah could probably give him some tips, and this didn't have to be the end of their contact. "I think having something like that at Smith Rock would be a good idea. It could be educational for visitors because they can learn about local animals, including crows. Plus, we can help local wildlife that needs it."

"Yeah, I like it. It doesn't hurt to at least try, right?" she said.

"Of course, it won't be easy." It might even be impossible, but Dex was excited by the prospect, anyway. "I'm just a ranger without much pull, and my boss is probably going to tell me no because governmental earmark money for park improvement projects is already tight, and this would probably be really expensive."

"Doesn't the park sometimes get private donations for something like that?"

"Well, yeah, maybe. I just have never tried to undertake something like this before."

"Neither myself nor High Desert Tours has that kind of money, but we might be able to help in a small way, at least with visibility. You know, if you ever need that."

"Really?" He'd love to have the prospect of seeing her again, even if there was no future between them, other than as acquaintances. Any excuse was better than none.

"Sure. For Harper."

"Oh, yeah. For Harper." Dex shouldn't lose sight of this. Getting to see Selah was a bonus. Harper shouldn't always get shafted in attention, and he could relate. In a world where majestic eagles and beautiful peacocks existed, some people were simply crows, like Dex.

"I get it, though. We here at High Desert Tours could use the exposure too. We're getting closer to the end of summer and things always get a little tight around here once the weather turns cold."

"You still fly in the winter?" he asked.

"Sure, if the weather's good. I'll fly anytime. Do you

have any ideas on how to go about starting the rehab?"

"Uh, not yet." He wished his brain was quicker this morning instead of sluggish due to a recovering hangover.

"Well, if you ever need a brainstorm pal . . ." She let the sentence linger, but it felt like an opening, something full of possibilities.

"Okay. That sounds great." Even if the whole thing didn't work out, at the very least, it was a consolation prize. "Maybe . . . I can text you later to discuss it?"

To his surprise, he left the farm with her number in his cell phone and his in hers. It buoyed his soul in a way pain relief pills couldn't touch, and it was all thanks to Harper.

Chapter Nine

S HE WASN'T SURE what made her agree to give Dex her
phone number or to imagine there was anything worth
developing between them, even in a business sense. Especially since a wildlife center didn't have any connection to High
Desert Tours or her goal of becoming a real pilot.

But Selah also knew they had to do something for her
family's business. Naomi was right. While her sister's ideas
were sometimes out there, like kids' birthday parties in a
balloon—which sounded like trouble and a huge liability—
their attempt at finding their footing the normal way was
becoming discouraging, and their father's debt wasn't
disappearing at a satisfying rate. Before Dex had shown up
with her phone, Naomi had given her the news that their
attempt to be featured in the *Bend Bulletin* had been pulled
because the newspaper decided Soaring Over Oregon would
make for a better story and went with them. No matter how
hard Selah worked, there were constant roadblocks being
dropped, and she was beyond frustrated.

Regardless of the reason for exchanging numbers, Selah
liked talking to Dex. He was a nice diversion from her
normal, everyday life, especially since at the beginning, their
messages had little to do with business.

I get what your phone sticker means.
It only took an embarrassing long
time to finally get it. AV8R. Aviator!
Clever.

> *Oh yeah. My dad gave me that when*
> *I got into flight school.*

The same sticker had been on Robert's phone as well, which now sat dead, propped up next to his urn, somewhere on her mother's cluttered dresser.

Sounds like he's proud of you.

> *He was.*

Selah should have replied, *yup*, and kept things moving. Those two words could pack a lot of meaning in any number of ways and, obviously, Dex wasn't going to know, nor did he need to.

Except his comment about her dad being proud of her pricked at some emotion. In the privacy of her vehicle, currently parked in the spot behind the townhome she shared with her sister, she wanted to feel the prick, to know she still could feel it. Selah could be as cool as marble when she needed to, but right now, she allowed herself to feel something different, to feel some of the loss.

It took several minutes for Dex to respond, the minutes long and agonizing as she watched the conversation bubbles appear, disappear, and then reappear and disappear again. Whoever invented this feature on phones did it as a cruel joke to torture people.

His response came before she could change the subject to

something else and end the misery.

*Sorry. Did I just step into something I
shouldn't have?*

No. It's fine.

She wasn't sure if this was reassuring or not, but she was used to managing. She could be fine. Selah was always fine these days.

*I don't think anyone has ever given
me a sticker before. I get other
things. Do you know that crows are
generous gifters? When they like you,
they bring you gifts. Today, Harper
left this for me.*

Under the message was a picture of Dex's palm. In the center was a small, grimy, heart-shaped button.

*That's cute! Do crows actually un-
derstand the significance of a heart?
My mind is blown.*

*No . . . at least, I don't think so. She
just likes finding things that seem
unusual to her. Yesterday, she
brought me this.*

The next image was a single metal dangle earring, dirty and bent.

*To raise money for the wildlife reha-
bilitation, you can loan her out to
find lost items at Smith Rock, like a*

*crow search and rescue, but instead
of people, she's looking for earbuds
or lost wedding rings.*

*See! I knew it was a good idea to ask
you for help. You're already coming
up with good ideas. I was just going
to throw this away.*

*Noooo, you can't do that! She prob-
ably went to a lot of parks and dirt
paths to find the perfect gift for you.
What does a crow get for a park
ranger that has everything? Sorry,
but you have no choice but to pierce
one of your ears and wear it.*

*I get one gift from a crow, and now I
have to be a pirate?!*

*Yup. Pretty sure that's crow law. You
can thank the founding fathers for
that one. I believe it was Benjamin
Franklin who fought to get it included in the Constitution.*

He reacted to her text with a laughing emoji and she liked it because she was laughing in her truck as well. Her whole mood completely turned around.

This might be why, after a couple of text conversations during the week, she agreed to meet at his place after work to brainstorm about the wildlife center. They kidded themselves into thinking they'd be less likely to get sidetracked if they were meeting for a specific reason. Or maybe she was the only one kidding herself because she wanted to hang out, to feel like she could be a different version of herself with Dex. She needed some space where she didn't have to be anyone's rock.

"Hey," she said as she exited her truck, a small swarm of butterflies buzzing through her stomach.

He sat in one of the red plastic Adirondack chairs on the porch, drinking a bottle of some kind of kombucha drink. Besides warm tanned skin, he didn't look as if he'd spent the day under the hot sun at the park. He looked refreshed, wearing a simple dark green T-shirt and jeans, no uniform in sight. It was still odd to imagine Dex had a full wardrobe in his closet other than hangers upon hangers of park ranger uniforms—almost the same as a kid discovering their elementary school teacher also went to grocery stores and didn't live at the school.

Harper, perched on one of the porch railings, cawed twice in greeting. Dex lifted his head from his phone, a smile slipping into place. Selah was a touch nervous about if she should hug him in greeting or what. Her family were big huggers. She was relieved when the decision was made for her because he didn't get up from his seat, only did a small, playful salute and said, "Captain."

"Captain was my father. Selah is fine."

"Selah, then."

"Ranger Dex." She took a seat in the other Adirondack chair, sliding her sunglasses to the top of her head. Dex offered a chilled extra bottle of kombucha. "Thanks," she said, twisting the lid off and taking a healthy sip. It had the sweetness of marionberries, mixed with the zing of ginger, the flavor fizzling on her tongue.

While Dex did have neighbors, there was a healthy distance between them. Real space, with plenty of old-growth trees, and it smelled warm and earthy. If she couldn't be in the sky, this was a fine spot at ground level. She leaned back, her nerves leaving her and a sense of relaxation and calm taking their place.

"You ever meet Smokey the Bear?" she asked, taking another sip from her bottle.

"Have you ever met the Red Baron?"

She almost choked on her drink because his quick follow-up question was unexpected. "Excuse me? Is that a dig at my age?"

He shook his head, laughing. "No, but Smokey the Bear died sometime in the seventies. How old do you think I am? Or how old do you think Smokey the Bear is?"

She studied him, feeling brave enough to take a guess. "Thirty?"

Dex was in the middle of taking a sip and held up two fingers.

"Aw, thirty-two then."

He turned a scrutinizing eye in her direction. She returned this with a coy look, raising an eyebrow. She wasn't sensitive about her age. It was just a number and, whatever, she didn't care. It was more that Selah enjoyed seeing guys squirm at having to choose a number. It was her turn to see how courageous he was.

"Twenty-two?"

She flicked her bottle cap at him. "Shut up. You don't honestly think I'm twenty-two."

Harper responded with her own squawk.

"Yes, exactly! I agree with Harper. You're nothing but a big caw-ward," she said to Dex.

"Ha! I didn't know you did dad puns. Okay, then. Thirty-two?"

"Oh my God! You think I look thirty-two?" She feigned shock. "You think I'm an old crow?"

"But *I'm* thirty-two. Are you saying that's old? How old are you?"

Selah schooled her features into prissiness, replying, "Thirty," before taking a sip.

Dex laughed heartily, sending bright bubbles of pleasure through her chest. "Get out of here with that fake outrage."

They soon got down to real business, but only after Selah begged him to drag his coffee table onto the porch so they could work on his current jigsaw puzzle while they chatted. She found it easier to keep her focus on something else, instead of catching herself gazing into his hazel eyes.

"Did you talk to your boss about your idea already?" she asked.

"Oh, yeah, that went great," he replied with sarcasm. "She basically laughed me out of the yurt. You have no idea how damaging it can be to your ego to be laughed out of a yurt. As expected, the answer basically boiled down to no budget, no interest, and, most importantly, no budget."

"Wait, so is that it?" If the whole thing was impossible, what was she doing here?

Unless he wanted to hang out with her too? But why not say so instead of creating an excuse? There was a part of her wanting to believe this was true.

Selah reached for a puzzle piece within the box, the same

one as him, and their fingers tangled together. His felt strong and tender. Her gaze lifted, which was a mistake, because exactly what she had feared happened. She got lost staring into his eyes. She counted on him to put an end to it, to stop touching, to break this connection, but he didn't move either. Her skin flushed hot.

Harper's squawk startled them both, bringing them back to their senses. Dex muttered an apology before pulling his hand away and surrendering the disputed puzzle piece to her.

Selah cleared her throat. "So, about the project?" she said to remind both of them of the conversation they were having while concentrating extra hard on fitting the puzzle piece together with its correct partners.

"Oh, well, Chris said, *Go find yourself a wealthy benefactor who cares about crows and ducks.* And, yeah, I guess she was being sarcastic, but then I thought, why not? Smith Rock is famous, so it's easy to believe that wealthy people visit just as much as poor people. If we can get enough attention, maybe it'll generate some kind of interest from the right person."

"Except getting people's attention these days isn't easy."

"True. Although, a hot-air balloon always catches people's attention. I know it catches my eye when I happen to see one at work."

Considering *The Blue Wonder* was most likely the balloon nearest to him when he was at work, she wondered if he'd seen it and thought of her. Or would he only think about what a bad experience that flight was? Maybe he hated the sight of her balloon, its whole association tainted because of one bad proposal. It was hard to tell from his words whether this was a good thing or bad. If anything, it reminded her the guy was fresh off the relationship wagon and she should be more careful when choosing and picking puzzle pieces.

"Well," she started, "it's not like I can give people hot-air balloon rides inside the park as it wouldn't be very practical, and I don't know how we can connect it in people's minds to wildlife or rehabilitation or any of it, although . . ." An idea struck her, and she wasn't sure if it would work, but decided to blurt it out, anyway. "What if . . . what if the park had some kind of educational event, but we turn it into a picture slash Instagram moment?" Her pointer finger rubbed across her bottom lip, a habit she was prone to do while concentrating.

Dex leaned his head against a hand, his attention focused on the movement, his eyes softening. It wasn't clear if he was listening, but then asked, "What do you mean?"

"Okay." She spread her hands in front of her as though about to reveal something big. "Tethering. We set up the balloon in some flat area at the top of the park, like maybe the RV parking area, but it'll be tethered to the ground. I'll use my whisper burner mode to keep the envelope inflated and people can take pictures in front of it. We're getting closer to the end of the season, so people are going to be looking for opportunities for family images to use on this year's holiday cards, or maybe they just want to take a nice image for their social media. And what cooler image can you have than taking a picture in front of a hot-air balloon with Smith Rock in the background? Right?"

"Yes." He pondered this for a moment before nodding.

"I think my boss would really like this. If we can promote it, it might draw people in. And balloons are in the sky, just like crows, so maybe we can connect these two things. Harper and I can have a table nearby. Help Harper's friends. If people take pictures, learn about Harper, they might be more willing to make donations to the Smith Rock non-profit organization. It might not be enough to get the wildlife rehabilitation center, but it'll still help the park."

"As long as you think Harper will be okay around people. We don't want to stress her out and have some bird accident with someone or the balloon." She didn't want to imagine what that could be, but she'd feel bad if something were to happen. Tethering wasn't the easiest thing, as balloons wanted to soar away, but it might be worth it for the attention. Naomi would be proud of her for coming up with this out-of-the-box idea.

Wrapped inside the Moreno barn was the new envelope her dad had purchased. All this time, she hadn't been able to bring it out. It was his. But this might be the opportunity they needed to drum up business for High Desert. They needed a balloon that would pop against the background and get people to remember them. Maybe this was the nudge she needed to finally face it.

"Harper should be okay. I've brought her to the park half a dozen times already, mostly in the hopes she'd want to stay, instead of living with me. The problem is that she's not afraid of people and prefers my food, so you can see how well that turned out." He did a half eye roll in the same direction as Harper with a smile, which was the most charming version of an eye roll she'd ever witnessed, more playful than sarcastic. "As long as people give her space and don't crowd her, she might even pose for a picture or two and not be an asshole about it."

Her brain couldn't stop zipping along. "Oh, you know what? I can get my sister, Hailey, to do some social media videos for us so we can get the word out to even more people. If they're able to donate online, it might mean more money."

"Your sister would do that for us?"

Selah tried not to focus on the word "us" too deeply. There'd never been an "us" between them before. She casually flicked a hand through the air and replied, "Oh, sure. She owes me. Plus, she supposedly does really well on the Loop app. Her channel is some kind of gossip thing. Her handle is @HaileyTeaTime. I don't really get it, but I know she gets a lot of views. As long as we're okay with her having creative license, I think she'll be willing to do it. But this way, we can cast our wealthy benefactor net even wider than just local park visitors. You never know."

Harper hopped off her perch onto the table and grabbed a bright blue piece from the puzzle box, dropping it into Dex's hand before returning to her spot. Like some kind of magic trick, he put the piece in the exact spot it belonged, snapping it together with an easy click, his gaze flicking to Selah's with a grin. "Well, friend, I think you, me, and this plan are going to fit together perfectly."

It was all so smooth, Selah almost swooned right there. It was too bad she'd declared swooning was prohibited. She laughed it off instead. There was nothing else to it. Friendship with Dex would have to do.

Chapter Ten

WHEN PRESENTING HIS and Selah's idea to his boss, Dex worried he was about to be laughed out of the yurt again. He'd also talked it over with Jon, who raised his eyebrows at the mention of Selah's name but, in the end, was encouraging and offered his help if they needed it. Jon even offered some good suggestions, such as where would be a nice spot to set up the balloon and they should make a designated spot for people to line up to take pictures. This way there would be a safe distance around the balloon, and people would be able to get the whole balloon with Smith Rock in the background. With both Selah and Jon helping him, it gave Dex the confidence he needed to talk to Chris.

As much as Dex gave Chris a hard time about shooting down his ideas, the old-school, stout woman was a fairly reasonable person, even if she insisted on wearing the traditional campaign-style hat. Chris wasn't a bad boss. She tried to give the rangers under her leeway in running the park, as long as things ran smoothly.

This time there was no laughing. In fact, Chris loved the idea and asked if she and her wife could get a picture in front of the balloon so they could use it for this year's Christmas card. After the date was picked, with confirmation from

Selah and her team, everything for *Postcard Day at Smith Rock* was settled.

Dex was pleased with the possibility of having a reason to talk to Selah. He'd had friends before. There was Jon, who'd become a good friend, but this thing with Selah was different. Maybe because she was funnier than Jon, made him think about things in a different way and, also, he could feel at ease around her—he didn't always feel awkward and strange in her presence. He might still be a human-version of a crow, but she didn't seem to mind. His world was that much brighter when she was around. Maybe what they said was true and there were three hundred days of sunshine a year. At this point, he'd lost count, anyway.

It was weird. Ava had been a part of his life for at least a year. They'd been broken up for three months, and yet, it felt like a lifetime ago. It was one phase of his life, and he was entering into a new one, a better one, and rarely looked backwards. He supposed that in itself was telling about his and Ava's relationship.

But, obviously, this thing with Selah wasn't a romance or even the beginning of one. She had made it clear her plans didn't include staying in Central Oregon and she had no interest in dating him or anyone else. His only hope was friendship, and there was no "taking this friendship to the next level." What did that even look like? Was it things like agreeing to be godparents to each other's kids or donating a kidney if necessary?

Whatever this was, he would have to be satisfied, because he wasn't going to get anything else. This was easier in theory than in practice, and nothing tested him more than the morning of their shared event at Smith Rock a few weeks later, in mid-August.

Their trucks and the white High Desert Van arrived early, parking in a designated area. From the van came her mother, sisters, and some guy he thought was also at the launch on that fateful proposal flight. Selah slid out of the driver's side of her truck, dark wavy curls framing her heart-shaped face.

Selah wasn't like Ava, but he no longer wanted someone like his ex. Selah was a special mix of cute and tough, which he thought was impossible, but she did a good job of proving him wrong. With the aviators in place and wearing a tight white tank top, navy pants, and black boots, she looked confident and competent. Dex was beginning to understand the preference for people in uniform . . . not his uniform, of course. Park rangers were rarely asked to pose for provocative calendar spreads, and probably for a good reason. Selah's clothes weren't necessarily classified as a real uniform, but it was her flight getup. It meant business. And on her, it looked sexy as hell, and he'd quickly part with his money if someone was offering a calendar featuring her.

Jon snapped him from his hot-air balloon pilot calendar fantasies by strolling toward the group with a hand raised in greeting before saying, "Hey there."

Selah greeted Jon warmly, hugging him and then introducing the ranger to the rest of her family, who all hugged him as well. Dex had never seen so much hugging in his life. There was no reason to be jealous because he didn't need hugs. He'd gotten this far in his life without many of them. It simply made him curious what it would be like to be in a hug-heavy family. He also wondered if living with Harper made him smell a certain way and this explained his lack of hugs.

"Hey," he said, interrupting the group, his hands stuffed deep in his pockets.

"Hey, Dex." Selah gave him a soft smile in return before sliding past him to drop the tailgate of the truck transporting the balloon equipment. She hopped up, along with Naomi, and they started undoing its ties. The other man quickly introduced himself as Boone, and he helped wrestle the basket off once the tailgate lift lowered it to the ground before tipping it to its side.

Selah's mom approached him. "Dexter. It's good to see you again. You're still invited to dinner one of these days. You need to come. I'll make you something special." She wrapped her arms around his middle, squeezing him warmly. He was so taken aback, all he could do was return the hug with an awkward back pat, proving he was the hug amateur. Even his own parents never called him Dexter. It was a reverse nickname, but was genuine in sincerity, and he liked it.

"Yes, ma'am. It's good to see you too. What happened to the other balloon? The blue one?" He watched as Selah, Naomi, and Boone unfurled and unstretched this current one, revealing bright rainbow colors instead of the sun-bleached solid-blue one.

"Oh, we still have *The Blue Wonder*, but Selah thought this one would stand out better for pictures," her mother said.

"You name your balloons?"

"Their dad started the tradition, my Robert. God rest his soul." Her eyes grew sparkly with unshed tears. "He said his balloons were like big ships of the sky, and like ships, it needed a name. He bought this one shortly before he passed away. It's never been used before."

Dex's gaze couldn't help but seek Selah out, wondering if this balloon, and the moment, was affecting her. It was hard to tell behind the reflective sunglasses. Her motions were mechanical and efficient, like she'd set up hundreds of balloons before and this time wasn't any different.

"What's the name of this one?"

Selah's mother shrugged. "It doesn't have one. Not yet. I'm hoping when she stops thinking of herself as Number One and sees herself as a captain, it'll get one."

Dex didn't entirely understand what Elena meant, but it felt rude to pry. "I should go see if they need any help," he said.

"Yes, that's a good idea. Selah doesn't really ask for help very often, but it doesn't mean she doesn't need it. Be careful, though. It's easy to forget that a tethered balloon can still be a little dangerous. They, like their pilots, don't like to be tied down, when all they want to do is take off."

"Uh, okay, I'll keep that in mind," he said before heading over.

By that time, the team was almost finished and there wasn't much for him to do. But he, with the rest of the group, watched with amazement as the balloon filled with air, slowly growing fuller and rising into the air until it was perfectly over the basket. The moment was the same as witnessing magic, and Selah was the magician who controlled a giant flame thrower. Witnessing her do this would never not be cool. The final reveal drew claps from nearby visitors, and Selah's sisters hugged each other and then their mother.

The balloon's colors were bright and pristine, standing in contrast to the sky. It had rainbow vertical stripes with bright white font reading *High Desert Tours* and there was a silhouetted flock of birds in flight above the words. Early visitors broke out their phones to take pictures.

Selah, of course, stayed with her sky ship, remaining stationed inside the basket. Her arms were crossed over her chest, and she peered upward into the center of the balloon. Even as an amateur hugger, he wanted to wrap his arms around her and hold her to his chest. Now that he knew something about the history of the balloon and the loss of her dad, he wanted to hug the whole family, but he especially wanted to hold her. He couldn't deny it anymore. Dex was simply inexplicably drawn to her like she embodied her own gravitational pull.

"Hey," he said as he approached. "Everything okay?"

She continued staring upward, facing away from him. "Yup. I'm fine." She finally turned, but the most important part of her expression was hidden behind the aviators. "Just make sure Jon knows that we don't want people coming up to the balloon if we can help it. These things can still be a little unpredictable even when tied down. I don't want anyone getting hurt. So, if we can keep pictures over there, by your table, then that's probably for the best." She was in full business, piloting-mode. It was hard to see the other Selah he had gotten to know these last couple of weeks. It made her feel untouchable again.

"Okay, well . . . if you need anything, water, something to eat, you can just text . . . or holler at me." He threw a thumb over his shoulder at the spot where his area would be with Jon. His fellow ranger was in the process of setting their table up. He felt silly pointing out the obvious, since she already knew where'd he be. "You know, in case you need me."

"I should be good. I have Boone here to help me." She tipped her head toward the man who sat perched on the side of the basket as if he was a human sandbag. Had he been there the whole time? Boone only grinned knowingly in his direction for some reason. "And my mom set me up with this." She held a bright-pink drinking canister and pulled a child-sized granola bar from her pocket, as though she were prepared to survive a week in this situation.

"Oh, okay, good." Dex didn't have anything else to say, but for some reason, added, "Good luck," making him want to do a full-face cringe before turning and leaving to retrieve Harper, who was waiting in her carrier in the visitor center.

For him, the day was fun and busy. It was exciting to see people come specifically because they heard about the event he helped create. At one point, there was a long line to participate. In addition to this, he got to do his favorite thing, which was talk to guests about the park, wildlife, and Harper. Many people donated, leading him to feel successful, no matter what.

There was a flaw in the whole plan, though. He didn't get to hang out with Selah. He had more interactions with her sisters and mother than he did with her. Naomi and her mother chatted with people, using people's phones to take pictures while slipping them High Desert Tours business cards. Her other sister, Hailey, flitted about with her phone like a busy hummingbird, taking images and video. Sometimes he or Harper was her focus, but he tried to ignore it because he wasn't sure what to do that would appear natural and not awkward.

None of this stopped Dex's attention from sliding in the direction of the balloon or its pilot. It was a huge distraction. Literally. His focus drifted her direction more than once, and she may have even returned his look. It was hard to tell with the sunglasses, but she leaned on the basket, propping her head on the bent arm resting on the basket's edge, facing him, before suddenly snapping straight to turn on the flame to add more air to the balloon or talking to Boone and—

What was Boone's deal? Was there a reason he was chosen to stay with her instead of somewhere else? Was there something between them? The situation annoyingly picked at Dex and he wished he wasn't stuck here while she was over there.

At one point in the early afternoon, Selah and Boone swapped spots and Naomi joined the basket. Selah left her post, heading toward the restroom.

"Can you hold down the table? I'm just going to take a quick restroom break," Dex said to Jon.

"Is your bird going to be okay without you, or are you taking it with you?"

"I'll just put her in her carrier." Dex removed Harper from his shoulder, where she'd spent most of the day, keeping herself entertained by latching onto one of his earlobes and tugging, as though he were a slot machine, and this action caused treats to drop out. He put the bird in her carrier before walking toward the restroom and dusting off the top of his shoulders in case there were any feathers or bird dandruff.

As he reached the corner of the cinder block public restroom building, Selah rounded the corner. Almost bumping into each other, her damp hands pressed against his chest and his went to the tops of her arms, stopping a full collision.

"Oh! Sorry," she said.

"Hey. Funny seeing you here. You come to this restroom often?"

She released a laugh, her eyes lighting with warmth. Her sunglasses were on the top of her head, holding those dark wavy curls away from her face, giving her a more open and approachable look again. This was the version of Selah he'd been hoping to see all day.

"Only when my mother insists I drink a whole canister of water. Oh, sorry. I didn't mean . . . it's just water," she replied, removing her hands from his chest, leaving behind damp splotches on his clothes. "There were a couple of kids playing with the hand dryer and I didn't want to wait."

He hadn't removed his hands from her arms, continuing to hold her, liking how she could feel tough and strong and yet there was something delicate about her, something that made him protective. He didn't want to let go, but he did anyway. "You doing okay over in your area?"

She peeked upward at him, smiling softly, "Oh, yeah, doing okay. Boone does a pretty good job keeping curious people from getting too close and he helps keep the basket stabilized."

He supposed Boone's involvement made sense in that respect, but he still felt like a villain, wanting to shake his fist and curse the other man's name. All he could do was respond, "Good. Well, if you need anyone else to stabilize your basket, I can help too." He nearly closed his eyes at the cringe of it all. Did that somehow sound sexual, or was it just him? Either way, he quickly followed with, "Or tackling. You shouldn't have to do it. You're too short."

She flicked him a playful look. "Aw, okay, I see how it is. I must be *this tall* to tackle and, apparently, to date. Is there anything I'm not too short for?"

His suddenly dirty mind came up with some things, but it wasn't appropriate to voice, especially for a friend he hoped to elevate to the next level of friendship. "Piloting is clearly something you're not too short for. And who said you were too short to date?" It had to be another asshole dump truck, and he considered sending Harper to shit on their head as payback.

"Now let me think. Who was it that said I was too short to date?" Selah did that thing where she rubbed a pointer finger against her bottom lip while thinking. It was cute and got him entirely too focused on her mouth. "I think it was some tallish park ranger. He might have a crow as a roommate."

"Me?" *He* was the dump truck? In response, his ears grew hot. He regretted wearing his standard baseball hat instead of something more practical and fashionable, like Chris's campaign-style headgear that was able to hide the tops of his ears better. His boss was clearly onto something. With this reminder, Dex was beginning to remember the whole height conversation and kicking himself for suggesting such a thing. These days, he didn't consider her to be "too" anything.

"I'm also apparently *too cool* to date or something, which I don't even know what that means." Selah did the most sarcastic finger quotes he'd ever seen.

This point remained true. "Yeah, it's all coming back to me now. Hmm. I seem to recall you saying I'm too tall, so it's clearly not just me."

"Exactly. It's all so impossible."

Her face tilted upward and was entirely too pretty. Huh. There was something she was "too" much of, after all. "Yeah, impossible. Can you imagine? What am I supposed to do, hunch over like this?" He tipped over her, coming closer to achieving a new goal of his and still feeling much too far away. "It's not recommended for anyone's spine to bend over like this for any length of time."

"True. Spine health and posture are too important to risk long-term back pain. And what am I supposed to do? Go up on my tiptoes like this?" Selah rose a few inches, their faces now close enough for him to imagine all kinds of obstacles he'd be willing to overcome in order to close the gap, even poor posture.

"What am I? A ballerina?" Losing her balance, she stumbled backwards, her back hitting the building's cinder block wall, and she giggled. "See? It wouldn't work. I have to be the worst ballerina."

Dex couldn't help smiling as he adjusted his position, using a hand on the wall to support himself as he leaned into her space. "So, a better pilot than a ballerina?"

"I guess so. So, again, the whole thing is . . . impossible." The last word was said on a light breath and paired with a coy smile. He was coming to appreciate those smiles. They were the type that made it seem she was holding back intriguing thoughts. He wanted to weasel his way into her brain, to uncover every single one of them, because based on her expression, they were something good.

Before he could reply, Selah's name was called from beyond the building, and she snapped from this intimate bubble. "Oh God. That's my mom. I need to get back to the balloon." Due to her short stature, Selah easily ducked under his arm and jogged to the event area, leaving Dex behind to pick up the pieces of his scattered self. He took a moment to lean against the cool surface of the concrete wall, closing his eyes, and taking deep breaths.

She wasn't supposed to affect him like this, but fighting it also felt like a lost cause.

Chapter Eleven

A S MUCH AS Selah wanted nothing more than to fulfill her dad's dreams of piloting an enormous jet, there was something to be said about the hot-air balloon life. Somehow, even in the higher altitude, where the air was thinner, she could breathe easier. This height had a way of making all the stress slip away, letting her forget about her family's bills and business worries and allowing her to re-center. She understood why people loved it and why, every time she had a scheduled flight on the books, her heart lifted. There was a bright spark of happiness in the knowledge that she got to go up again. The mechanics aspect may be simple, compared to a real cockpit, but hot-air balloon piloting truly was an art, and she was feeling better about her skills all the time.

It almost made the pain of missing Robert a little less. Although, she still missed those hours spent watching *Star Trek* or *Galaxy Quest* together or studying the pi-ball on frosty mornings with fresh coffee in their hands, or just discussing things going on in her life in general. While the hole in her heart remained, and she wasn't sure it'd ever be filled, things were made easier when she focused on the things she could control. The flights, the business, making sure her mom stayed on top of things like paying the bills and taking care of herself. Some days, Selah felt as though she was doing the minimum and yet, she was exhausted by the end of it.

When she had trouble falling asleep, she lay there, thinking about pleasant things like Dex and that goofy crow of his. Her finger itched to send him some random text, wanting to take a chance to see if he was up and would still talk to her now that their shared event was over and there was no excuse to continue communication. Their chats were becoming a bad habit. It wasn't smart to have one person who could turn her whole mood around, to become dependent on someone she would eventually have to part with. But it couldn't be helped. She craved the connection with this man, regardless of what the logical part of her brain said.

One good thing was that business did pick up in the week after their event. So much so, she got to spend nearly every day in the air doing what she loved most. She returned to using The Blue Wonder as her main envelope. While it had seemed to be a good idea at the time to use Robert's new, more colorful one, the prick of pain at Smith Rock had hit a little too strong. It took some clamping and grinding her jaw together to keep her emotions at bay. If she was going to get actual work done, it was better to keep things, like feelings, to a minimum.

Today she had a group of four people scheduled for a flight—a pair of friends and a couple who were celebrating their fortieth anniversary. It was common and more economical to combine groups of people whenever possible. A flight of two people, like those who wanted something more intimate, only happened if they were willing to pay extra.

She preferred groups because it was chattier and full of energy, and it was less likely for her to get wrapped up in her own thoughts.

The flight went well until the older woman, one half of the anniversary couple, took a picture with her cell phone, placing it over the basket's edge. Selah was about to remind the woman this wasn't a good idea when the phone slipped from the woman's hand, plunging to the ground below. The woman became irate when Selah didn't follow her demands to land the balloon immediately so the woman could retrieve her phone.

The woman refused to listen to Selah's explanation that landing on the spot wasn't possible, nor was she going to radio her chase crew to go on a scavenger hunt in search of the phone. Getting mad and blowing up in response to an irate passenger, especially when Selah was responsible for everyone when they were two thousand feet above the ground, wasn't an option. All she could do was flick every emotion off and maintain a piloting frame of mind, one that was emotionless and cool. This mode was becoming easier to switch to.

Either way, being yelled at by someone who was angry wasn't fun. After the tour, Selah returned to the portable office trailer crabby and with a pounding headache. High Desert Tours was no doubt going to get a bad Yelp review, and there was nothing she could do about it.

With a resigned sigh, she took a seat at her desk, undoing the cap on her water canister so she could wash down a couple of pain relievers before tapping her laptop to life.

"Good God," Naomi said, popping in through the door

while pulling her long, wavy hair into a ponytail. "The witch finally left. She was trying to get me to agree to buy her a new cell phone. She thinks that our insurance should cover things like that. I swear that no one reads any of the pre-flight paperwork before they sign it. Are you feeling okay?"

"Headache."

"Understandable. In fact, give me a couple of those."

Selah handed over the bottle of pills. "We're booked tomorrow, right?"

"Yup. It's wild to be this busy this late in the season, but I'm loving it. You know, with fall just around the corner, I was thinking . . ."

Selah didn't hear what her sister said next as she had pulled her phone from her pocket, revealing a text from Dex.

Did someone from the local Bend
news station reach out to you?

"Hey, you didn't hear anything from a local news station, did you?" Selah asked, interrupting her sister.

"No. Were we supposed to? Are we getting featured finally? It's not fair that Soaring Over Oregon always steals the spotlight. This is why I think we should just switch to the new envelope. It caught a lot of eyes when we were doing that thing at Smith Rock. I keep telling you that."

Selah responded to Dex with a negative answer.

They'll probably be reaching out
soon. I got a message from them this
morning about doing some sort of
news segment on Harper and the
park and stuff.

That's great!

They want to talk to you too.

Me? Why?

Selah would rather let Naomi handle this kind of thing, as she was better at it and way less awkward on camera.

I don't know what kind of magic your sister did, but something worked.

Did you get your rich investor?

Not yet. But I also was contacted by some radio station in Colorado for an interview. Not sure what kind of a show it was, but they asked some weird questions.

Colorado? How would anyone there know anything about the event?

Like what kind of weird questions?

She watched the bubbles appear and then disappear again before he finally responded.

I don't know. Just stuff I wasn't expecting. It's not that big of a deal.

Selah was curious, because maybe he was right and Hailey had done something magical for them. It would be nice for her youngest sister to finally do something to benefit the business for once, even if Selah didn't consider it to be real work. "Have you been on Hailey's Loop account lately?" she asked her sister.

"You know I stopped using that app. It was too much of a time suck."

"Yeah," she agreed, going to the barely used app that she'd only downloaded because Hailey kept sending her links to videos, and it was the best way to view them. She went to her sister's page, clicking on the video with a thumbnail of Harper. The video was the crow with some kind of sparkly flashing filter, giving Harper different looks as though she was going to visit the bird version of a dance club or something. Sometimes different accessories and outfits were superimposed over Harper's image, like a crown or heart sunglasses.

Her sister, Hailey, appeared in the corner of this changing imagery of sparkle vomit, wearing a feather boa and singing what sounded like some made-up-on-the-spot song. Her sister had a good singing voice, but this was some weird catchy jingle where she repeated the words "the crow" over some generic beats. Selah had no idea what she was even watching and clearly didn't understand today's youth. At least her sister ended the song with "Harper needs your help" and added a link to a donation page.

"What in the world was that?" Naomi asked her, while inspecting the ends of her hair.

"I don't know. I just asked her to do a few simple videos of the event and that's what she did."

Her sister looked at the screen over Selah's shoulder. "Wow, it got a lot of views, though."

"Yeah, I guess people really like nonsense these days." This was why it was better for Naomi to deal with PR for the company instead of Hailey or Selah.

Her sister laughed. "Hopefully, it translated into a lot of donations for that crow. Do you think that explains the extra business?"

"Maybe—but she didn't even mention High Desert Tours. Why can't she just do what I ask?"

"We're your sisters. I think sometimes you forget that."

She wasn't sure this was true and the words annoyed her, which didn't help her current bad mood. Before she could say anything in her defense, her sister said, "Wait . . . what video is that?"

When Naomi pointed to it on Selah's phone, she accidentally touched it and it started playing.

It was filmed in Hailey's bedroom, the camera set in front of her while she did her makeup, talking as though already in the middle of a conversation. "Gah, stop asking about R. No updates except hate him with my life."

Selah was about to flick the video away, because she couldn't care less about any of this, but before she could, her sister rambled on. "Besides, I have some new tea and this is delicious, so you're gonna want to pay attention, besties. Okay, so, that video with the crow, my sister asked me to do that. This crow was injured and one of the park rangers rescued it and now he wants to do a rehabilitation thing to, I guess, rescue more crows. I mean, crows can be in my crew and are cool but, whatever, it's weird." Hailey moved on to applying eyeliner. "Well, this same park ranger actually took a ride in my sister's hot-air balloon a few months ago. Remember, she's a pilot for my family's business and stuff. He took the ride because he was planning on proposing to his girlfriend. This is the guy." An image of Dex from the Smith Rock event appeared behind her sister's shoulder.

"Yeah, he's nice, but so mid, like mid-mid. And a hot-air balloon ride proposal? Yeah, okay, like watch a TV show or something for some inspiration, friend, because, ugh, cringe. Anyway, the girl said no. She didn't want to marry him. And then when they landed, the basket tipped over and my sister fell right on top of him. Literally. One hundred percent true story."

Selah's heart dropped, making her want to crawl into the deepest hole. What the hell was she going to tell Dex? She had told her mother about the failed proposal and what had happened afterwards, but she hadn't told anyone else. Naomi had kind of been there and only knew some of it. It was clear her mother wasn't the most discreet person and neither was Hailey. Either way, it was Selah's fault her family was publicly humiliating him.

Hailey pulled out a tube of lip gloss, going back to putting on her makeup. "But that's not the end of the story. Because he's been totally making eyes at my sister, the same sister who was at his proposal rejection. I'm not even lying. Look at exhibit one."

It cut to a video from the event and her sister had caught a moment where Dex happened to be looking off in the same direction of her balloon. He could have been looking at anything or nothing. The park was a large place with a lot of activity. Of course, it didn't help that Selah herself seemed to be gazing in his direction at the same time. As if to emphasize the point, cartoon hearts were added to the video before it cut back to Hailey. "Yeah, and that happened all day. I mean, God, they weren't even being discreet about it. And Selah is super insistent that there's nothing between them, but like, be for real with us, sis. They went through this whole thing about why they'd never get together. Doth protests and all that. So is my sister secretly dating the crow park ranger guy? The same guy she had a front row seat for him getting his heart stomped on? Did something else happen on that balloon ride? Did the basket and her falling on him really happen by accident? Hmm."

It cut to another video, this time taken from a slight distance away but showing the area near the restroom where Dex was leaning over her. They looked as if they were involved in an intimate conversation instead of something that could be innocent for a number of reasons that Selah couldn't think of at the moment. "Gross. Seriously. Get a private hot-air balloon, you guys. Ha!"

Her sister then did several rapid air kisses by pressing her palms to her lips and said, "This has been your Hailey Tea Time, besties!"

Selah turned off the video, setting her phone on her desk before turning her focus on Naomi and crossing her arms. "Did you know about this?"

Her sister's eyes widened as she lifted her hands in surrender. "No, I swear. I had no idea she—"

At that moment, the sister in question came parading through the door with an iced coffee drink in a teal tumbler. "Oh my God. I have to show you the color of this nail polish, because it's about to become my whole personality—"

"What the fuck, Hailey? I am so pissed off right now, I don't even want to look at you."

Her sister paused, her shocked gaze switching between Naomi and Selah. "What did I do?" If she suspected the reason for Selah's anger, she was doing a good job pretending to be ignorant because, by all appearances, she was perplexed.

Naomi cut in. "We saw the Loop video you did about Selah and the park ranger—"

"Oh, is that what this is about? Gah, you made me think it was something worse. You need to go touch grass, Selah." Her sister collapsed in one of the office chairs, sliding into a slouched position as she took a sip from the straw in her tumbler while inspecting the paint job on her pointy, perfectly manicured nails.

"This isn't a joke. That was a horrible video, and you need to take it down right now. I'm not kidding. I want it down. I can't believe you would do something like that to Dex and me." Selah hadn't even perused any of the comments, which she was sure were riddled with commentary and would result in her becoming angrier. At this point, she felt bad for Dex for getting involved with the Moreno family. He didn't deserve any of this. Maybe she did, though, for trusting her sister with this one small thing.

The straw popped from Hailey's mouth. "I can't do that, especially not without an explanation. Did you see the numbers on that post? If I take it down, it's just going to make everyone suspicious, especially since it's still making rounds."

"Does it look like I care about your numbers? Take it down."

"*You* told me to work my magic. You said I could do whatever I wanted. I got the spotlight right on the event, just like you asked."

"You think this is what I wanted? For Dex and me just to be tossed under a bus for your entertainment and social media clout? You were supposed to be helping us. If this is your idea of help, I don't want it."

"I was helping! Do you know how hard it is to cut through the noise and catch people's attention? These days you have to either intrigue people or make them mad—"

Selah released a bitter laugh. "Oh, well, that's just great. Congratulations, I'm mad. Do you not get it? Do you not understand anything? Maybe you don't take this seriously because you can just stay with Mom and live off of her good graces forever, having her cater to you while you just do whatever you want and make your silly videos—the rest of us here are trying to keep the business afloat. And maybe it's not important to you, but it's important to me.

"Do you have any idea how hard it is for someone like us to be taken seriously in this business, or really *any* business? To be a young Latina woman trying to be a pilot? I've had to work my ass off. And you're out there telling the whole world I'm crash landing baskets. With one video, you just threw away not only my reputation, but the business's reputation—right into the shit can. And then what are we supposed to do? What is Mom supposed to do?

"And this is not even taking into account how Dex might be affected by all this. What am I supposed to tell him? That my sister blabbed his private business all over social media? That I can't be trusted, either, because it's my fault that I told Mom, and she told you. What if he gets in trouble at work for this? It's easy for you, but this is our reputation that you're playing with.

"We're family. We're supposed to have each other's back, but it's clear I can't trust you to have mine."

Her sister blinked for the first time, her eyes welling up with tears but none of them spilling over, and her expression still one of defiance. "You don't know how hard it's been for us since Dad's been gone. What we've been going through. Not all of us can just pick up and move on as easily as you."

Selah's anger blazed hotter. "Excuse me? *I* don't know how hard it is? I've been suffering right along with the rest of you."

"Even Naomi says she's never seen you cry." Hailey flung an arm in the direction of their other sister.

Selah glared at them. "I'm sorry. I didn't realize I needed to have my heart laid out on a platter for you two."

"Se—" Naomi started to say, but Selah was mad at both of them, mad at the whole damn, rotten world. In fact, she wanted to go into the barn and shred *The Blue Wonder* to ribbons.

Hailey wiped all the tears away with a hand, finding her footing again. "Sometimes I don't get you, Selah. I really don't. And I have been trying around here. Really trying. But you don't see any of it. You want your sisters to have your back? When was the last time you saw us as sisters instead of just employees? And why does it even matter when you're just looking to leave, anyways? Do you even care Dad is currently under a pile of clutter in Mom's room? You were his Number One. You were chosen out of all of us, and you can't get away fast enough. It was clear he loved you best and you weren't even his real daughter. It wasn't your father who died."

Selah didn't have anything left after that. She simply got up, walked out the door, and slammed it behind her.

Chapter Twelve

D EX WAS DISAPPOINTED the only reply he received from Selah, after his last message regarding the reporter wanting to talk to her, was *k, thx*. He wasn't sure what she was thanking him for or if this was an accidental message meant for someone else. Either way, it didn't give him anything, and while his message hadn't required a response, he'd wanted one, anyway.

The whole week had been odd. The news station in Bend wasn't the only one, as he had received other requests from random media sources around the country, most of them being blogs or YouTube personalities. He hadn't replied to those emails yet. Regardless, he needed to talk to Selah about the interview he did for the Colorado radio station. She may never come across it, but it seemed important to at least give her the heads-up on the off chance she did.

"What's going on between you and the sexy hot-air balloon pilot? What's her name? Sara? Are you guys hooking up or what?" the radio personality had asked him.

Dex had been caught off guard by the question. All he could do was release a nervous chuckle and reply, *"It's Selah and, uh, yeah . . . we're just . . . you know . . . friends,"* which didn't sound convincing, even to his own ears. He'd been debating telling her ever since, even though nothing could be changed and—It was only the implication of it all.

Also, it didn't help when his boss, Chris, pulled him aside at work to tell him she didn't care what Dex was doing in his personal life, but maybe take care of it outside the park when he wasn't wearing his uniform. He wasn't sure what Chris had witnessed, but it worried him all the same. Dex should never doubt that his campaign-hat-wearing boss and fellow rangers were as perceptive as hell, and their eyes could be anywhere. The point was, he should know better than to try anything on park property, no matter how big—or, in this case, short—the temptation was.

It was a good thing Chris got a call from the Smith Rock nonprofit, congratulating her on a healthy amount of donations. Also, Chris's wife was quite pleased with their new family photo, so it was more of a discussion than Dex getting written up. He tried to shrug the whole thing off.

After he got home that day from work, he took another chance and sent a text to Selah.

Got a new one if you're interested.

He sent along a picture of a jigsaw puzzle he'd recently ordered online. It was a stylized image of a crow posing inside of a gothic library because Selah once mentioned it would be fun to do something different from landscape images.

She responded after a few minutes.

I haven't had the best day.

He frowned, wondering how to follow up. After thinking and rethinking, causing several false starts which he deleted and then retyped, he came up with a response.

> *Oof, sorry. Today wasn't great for me either. But if doing a puzzle and eating pizza sounds like something you can handle, you should come over.*

It was after the message had been sent did he regret using the word "handle." Shit. He should have picked a word that sounded less of a challenge.

Actually, that sounds pretty nice.
Okay. :)

Suddenly, he had all kinds of things to do as he ordered the pizza and rushed to do the dirty dishes in his sink. He'd at least taken a shower to get the park dust and sweat off before he'd decided to text her. He was putting the last of the dishes in a small countertop drying rack when Harper cawed twice from the porch railing, as though she'd assigned herself guard bird duty. This notified him of the arrival of Selah's dark-green pickup. He tapped a wet finger on the window above the sink, warning Harper to behave herself because lately she'd been in an ornery mood.

Grabbing a towel, he wiped his hands as he opened the front screen door.

"Hi." Selah gave him a warm smile as she approached, and his heart stopped inside his chest. "Hey, Harp. I brought you something." Reaching into her pocket, she removed a small trinket and dropped it onto the wooden railing. "It's just a broken metal zipper tab I found on the ground today. Is that okay?"

"Oh, yeah. Should be fine." He was just happy the bird didn't attempt to snap at Selah. Instead, Harper cocked her head, studying the zipper tab, tapping it with the tip of her beak, before picking it up and hop-flapping away. "Where's my broken zipper tab?" he asked with a grin.

"Here. I went to the dentist earlier this week and they let me pick out a sticker from the kid box. You said you'd never gotten a sticker gift before, so I picked this out for you."

She handed him a small, round sticker featuring a cartoon hedgehog holding a yellow flower. He made plans to put it on his phone case as soon as she departed. The real gift would have been if she would have allowed Dex to wrap his arms around her petite, curvy frame, especially since he knew she had a rough day. Instead, he could only invite her inside. "Come on. Maybe Harper will be too occupied with her present and leave us alone this evening."

Selah took a seat on the couch, dropping a small, worn canvas bag on the ground as she studied the image on the puzzle box.

"The pizza isn't here yet. You wanna talk about your bad day?" he asked, taking a seat beside her.

Her focus remained on the puzzle lid. "Not really." There was a strange vibe coming from her, something cool and closed off. It was clear she wasn't in a talkative mood, and he wasn't going to force the issue.

"We can stream a movie or something if you want."

"Sure. Okay."

Movie. Pizza. Puzzle. Plus, hanging out with Selah. As

far as Dex was concerned, this was a solid Friday night for him.

That was until he switched to a streaming platform and found himself faced with an impossible task—finding the perfect movie. It had to be one that didn't have any sex scenes to prevent things from becoming awkward. Also, he probably shouldn't choose anything too romantic, too dark, too heavy, too anything. He asked her if she wanted to watch anything in particular, and she replied with the dreaded, "No, you can pick whatever you want. I don't mind."

Heated beads of sweat popped along his neck as though this was some sort of test, and he was about to royally screw it up by choosing wrong. His insecurity at being out of touch when it came to good movie choices was putting him on edge.

Finally, he struck guaranteed gold, pushing the play icon. "Oh. Let's watch *Galaxy Quest*."

Her body stiffened, but her gaze remained downcast, focused on the puzzle.

"You don't like it? I can pick something else," he said, reaching for the controller again.

"It's fine," she replied, but she didn't look fine. She appeared pale and uneasy. But she kept her head down and concentrated on gathering edge pieces from the box.

This was how it went for about ten minutes, with only the sound of the movie filling the space, until she hyperfocused on a single piece in her hand. She appeared frozen, except for her chest moving at a rate too fast for normal breathing. He was having trouble paying attention to anything else, certain something was wrong, but not knowing what. Dex opened his mouth to ask her, when she suddenly grabbed her bag, sprung to standing, knocking several puzzle pieces to the floor, and said, "I—Sorry, I need to go. I can't—I need to go."

Dex checked his phone. "The pizza should be here any minute. Why don't we—" but he was cut off with the door slamming shut, leaving him confused. Worried about her unexcepted change in demeanor, he rushed from the house to see if he could catch her before she left. Maybe she had heard his Colorado radio interview and she was upset about—

Dex did a dead stop on his porch. Selah had made it to her truck, but she stood hunched over at the passenger side, bracing herself against it, her breathing heavy and approaching hyperventilation.

Seeing her like this made his blood run cold. It terrified him. He wasn't used to handling whatever heavy emotion this was. Someone else would be better than him. Except there wasn't anyone else, and this was Selah. He strode to her, taking her by the shoulders, and the large dark eyes that met his were filled with so much pain and sorrow. It didn't come as a surprise when she burst into tears.

He pulled her into a tight embrace. Her face pressed into his chest as her whole body racked with sobs. It absolutely killed him, his own chest tightening with helplessness at not knowing what was wrong or how to fix things. All he could do was hold her and murmur, "It's okay" over and over again.

After a while, her sobs lessened, though she remained in his arms, the fabric of his shirt clutched within her fists. "I'm sorry," she said through tears, pulling back. She sounded small, as though every part of her was cracking apart like fragile glass.

He readjusted his arms to fully embrace her body again, settling his head on the top of hers. "You don't need to be sorry."

"I should go home."

Dex hadn't cried when Ava rejected him, or even when Rachel left. It was more of a dark, bitter pit of emptiness moving into his chest. At some point, this dark pit had moved out again. He hadn't noticed when it happened, only that it had. What Selah was experiencing was something else entirely, and he didn't feel great about her leaving until he knew she was okay. "I think you should stay . . . just for a little bit. Until you're feeling okay. Wanna eat some food? Get something to drink?"

"Did the pizza come?"

In fact, the food delivery driver had shown up about five minutes after Selah had started crying. The woman had looked unsure at what she should do in such a situation, choosing to walk delicately to Dex's porch, gently setting the pizza box down and then quietly getting back in her car.

"The driver left it on the porch. It's probably cold by now, but I can heat up some slices for us. Come on." He led her back to his house, one of his arms still wrapped around her shoulder, not wanting to let go yet. It was amazing how holding her felt entirely natural.

"Oh God. Really? So, the delivery driver saw me being a mess too?" She rubbed a hand across her cheeks.

"I shielded your body. She probably thought it was me."

She released a stuffed-up, watery laugh at this. "God. Sorry."

Dex had to let go to pick up the pizza box and opened the door for her. He immediately turned off the movie and got her situated on his couch again. As he heated a plate of slices in the microwave, he brought her a glass of water, and she downed half of it. He pushed the puzzle in progress to one end of the coffee table—they hadn't gotten far, any-way—and put down the heated slices with some napkins. They each grabbed a slice, and she didn't fight him when he relaxed against one end and brought her with him. In fact, her head settled right on his chest and his free hand rubbed along her bicep as they each ate with one hand.

"You wanna talk?" he asked carefully.

"I've just had a really bad day."

"Apparently. Must have been a real doozy. Was it even worse than tipping the basket over and landing on one of your passengers?"

"Oh God. Are you ever going to forget that?"

"Nope. Your website promised a once-in-a-lifetime expe-rience and, boy, did you deliver." He'd probably never forget anything relating to her. Every memory was being locked inside a special chest in his brain.

He took a huge bite from his slice and thought it over. "If you're not going to give me details, I'll just have to guess. Let's see. Some big VIP, let's say the governor of Oregon, booked an important flight for some kind of PR thing and you didn't have the balloon completely hooked in. So just as you were about to take off, the balloon detached from the basket and you all had to watch it swirling about like a helium balloon losing air." He demonstrated this using his pizza crust as a stand in for the balloon in this story.

She laughed and lowered his hand with hers to stop the pizza crust from continuing to make wild loop-de-loops. "Come on. I don't even think that's possible unless you're talking about cartoon physics."

"Okay, then. Maybe this is about a flock of birds with a bad case of diarrhea and they flew over the balloon and—"

"Stop! I'm eating! I don't want this to even have a chance to enter my imagination."

"I'm just going to keep guessing until—"

Selah sat up and he instantly missed the warmth of her body pressed against his, but at least her mood was improving. "Okay, fine, I'll tell you. During the tour today, this old lady passenger was taking pictures with her phone, and she put it over the edge of the basket and . . ." She whistled as one of her hands demonstrated a death spiral downwards.

"What? Why would she even risk that?"

"You work with the public too. You tell me. And then she was like *Well?* And I said *Well, what?* She actually expected me to immediately land the balloon, so she could go get her phone."

"Are you kidding? That phone had to be toast, anyway."

"Right? And I'm just going to randomly land a balloon somewhere with no ground crew? No, I don't think so."

Dex couldn't help grinning at how animated she was getting in retelling this story. It was a completely different side of her. She was lively, full of energy, and hilarious.

"And she was yelling at me because why didn't the basket have smaller baskets on the outside to catch things? Because this kind of thing must happen all the time. Then she came up with some wild theory that I probably had some side hustle in collecting people's dropped items and making money off of it by selling them. She kept saying, *My pictures! What about my pictures?* Apparently, that phone had three years' worth of pictures on it and she hadn't downloaded it to her computer yet or put it on the *flashy* thing her son gave her."

"Come on!" Dex was laughing hard, and Selah was as well. Every additional sentence made the story more ridiculous and funny. "Did she call it a 'flashy thing'?"

Selah wiped a tear away from the corner of her eye. "Yes! And she kept yelling at me that now she no longer has the photos of her third grandson's birth and unless I'm going to make her kids have another baby, I've just ruined her whole lifetime of memories."

Dex almost choked on his pizza. "Stop."

"So, yeah, anyway, I'm expecting to hear from her lawyer any day now and need to start practicing for my deposition."

"She's not really going to sue you, is she?"

Selah wiped her hands with a napkin, not appearing the least bit worried. "She can try, but the form we have everyone sign pre-flight is very extensive, especially in regards to these kinds of accidents."

"Dropping things is on the form?"

"Seriously? You didn't read it? Why doesn't anyone read?" she asked.

"Why doesn't anyone stay on the path?" he asked, equally exasperated.

She threw her used napkin at him. "I'll have you know

that I'm very good at staying on the path. That was an extenuating circumstance."

"Oh, sure. It's always extenuating circumstances for you, but not for little old ladies who drop their electronic photo album with the only known pictures of their grandson's birth on it."

Selah did a cute little snort laugh. "Stop. It's not like I got away with it either. You were an asshole, and one step away from pulling out your ranger cuffs and throwing me in ranger jail."

"I wasn't being an asshole. I was in professional park ranger mode." Although, imagining her in handcuffs in his bedroom was a new fantasy unlocked.

"You called me *ma'am*! And you were *very* stern." She was obviously offended by the first part, but the second part intrigued him because her gaze flicked over him in a flirty manner. It was a look that made his blood heat.

"Se—"

"I should probably be getting home," she said, interrupting him. "I'm feeling okay now. I hope I didn't completely ruin your Friday night."

Dex didn't want her to leave, but he had no excuse to hold her. He was beginning to understand her, to unlock what made her tick, and, yet, he had many questions remaining. While he had no doubt that Selah did have a terrible day with a ridiculously difficult passenger, this didn't feel like enough of an explanation for everything that had happened tonight. Something like that wouldn't have caused such a big crack, to change her from a person who was unflappable to completely vulnerable. He wanted to know more, but was afraid to push.

"All right," he said as she grabbed her bag from the floor. "Let me just walk you out."

She didn't fight him as they walked the short distance from his house to where her truck was parked. Even with her keys in hand, Selah didn't make a move to get in once they arrived. "Thank you for, you know, everything."

He took a chance, opening his arms, and she instantly fell into them. Maybe he was becoming a hugger, after all. He liked it, especially because hers were warm, fully invested hugs. She made him not want to half-ass it or pull away too quickly. They could sit with the hug, enjoy it. She released the longest, deepest sigh within this one, like she could live here, and this was now home. Or perhaps that was wishful thinking on his part.

When they did pull back, he noticed a light blue fuzz sticking to one of her curls, probably from the blanket thrown haphazardly on the back of his couch. Dex couldn't resist pulling it out, her hair like silk between the pads of his fingers. "You going to be okay? You can always call me or text me later?"

"It's getting late. I'm sure you don't want me calling you in the middle of the night?"

Except . . . he did. "If you need to." That beautiful gaze of hers rose to him. Though there was a clear height difference between them, tonight it felt less significant. His hand continued to lightly touch the ends of her hair. The air around them grew heavy, enveloping them in this bubble of tension.

A hazy memory reminded him that nothing was ever going to happen between them. In fact, she had once said it was *impossible*. Many of the reasons given then sounded silly now. These same reasons transformed into unwarranted excuses as her own eyes softened and drifted toward his mouth. His fingers secured themselves to the delicate skin of her jawline.

Impossible.

Except the word applied more to inaction rather than action. To keep doing nothing? *That* was impossible. To not close this confounding distance between them and kiss the hell out of this woman? Yeah, that was impossible too. A need was building inside of him, his own breaths becoming shallower as he trailed his fingers from her jawline to the nape of her neck, those dark wavy strands brushing the back of his hand, setting his nerve endings on fire.

Something was going to snap this tension between them, and he was afraid it was going to be him. Dex worried he wouldn't hold anything back and completely devour her in heat and fire, if given the opportunity.

Before he could do anything rash, Selah slid her hand up his shirt, grabbed the neckline, pulled him down as she lifted on her tiptoes, and planted a solid kiss on his lips. It took him by surprise. It didn't last nearly enough time, especially not enough for him to react and kiss her properly in return. In a flash, she let go, got in her truck, and left. Dex remained there, dumbfounded and dazed.

She'd kissed him. *She* had kissed *him*. His bewilderment was promptly replaced by a goofy grin as he made his way back to his home, hopeful at what else might be possible.

Chapter Thirteen

S ELAH DROVE THE short distance to her townhome with tiny bubbles in her chest. These bubbles must have traveled upward, like carbonation, because the corners of her mouth wouldn't stop lifting of their own accord. She chewed on the edge of one of her nails to stop her lips from pulling into a smile, but it was of no use.

Oh, come on, she told herself.

She tried to make an argument that, by most people's standards, the kiss wasn't close to being the hottest one on record. There wasn't any tongue involved or heavy petting. She did nothing more than grab and plant one on him.

Remembering his shocked expression, she smiled again. In her defense, if he was going to keep looking at her with that particular heat in his eyes, one which said he wanted to claim her right there beside her truck—Well, she couldn't be responsible for the action she was forced to take to break the tension. Yes, true, there was no tongue, but she had felt that kiss everywhere. Everywhere. Her soul was so light, she might not need a balloon to get in the air anymore.

One moment, Selah was telling herself she had too much self-respect to be anyone's rebound, even for a cute park ranger. In the next, she decided self-respect was an overrated quality. If she had any, she wouldn't be sitting in her truck at this moment, chewing on her nails to keep from grinning like a loon.

Why shouldn't I kiss him? she asked, while slipping her key into the lock of the townhome's back door, quietly letting herself in so not to disturb her sister. She merely wanted to float upstairs to her bedroom to daydream a little—

She gasped after turning on the hallway bathroom light and—*Holy hell!* She was a messy, gross disaster with puffy eyes and blotchy skin. It was not the appearance of one who should be throwing herself into anyone's arms and confidently giving kisses. No wonder he was surprised. Perhaps he wasn't besotted with her lips as much as horrified because, again, *holy shit.* As a friend, he should understand why she'd never be able to see him again after this.

"God, Selah. What's wrong?" Her sister must have heard her strangled gasp because she appeared beside her.

"Nothing." Selah closed the bathroom door for privacy.

"That's not going to work. I'm going to stand right here until you come out," Naomi said from the hallway.

"There's nothing wrong. I have to pee. Are you going to stand there and listen to me pee?"

"Yes, because you don't look good, and I want to make sure you're okay."

"I'm okay. I just went to a friend's house and the movie we watched made me cry." Technically, it was the truth.

"What friend? You never go to any friend's house. And since when do you ever cry over movies?"

"Why does everyone think I'm some kind of unfeeling

robot?" She definitely wasn't a robot because if she were, Selah would have been able to keep a secure lid on her emotions. Except it wasn't a small prick this time, and she could, usually, prepare herself. She'd gotten good at knowing when there might be things that could trigger the pricks in her life. To the point where she thought she had total control and could be a human pincushion, no problem. She could be a rock nonstop.

Tonight, though, had been different. It wasn't a prick as much as it had been a surprise stab to the gut. All it took was that first few opening scenes of *Galaxy Quest* and the lid on her emotions hadn't simply come off—the whole thing had tipped over and everything spilled in a full containment breach. Doing a puzzle at Dex's place was not the time nor the place for her to be hit with an emotional tidal wave, one she wasn't able to stop.

He'd been sweet and gentle, even without an extensive explanation from her. Selah didn't know how to reveal that this sudden outburst was a result of nothing more than a silly movie.

So, yeah, she was clearly mentally confused and out of control. It was no wonder she kissed him, for the last and final time. Selah should have used tongue while she had the opportunity. If a closed-mouth kiss was hot, she had no doubt that an open mouth one with tongue would have melted her bones down to their marrow.

Of course, she wasn't going to explain all this to her sister, the romantic one in the group. She'd, no doubt, try to talk her into something ridiculous like making out with Dex, and Selah was much too fragile to risk it.

It was quiet outside the door. Maybe Naomi took the hint, leaving Selah in peace. She washed her hands and dabbed some cool water on her eyelids as if this might magically transform them into a normal appearance.

When she opened the door, her sister hadn't budged, leaning against the wall. "I'm sorry," she said in a sincere tone.

Selah shrugged, moving past her. "Why? What do you have to be sorry about?"

"I don't want you to believe that I think you're an unfeeling robot. I don't think that. And what Hailey said today wasn't fair. He was your dad as much as ours. She doesn't believe that, either, but I think she's seriously bothered that Dad . . . well, that his ashes aren't being respected, and she doesn't know how to talk to Mom about it, so I think sometimes she finds it easier if she takes out her frustrations on you."

The pinpricks of heated tears had returned again to her eyes, which was annoying when she thought she'd cried them all out earlier in the evening. Whether what Naomi said was true or not, it didn't matter at this moment. Selah didn't have the energy to take it. She sighed. "It's been a very long day and I'm tired. I'm going to bed."

"Did you at least have fun at your friend's, even though the movie made you cry?"

"Yes." Thankfully, her sister didn't ask the name of the movie. Otherwise, it would have given the whole game away. Selah hadn't lied. She did have a good time at Dex's. Yeah, the whole emotional breakdown part sucked, but the rest of it was nice. It was those moments she held onto as she lay in bed that night.

The next morning, Selah was in the office going over finances when her mom brought her homemade breakfast bars and coffee. "What's all this for?"

"I just wanted to see mi roca and bring you breakfast. I'm trying a new recipe with the fresh peaches I got from your auntie. You work so hard, mija." Her mother brushed back some of Selah's hair. "Also, I need to apologize."

Selah gave her mother an odd look. "What do you need to apologize for?" As far as she was concerned, there was too much apologizing going on, except from the one person who needed to.

"So, yesterday, there was a call from Bria, a reporter at the Bend news station, and I forgot to give it to you. I put the Post-it with the number and her email right there."

Selah picked it up while taking a bite of food. "It's not a big deal." She wasn't sure she wanted to talk to the news organization, anyway.

"I know, but it could be very important for the business, and I should have been more on top of it."

Selah set down the Post-it, turning her chair to face Elena. "It's not even your responsibility. You and I both know that Hailey's supposed to be taking calls and emails and, as usual, you're picking up the slack for her. That's not fair to you."

"I think you should talk to her. She was crying a lot yesterday after you left."

Selah did her best not to roll her eyes. *She* was crying? There was a part of Selah who could understand Hailey's frustration in regard to their father's urn, because talking to their mother about that stuff wasn't easy when Elena did her best to avoid such conversations. It had taken Selah two months to get her to agree to let their father's cell service drop to save money and, even then, there'd been a lot of tears. But, despite Selah having sympathy in this area, it didn't excuse her sister's other actions. Hailey was the one who purposely created the gossip surrounding her and Dex.

"You know what, Mom? I really don't have time to baby her. She's twenty-three years old. If, at this stage of the game, she needs to hear it from me that maybe she should treat people with a little more respect and take some responsibility in her life, then I don't know what to say. We're all here doing stuff, and yet, I'm supposed to stop working to make her feel better? You weren't there. You didn't see the video and you didn't hear what she said."

"You know your sister means well and she loves you."

"Yeah, well, right now, I don't care," Selah said as she wrote down a note to herself.

"Don't say that!" Elena cried, instantly becoming weepy. "You all need to love each other. And you do. You do love each other. Your dad would want you to work together and to love each other. You're their older sister, our Selah, our rock. They're not like you. Hailey is just doing the best she can."

Except, at the moment, Selah didn't feel like the rock everyone wanted her to be. She was more like aging, crumbling concrete. Last night was proof that she was full of pits and not structurally sound enough for everyone to lean against.

"I'm also doing the best I can and, right now, I can't talk

to her. She needs to grow up, just like I've had to do." Selah had a lot more to say, but she couldn't say it without making Elena more upset. Instead, she pushed everything down and focused on work.

After her mom left and she was alone, Selah called the number from the Post-it. "I appreciate you giving us a call back. We've already been talking with Dex Westerly, your . . . ?" Bria from KTVZ didn't finish the sentence, prompting Selah to do so instead.

"Uh. Friend?" She wasn't sure which direction the woman was trying to push her, but this was the best way to describe their relationship, even with one quick kiss in the books.

"Yes, sure, of course. Anyway, we're planning on sending a crew to do an interview and get some footage for a piece we're planning to air this coming week. I think . . . yes, Clint and I are coming to Smith Rock tomorrow and thought it would also be nice, since your business is so close to the park, if we can swing by afterwards to talk with you as well."

"But this story is about Dex's rehabilitation center, right? Not that I wouldn't love to have our business in the news, but I'm confused about what I'm going to contribute—"

"This is simply one of our human-interest pieces for a special segment we've been doing called *Stories from the Heart of Central Oregon*. You worked with him on an event recently, correct?"

"Yes, but depending on what you want to know, my sister Naomi might be a better person for you to talk to."

"Is that your younger sister? The one with the Loop account?"

Selah scrunched her features, her suspicions beginning to take root. "She's one of my younger sisters, but no, that's Hailey and, um, I just want to again mention that Dex and I are just friends. My sister can be a little—"

"Okay, I'll be there in a minute," she said to someone else on her end before continuing with, "Yes, yes, of course. I understand perfectly. We're hoping to get some B-roll with your balloon. Are you doing any tours this week?"

Selah informed her there was one tomorrow, but she flew early in the morning. Before she knew what was happening, she was booked for an interview soon afterward and Dex would be there too . . . which sort of threw a wrench into her whole plan of never seeing him again.

SELAH TRIED HER best not to show any anxiousness on her tour the next morning. It was a calm, uneventful flight, but she was as nervous about seeing Dex as she was seeing the news van with the letters KTVZ parked beside her mother's vehicle when approaching the landing spot.

There was a man with a camera on his shoulder, completely focused on her and *The Blue Wonder* and . . . What if she tipped the basket over for the whole world to see? If this were to happen, she'd never be able to pilot anything again, let alone a hot-air balloon, due to humiliation and what people would see as incompetence. It's not like she'd get a reshoot.

Dex also made her nervous. He'd sent a text yesterday with a picture of his crow, reading,

*Harper and I are wondering how
you're doing this morning?*

Sure, it wasn't *I couldn't stop thinking about you and your lips since last night.* This was probably a good thing, since Selah wouldn't have known how to react to something like that. Instead, he and Harper were being nice because he was a sweet guy and wanted to make sure she wasn't an inconsolable puddle on the floor. She'd replied with an emotionless thumbs-up emoji, which had to be confusing, but she was still in the process of packing herself up again.

Her reflection in the mirror when she came home that night was burned in her memory. This morning, she rose earlier than normal and did her makeup. Not full nightclub face, but somewhere between being barefaced and looking "natural," but with makeup. Hopefully, no one would notice her obvious effort when she was simply trying to avoid appearing exhausted.

"Oh, good, you did your makeup," was the first thing her mother had said that morning.

"No. Yes. Just a little. I'm going to be on the news, for frick's sake. I had dark circles under my eyes."

"Well, you look very pretty today," her mom had assured her. "They're going to love you, and your dad would be so proud of you flying his balloon on the news."

Except it was one thing to look pretty before a flight and quite another thing afterwards. Selah did her tour with the sun beating down on her and the wind whipping hair into her face and, also, forgetting and rubbing her eyes. She got tired of it, putting on her regular baseball hat and aviator sunglasses. In the end, she got up early for nothing.

As she and *The Blue Wonder* approached closer to the landing spot, she sucked in a steadying breath, begging the universe to please give her a perfect landing with no tipping. The camera lens was an unflinching witness. When she saw Dex, her heart skipped. He peered upward as the balloon approached but, while most people focused on the envelope, he looked directly at her. He had a huge smile on his face, as though thrilled to see her, raising a hand and doing a small subtle salute in greeting. Her heart continued skipping, her nervousness washing away at the sight of it.

To her relief, the balloon cooperated, landing perfectly. Naomi and Boone went to work securing and tethering the balloon as they had previously agreed, so the camera could get a few shots of it on the ground for B-roll.

Dex strolled straight to the gondola as though he were part of the team. He helped the passengers disembark as they climbed from the basket, chatting with them like he was the hot-air balloon flight attendant.

When the passengers left to get into her mom's van, it was just the two of them, besides Boone and Naomi, who were still tethering. But she could tune out their activity, and even the camera crew. It felt like only the two of them.

"Hey, Pilot," Dex said as he gripped the edge of the gondola from where he stood outside of it.

"Hey, Ranger," she replied, her lips again being uncontrollable as they pulled into a smile.

He held out a hand. "Can I help you disembark?"

"Actually, do we think we can get Dex inside the basket as well? I think it would make for a nice visual for us to use.

Is that okay?" This was yelled by a woman with wild red hair standing beside the cameraman. She then waved to Selah. "Hi. I'm Bria."

"Hi there." It served as a reminder this wasn't a nice moment between her and Dex. He was here for a reason and, apparently, they were also being directed, which was weird. They shared an amused expression at the ridiculousness of it all. After shrugging, Dex climbed into the gondola, this time with Selah assisting him. While it was probably safer to have a wicker wall between them, she liked having him on the same side and—

"Can you remove your sunglasses and hat? There's too much shadow and we can't see your pretty face, Selah!" Bria yelled from twenty yards away. "Can you two just chat with each other for a minute while we get this?"

With a sigh, Selah did as she was told, tossing the items onto the gondola floor and doing her best to fluff her hair, hoping she didn't look too awful.

"Having an eventful day so far?" she asked Dex in the hopes of keeping the mood light and casual.

"It's definitely improving."

"It has to be better than the last time you were in my basket." As soon as it left her mouth, she froze, biting her bottom lip. Reminding him of that awful day must make her as bad as Hailey. "I . . . what I meant—when the basket tipped over and . . ." she stumbled, trying to save the situation.

"Selah, it's fine. And, yes, so far, it's much better than the last time." One of his fingers did the softest glide against the outside of her hand, so light it could have come from a breeze. Her gaze dropped to the movement before lifting again to his face. There was no way the camera or the people outside the basket would observe any of this, as their hands were below the top of the gondola. But she knew. Her heart took the biggest, sweetest breath, one that could fill her whole chest cavity, one she usually only took when she was high in the air, where she belonged. This didn't usually happen when she was still on the ground.

She adjusted her hand closer, leaning into the touch. Selah turned her attention toward the camera as though nothing was happening at all, not in the basket and not in her heart.

"Of course, I suppose it is possible for you to tip the basket again, but this time I get to be on top," Dex said.

A loud laugh burst from her, probably ruining Bria's B-roll take.

Whatever. She didn't care.

Chapter Fourteen

WHEN DEX ARRIVED with the news van that morning, after they finished his individual filming at Smith Rock with Harper, he watched her balloon come in. It was corny, but it was as if she were some aviator-wearing angel coming down from heaven. He didn't notice any of the other passengers until they attempted to disembark, and he'd been so single-minded he'd been in the way.

She had smiled at him sweetly. A single wavy strand had escaped her hat, brushing against her cheek in a breeze, and her skin was pink from the flight. When Bria requested he get in the basket as well, he practically catapulted himself in there, probably appearing too eager, but whatever.

God, she was pretty. His carefulness at holding back and not touching her eroded quickly. Dex reached out a single finger to touch her because something was better than nothing. Her laugh lit up his whole world. Her smile dazzled him. He'd take her tears, but he wanted her joy.

"Okay, I think that's good enough," Bria said, interrupting everything. "Would it be okay if we could interview you, but over there, where we can get the balloon in the background?"

Dex and Selah climbed from the basket, Naomi taking

over in watching the balloon. Resetting the camera, Bria told them about the process—how she was going to stay off camera and let them answer. He'd already heard this once before when it had been only him rambling about Harper, the park, and how important conservation, education, and wildlife rehabilitation were.

"How long have you been flying balloons for?" Bria asked Selah.

"Oh, uh, well, as an official job, I've been doing it for almost two years. But because it's the family business, I had experience for years before that."

"The business was started by your father, right? That's what we read on your website."

"Yes, High Desert Tours was started by Robert Moreno, my dad." She pulled away one of the loose curls from her forehead. He could feel the tenseness radiating from her frame.

"And he died? That's why you're flying for High Desert Tours now?"

"Mm-hmm. Yup," was the only response as she fiddled with her hands before crossing her arms.

At this point, Dex didn't care if this media exposure was good for business or if it could bring the park some rich benefactor. He didn't know what it was about this woman that turned his normally easygoing soul into a feral Viking warrior, ready to burn down villages if anyone so much as bothered her. Because if they made her cry, he swore to God he would shut the whole thing down. Especially since everything Bria was asking didn't have anything to do with what he thought the interview was going to be about.

Dex was stuck, not being able to touch her or put an arm around her. It was his pet project that was the reason they asked her these personal, intrusive questions, making him partly to blame. He eyed the cameraman, wondering if he had the advantage to take the camera away and smash it on the ground if necessary. Then he and Selah could jump into *The Blue Wonder*, making a cool escape, and maybe do some more kissing.

Luckily, the line of questioning shifted to another topic, but he wasn't sure it was any better. "So, tell us how exactly you met."

Both he and Selah eyed each other for a moment, each wondering how they were going to answer before he said, "Well, we met when I booked a hot-air balloon ride. She's one of the top balloon pilots in the area. I highly recommend High Desert Tours." He didn't know if her being a top balloonist was true, but he didn't think anyone, including Bria, was going to fact-check him. How many could there be? Besides, this was a way to at least push her business. "Her and her family's business have been a great help in making our event at Smith Rock a success. We wouldn't have gotten as many donations as we did without her and the balloon."

"But you hired her initially to propose to your girlfriend, right? And Selah was your pilot and now you're . . ." Bria prompted him to finish wherever she was trying to direct him with a sweep of her hand.

"Um, well, yes, but . . ." Dex found all of this odd. Why would anyone in the news care about this? How was his personal life interesting to anyone?

"We didn't know each other then, but, after that flight,

we kept running into each other, and we're just friends," Selah jumped in. "And he truly cares about Harper and Smith Rock. It's . . . hard to resist that kind of sincere passion." She paused to drag another curl from her cheek, glancing up at him. "When he asked, I couldn't say no. Plus, in our business, we want people who ride with us to get an appreciation for all the natural beauty the High Desert has to offer, and that includes the local wildlife."

Selah's answer was as lovely as she was. He continued with, "That's right. We're essentially on the same side, and I think that's why the event at the park was so successful and why we're hoping it continues to draw attention to a very important cause. I guess it doesn't matter how it started or how we became friends. Life is weird and funny and compli- cated. Sometimes, things just happen."

Selah smiled at him. "Yes, exactly. You never know when your basket will tip over or something will just fall out of thin air and land in your lap. Hopefully, the same will happen for Harper and all her wildlife friends too."

This morning, during his solo interview, he stumbled around and wasn't as eloquent with his words. Dex was used to talking to the public and educating them, but doing so in front of a camera was something else entirely. By doing this with Selah beside him, all the awkwardness melted away. They didn't need to be prompted and directed. Together they could control this interview. He felt proud of her and proud of himself.

Bria continued asking her questions, but he no longer worried about what she might lob at them or how she somehow seemed to be knowledgeable about things in his life. He shrugged it off because the woman was a journalist. She had to be good at digging information up. Regardless, he was happy with how the interview went.

Two days later, Dex was again waiting for Selah to come over after work because an email came, informing them the story would air that evening toward the end of the news hour. They agreed it would be fun to have a watch party together, and Selah volunteered to bring some food with her.

Except they didn't know how to watch the local news because it wasn't streaming live on any website and neither one of them had cable. But if there was a will, there was a way, and Dex had a lot of "will" where Selah was concerned. After work, he went to the store and purchased a bunny ears antenna for his TV after learning such things still existed. He hadn't seen them since he was a kid and hung out in Lincoln's bedroom. He was setting it up when Harper cawed from her usual perch on the porch and heard the bird's nails pattering excitedly against the wooden railing.

"Here you go, Harp," Selah said outside before the bird flapped away.

"Are you bringing more gifts for her? She doesn't need to get any more spoiled," he yelled from behind the TV as he plugged in a coaxial cable.

"Don't get jealous. I brought something for you too," she responded after letting herself in through the screened door.

That perked him up. "Oh, yeah?"

"Don't get too excited. It's just dinner. But between delicious homemade Mexican food and a dirty old clip from a lanyard, I think you have the better end of the deal."

He laughed while setting the bunny ears on the TV

stand. Selah had taken a seat on the sofa and was bringing out small Tupperware containers from a paper bag. Putting them on the coffee table, she was careful not to disturb the in-progress jigsaw puzzle there. While he would have preferred his "gift" to be something more personal, like a kiss, he was also excited about the food.

"My mom's annoyed we're not watching this news segment at her house because she still wants to have you over for dinner." Selah rolled her eyes good-naturedly. "But sometimes I just have to, you know, get away. She still insisted on me bringing you over some food, though."

While he was touched Selah's mom was sincere in her invitation to have him over, he also didn't mind having Selah all to himself.

Dex played it casually, taking a seat beside her, accepting one of the plastic containers filled with some type of enchiladas and Spanish rice. The delicious smell enticed him to take a bite, the food still warm. "Oh God. I will go over to your mom's any day she will have me. Tell her I adore her," he said, helping himself to more. This was the best thing he'd eaten in a while. His normal fast, easy, and often frozen meals weren't close in competition to this.

"If I told her that, she'd have you over every day."

"You say it like it's a bad thing, but I don't understand how it could be. I can make stretchy pants on a park ranger look sexy."

She snorted a laugh, almost losing her own bite of food and quickly lifting a hand to cover her mouth. "No, it's not . . . let's just say that it's pretty clear you don't have younger sisters."

"Only child," he responded.

"Well, now everything about you makes sense."

It did? He wasn't sure how to take that. "Your sisters don't seem that bad."

Selah raised her eyebrows, tilting her head as though she was about to add something to the conversation when his phone alarm went off, a reminder the news was about to start. Picking up the remote, he fiddled with it, trying to find the correct input the TV should be on. It took him roughly ten minutes to get it working and find the right channel. It'd been so long, it's as if he forgot how to use TV the old-fashioned way.

"Oh, I think this is it!" Selah said, touching his arm. They finished eating their dinner and watched several news segments, with theirs coming at the tail end of the hour. She'd long since taken off her shoes and brought her legs up on the couch, shifting to get comfortable.

He'd miss hearing the lead-in playing over a graphic showing an outline of the state with a heart at the center. The text read, *Stories from the Heart of Central Oregon*. He'd been distracted by Selah, but attempted to focus, feeling nervous at how he was going to look on camera. The segment began with the early morning shot of both of them chatting inside the basket, Bria's voiceover playing over it.

"When Dexter Westerly, local park ranger at Smith Rock, booked a romantic hot-air balloon flight with High Desert Tours, to propose to his then-girlfriend, he, like many hopefuls, probably imagined it would end in wedding bells. But this story took a different turn."

It then cut to him saying, "Life is really weird and funny

and complicated. Sometimes, things happen."

Dex felt his color melt away at this. Every good thought he'd had at the end of filming the interview vanished as he sat there dumbfounded, watching whatever this was unfolding on his TV screen.

This was going to be a train wreck.

Chapter Fifteen

S ELAH BROUGHT HER hand up to cover the lower half of her face as she watched the pre-taped segment continue on screen, her gut already churning with anxiety as it continued unfolding.

Bria's voice cut back in. "Little did he know how true that would be when a sudden gust of wind tipped over the basket upon landing, and the pilot of the balloon ride, Selah Moreno, would land on top of him."

Selah was in the next cut. "You never know when your basket will tip over or something will just fall out of thin air and land in your lap."

Okay, well, she was going to throw up. While the whole misunderstanding wasn't Selah's fault—that would be Hailey's doing—she would have no choice but to confess to Dex. She'd have to explain how the news crew got this story and why they were treating it like salacious, local gossip. She didn't want him to be pissed, but would understand if he was.

What followed was a shot of them walking side by side across the field and Bria's voiceover continued, "Truer words were never said as the couple kept running into each other, going from strangers to becoming something more, even deciding to come together for a good cause."

When it cut to her saying, "It's . . . hard to resist that kind of sincere passion. When he asked, I couldn't say no," Selah may have released a small gasp beneath her hand. Oh God. What in the hell was happening here? Was everyone in cahoots with her sister?

Her phone rang, and the caller's name provoked a groan. She answered, even while regretting it. "What?"

"Selah María Moreno," her mother said in an excited breath before switching tones. "Don't you what me. Are you going to finally explain this?"

"Mom, it's not—"

"You and Dexter?"

"No, that's not what's hap—"

"I'm watching it right now. It's on the news. Naomi! Naomi, you're recording this, right, mija? I want to send it to your auntie and show her my Selah has a sweetheart, and they're on the news."

"I've already told you. We're just friends. Are you going to believe me or the news?"

"The news, of course. I see how you two look at each other. And you brought him dinner. Did he like it? When is he coming over for a proper meal? Even Boone comes over for dinner."

In the background, Naomi said, "And I keep telling you to stop inviting him because I don't want to spend any more time with the guy than I have to."

Her mother ignored this, rambling to both her and Naomi at the same time and making her own plans for trying new recipes. Selah half listened, waiting for the moment her mother took a breath so she could jump in and end the torture. This whole thing was embarrassing. She was putting Dex in the most awkward of positions, and it was all her family's fault.

"I love you, but I'm hanging up." Selah promptly ended the call. Her saving grace was choosing to watch this at Dex's place instead of going with her mother's proposal of watching it all together. The decision was made because she needed to get away, to have some moments just for her. After spending the day going through finances and discovering her mother had indeed renewed her father's yearly fishing magazine subscription behind her back, she deserved it.

Selah didn't know what she had missed, due to her mother's phone call, but it couldn't have been a lot, because there wasn't much to the story. Why would anyone care when both she and Dex were nobodies? Central Oregon must be starved for stories.

With a sigh, she returned her attention to the segment, wanting the whole thing to be over, so she could stop feeling guilty and confess her sister's deeds and apologize. And then she'd promptly get in her balloon and fly off into space, where she could live with her shame in privacy and peace.

"Dex's love of wildlife and his pet crow, Harpo, provided the perfect opportunity for them to work together as they put together the biggest event at Smith Rock this year where guests were allowed to take an Instagram-worthy picture like this one," Bria's voiceover continued. "Creating their own memorable moment is something Dex and Selah know a lot about."

It cut to a shot of Dex from his solo interview with

Smith Rock behind him and Harper on his shoulder. "I want people to see her like I do. She's truly magnificent."

Selah had enough courage to slide a look in his direction because . . . *what in the what?* Dex slid his hand over his eyes, his head tilting down and the tips of his ears turning a bright shade of pink. He appeared as if he wished he had access to a space balloon himself. It was doubtful this night was going to get any better for either one of them.

The pre-taped segment ended with them back inside the balloon and Bria saying, "For these two lovebirds, the sky really is the limit." It cut to a live feed of Bria standing in some empty field, a microphone in hand and her other hand pressing a finger to one of her ears. "Dex Westerly hopes this will bring attention to the Smith Rock NonProfit Org, in hopes of creating a wildlife rehabilitation. If folks are interested in donating or they want information on the park's conservation efforts or to learn more about the local business, High Desert Tours, they can check the story on the KTVZ website. Samantha, back to you."

Dex snapped up the remote and turned the TV off. They both sat staring at a black TV screen for a few long silent minutes, the tension becoming unbearable.

"My sister posted a Loop video that made it seem like we were together," she blurted.

At the same time, he said, "The radio interview might have gotten the impression we were more than friends, and it might be my fault."

"What?" she asked.

"Your sister did what?" Dex replied, equally confused.

"I'm so sorry. It's not your fault, it's mine. I shouldn't

have asked her to create content for us. It did get the word out, but she took a lot of liberties in creating something, um, sensational, so that's where all this might have started. I've already had a talk with her and tried to get her to take it down but . . . these things tend to have a life of their own. And now it appears that no one is listening or cares."

Dex dropped his head against the back of the sofa and rubbed his eyes. Her anxiety in anticipating his reaction, one involving him kicking her out of his house forever, caused her heart to race. "I'm really, really sorry. It's not fair for your personal life to be on display like this when you've been great and trying to do something good here. You definitely don't deserve to get mixed up in the chaos of the Moreno family, and I understand if you want to drop us."

To her surprise, he laughed. "Oh, God. I thought *I* had screwed up."

"What? How?"

"That interview I did for the Colorado radio station. They kept asking me if there was something between us and what was the real story. I was so caught off guard, I sort of stumbled through it and may have given the impression that, yes, it was true. And then this"—he motioned toward the TV—"and I thought, oh shit, they heard about that interview and I really screwed it up. Now this reporter is twisting my words even more."

Her panic gave way to mirth. "So, it's not true? You don't think I'm magnificent?"

"I was talking about Harper—or I guess 'Harpo,' since they screwed that up too." He shook his head while chuckling exasperatedly. "Not that you're not magnificent, but . . .

well, you know."

Selah hid a smile behind one of her hands, barely able to contain her reaction at the whole ridiculous situation. Maybe someday they would find the whole thing funny and laugh but, truth be told, she wanted to laugh now, especially after spending so much time worrying about it. "It's okay. I hope you feel better, knowing it wasn't your fault."

"I don't think it was your fault, either."

She scrunched her nose. "But it kinda was."

"I've known you long enough to see you put a lot on your shoulders. You don't need to do that."

Selah realized she was doing the same thing she'd accused her mother of. She was covering for Hailey, shifting the blame to herself to protect her sister. This time she did laugh, shaking her head, absentmindedly touching Dex's forearm. "What my sister did was a really . . . jerky thing to do." There were better ways to describe her sister's actions, but Selah took baby steps at saying it out loud. "Just do me a favor. If you ever come across her video, don't watch it."

His eyes glinted with humor. "Why?"

"It's *really* embarrassing."

"For me or for you? It can't be any worse than everyone knowing I'm a loser that got dumped on a hot-air balloon ride and it being blasted on the local news."

"Yeah, I—You're not a loser, Dex. And if that's what someone takes away from 'our story'—and she did finger quotes around the phrase in hopes of lightening the mood—"then they're missing the bigger picture."

"A story where we're just friends." It was weird how his statement also sounded like a question.

She shrugged. "People see what they want to see, I guess."

He laughed again, but this one was short and tinged with bitterness. Selah wished she could peer into his brain, read his thoughts. Was he thinking about Ava? Or was he worried about people mistakenly thinking he and she were together? Did he really see himself as a loser because of one silly event on a balloon ride? She didn't want this for him, preferring to gather up all his worries and carry them herself, as though her emotional backpack had plenty of room inside.

"Dex," she started, unsure how to finish it. Selah wanted to say something about how she appreciated his friendship and everything he'd done for her. Everything could have turned out differently after his initial balloon ride. He could have walked away, not wanting to be reminded of it, and she would have understood. But he hadn't. Instead, she had received an unexpected miracle of a relationship, one that was a friendship unlike all the other ones she'd had before. It was like being thrown into a new plane, one she'd never trained on before. She could have basic knowledge while being terrified of mucking it up.

She continued sliding her fingers across his forearm and, like a fog being lifted, suddenly saw all the other parts of the picture. Selah wasn't sure how he did it. How being around him made it so easy to slip into this comfortable space. How she could feel so at home with a person. She'd thought nothing of shucking off her shoes, reclining into him, her bent legs snuggled against his thigh, practically on his lap, and thought nothing when his hand slipped over her knee.

Her hand stilled. His hazel gaze drifted across her face,

taking her all in. The strength of her pulse and breath increased.

She'd been kidding herself.

There was something always passing between them, electrified molecules zipping back and forth. Her family had seen it, along with the news, and probably countless others.

Except, the timing wasn't right. He'd just gotten out of a serious relationship and she had bigger things in her life to worry about. The two of them getting involved would do nothing but make things messy. Only fate didn't care about her excuses. In fact, fate was having a big laugh at their expense as it flung them together like some chaotic game of chess while including pieces from other board games. None of this was fair.

She drew away from him, bringing her feet to the floor and gathering the dirty Tupperware pieces together. If she had any chance at all of escaping temptation, she needed to leave and do it without making eye contact with him. Her willpower was held together by a delicate thread at this point.

As she went to stand, he grabbed her elbow. His voice was a little rough, full of some unspoken emotion. "Ma'am, I'm gonna need you to get off the path you're currently on." His voice gentled with, "Stay here in the brush with me, Selah."

She froze, taking a few slow breaths, every atom screaming for her to give them what they'd wanted this whole time. Him. The way she justified it—she'd already kissed him, so she was already his emotional rebound. Selah might as well take all the perks that went with it. Besides, she wasn't hanging around long, anyway. A rebound was probably the best thing in this period of her life. It might make things easier for both of them.

Selah turned, seeing the same hungry want in him. Before debating it any further, she launched herself and he caught her easily, his arms wrapping fully around her as she straddled his lap, finding his lips with her own, cradling his face between her palms. His hands did a long slide along her spine, before gripping and clasping her shoulders, pulling her to him, as though trying to ease her into his soul. The kiss was a little feral, a little messy, a little out of control, but that happened when something was denied for this length of time. The longing and emotion couldn't help but burst from them.

"You are magnificent," Dex said between kisses.

"Not too short, then? No danger of spinal misalignment."

"No. I guess we just had to figure it out." He smiled against her lips, and she returned the expression as she kissed him again, loving how his tongue slid rhythmically against hers.

Every part of him touching her felt so good and, after everything, Selah needed to feel good right now. She wanted it all. Messy or not, she didn't care. She needed to feel him. When one of his hands slipped across the side of her rib cage, a thumb sweeping over one of her breasts, she didn't stop the small moan she made against his mouth. She was about to melt off his lap and let him do whatever he wanted with her.

"I can't resist your stern park ranger voice," she said.

He released a small, "Hmm," the sound vibrating deliciously against her skin. Dex's teeth scraped against her neck, before he sucked a spot and said, "Ma'am, are you going to come to my bed or am I going to have to throw you over my shoulder?"

She gave him a coy look, pushing one finger into his chest. "You call me 'ma'am' one more time and I'm going to do some bad things to you."

The tips of his mouth kicked up mischievously. "Ma'am."

"Take me to your goddamn bedroom right now."

He tried to stand with her clinging to the front of his body like a horny koala, but they nearly tumbled to the ground, her giggles filling the air. It was safer if they both walked there on their own two feet, but there were many pit stops on the way, such as when he peeled off her shirt, then his own, before pressing her into a hallway wall to kiss the breath from her lungs. His park uniforms didn't do him any favors, as they hid much of what was underneath, making this moment feel like a mirage. Dex was lean and, yes, on the lanky side, but the leanness was firm, and he clearly had muscles. Having them pressed into her body, she could feel his strength, and it excited her as she dragged her fingernails along each ridge.

She was never more grateful when the destination of his bedroom was reached. This room was less dated than the rest of the house, with white walls instead of wood paneling. There was a simple modern bed butted under a window with basic gray bedding, the rest of the room was uncluttered. Not that any of this mattered. At this moment, he could have sex with her on a beanbag for all she cared.

When her legs hit the bed, she fell onto it, dragging herself backwards across the comforter's surface in order to secure a more optimal spot. He crawled after her, his mouth finding hers easily, as if tonight a homing beacon had been established between them. His hand slid across her thigh, reaching the top of her pants as he undid them.

"Dex," she said his name between light breaths.

"You want me to stop?" He was panting as well, his eyes dark and wild. She liked being the one to evoke this kind of reaction from him.

"No. It seems a little silly to be bringing this up now, but I just want to make sure you have a condom."

He gave her a funny look. "Why would that be silly? My whole job is trying to make sure people stay safe. You're allowed to feel safe." Dex reached to his nightstand, rummaging through the contents of a drawer before removing several squared packets.

Well, okay then. Apparently, she was about to get the perks of being a rebound several times over. She wasn't about to complain, biting into her lower lip to prevent even the chance.

He pressed his finger against her mouth, running along the entirety of it as though to test the plushness of it. "God. These lips of yours are going to be the death of me." His words made her melt a little more as she pressed a slow kiss on the end of his finger.

Returning to his task, Dex pulled off her pants, tossing them on the floor behind him. His movements and touches were sure, like he'd spent a long time planning his seduction of her and could execute it blindfolded. He faltered, though, when she unzipped his pants, slipping her hand past the elastic band of his boxer briefs to stroke him. His breath came sharply before morphing into a groan, and he sunk his face into the nook in her neck. "Fuck," came his muffled response. "I want to be gentle, but I don't know if I can."

She laughed because she didn't think rebound relationships were supposed to be soft and gentle. "It's okay. I know you think I'm this short little thing, but I'm tougher than I look. I can handle it." Besides, *gentle* sounded slow and she'd been waiting long enough.

He rose on his forearms, pinning her with a serious expression. "I definitely do not think that you're a short little thing, and I know you're tough. But also, you don't have to be that way with me if you don't want to."

"Okay." She could have said a lot more, but Selah didn't trust herself. The sentiment of his words struck her, and if she thought about it too long, she'd probably cry again and she didn't want tears at this moment. She preferred instead to keep things simple so he'd keep touching, kissing, and showing her all the physical affection she craved from him.

As much as he stated he didn't know if he could be gentle, Dex seemed to find inner strength as he encouraged her to lift so he could reach behind her and undo the clasp of her bra, slowly sliding it away. He shifted downward, pressing his face into her chest as he trailed hot open-mouth kisses across her breasts, and slipping his hand into her underwear as he slowly stroked her there. Selah arched into his touches, her skin tingling hot as she moaned with pleasure, weaving her fingers through the soft strands of his hair.

"I know you're going to feel good," he said. "You already feel good."

"Yes," she sighed.

"Do you want me?"

She nodded her head, having a difficult time attempting to find words.

"I need more than that, honey."

"Yes, Dex. I want you."

She was somewhat frustrated when he stopped touching her, but watched with interest as he slid his pants and boxer briefs off and grabbed one of the packaged foils from the nightstand. Her gaze drifted across his body with appreciation, her soul feeling an extra glow of happy gratefulness because he was going to give her what she needed, and she wanted to do the same for him.

After rolling the condom on, he removed her underwear before sinking back over her, kissing her soft and gentle, his tongue caressing her own. His strong fingers wrapped themselves around each of her legs, positioning them around his hips—the anticipation of it all vibrated throughout her body, and she pulled him toward her.

When he did finally push into her, there was a brief moment of mutual relief, their foreheads touching as they took a shared breath. Her arms wrapped around his neck. His pulse was so strong, she could feel it through her fingertips and was sure it was pulsating into her own bloodstream. Groaning, he pulled out before pushing back in, his rhythm growing in strength and determination, as if he would take everything he could from her. He pushed her closer and closer to the edge of a cliff, her whole body tightening and her moans becoming rougher. Selah begged him not to stop as she dug her heels in until she cried out, leaning into him, wringing out every single sensation she could as he grunted toward his own finish line before collapsing.

Clinging to him, she struggled to catch her breath, not sure if she ever wanted to let go, scraping her fingers along his scalp and enjoying the weight of him pressing onto her.

The aftermath didn't last as long as she would have liked because he soon rolled off of her, muttering some apology for who knows what, and went into the bathroom, shutting the door behind him. Left behind in the messy remnants of his bed, she lay there exposed, tossing an arm across her eyes, wondering how the hell they'd gotten here. One moment, she was bringing a friend her mother's homemade enchilada verde, and the next, she felt like she was going to wilt up and die if he didn't touch her and take her to bed. If this was some weird mood or phase, it wasn't out of her system yet, because she was already hoping for a next time—

And how long was he going to spend in that goddamn bathroom and leave her alone to ponder all these thoughts? The bathroom faucet ran for an awfully long time. Was he figuring out a reason to get her to leave? Her previous rebound relationship never tiptoed around the matter. The man was always quick to tell her it was getting late, and he'd see her around. Was Dex stalling in that bathroom now, regretting things? Did this ruin what they had?

Selah sprang into a seated position, pulling the gray comforter around her body as she tried to locate her clothes among his.

"You're not leaving, are you?" Dex asked as soon as he emerged, beautifully naked and rubbing a small hand towel over his face, a frown settling on his lips.

She froze. "You want me to stay?"

"Well, yeah, I want you to stay. Sorry. I should have offered you the bathroom first."

Slowly unwrapping the comforter from her body, Selah became awkwardly shy, even after having sex with the guy not five minutes ago. He studied her and she blushed while slipping past him to get to the bathroom.

When she reemerged, he scooped her into his arms, literally sweeping her off her feet. Selah gasped and then giggled. "What are you doing?"

"I'm not taking any chances with you." He deposited her on the bed, pulling the covers over both their heads, plunging them into a more private oasis beneath his bedding.

Tonight they'd forget about the rest of the world for a little while longer.

Chapter Sixteen

*T*AP, TAP, TAP.

Dex pushed his face into his pillow, ignoring whatever was attempting to wake him from the deepest, best sleep of his life. The source of the taps was obvious, but he hoped someday the bird would get the hint and let him sleep in at least one morning. Dex was beginning to forget what it was like.

Unfortunately, this was followed by more tapping and some loud cawing.

Oh, for God's sake.

He blindly reached for the window above his headboard, pushing it open and letting a rush of cool morning air flow into his bedroom, along with the crow. Hopefully, Harper would find some way to keep herself occupied and leave him alone.

Pulling his bedding closer, his hand made contact with soft, warm, and, more importantly, naked skin. Cracking a single eye, he was rewarded with the vision of Selah's delicate back, as she slept facing away from him.

What an instant hit of joy it was to discover last night hadn't been a dream. He'd had her and was hoping to keep having her. Sex with Selah may have blown his mind. Not that he hadn't enjoyed it before. He wasn't sure if it was because he'd been pining over Selah for a while or maybe because she kept giving reasons on why they couldn't be together, making everything extra thrilling about doing something they shouldn't. Either way, he'd been so taken by her, both in the physical sense and also on an emotional level, he'd nearly lost his mind when her body had tightened and pulsed around him. Last night they'd existed in a bubble of their own making. She was beautiful and tempting and within easy reaching distance now. He wanted to live in the moment again, take up permanent residence within the bubble.

He liked having this. In contrast, Ava appreciated her space, to the point where there weren't many overnights together. She'd push him away with a shoulder when she felt he'd done enough, making him feel that any above and beyond physical affection was clingy. Because his parents were also the same way, he had wondered if he was the odd one for aching for something more.

In the bathroom last night, he'd had an epiphany that his relationship with Ava had been one of easy convenience. It was what his friend, Jon, had seen but hadn't overtly said. There wasn't anything of substance between Dex and Ava. They hadn't fit together easily, like puzzle pieces meant to match. It was glaringly obvious now because he clicked with Selah without much effort at all. The difference was significant and eye-opening. Getting married to his ex would have been a huge mistake. He was grateful Ava had seen this and had given him one last figurative shoulder push, shoving him into something better. It was then Dex had realized he'd spent way too long in the bathroom and Selah was probably wondering what had happened to him.

But she had stayed. She was here this morning. He ached to touch her, deciding to try sliding his arm over her hip, tucking her into him, slipping his face into the crook of her neck. Selah smelled sagey and sweet, and he inhaled as much as he could in a deep contented breath.

She stirred, made a soft "hmm" noise before sighing and snuggling into him. His heart broadened to fill every inch of his chest, and he looked to Harper, who perched on his headboard. Dex lifted his brow at the bird as if to silently tell his feathered friend, *Hey, look, buddy. Found a real treasure with this one.*

Harper's black eyes studied him, cocking her head one way, then the other. She held one of her gifts in her beak, a bit of colored glass. It was one of those flat marbles his mom used to put in candle decorations and flower vases. After more head cocking, Harper made her way across the top of the headboard, setting the flat yellowing marble on the nightstand before hopping onto the floor and leaving the bedroom for the kitchen.

The crow had chosen to leave the gift on Selah's side of the bed, not his. This made his heart even fuller, giving him hope things were going to be okay. Maybe Harper would learn not to be an asshole. Maybe Selah would continue coming to his bed. And maybe he could relax in the knowledge he'd found someone who seemed to get him. He wanted her to feel the same way, to let her guard down and tell him what she wanted and what she was worried about. But, most importantly, he wanted insight into what that tattoo of the three circles on her wrist meant.

Her right arm was stretched across the bed, palm facing up. He stared at her tattoo, couldn't stop pondering it. He didn't have one, but he knew tattoos were personal, a clue into the person who possessed them.

He pressed a soft kiss to her bare shoulder.

"Mmm," she said sleepily. "I like it when you have a little scruff. The scratchiness against my skin is the best."

"What?"

"You shaved for the news interview, but now you have a little bit of facial hair again. I like this better."

"Oh." Dex had always been a meticulous shaver before. It was neater, cleaner, more presentable. It had fallen to the wayside after Ava broke up with him. Somewhere along the way, he stopped thinking about it as much. He didn't want to shave every day and, since he wasn't dating, there was no need. Except Selah liked him better this way. He found himself pleasantly surprised again.

He began kissing her shoulder, her back, her neck, wherever he could. She arched into him, stretching her neck to give him better access to the soft, sensitive spots of her anatomy. He gladly took advantage, sliding the hand he'd draped over her hip to the lower part of her body, taking note of what drew small gasps and shallowing breaths.

"I really shouldn't stay very long," she said. "Naomi is definitely going to notice my absence and she'll probably tell my mother, and then there will be all kinds of assumptions that will most definitely be correct, because the Moreno women are hardly ever wrong."

Dex didn't stop what he was doing. It was too enjoyable,

and he was working himself up as well as her, unable to stop pressing himself against her ass, his dick desperate in its attempts to be noticed. He smiled at her excuses as he continued kissing her skin. "Yeah, uh-huh. I'm sure you're eager to get home, strike some notch on your bedpost, and brag about how this pilot just bagged herself a park ranger."

She turned to face him, her hand going to his neck, humor lighting her beautifully dark eyes. "Why do you act like I'm some kind of *Top Gun* Maverick fighter pilot? I fly balloons. I think that makes me the lowest level of coolness in the piloting world."

"I've seen you in those aviators. You're cool. Definitely cooler than me."

"Were you a nerd growing up?" The question was softened by the gentle kiss pressed to his lips.

"Not sure what gave you that impression. You don't develop this kind of a body being really good at sports. No, you get it from spending countless hours playing video games at your friend's house. We were knee-deep in a hoard of imaginary ladies."

She giggled at this, pressing a kiss to his neck next. "Your efforts were clearly well spent, and have been noted and appreciated. I like it."

"And I think it's pretty obvious the feeling is mutual." His body liked her more with each passing second. She was cute with her sleepy eyes, her slightly wild, wavy hair that would curl into her cheek and neck, and her warm, light-brown skin that was more than kissable this morning. Dex kissed her again, this time in earnest, letting go of his usual morning-after related anxieties when she responded to him in equal eagerness.

Selah suddenly broke it off, pushing him with a hand, a sly smile on her lips, until he was on his back. She climbed on top, straddling his hips between her thighs. "I just realized you probably don't want to be kissing me before I had a chance to brush my teeth, and it's even worse, because I don't have a toothbrush here."

Dex made a mental note to fill his whole medicine cabinet with extra toothbrushes. Except his brain didn't dwell on his future shopping list for long, as he became preoccupied with this new and more alluring view before him. He slid his hands along her stomach to her breasts, cupping them. They fit perfectly within his grasp.

Before he could do more, she took hold of his hands, pressing them into the mattress beside his head. "Nope, nuh-uh. It's my turn," she said, her morning voice huskier and sultry. "Let's make this park ranger happy he bagged himself a pilot."

She stretched to his nightstand, taking one of the condom packets and making a big show of tearing it open, taking his dick in hand and rolling it on, as if it was a striptease in reverse.

Reaching to touch her again, she swatted his hand away with a light smack. "Sir, I'm going to need you to keep your hands stowed and secured. I'm in charge of piloting the cockpit this morning." Leaning, she pressed a soft kiss to the corner of his mouth before saying lightly, "Now sit back, relax, and enjoy the ride." He was so turned on at this moment, he was ready to explode then and there, and she wasn't even wearing her aviators.

She lifted herself to take him inside her, her head dropping back and releasing the most breathless, sexiest moan. This, combined with the absolute feel and heat of her, had him clasping the sheets in a death grip.

As she started riding him, she whimpered, "Oh, Dex." One of her hands were splayed on his chest to anchor herself while she drew a path with the other hand along her neck to her breasts, fondling herself. Dex gritted his jaw, his heart racing along with his breath, trying not to lose control too quickly. It was a miracle he was able to hold on as her pace increased, working him over.

She moaned again, an attractive flush spreading across her skin and her nails scraping along his chest. Dex swore as the thinnest string of self control broke. He gripped her thighs so he could press upward into her, meeting her as hard as she met him, unable to resist grunting through it, completely swept away. This kind of wild, mad turbulence had the potential to fling him right out into the atmosphere. He was pretty sure it did, right into the sun, as they shattered together in a thousand starbursts.

He hadn't known something like this was possible or how he'd ever be able to accept anything less in the future. As their breathing slowed, she slumped forward onto his chest, releasing a sigh of satisfaction, and he wrapped her in his arms. Inhaling her lovely scent, he appreciated the weight of her. It was an anchor to his soul. He closed his eyes, taking deep breaths, wanting to be like Harper and shower this funny, cute woman with a bunch of trinkets. Wanting to give her everything he had.

"Thank you," was all he could manage to say.

He couldn't see her face, but he felt her cheeks pull into a smile against his chest. "Oh, you liked that?" she replied as though it was nothing and not absolutely everything. "You're welcome."

She might have assumed he was thanking her for sex, which would be a weird thing to do. Maybe she thought he was drugged up in orgasm heaven and his brain had stopped functioning. This was half true. But when he said, "Thank you," it was a fraction of the sentence and meant so much more. The rest of it, the implied part was, *Thank you for showing me that there were still sunny days to wake up to.*

Chapter Seventeen

"**D**ID YOU SEE Chris?" Jon asked when Dex appeared at work the following day.

"No, was I supposed to?"

"She said that hikers are worried about some injured hawk at the top of Misery Ridge."

Dex released a short laugh at this news. "What am I? The bird guy?"

"I believe she did say, '*Dex is good with birds, right? Have him go up there.*'" Jon eyed him with greater scrutiny. "Everything okay with you? Is your pet crow giving you problems? You're still the bird guy, right?"

"Yeah, she's been fine." Better than fine. After discovering the yellow marble on the nightstand, Selah fawned over it for Harper's benefit, who then flapped to Dex's desk and returned with a pen cap to add to the collection. So it seemed Harper was now giving Selah his stuff. Not that he minded.

Jon nodded, then seemed to think about it some more before replying, "And how's Selah doing?"

"Fine. Why?" This was also better than fine, but he wasn't going to give Jon the details, as much as he wanted to tell the whole world about his incredible luck lately. Happiness had taken up residence inside his chest, and it wanted nothing more than to burst and cover people in heart-shaped confetti. On the other hand, Selah was right—he'd just gotten out of a longish relationship with someone he'd proposed to and had planned to marry. Him already feeling serious about Selah might give the impression he couldn't trust his own emotions, and, considering how it all turned out with Ava, he sometimes had his doubts.

Also, he never thought of himself as the type of guy to sleep around. For one woman to jump into his bed not too long after another one vacated it, made whatever he felt for Selah seem less significant, which wasn't the case at all. She wasn't just any woman in his bed, she was someone much better than he could have hoped for. In the end, it was better to keep this part of his life private, especially considering that much of his previous romantic life was currently not private at all.

Jon gave him a smirk, tilting his head knowingly. "I saw that news story you guys did. It was definitely something."

"Oh God."

"Was she mad?"

"Who?" Dex asked.

"Selah."

"No." He threw Jon a confused look, since he didn't understand where any of this was going.

Jon merely made a pointed look at his neck again, his eyebrows lifting as he made a "Humph" sound of amusement. "Okay, well, good for you, then. Glad to hear things are working out between you two."

"What the hell does that—" Dex stopped, stooping to

inspect his neck in a side mirror of one of the park ranger's vehicles beside him. There were some scratch marks he'd failed to notice earlier, going up one side of his neck due to some of Selah's over eagerness in bed. He rubbed at them as if they were ink marks and would disappear with aggressive scrubbing. The irritation to his skin made the evidence more pronounced.

"Dex," Chris said behind him, causing him to almost jump out of his skin, like he'd been caught at something.

"What?"

"What happened to your neck? Did that crow of yours do that?"

"No. I just . . . must have happened while I slept." It at least happened in bed, so it was technically true. Jon, who continued hanging around, hid a cough-laugh behind a fist at Dex's awkward situation.

"Okay, good, because you're our bird guy and hikers are reporting there's some injured hawk on the trail at the top of the ridge. Go check it out and see if we can't find some rehabilitation center to take it."

"It's probably going to take me most of the day and a lot of those rehabilitation places are pretty maxed at capacity. This is *why* we should have something here."

His boss waved him off. "Look, I know. But you know how hard it would be to pull something like that off. If it makes you feel any better, the attention you've been pulling into the park is having an effect, so maybe you are onto something. By the way, some morning show on the East coast sent me an email trying to get ahold of you. I forwarded it to you, so you might want to reach out to them. Bring more of that good attention and donation dollars our way while the attention is hot."

"Something is definitely hot," Jon said under his breath as Chris walked away.

"Hey, Chris," Dex called to his boss, "I might need some help, and Jon volunteered. Okay if he comes up the ridge with me?"

"Yeah, sounds good," Chris replied.

Dex gave his friend a shit-eating grin because he was only too happy to return the favor.

Jon released a big sigh before saying, "All right. Come on, bird guy, let's get moving. That hawk isn't going to rescue itself."

Chapter Eighteen

"OH MY GOD! Is that a hickey?"

This was exclaimed by her sister Naomi, when Selah showed up to work after spending much of the previous day avoiding her sister and questions like this. She'd done her best to cover the mark on her neck with makeup. To be fair, Selah wasn't a makeup artist like Hailey, and she'd probably rubbed off half the cheap concealer by the time she arrived at the farm. She didn't respond, choosing to zip her fleece jacket to the very top and popping the collar, as if this was a solution to making the hickey disappear from sight and everyone's attention.

Her mom grabbed her, yanking the collar away to inspect her neck like she was a dejected show dog. "Selah María Moreno," her mother said while *tsking*. "What do you think you're doing? I raised you to be a good girl. Your passengers are going to be here any minute. What will they think?"

She looked to the heavens, praying for strength. "Okay, can everyone stop? I'm a thirty-year-old woman. I'm going to do whatever I want." She most certainly had done whatever she wanted to Dex. If that made her a bad girl, she was more than happy to be one with him. In fact, she was hoping to be both a bad and good girl several more times.

Naomi grinned while pumping her eyebrows. "Well, it certainly explains why you never came home the other night. Seems like you and Dex had a lot to, uh, talk about after that news segment."

"Dexter did this?" Her mother grabbed her again to inspect her neck. "Ah, see? Hailey did you a favor, and now you're so happy, you can forgive her and you girls can go back to loving each other. I knew it would all work out. You and Dexter together. This is wonderful. And maybe you'll stay here and not leave to go to some strange city away from me and your family." The change in her mother's demeanor was funny. It would appear Elena had no problem with her "bad" behavior if it all worked out in her mother's ideal favor.

At the same time, she didn't want to give her mother false hope. One, admittedly, amazing night (and morning) with Dex wasn't about to alter the trajectory of Selah's whole life. "Mom, come on. Nothing's changed. I'm still mad at Hailey. Dex and I are still just friends"—because the last thing she wanted to explain was the concept of rebound relationships—"and I've reached out to my old flight instructor to see if he knows of anyone who might be interested in piloting for High Desert Tours."

The way her mother's expression dropped made Selah regret being blunt, but none of this should be a surprise. Her anger at her youngest sister was more than just Hailey starting a rumor. Her sister had no qualms about embarrassing her, Dex, and the whole business in such a public way. Also, she'd said some hurtful things to Selah and there wasn't an apology anywhere. In fact, it appeared as if Hailey was hiding from Selah because her work schedule went from sporadic to nonexistent. Selah was about to suggest they hire a new office person, along with a new pilot, because it appeared her sister didn't care about anything other than her own selfish needs.

Selah did feel bad, as if she was abandoning her mother. She decided to throw Elena some kind of bone. "But I do really like Dex. He's been, um, really nice to spend time with." Even this was insufficient to describe her real feelings—as though Dex was some nice acquaintance of hers. The truth—he was not only an attractive man, but someone who was beginning to have this ability to strip her down to her bare bones and give her the lightness and happiness she'd been missing from her life for some time. She never known anyone quite like Dex, someone who was not only endearing but made her feel as if she could lean against him and trust him to take some of the weight.

Her desire to want it all, to fulfill everything she'd put on her figurative to-do list, was becoming a complicated dilemma. Life never made anything easy. If anything, perhaps this relationship was simply another roadblock to hamper her. As wonderful as Dex was, she couldn't throw away her goals and her dad's dream for something that was more than likely a temporary relationship. Dex was trying to find his footing after Ava and, she had no doubt, he'd eventually find someone else. She was a Selah blip between the Avas. She'd been here before, but this time she didn't have delusions about how any of it worked.

Her mother had her own ideas, though. "I'm sure Dexter

is already halfway in love with you. Who wouldn't love my Selah? You're so strong. You're such a rock." Her mom stroked her cheek with tenderness and she tried not to think about it too much because passengers were about to show up. Boone arrived, getting out of his vehicle while eating an apple and casually strolling over to the group while holding a basic blue balloon for her pi-ball test.

"Everything okay?" Boone asked, tossing his apple core into the field after handing the balloon to Selah and scraping his fingers through his slightly messy rock star hair.

"Yup," Selah replied. "My mom is just trying to convince me that everyone in the world loves me. And here's a perfect example. Boone doesn't love me."

"Of course I do, darlin'," he said in a slight Southern twang. "All the Moreno women have won my heart, some more than others . . . like your mother and her cooking."

"Good grief," Naomi responded flatly while their mother giggled.

"You can cook for me anytime too, honey," he replied to her sister, throwing her a quick wink.

"Great. I hope you like your dinner with a giant side of laxatives."

"Naomi Rosa Moreno, hush now. I didn't raise you like that. I raised my daughters to be good girls. Boone, come to dinner on Friday, okay? And, Selah, you make sure to invite Dexter. If you don't, I'll find him on the Facebook and ask him myself."

She opened her mouth to object but there was a side of her that didn't want to fight it. She wanted to see Dex again and her mother gave an easy excuse. "Alright, fine. I'll ask him."

After that morning's flight, she returned to the office trailer, pulling out her phone. She wasn't sure how to start a conversation after they'd slept together. *Hey, buddy* was weirdly casual. *Hey* also didn't feel right. How could a single word appear both aggressive and standoffish at the same time? She didn't want to call him in case he happened to be at work. What if she interrupted him while he was in the middle of rescuing someone hanging off a cliff? Was that even part of his job? In the end, she didn't care if it was true or not, because fantasizing about Dex rescuing someone off a cliff was hot.

Selah typed, *Hi there, friend*. After a second, she backspaced the word *friend*, removing it from the text, and hit send.

A few minutes later came the response,

Hey! Made a new friend today.

A selfie followed. It was a picture of Jon and Dex beside each other. Dex clasped a swaddled old towel to his chest with what appeared to be a hawk head peeking from the top of the bundle. The bird's face expressed bewilderment at being included in this selfie, its yellow eyes wide and its beak held agape. The picture made her smile and, to be honest, it was hotter than imagining him hanging off some cliff, rescuing some careless human.

Oh no. You're getting another roommate? I don't know how Harper is going to feel about this.

This was better than her first instinct, which was to express worry that an injured hawk could hurt him. Already feeling protective of the guy wasn't a great sign when it came to her determination not to catch serious feelings.

> *It's all good. Jon and I are on our way to a rehabilitation center near Warm Springs. Gonna get some fry bread for lunch while there. How's your day going?*

> *Any day I get to go up is a good day.*
> *:)*

Selah was beginning to truly feel this way. Sure, this morning's conversation with her family was slightly uncomfortable, but being able to escape into a hot-air balloon was about as close to heaven as she could get, outside of being with Dex. On today's flight there was an older gentleman who, at one point, closed his eyes while taking a deep breath and smiled, like he'd been transported somewhere else, somewhere wonderful. She found herself closing her eyes to take a deep breath as well. Being the person able to take someone to this peaceful place made her feel good, like she had the ability to give them something special. Selah was fortunate to experience this all the time.

> *No one lost any irreplaceable electronic photo albums off the side of the basket?*

Selah laughed.

> *Nope. No phones lost. We in the pilot-ing world call that a successful flight.*

That's my girl.

His response made Selah freeze. The sentence expressed both pride in her and a certain amount of possession. She didn't know which aspect she liked more. Regardless, it shouldn't send warm tingles coursing through her body or produce longing for the man over one silly expression.

It was also possible he'd said it without thinking it through because, on his side, there were those damn reappearing and disappearing bubbles again.

She did her best to brush it off and not read too much into it.

> *Anyway, the reason I'm texting is Mom's insisting you join us for dinner this Friday. Obviously, no pressure if you can't. But if you want the whole experience of her home cooking, you should come.*

Yes!

This was quickly followed with another text.

Was that too desperate? Should I have been more aloof?

She laughed again.

> *It's okay. We're kind of used to peo-ple reacting that way with her cooking. She uses it to her ad-*

vantage.

Especially these days. After her father passed away, her mother used her cooking to draw not only her immediate and extended family closer, but to adopt new members into it. If the house was always full, it was easier to ignore the one member who was missing. It might explain why her mother's interest in cooking and baking only increased in the aftermath and, many times, it completely absorbed her attention.

I mean, the food is a nice perk, but getting to see you is the main attraction for me.

And there it was. He was right back to sending those warm tingles into her chest again.

Chapter Nineteen

WHEN DEX PARKED at the Moreno farmhouse, he searched for Selah's truck, but there wasn't any sign of it. Checking the time, he realized he was a touch early. He wasn't sure if he should text her or wait for her or what. He was nervous about this dinner and not sure why.

It didn't make sense since he'd met the family before and they'd been warm and welcoming. But, then, he'd merely been an acquaintance. Things were different now because he and Selah were . . . he didn't know if he could say they were officially together, but he had feelings for her and it was clear she felt something for him. They were in an awkward period of their relationship, sort of a no-man's-land, each one too nervous to crawl from their respective foxholes and say things out loud. If their previous text exchange was any indication, he hadn't become courageous enough yet and neither had she.

Dex ran his hand over his newly showered hair and across his jawline. Why hadn't he shaved? He should have, instead of showing up at Selah's mom's house for dinner looking like a slob. Ever since Selah said she liked it, he'd preferred the unshaven lifestyle, as well, but his doubts were creeping in. Knowing his mom's opinion on the subject increased his anxiety.

Grabbing the bottle of wine Jon had recommended, he got out of his truck and smoothed a hand across his shirt. Was the wine too much? Or would it have been rude to show up empty-handed, especially since Selah's mom was feeding him? Before he could overthink and change his mind about everything, he knocked on the door.

It swung open and Elena greeted him with a large smile, pulling him in by the arm. "Dexter! It's good to see you. Girls, Dexter is here!" She fawned over the wine, yanking him into the biggest hug and—He noticed a small clump of dirt on his boots, which he was currently getting all over her floor. His chest seized with a moment of panic.

"Ms. Moreno, let me just take my shoes off, so I don't—"

"Call me Elena. Don't worry about it. It's just dirt. We live on a farm, so we're used to it. You should have seen all the dirt my Robert used to track inside. Drove me bananas. Now I miss it, so you're really doing me a favor. I'm so glad you've come. Are you hungry?"

Dex had a moment of bitterness sweep over him. He got more from this woman he barely knew than his own parents. He wanted to soak up this family like a sponge.

He wasn't able to think about it too long before Selah's sisters came into the room to greet him. Naomi pulled him into a sweet hug. "Hey, Dex. Selah should be here soon. We were out of paper towels, so she just ran to the store for my mom to pick some up."

"And we're still waiting for Boone. You remember Boone, right? He helps us at the balloon launch. But come, come, make yourself at home. You can relax until the food is ready. Do you want to sit down?" Elena asked.

She pulled on his arm, leading him into the living room. "Here, you can take Robert's recliner. It's very comfortable. He said it was the best napping chair." Dex allowed himself to be pushed into the chair because it felt rude to resist, but he definitely didn't feel he deserved to occupy another man's throne, even if he was no longer around. "Here's the remote. Feel free to watch whatever you want. I'm sure you can figure it out. It's Robert's remote, as I hardly ever watch TV, except sometimes Hailey will put on baking shows for me. There now. Are you okay? Do you want anything to drink? Water or some of the wine you brought?"

"I think I'm okay," Dex said, somewhat overwhelmed with this level of attention, as he sat stiffly in Robert's recliner. Although it was hard to feel nervous when someone was bending over backwards to make sure he was comfortable.

"Okay, I'm just going to check on the food. Naomi, can you set the table? Hailey will keep you company until Selah arrives."

Hailey stood near a darkened staircase. She approached tentatively and took a seat on the couch closest to the recliner, giving him a small smile. "Did you want to watch TV?"

"I'm okay. Thanks." An awkward quiet descended around them.

Dex took the opportunity to inspect the room. It was a very lived-in, older home, closer in style to his own place. It was different from the bright, minimalist style of his parents' house. His mom would hate it. There was no way to play it up as farmhouse rustic chic or whatever they called it. It wasn't dirty, but it was filled with all kinds of knickknacks, mementos, and untamed house plants. The walls were covered in family photos—lots and lots of photos of hot-air balloons, in particular *The Blue Wonder*. Dex assumed the older man featured in many of the pictures was Robert. Sometimes other members of the family were with him, but many featured Selah and Robert.

He was an older white guy with windswept salt-and-pepper hair and a beard. A chip on one of his front teeth revealed itself when he smiled, giving him a roguish, but fun-loving pirate vibe. Besides the shared love of balloons, Dex didn't detect any physical resemblance between him and Selah. But her dad always held his daughter close to his side in the pictures, and she glowed with happiness. Dex was glad he knew her now, but there was a part of him wishing he'd known her then too. He wanted the opportunity to know her at every stage of her life.

"Can I talk to you before Selah gets here?" Hailey asked, interrupting his thoughts.

"Oh, uh, sure." She wasn't a kid, but she looked very young. He had enough trouble connecting to people in his own generation, let alone a younger one.

Her gaze dropped, one hand fidgeting with the hem of her sleeve. "I'm really sorry if I hurt you or made you angry with the, um, video I posted on Loop."

"Oh. Okay." Her apology was unexpected, and Dex wasn't sure how to respond. He hadn't seen the video in question. Truthfully, he forgot about social media most of the time, unless one of his fellow rangers roped him into recording something ridiculous for the park. He was curious, though, because both Hailey and Selah had brought it up, each one prepared for him to blow up in anger as a result of its existence. Except he'd had much better things to occupy his life with than to worry about it. It certainly couldn't be any worse than the interview he and Selah did for KTVZ.

"I hope I didn't get you into trouble with your job. And I really was just trying to help. I'm just not very good at it and, as usual, I screwed it all up." Hailey hung her head, continuing to fidget, looking miserable about the whole thing.

"Hey, it's okay." Dex felt bad if she was beating herself up over something this silly. "I'm fine. And it did help. The park actually got a lot of donations, and I think most of it was thanks to you."

She snuck a look at him, possibly checking his sincerity, before smiling brightly. "Really? Oh, I'm so glad to hear that. If you ever need another shout-out or something for your crow, I'm happy to do it. This time I'll do something much better. And Selah really does like you. She sometimes fights to prove otherwise on how she really feels about things, but it's not always true. That's just how Selah's been lately."

"How have I been?" Selah asked, coming into the room with a large pack of paper towels under her arm. Dex stood, thinking he should take the load from her arms, but before he could act, Boone followed into the house behind her and took the paper towels himself.

"Hey," Selah said in greeting him, having no qualms about pulling him into a quick hug which he gladly took. "How was your day?"

They'd been chatting off and on throughout the week so there wasn't anything new to share, but he liked that she asked him, as if things were so comfortable between them they could talk about mundane things such as how their day was. When she ended the hug, he kept his hand on her back, lightly rubbing it along her spine. "Better now. I've been looking forward to this all week. How was your day?"

"Good, I think. Were you guys talking about me?"

Hailey appeared somewhat stricken, her gaze darting away and her body posture pulling into herself. There seemed to be some tension between the two sisters. He didn't think Hailey's words would upset Selah, but it felt as though the younger sister was confiding in him and he didn't want to ruin it. He simply pulled Selah into his side. "She was just telling me that you liked me. I think someone found your diary and my name was covered in hearts or something."

"Oh," she replied, easing into him. "I guess I should do a better job at hiding it then. Are you hungry?" She led him to the dining room, but he caught Hailey giving him a grateful smile.

As expected, dinner was delicious. Even better, he'd found a family as welcoming and lively as he remembered Lincoln's home being. Despite the weird vibe between Selah and Hailey, the rest of the family had an easy camaraderie, although they did like to tease each other. The daughters found great delight in riling up their mom and getting her to say things like "Mijas, no. I raised you better than that." But it was clear everything was done in love and Dex enjoyed being a part of it.

Even Boone wasn't as bad as Dex assumed. Perhaps jealousy had colored his initial opinion. The guy was easygoing and seemed to love charming Elena. Even better, there wasn't anything romantic between Boone and Selah. In fact, Boone focused more on annoying Naomi and did so easily.

"Do you want some more, Dexter?" Elena asked him. "There's plenty of food."

"Oh, no, thank you, ma'am. I'm full. It was the best thing I've eaten all week." He draped an arm across the back of Selah's chair, feeling satisfied and needing to give his body some space after eating too much. Selah's mom was an excellent cook and he hoped to score future invitations. The plate of rosemary roast, garlic buttery potatoes, and grilled leeks was something he only ever expected to eat in restaurants. Dex rarely went to those kinds of places after Ava departed from his life, and this situation was more enjoyable.

"Dexter. What did I tell you at the door?" her mother asked quite seriously.

"Uh . . ." He wasn't sure, glancing at Selah for a hint to this pop quiz. She gave him a light shrug and smile because, of course, she hadn't been there. He was on his own.

"I told you to call me Elena."

"Oh, sorry, ma—Elena."

"God, Ma, it's so unfair," Hailey said, jumping into the conversation. "All this time you keep telling us you want us to behave better, to have good manners, that you raised us better. And yet, Dex and Boone get in trouble for having too many manners. Make up your mind."

"They're not in trouble. I just want them to feel comfortable, and they're our special guests. We should treat them as such."

"Did you hear that?" Boone said, leaning a bent elbow on the table and resting his head against his hand, his attention again on Naomi. "You should treat me like your special guest."

"Gross," she replied with an eye roll. "You're Mom's special guest, not mine."

"You be nice to Boone," Elena said, admonishing her daughter. "He's been a great help with the business." She stood and started gathering the dirty dishes.

"Here, let me help you," Dex said, pulling his dishes together.

"Dexter, no, stop it."

"I got it," Hailey said, taking his and Selah's plate. "You are our special guest, Dex. I'll do cleanup and dishes tonight."

He thanked her and she smiled in return. He noticed Selah raising her brow, but she didn't say anything.

"Ah, thank you, mija!" Elena was pleased by her daughter clearing away the table, but couldn't stop herself from helping as well.

"You wanna take a stroll to work off dinner?" Selah asked him.

"Yes, you kids go for a walk. I'll pack some food up for you to take home whenever you leave. Is that okay, Dexter?"

She wasn't going to have to twist his arm over it, and he readily agreed as he stood up with Selah. Naomi also moved to get up, but suddenly stopped and slid back into her chair.

"Did you want to walk with us?" Dex asked because he didn't want to be rude, even if he greedily wanted Selah all to himself.

"Oh no, that's okay. I think Boone and I will just hang out here to . . . um, I don't know, do something . . ." Naomi looked to Boone, as though he could help her finish the sentence.

"I'm sure we can think of something. Maybe you can show me your old bedroom. I bet that'd be interesting." Boone pumped his eyebrows while giving her a sly smile.

With that, Dex was allowed to follow the woman he wanted most, and he did so right out of the house.

Chapter Twenty

EXPECTING NAOMI TO stay in the house with Boone was asking a lot. Selah definitely owed her. She'd been worried her sister's general annoyance with Boone would have been enough to accept Dex's invitation to join them. She was lucky Naomi could read facial expressions, especially the pointed one that said, *Don't you dare come with us.*

Selah burst out of her mother's front door, the September evening still warm from the day. She grabbed Dex's arm, practically dragging him, as she power walked from the porch, past the edge of the house, and to the barn like a woman on a mission. It wasn't the casual after-dinner stroll she'd promised him.

As soon as they rounded the corner on the far side of the barn, away from any curious eyes who may be peering through the kitchen window over the sink, Selah pulled him to her. Perhaps a warning would have been in order because he did a small stumble, putting his hand on the barn wall to steady himself. He didn't fight her, though, as she clasped his neck and she brought her desperate lips to claim his.

After their sudden and explosive coming together the previous week, she wondered if some of the frenzied hunger would have subsided. She at least hoped she'd be able to manage all of this better and not attack the man as soon as they had a moment alone. Her current actions proved otherwise as her desire continued to be out of control, possibly worse than before.

She opened her mouth to him, sliding her tongue with his. Dex returned her actions with his own fervor, pushing her against the barn wall. One of his hands went to her thigh, encouraging her leg to drape over his hip so he could press himself into her. He moved his hand to her neck, tilting her jawline to a better position. Their kissing started heavy, but soon morphed into something less messy and more coordinated and satisfying. A sexy groan rumbled in his throat.

When he broke their kiss by resting his face on her neck, pressing his lips there, he said, "Looks like your sister provides some good intel. I guess you do like me. God, you always smell so good."

She laughed, feeling calmer since she was able to freely touch and kiss him, without having to keep her hands to herself because her whole family was around. What she signed up for in a rebound relationship was more hot make-out sessions and a lot less normal-ish family dinners in her childhood home. Selah was clearly doing it wrong. Although she had to admit she liked having him at the table with her. He fit in well with her family. It had felt uncomplicated and natural, even though their situation was tricky.

Regardless, she was happy they got to the hot make-out part eventually. Some of the wild frenzy steadied, which was probably a good thing. Selah didn't want to get caught having sex next to her family's barn. Kissing him would have to do. She trailed a hand along his chest, gripping the button placket of his shirt, while also brushing through the shorts hairs on the nape of his neck. He returned to kissing her lips and it was heart-meltingly lovely, his hands stroking down the sides of her torso before landing on her hips.

"Did you miss me this week?" She shouldn't have asked. It made her sound like a desperate girlfriend when she didn't consider herself either one of these. Even when she'd been a girlfriend, at various points in her life, she'd never been this pitiful.

"Mm-hmm." He kissed her slowly. "I hope I get to go home tonight with both your mom's leftovers and you."

"You're not *hoping* very well. You just put me second to leftovers."

He stopped, his eyes growing wide at possibly getting caught. "I don't even care about the leftovers. Let's leave right now. Come home with me."

She slipped from his arms, walking away because maybe things were getting a little out of hand. "Nope, sorry. I can't."

"Ah, shit. I'm really sorry. I didn't mean that. You're much better than leftovers." He sounded genuinely worried she was offended. She wanted to laugh until she turned her head and saw his expression.

"Dex, seriously? I'm just giving you a hard time. Why would I get mad over something so ridiculous? It's okay for you to get excited about leftovers."

"So you'll come home with me tonight?"

"Um, no, that's still a negative, but it has nothing to do with you liking leftovers more than me. I mean, it's my mom's cooking. Who's not going to feel that way?" She gave him a flirty look before pushing the barn's side door and slipping inside. The barn's interior was dark, drafty, and musty with old hay and the remnant scent of livestock that used to occupy the space. It hadn't been used for its real purpose for a while. Instead, there was old farm equipment, tools, but, most importantly, it housed the gondola of the hot-air balloon and the large wheeled cart holding the stored envelope. She approached the basket, sliding her hands along the brown fabric bumper wrapped along the top edge of the gondola's wall, wishing she could go up with Dex at this moment. Then she'd have the two things she liked best with her at the same time.

Selah wasn't sure when he'd become one of her favorites, only that he had. They hadn't even known each other for long. This time last year, her outlook on life had been quite different, understandably. Things had been tough and darker for her and her family. It was strange to think about a period of time when she hadn't known Dex. He'd probably been with his ex then, had been happy and kissing Ava. If Selah had any guts, she would have asked him if he missed his ex-girlfriend, but she didn't want an honest answer, one she might not like.

He'd entered the barn, coming to stand behind her. "Selah." Her name came out in a rough voice as he slid a hand around her hip to her stomach, pressing his face to the back of her neck, his breath hot on her skin. She didn't stop herself from leaning against him. "Do you want me to beg or something?"

Imagining him begging was doing all kinds of things to

her, mostly setting her insides on fire. As much as it would please her, it wouldn't be fair to him. "I really want to go home with you, but I can't. I have to get up early tomorrow—"

"That's okay. I'll get up early with you."

She smiled at his willingness. "And I can't stay up late. I have to get a decent amount of sleep since I have an early tour. I'm trying to be rational, as it's a safety thing, and I have a responsibility to my passengers and to my family. No one wants a pilot working on three hours of sleep. And if I go home with you, it's going to be really hard to just sleep and not do a bunch of other things."

"Ah," he replied. "I get it. But, also, I have to tell you that a responsible, safety-first woman is a real turn-on for me so . . ." Dex pressed an open-mouthed kiss to the back of her neck, his arm pulling tighter on her waist.

This she could allow, this she could get into. She gripped one of the fabric-covered steel support struts extending from the top of the gondola, and he closed one of his large hands over hers. His other hand, the one on her waist, drifted to a breast, fondling it until she whimpered against him.

"I don't know how you can calm me and get me worked up at the same time," he said.

"Maybe it's a pilot thing," she suggested between moans.

"I think it might just be a 'you' thing. *You* do this to me."

As much as her brain didn't want to fall into a trap and believe him, she had to admit he was making a good argument. She tried to enjoy this, even while knowing it wasn't going to go nearly as far as she would like.

"Tell me about your tattoo," he said, stroking one of his long fingers on the inside of her wrist.

She stiffened, like she was being tossed from a hot bath into a frozen lake.

His grip on her softened as he dropped his head against hers. "It's something important."

Selah fought the urge to push him off and tell him good night. Instead, she said, "No, not really. It's just a little silly."

"But you don't want to tell me."

Selah took the gondola footholds, climbing inside before turning to face him. If she was going to talk to him, she'd rather do it with some distance and a wicker wall between them. She took the farthest side she could, thankful he didn't move to join her. Dex leaned against the top of the basket and waited patiently. She kind of hated him at that moment—for being that way. He made her want to confide when she preferred not taking anything out of her carefully protected shell.

Crossing her arms and steeling herself, she leaned against her side of the gondola. "You ever watch *Star Trek*?"

"I know I come off as a nerd, but I'm not into every fandom out there."

Huffing a laugh eased some of the tension from her body. "My dad loved that stuff. We'd watched the original series, movies, all the new series, but his favorite was TNG. I think I've seen every episode at least five times. It was kind of my dad's and my thing, like flying."

"And *Galaxy Quest*?" he guessed.

She bit her lip, nodding and taking a moment to blink away any tears.

"Permission to come aboard, Captain?" He didn't wait for a response before climbing into the gondola.

She sniffled. "I'm not a captain, just a pilot. Plus, I think that's more of an ocean ship thing than aviation."

"Except I heard that hot-air balloons are the ships of the sky."

Sucking in a breath at his unexpected words, it sent a prick right into the center of her chest. "Where did you hear that from? That's my dad's thing to say." It came out accusatory, as if Dex had somehow stolen something from Robert. He had no ownership to say things like that.

He didn't flinch at her tone, but his next words were low and calm. "Your mom told me."

"Oh." She felt herself detaching, becoming muted.

Dex took her arm, placing it against his chest, gently stroking over the same tattoo in question with his other hand. Was this how he was when he'd first found Harper as a poor injured crow? His touch felt as if it was capable enough to hold the most fragile of things, like hollow bones. There was nothing more fragile than her at this moment. One rebel tear managed to break free from the others as she watched his finger smooth over her skin where the tattoo was.

"He wanted to be a commercial pilot so badly, but, you know, life kept throwing him a lot of curveballs. When he started this business, he was so excited and I used to . . ." Selah swallowed a painful lump, her voice cracking into pieces. "I . . . used to call him Captain Picard . . which everyone knows is the best captain in all the *Star Treks*. My dad was *my* captain. When I didn't have school or wasn't working, I was right here helping him, because I was going to be a pilot too. He'd call me Number One because I'd like to pretend I was his first officer, like Commander Riker."

She roughly dashed a tear away from her cheek. "When I registered for flight school, I got this tattoo. It's the flag rank of Riker, the little, um, insignias, or whatever they call it on their collar. Riker has three of them. I wanted to show my dad that no matter how high I fly, I'd always be his Number One."

"Oh, honey, I'm so sorry," he said, drawing her to him, her tears soaking into the fibers of his shirt as he ran his hand soothingly from her head down her spine. "I think your dad would be very happy you're the captain of his balloon."

She took a steadying breath. "I'm not, though. I'm not a captain, at least not yet." Selah pulled from him, raising her gaze to his. "They don't just give it to you. You have to earn it, work your way up. So that's what I'm going to do. That's why I can't stay here. I need to get my commercial piloting training, because the license I have is only for small planes and I need to go bigger. Then get on the crew as a copilot or first officer, and then, you know, after some time, maybe I'll eventually work my way up to captain."

"Wait, so that's what your dad did?"

"Well, no, but that's different because he couldn't. I can." It pained her to put it that way, because Robert had worked hard to get what he had. He was the captain of his operation. He deserved his nickname. Selah was happy to be under him, to learn from him, to do what was necessary to keep his dream afloat. But she didn't have a Number One by her side. She had two sisters, a mother, and Boone, and one of those sisters clearly resented and didn't respect her. Naomi and Boone helped, but they weren't invested like she and her father had been. Flying didn't take up their whole soul. Maybe she was a captain, but it was to herself alone, and that might as well be nothing.

"Yeah, I get your dad's dreams. But what are yours?"

She grew slightly aggravated. Dex hadn't been listening. "I just told you I'm going to go into commercial piloting."

"Simply to become a captain for your dad?"

"No," she said, even if part of it was true. But he didn't understand. "Not just for my dad. I love flying and I don't care what kind of aircraft it is, as long as I get to go up. I don't care if it's a damn weather balloon and, yes, I get that weather balloons don't have anyone inside them, piloting. I know how it works. I'm an aviator, for God's sake. I just need to find someone else to take me under their wing, another captain to make me better. I can't do this alone."

"Selah."

"What?" Her impatience found its end as she considered kicking the man out of her gondola and never seeing him again. She didn't need this level of grief from anyone, let alone from him.

"Honey, you're the one who's doing all the piloting here. You're running the show. You're a captain."

"I'm tipping baskets over is what I'm doing."

"You do that a lot?"

"Well, no, that was the only time it's ever happened to me."

He crowded her again, pressing kisses to her temple along her cheekbone. "I won't tell anyone if you won't."

"And what if everyone already knows because of my sister?"

His kisses moved from the shell of her ear to the curve of her neck. "I have a feeling you're going to be okay, Captain. You're still an excellent pilot."

She clucked her tongue, even while parts of her were softening with his touches. "Okay, but I'm still not a captain."

"Hmm. I think"—he skimmed his hands over the skin along the bottom of her shirt—"that you just haven't allowed yourself to get used to the title yet, Captain."

"Oh, is that how it works? Why don't I also just get used to people calling me Professor Moreno, and then I can—"

"Permission to go down on you, Captain."

She nearly choked on the saliva in her own mouth. "What?" Selah was certain she'd misheard the man until his fingers started undoing the button and zipper of her pants.

"Is it still the Mile High Club if we're in a basket and it's on the ground, Captain?"

She looked toward the barn door, checking to make sure it was shut, worried a member of her family would pop in any minute. "Okay, look, I don't think this is a good idea—"

"There you go, Captain, being all responsible again. You have no idea how much of a turn-on that is for me." He sank to his knees before her.

"Dex."

"Captain."

"Stop calling me that!"

He slid her pants and underwear down her legs as much as they would go without taking them off, since her shoes remained on. "I think the only one that can officially give orders in this basket would be the captain, so are you conceding that it's you?"

"No. I don't need to concede anything." She attempted to put some toughness in her voice, but it was difficult to pull off when he was face-to-face with the lower half of her naked body, using his strong thumbs to widen her stance.

When he pressed kisses to her thighs, all she could do was raise her face to the heavens, begging for some kind of strength. "Oh God."

Selah gasped at the first stroke of his tongue, nearly melting right there.

"Captain," he said in a low voice before stroking her again.

"Yes," the word released as half sigh, half moan.

His gaze rose to hers, those hazel eyes glittering with pleasure. "That's my girl." She really did feel like she was his. She wanted to be taken by him, to be something more than temporary, to be able to float up as high as she wanted, but know he was there as an anchor to keep her steady.

He returned to his ministrations, his tongue continuing to stroke through her. Selah's head dropped backwards as her heartbeat built upon itself. Her fingers dug into the fabric-wrapped struts of the gondola. Every time he murmured the word *Captain*, she panted a *Yes* because she couldn't refuse him. It led to more effort on his part. It turned out that concession, in this case, was not a depressing sense of loss, but a blissful explosion of ecstasy. She hadn't realized this was a possibility.

Selah's body wound itself tighter, her pants and moans increasing between beats of his name. When he wrapped his arms around her, pressing his mouth and tongue hard and fast against her, her release burst from her with a cry. He held her there against him, giving her his strength to remain standing as she allowed herself to bask in this.

Shortly after, Dex got up, and redressed her, which was the help she desperately needed. She was so boneless, if she bent over, she'd fall to the floor in an undignified heap. All she could manage was to cling to him, one of her fists gripping his shirt.

Selah needed some time before heading into her mother's home again. Who knew what her facial expression was at this moment? Probably something close to drunk love. She definitely wasn't either one of those things. She hadn't had any of the wine Dex had brought because she didn't like drinking, even a small amount, the night before a flight. Selah also refused to fall in love with a guy over sex. She couldn't allow herself to be this pathetic, not when she was destined to be a city girl and he'd always be a state park guy. She wasn't in love. He wasn't in love. It was sex. Nothing more.

After he finished fastening her pants, he stood beside her, his focus lazily dragging across her face, his expression similarly close to that of adoration. He sweetly brushed his thumb across her cheekbone. "Hey, Captain," he said in a soft tone.

"Hey." She continued gripping his shirt to remain steady, a giggle escaping her lips. She was grinning too hard for it to be normal. Dex may be getting the mistaken impression she actually was drunk love.

He kissed her temple gently before saying, "Good. I

don't want you to ever forget."

Selah wasn't sure how she could be in this gondola again and remember anything else.

Chapter Twenty-One

A FEW DAYS later, Dex was cleaning his place while waiting for Selah to come over after work. She'd mentioned to him earlier, she didn't have any tours booked the following day and so he was anticipating being able to enjoy and take his time with her all evening long.

"Hey, Harper," Selah said from the front porch after the rumble of her truck parked in front of his house. Harper replied with excited caws from her normal lookout spot on the railing.

Going to the door, Dex leaned against the frame, watching through the screen as Selah handed something to the bird before she flapped away with her goodie.

"I keep telling you, you're going to spoil that bird. You don't need to bring her something every time you come." Although part of him loved that she did.

Selah smiled. "Stop getting jealous, Ranger. I brought you a gift too."

Perhaps getting spoiled wasn't such a bad thing. His excitement at receiving a gift was weird, considering he was a thirty-two-year-old man, who was serious and had a serious job. He wasn't a child nor a bird with an affinity for tiny trinkets—unless the tiny trinket became a cute nickname pertaining to Selah. Either way, he swung the screened door open, welcoming her inside.

Her hands remained behind her back, doing her best to hide his gift as she entered the home. "Don't get too excited. I wasn't very creative this time, so you both get the same thing."

He hadn't paid attention before Harper had flown off, so he had no idea what it could be. "I'm hoping for something better than literal trash." In his mind *better* implied something physical with the woman, and he didn't need a special gift as much as he needed her naked.

"It's not trash to Harper as much as it's finding a treasure. I think it's kind of fun looking for things, like a scavenger hunt. I can see why it appeals to her. Now quit stalling and pick a hand." Her expression was one of mischief, and he wanted to kiss it right off her face.

Dex approached until he was close enough to loom over her, encroaching into her space as though he was going to kiss her. He was tempted, really tempted, but he also enjoyed her reaction to his proximity. Her breath quickened, her lips parted, and her gaze dropped. His own body reacted to this of its own accord, as though she couldn't get worked up without him getting worked up alongside her.

"Right," he said.

"You sure?"

He snaked his arm around her side, sliding it to her hand until he could claim whatever was inside. "Looks like I chose correctly."

"Mm-hmm." She surrendered the item, her skin tone blushing. He took advantage of the situation, kissing her lips and her mouth opened to him readily, letting him appreciate the taste and feel of her like enjoying a fine wine. He considered dragging her to his bedroom or the couch . . . even the small kitchen table he never used was becoming a good option. Why settle for a party favor when he could take the whole grand prize?

Before he could make a decision on where to drag her to, she pulled away. "What are you trying to do? Seduce me?"

"If it's not obvious, then I'm not doing a very good job. Let me try again."

Selah laughed, slipping away from him. In her other hand, she held a small brown lunch bag filled with something smelling delicious, taking it to the couch and removing her shoes.

The goodie bag left in his hand was a small Ziploc bag of marionberries.

"Those are what was left on my mom's plant. They're very sweet and pretty ripe, but not enough of them to make a pie or anything. My mom's been making jam and trying to sell them to passengers. I'm sure Harper is in heaven right now." She popped a berry she had in her hand into her mouth before pulling the tinfoil wrapped items from the bag. They were about the size and general shape of burritos. "Can you get some napkins for us?"

"Did you know marionberries are pretty much grown exclusively in Oregon?" he informed her as he went into the kitchen to grab some paper towels.

"I did know that, Ranger Dex. Although they're not really as common in Terrebonne. My mom loves them and whatever my mom wanted, my dad made sure to get her. He bought a giant plant at some special nursery years ago and set up an irrigation system for it, just so my mom could have berries without having to pull off the highway near Sahalie Falls to scavenge for them. I don't think you could kill that thing now if you tried. It's turned into a beast and will no doubt outlive us all."

He took a seat beside her and she handed him one of the burritos. She curled up with hers like a squirrel, sitting on the couch with her legs bent over his lap. If she expressed a desire to have her own marionberry plant, he'd also drive to a special nursery to pick one up for her and set it up with its own irrigation system, even if he had no idea how to do that. How hard could it be? While knowing it was too soon in the relationship to be this way, it didn't stop the feeling, regardless. He couldn't help it at this point. She had completely won him over.

He ran a hand along one of her calves. "Okay, but did you know marionberries are considered the king of blackberries?"

"That, I did not know. Do you feel better now that you've taught me some facts about Oregon today? Is this a park ranger thing for you?"

He chuckled. "I think it is a park ranger thing. Is it annoying?"

"No," she said. "I like it."

And he liked her, so he kissed her before unwrapping the tinfoil. "Harper and I thank you for the gift. And for bringing dinner with you."

"You're welcome," she replied, waving him off.

"I hope your mom doesn't think she always has to make

food for me. I mean, it's delicious and I love it, but she really doesn't need to. I'm happy enough to pick something up for us and give your mom a break."

"I tell her the same thing and then before I leave, she's suddenly handing me a bag of food that she made when I wasn't looking. I think it's how she shows love."

"So your mother loves me?" It was nice to know there was at least one Moreno who did and, with any luck, the feeling would spread to the rest of the family.

"Or she sees you as some poor bachelor she must adopt and take care of."

The status struck him as odd. Yes, he supposed he was technically a bachelor, since he was unmarried, nor had he ever been so. At the same time, he didn't feel the description necessarily applied to him, at least not in the stereotypical version he imagined in his head. He wasn't some young guy swinging through the world without care or attachments. Dex had plenty of things he'd become attached to, mainly the woman sharing her dinner with him. Which reminded him . . .

"Hey, so another interview request came in regarding *our story*." He did a small, amused eye roll at this. "Well, actually, they contacted my boss and then she told me and—"

"God. People are still interested in that? I hope this time they can focus on the wildlife rehabilitation part, which is much more important than anything involving me. Although I'm not going to complain, since the business has turned around and is even more active than before my dad died." Selah took a bite from her burrito, apparently more interested in it than the interview.

While Dex agreed that helping wildlife was an important cause, he also didn't see anything more important than her and was happy some good was coming out of the attention. While it was true he hadn't accomplished his goal of getting a wealthy benefactor who had a soft spot for crows, he was pleased to hear it had helped High Desert Tours. But he was selfish since he hoped, with success, Selah might change her mind about leaving.

"It died down a little," he continued. "But then it suddenly picked up again. I don't really get social media. It remains a mysterious puzzle to me."

"You and me both," she replied.

"Anyway, I've been ignoring some of these requests, but my boss is really encouraging me to do this one because it's *Wake Up, USA*."

Selah stopped eating at this, her eyes growing large. "Are you shitting me?"

"No."

"Oh my God. Well, you definitely need to do that one. I have to tell my mom. That's the only thing she watches regularly, besides her baking shows. She's going to become the number one fan in the Dexter Fan Club."

It was disappointing Selah didn't put herself first in what had to be a small group of people.

"What?" she asked after glancing up from texting on her phone. "Do you not want to do it? You don't have to if you don't want to. It's not like your boss can force you, right?"

Instead of making a big deal from it, he laughed it off. "So you're saying your mom is more of a fan than you are?"

She blushed and did a small stutter. "I . . . I said Dexter

Fan Club, which is a totally different fan club than the Official Ranger Dex Fan Club. Of course, I'm the president of that one." She smacked his shoulder playfully. "Stop it. But now you know how it felt to be second to leftovers."

"I like you better than leftovers." He liked her better than almost anything, but he wasn't quite comfortable telling her this yet. Relationship no-man's-land sucked.

She smiled sweetly at him over the top of her burrito. "And I like you better than my mom likes you."

"So you'll do the interview with me, then?"

Her face scrunched in displeasure. "Ugh. So they can screw up the intention of my words again."

"I think this will be more of a live interview thing, not something pre-taped. They said something about satelliting us in for some studio segment. It'll probably make your mom excited, since it'll be both of us. And it'll be easier, since they won't have to manufacture or create any leaps in our story since we're really together now."

"Ha, but not really." Selah peeled some of the tinfoil from her burrito.

"Funny," he replied.

"But seriously," she said.

He stopped eating as he stared at her, getting that horrible sinking feeling again, the same one he got when he realized he'd been wrong about Ava and her feelings for him.

Selah glanced at him and stopped too.

He swallowed whatever food he had in his mouth, but it was hard to push down. "Are we . . . not together? Is this a friends-with-benefits thing or something?" The status of being undeclared was bad enough. This, though, was sending hairline cracks across his heart. How could he have misread the situation this badly again?

Selah pulled her legs to her side of the sofa and sat up. "Dex, I . . . No, that didn't even cross my mind. I really do care for you. And getting to know you these last few months has been really great . . . the best, even."

While her words were nice, they weren't reassuring and, most importantly, they weren't some declaration of love, which was what he wanted. He was back on the edge again, wondering where he'd made a wrong turn. "But . . ." he prompted, expecting the other shoe to drop as soon as she opened her mouth.

"There is no 'but,' except that I know what I am. I've been here before. I know how this all works out."

Dex's brows pressed together in total confusion. "And what exactly are you?"

It was her turn to act perplexed. "Really? Let's be honest. I'm just your rebound. Not that I think there's anything wrong with that, but I'm not kidding myself that it's anything different."

He stared at her flatly. "You cannot be serious?" For one thing, he'd never seen her as "just" anything. He'd considered all that rebound talk from before as a joke, not something anyone would take as truth. "That's not a real thing, and I can't believe you would actually think that."

She threw him a dirty look. "Oh, okay, so my experience was totally my imagination, then."

"What experience?" If he was going to get thrown under this ridiculous umbrella, Dex needed to know what he was working against.

"I really don't want to talk about it."

"Come on, Selah. You know that isn't fair."

"Fine. While I was in flight school, there was a guy. He and his wife had recently divorced. We had a thing for a couple months. Then he dropped me and got together with the woman who became his next wife. I was just there to help him get his bearings until he found what he really wanted. See? There's not much to tell, but that's what happened. Happy?"

"Why would that make me happy?" If anything, it was worse, because the whole thing couldn't be boiled down to some silly joke. "Maybe that guy was just an asshole."

"Okay, well, news flash, Dex, most guys are assholes. That last date I went on, the one at the brewery, was more of the norm rather than the exception. This is why I don't like dating and try to avoid it as much as possible. And if we were together, why is it that we haven't done anything that most people would see as a date? I'll tell you why. It's because this thing between us isn't a real relationship, it's a rebound."

How could she be so calm, so matter-of-fact? Dex was to the point he wanted to rip his hair out. Had *he* screwed up? Should he have been winning her over by taking her on dates? Was she right? How had they skipped a step and moved straight into comfortable familiarity—something he loved. But maybe she'd been pissed about it the whole time.

"Okay, so this is all because I need to send you flowers and take you out to restaurants or something—"

"I don't care about any of that stuff. I just want to point out that six months or so ago, you were ready to marry someone else. You need time to work all that out. I get it.

I'm just a placeholder, someone to lean against while you get your footing again. I'm a rock. It's what I do. I knew what I was getting into and I did it because I like you. Besides, I'm not sticking around, anyway, so there's no point getting into anything complicated."

He felt like he was losing his mind. "So, this is a pity thing?"

She dropped her head back in exasperation. "Oh my God. No. I don't pity you. But how would this even work? I don't know where I'm going to end up . . . probably in some busy city hub. I need to be at some place where I can continue with the training I need, and you're going to be here."

"Couldn't you work at the Redmond airport?"

"Oh, you mean the smallest airport in the world?"

"Or I could move with you?"

"What if I end up going to some place like Chicago? You're probably going to be miserable. You know you love it here."

"Or I can Google to see what park jobs are available in the area. If being a captain is important to you, then it's important to me. It sounds like you're not even giving me a shot here. You don't even know when or what's going to happen, but—I want to go on that journey with you."

Selah appeared somewhat dumbfounded at this. "But why? You don't need me. You truly are a great guy. You can stay here, work at one of the most amazing state parks around, and find yourself another Ava."

"What?" Why in the fuck would he want another Ava? None of this made any sense. "Do you really believe I'm great? Because you're lumping me in with that asshole who flung you aside, assuming I'm just as bad. And you seem to be fine being treated that way. I don't get it. I don't know what it says about what you think about me or what you think about yourself. You're better than that." Selah's lack of faith in them terrified him. Dex was afraid she'd reject any of his efforts to put himself out there, to put his heart directly on the line. No-man's-land existed for a reason, after all. It was safer to remain in his foxhole.

The reality of this whole situation hit him like a brick. He pushed his face into his hands as he leaned forward onto his knees. How had he let this happen again? He was going to be sick.

"I don't think you're an asshole," Selah responded in a low voice. Her tone was dry, almost emotionless. "You haven't done anything wrong. I don't think you're a bad guy. It's just . . as I've said, I've been here before. I like to keep myself prepared."

He supposed she meant keeping her heart from being affected, unlike him, who hadn't wasted any opportunity to dive in. Perhaps all this time he hadn't given his parents enough credit. Maybe they had the right idea the whole time. A cool, carefully fashioned marriage kept oneself from getting too invested, preventing future heartbreak.

He rubbed his eyes, a sudden headache developing behind them. "Fine. Well, thank you very much for telling me exactly where I stood before I embarrassed myself on national TV. Again. That's Selah, always looking out for me." A dark bitterness crept into his words.

She didn't say anything for a moment until he turned to look at her. She sat on the far side of the couch, looking downcast and studying the burrito in her hands. He wasn't sure what he expected. She wasn't happy or mad or sad. She wasn't anything more than emotionless resignation. After releasing a long, slow breath, she put her burrito down, picked up her shoes, and, without giving him another glance, she said, "I think I better leave. I'm sorry."

And then she was gone.

He spent the rest of the evening staring at the opposite wall, feeling every bit of being dumped without having been in a real relationship.

Chapter Twenty-Two

WALKING TO THE High Desert Tours' office trailer, Selah removed her baseball hat and shook out her curls with a hand. She was worn out, even after a perfect flight. Flying wasn't enough to shake the funk she'd found herself in since leaving Dex's place a few days earlier.

She didn't know how to explain things to him. He already thought her whole belief in rebound relationships was ridiculous. She couldn't imagine how'd he feel about her theory regarding fate and how it had a habit of throwing up roadblocks, including her relationship with him, to keep her from her goal. Saying it out loud would sound silly, even to the logical, scientifically minded part of her brain. Except, she had lived it. She'd seen Robert live it. She kept it to herself because telling a person that fate had used them as some kind of pawn to mess with the Moreno family and . . . yeah, okay, it was ridiculous.

Regardless, she was cutting him from her life before the attachment grew any further. As much as she tried to convince herself she'd done the right thing, it hadn't made her feel any better. The absolute dejection on Dex's face would haunt her forever. It would have crushed her if she wasn't already crushed and hollowed out.

Selah spent much of her time waffling between what she did and what else she should have done. She felt like she'd lost the one person she could talk to, the one person she didn't have to be tough around. Returning to a life of mostly silence, when she'd gotten used to it filled with his text messages, was depressing. During those moments of misery, she wished she'd been smarter, less horny, and stuck with being friends only. Maybe they could have remained friends, even after she left Central Oregon.

Other times, she wished she hadn't said anything. She could have lived in the fantasy world a little longer, let the whole thing play out until its unfortunate conclusion. She still expected to get left behind at some point, but she'd already accepted this outcome. The only difference was she would have gotten more time with him. What she had received didn't feel enough.

But between those two things, it didn't add up to the number of times she wished she would have answered with, *Yes, we're together. You and I are now a "we."* If she'd gone that route, let herself completely sink into the relationship, it may have still ended in disappointment. But who knows how blissful life would have been before her two-year commitment to pilot at High Desert Tours had come to its conclusion. Unfortunately, life didn't work out that way. Sometimes one had to stay on course and fight through the turbulence the best way they could. Selah didn't know how to do it any other way.

Selah removed her aviator sunglasses as she climbed the few steps to the office door like she was trekking up Mount Everest. She was surprised to see Hailey at her desk, talking on the business phone line like it was a job and she did it every day. The sight took Selah aback, as though she had tripped into some alternate timeline.

She plopped into her office chair and took a long drink from her water tumbler as she woke her laptop from sleep.

"Yes, that's right. Just make sure to arrive fifteen minutes early to look over our safety contract, which needs to be signed before flight time. You can also read it on our website if you want to look at it ahead of time. Okay? Sounds great. See you then," Hailey said before hanging up.

Selah raised a brow at how professional and adult her youngest sister sounded. What was happening today? While Selah didn't have the energy to maintain the silent treatment, her time with Hailey could only be described as cool indifference with minimal interactions. Her sister avoided her more than the other way around. Not that Selah cared as she was too busy to worry about it. Instead of acknowledging Hailey, she focused on her laptop screen, searching for wind and weather forecasts for the following day.

"Mark called and left a message, saying he might know of another candidate for the balloon pilot position," Hailey said, after a few silent minutes passed.

"Okay, thanks." She only hoped it was better than the last guy her old flight instructor had sent her way. The man had spent much of the phone call talking over Selah and had a lot of high demands about how he expected things to work. The last thing she wanted was someone who'd push around her family when she wasn't there.

The quiet moment continued loudly ticking by before Hailey impatiently tapped a pen on her desk and released a loud sigh. "Do you hate me?"

Selah glanced at her sister, not in the mood to get into any sort of argument. "No, I don't hate you. I just don't always understand you, and you frustrate me."

Hailey gave her a dirty look. "Yeah, well, same."

Selah shook her head, returning to her work. They truly were different creatures, except she didn't consider herself difficult to figure out. She always thought of herself as straightforward. Although, perhaps, if she'd been more so with Dex, they would have been saved a huge mess. If only she'd been more upfront and honest. Lesson learned.

"Did you really break up with Dex?" Hailey blurted the question because she'd always been too impatient to ease into a discussion, preferring to jump straight into the deep end. Tact had never been her strong suit.

Selah nearly choked on the water from her tumbler. "What?"

"Mom said that you told her that you weren't going to see Dex anymore."

Earlier in the morning, her mother had pestered Selah about inviting him to another dinner. She finally had to drop the news that she and Dex weren't talking anymore to get her mother off her back. Of course, nothing secret ever remained that way in this family.

"I said I wasn't planning on seeing Dex anymore, which is an entirely different thing than breaking up because we weren't dating in the first place. It's not a big deal. I'm fine and he's fine." God, she hoped he was fine. She was tempted to send a message to check on him, even while realizing he most likely didn't want to hear from her.

"But why?" Hailey's brows pressed together, looking as crushed as Selah felt on the inside.

Selah released a deep sigh from her gut, not wanting to discuss it with her mother, let alone her youngest sister. She decided to be diplomatic about it. "Dex and I just decided—"

Her sister scoffed in disbelief. "I'm already calling bull-shit on whatever you're about to say. I know this was all you. Dex was a great guy. He was so hot for you, it practically oozed out of him. I can't believe you'd just drop him like that."

"Oh, I'm sorry. Weren't you the one who described him as 'mid'? Yeah, I'm pretty sure that was you."

"Is *this* because of me?" Her sister at least had the where-withal to appear horrified at the possibility her action had a consequence she didn't expect.

"No. Not everything is about you, Hailey. You really think I'd break up with someone because you think they're mid?"

"I thought you said it wasn't a breakup?"

"I—" Selah took a breath to restart the conversation. To be honest, she was surprised Hailey was coming to Dex's defense. She had no idea why her sister felt so strongly about this. But it was weird Selah wasn't the one standing up for him because Hailey was right—he was great and didn't deserve any of this. "It's not a breakup. I'm just pointing out that your original opinion of him wasn't very nice."

"And I changed my mind. He's perfect for you." Her sister's eyes turned dark with anger as she crossed her arms. "But *you* probably did something to ruin it. Why don't you just go ahead and leave already? I don't know how you can be so cold and uncaring. You're okay leaving us behind like we're nothing, like it's easy."

Aggravation flared inside Selah's chest. "Do you think any of this is easy for me? That I haven't worked my ass off? That I wouldn't love to be as carefree as you? Or be able to just throw myself into having something with Dex? How do you know my heart isn't always breaking?"

Her control over her emotions shredded as large, hot tears slid down her cheeks. "But I have to be the rock. I have to make sure Mom's bills get taken care of because some days it's just too hard for her to think about it. I have to make sure that Dad's shitty financial decisions don't come back to bite the rest of us in the ass. I have to be the one who holds herself together. If you don't think I'm not also pissed off at everything, you'd be wrong. I am. And the one person"—her voice cracked at the thought of Dex—"the one person who allowed me to lean on them when I needed it, I can't have, and I can't do anything about it. I don't know how it would ever work with us, and I have everything else to think about. So you can go ahead and believe whatever you want, but just know that everything I do is for a reason, and none of it is fucking easy."

Her sister stared at her during her outburst, dumbfound-ed, not saying anything.

Selah attempted to pull herself together, rubbing away any tears with the bottom of her fleece jacket while sniffing. She was exhausted, too tired from navigating through her days. She didn't want to talk about it anymore, returning to her laptop screen, leaning forward so she could press her pounding forehead into her hand. This blocked Hailey from her view and, with any luck, her sister would go back to being mad and ignoring her.

She sat like that for a minute or two, not reading or processing the screen in front of her, attempting to concentrate. Selah hadn't expected her sister to come to her and put her arms around her, stiffening from shock when she did.

"I'm so sorry," Hailey said, her voice broken with her own weeping.

This only ruined Selah more as the tears came rushing forth again, overtaking her. It was hard not to feel broken and not to see her sister the same way.

"I'm sorry that I hurt you—what I said about Dad, and for everything. I've just been so . . . m-mad. I've been pissed at Mom for not being able to make decisions without Dad and holding onto that goddamn urn. And I've been pissed at you because sometimes it seems like you don't even care. Maybe I did do that video to hurt you or get some kind of reaction. I feel like something is wrong with me, that I can't hold everything together—"

"You're just young. I know that, and I'm sorry I've been tough on you, but I can't always be everyone's rock all the time. I'm tired."

"I know. You're right. But I'm scared. I'm afraid I'm not going to be capable, like you. I don't know if I can."

Selah pulled her younger sister down until they were eye level, brushing her sister's wild, curly hair from her cheek. "Listen to me. We are Moreno sisters. We can do anything. You are capable. Don't ever let anyone tell you differently." As she said the words, she realized maybe this was where she'd gone wrong. She'd been so busy trying to be marble and do everything for everyone, she forgot that the best thing she could do was teach her sisters how to be their own rock for themselves and each other. Maybe her support, whether it was about their father's ashes or about other creative business ideas, meant more to her family than trying to be the perfect daughter and just keep everything going.

Hailey's large brown eyes were so sad, Selah wanted to hold her, to let her sister lean against her for a little longer. "Dad wanted to take me for a special hot-air balloon ride, just him and me before my last birthday," her sister said in a low voice, as though she was revealing a deep secret.

That would have been about a month before their father had passed away. This kind of thing wouldn't have been out of the ordinary for Robert. "Okay," Selah said.

"I did it, but I was kind of in a bad mood because I'd gone out with friends the night before, and we stayed out really late. I didn't want to get up early. But he'd already gone through the trouble of getting *The Blue Wonder* ready, so he said I had to, it was the golden hour. And he'd been so excited, but I was grumpy, so it kind of ruined the whole morning. I fooled around on my phone instead of talking to him. But then I said . . ." She burst into more tears, her skin turning red. "I said, *This is really your and Selah's thing. You should just do it with her. She's the only one who cares about your balloon.*"

Selah should have been angry because she knew those words from Hailey would have devastated Robert. He'd been trying to have a special moment with her sister, and she'd tossed it away. Except there was no reason to get upset when this memory had clearly been weighing her sister down all this time.

Hailey continued, "And I could tell he was mad. You remember how he used to grind his jaw together? Yeah, he was doing that. But he didn't say anything. Not for the rest of the flight. Just stayed quiet and landed the balloon. It's kind of like what you do. You can tell when you don't want to deal, and you just switch yourself over to autopilot mode." She looked away. "And the only thing he said to me after we landed was, *I don't care what you do, Hailey. Just do something that makes you happy, something as happy as you and your sisters and mother and this balloon make me.* I thought it was such a weird thing to say because I had hurt him and couldn't have been making him happy. And now it's too late and I'll never be able to go up in that big blue balloon with him ever again. So, yeah, I'm pissed off, too, but the person I'm most pissed off at is me."

"Oh, Hailey," Selah responded, hugging her sister, letting her cry on her shoulder. There wasn't anything she could say to make her sister feel better. If she were her, she'd feel terrible too. "You know Dad didn't hold a grudge. He wasn't like that. He was probably just disappointed. You know he loved you."

"You don't hate me, do you?" her sister asked through her sobs.

"No."

"Then stay. I don't want to lose you too. You can be happy here. We all love you, Selah, and so does Dex."

She considered correcting her sister. Even if Dex had loved her, he certainly didn't love her now. She imagined he'd get over her quickly, as most guys in her experience did.

Instead, Selah said, "We'll see."

She didn't like making promises she didn't know she could keep. There might be some truth in what Hailey had said about her. Selah had switched to autopilot after receiving that horrible phone call from her mother telling her Robert was dead. This had been the only way she knew how to deal with the magnitude of her loss. Since that point, she'd never switched back and wasn't sure she had the strength to manage piloting without it, to trust her own judgment. Selah was maintaining whatever course she'd set up and that was that. She hadn't taken into account any changes of feelings or circumstances, seeing them as challenges to overcome instead of something to be embraced.

Regardless, Selah lifted her chin and gave her sister an encouraging smile. "Either way, you're going to fly in *The Blue Wonder* with Dad again. We all are. We're going to make it happen, okay?"

Her sister sniffed. "You'll help me?"

"Yup. That's what I'm here for."

She hoped it would be enough. Something deep down inside told her she needed this too. Because, for any chance of moving into the future, whatever it might look like, they needed to follow Robert's last advice to Hailey and try to be happy.

Chapter Twenty-Three

"YOU DOING OKAY?" Jon asked. Dex stood beside a fence post as the audio guy fitted him with a wireless lavalier mic on the button placket of his shirt.

"Fine," Dex responded, regretting he'd agreed to move forward with this interview with *Wake Up, USA*, especially since he'd be doing it alone. He'd asked Jon to show up for emotional support but, so far, all his coworker had done was ask him annoying questions like *What happened to Selah?* and *Why is Harper being an asshole this morning?*

The answer to both of these questions was the same—*I don't know*. Both Selah and Harper were a mystery to him, and he was mad at both. In Selah's case, it was because he'd given his heart to a woman who didn't want it. And Harper? For some unknown crow reason, she was annoyed with him and wouldn't stop pecking and pulling at his clothes, skin, and arm hair. If he were to guess, it would be because she wanted to do her own thing while Dex forced her to stay on his arm with a bird lead attached.

It didn't help they'd been made to wait around forever because they'd shown up for a morning segment on East coast time, only for it to get pushed back an hour. They still had another forty minutes to go.

"You don't look fine." Concern was etched on Jon's face.

"I'm fine. I'm going to go on, talk about Harper and the rehabilitation center, and that's it." He didn't want to talk about Ava or Selah or anything else about his personal life. His life wasn't for the entertainment of others. He wasn't some chess piece someone could manipulate around a board for their own amusement.

Harper cawed loudly and pulled again at his sleeve hemline, nipping painfully on his arm in the process. "Okay, fine. You wanna leave. Go ahead. Leave." He unwrapped the small lead, detaching the bird, and Harper immediately flew away. Well, fine, now he didn't have Harper to do the interview with either. It would only be him.

The guy behind the camera exchanged a glance with the audio guy before saying, "Um. That bird knows to come back before seven, right?"

Dex shrugged, not caring about the situation anymore. The whole interview felt like a mistake. He wasn't sure if he should cancel or find a way to stumble through it.

"Dex?" Jon said.

"I'm fine. Really. Harper isn't a pet. If she wants to go, then she can go. I don't care. She can do whatever she wants. She's probably happier being free of me, anyway."

Jon motioned with his hands for Dex to calm down. "It's going to be okay. I'm sure she just needs some space. It's okay to step back and really think things over, you know."

"Yeah, okay," Dex agreed, but the ball of anxiety in his gut unraveled. "But what am I supposed to do in the meantime? I feel like I finally found someone who really got me, where I could just be my weird self, and it didn't matter.

And I thought she felt the same way. I'm just tired of being wrong all the time."

The cameraman and audio guy exchanged looks again. The audio guy then busily fiddled with his equipment, but under his breath, he said, "Man, that must be some crow."

"Yeah, and maybe you're not wrong. Maybe it's just complicated," Jon said.

Dex wasn't sure if he believed him. Maybe Selah did love him, but it was hard to see everything when he was so hurt and she never said anything. All this time, he thought he wanted something big and messy and complicated, but now he wasn't so sure.

His fellow ranger continued. "Hey, isn't that Selah's sister?" He pointed in the direction of a wooden picnic table not too far off in the distance, where the young woman sat on the table with her feet on the wooden bench seat, watching them.

While he sometimes searched the early morning horizons for any sign of a blue hot-air balloon, this sight was an unexpected one. "How long do I have until the interview?" he asked the crew.

The cameraman glanced at his smartwatch. "'Bout twenty-eight minutes."

"Okay, give me a minute."

He shoved his hands in his pocket as he strolled to the picnic table, but not before he heard the cameraman say to someone, "He's coming back before seven, right?"

When Hailey noticed him approaching, she appeared somewhat sheepish, but gave him a small smile. "Hi."

"A little early, isn't it?" Hikers at this hour weren't unusual for the park, as they opened at dawn, but Hailey didn't give the impression she was there for hiking.

She pulled a stray curl that had swept across her cheek. "Yeah, I'm . . . trying to get myself in the habit of waking up early. So far, I hate it. My dad was an early riser, you know. Selah's the same way. You think that's something that a person can change about themselves?"

"Sure, I don't think it's a personality trait set in stone." He hadn't been a morning person, either, in his youth, but with his job sometimes requiring an early start, he saw the appeal of doing things while most of the rest of the world remained in their beds. There was something peaceful about it.

Dex took a seat beside her on the picnic table. He wasn't sure why she was here, but he was interested in what she had to say. He wondered if this might be the closest he could get to figuring out Selah's brain, as though her sister might offer him a few crumbs and he could snatch them up for later study.

"You're getting ready for your interview?"

"Yeah, in a little bit, with *Wake Up, USA*."

"I heard about that. My mom loves that show."

"You wanna do the interview with me? You are the expert at this sort of thing."

She snorted a delicate laugh. "Oh no. I'm not risking getting into more trouble with my sister. It's already hard enough to not screw up things. I just stopped by because . . . I was hoping to talk to you. But I didn't know when you were in the park, and, I don't know, I just came here on a whim." Hailey scratched at the surface of the picnic table with a fingernail.

"Well, I'm glad you found me. I like talking to you." He gave her a friendly smile in return.

Her brow lifted in surprise. "You do?" She scooted closer, looping her arm through his and resting her head against his shoulder, as though they were old pals. Dex wasn't sure he'd ever get used to such a touchy-feely family as the Morenos, but he wanted to.

"You know, my dad was a really great guy. He was a little stubborn and sometimes goofy, but also calm and patient, and he loved flying that damn balloon so much. I didn't always appreciate it, not like Selah did. She's a lot like him. The ironic thing is that he was her stepdad. Or maybe it isn't ironic at all. Maybe she realized before all of us that there are some guys out there who aren't so great, and he was one of the good ones. He adored my mom. Oh my God, sometimes it was so cringe." She laughed lightly to herself.

"But even though my dad was a pretty happy guy for the most part, there were some disappointments in his life. Selah, I think, saw it more than any of us. And I wonder if because he loved her most when he didn't have to, she feels some kind of an obligation to him." She raised his gaze to him, her light-brown eyes sincere and serious, as though she was trying to push some kind of understanding onto him.

While Dex understood this was some kind of insight into the woman he'd given his heart to, he didn't understand what hint he was supposed to be receiving. Was Hailey warning him to give up? That Selah had no room in her life other than her obligation to her dad? Or that he should keep trying? He opened his mouth to ask some kind of question, but was interrupted.

"Dex!" the cameraman called to him. "Ten minutes." The man held up both hands in the air with all ten fingers splayed to reinforce the information.

Hailey released him. "You better go. It's almost time for your close-up."

"You gonna stick around?" He was hoping she'd say yes so he could talk to her about Selah further.

"Eh, I think I better head home. My mom and I will watch it together."

"Oh. Okay. You have a good day then. Say hi to your mom for me." It might be weird he didn't pass along a message to Selah, but "hi" seemed insufficient after all they'd been through. He wasn't sure he was ready to be at this level of casualness yet. Instead, he made his way toward the production crew.

"Hey, Dex!" Hailey called to him. She stood on the wooden bench seat, appearing ten feet tall. Her voice carried over the quietness of the area.

He turned, walking backwards, as he waited for her to finish, holding a hand to his ear.

"You didn't listen to what I told you the last time. Remember, I told you that Selah will fight to convince you that she feels differently than how she feels. Turns out she may even look indifferent. But then we're all still a little screwed up."

Dex didn't know how to reply to this and simply waved goodbye before turning toward his destination.

"Everything okay?" Jon asked.

"Yeah, fine." But Dex wasn't sure if it was fine or what

fine looked like. His mind was diving deeply into Hailey's words and what they meant, especially what it all meant for him and Selah. He barely paid attention to anything else, only to be slammed into focus when a voice popped in his earpiece, some kind of introduction, and then he was scrambling as he stared into the camera like a deer in headlights.

"Hello, Dex? Can you hear us?" the voice came again.

The cameraman made a circular motion with his finger over the camera in a signal for Dex to say something. Jon placed a hand over his mouth in an expression of worry.

"Uh, yes. Sorry. Yes, I can, uh, hear you." The words stumbled from his mouth.

"Why don't you tell us a little bit about yourself? How long have you been a ranger, and for which park?"

"Um, okay. Well, I've . . ." He cleared his dry throat, wishing he'd used his time more wisely and drank some water. "I've been a park ranger for . . ." His mind was so full of Hailey's words, he blanked on everything else. "Uh, Jon, how long have I been a park ranger for?"

His friend dropped his head, covering his eyes.

"Oh, uh, I don't know, years, I guess. I've been working here at Smith Rock in Central Oregon for a couple of years now. We're known for being the birthplace of sports climbing, but hikers from everywhere come to appreciate our beautiful landscape." Dex stiffly swept an arm toward the picture-perfect scenery behind him.

Harper glided into the frame, landing on his outstretched arm like a preplanned trick. He tried to not appear shocked, as though he'd expected this, even while gasps came through his earpiece at her sudden appearance. With the crow returning, his comfort in the situation shifted into something easier. "This is Harper. She's a typical American crow, not to be confused with a raven. The shape of the tail is different between the two birds. Although, she's also quite intelligent. She was rescued and rehabilitated less than a year ago, and we're hoping we can get enough donations to start our own rehabilitation center here at the park."

"Is there something in her mouth . . . uh, beak?" one of the women interviewers asked him.

This was an easy spiel for him, having said it several times before. "Sometimes, when crows love you, they will bring you gifts. Trinkets." He opened his hand and Harper dropped a bead. He held it to the camera to show it off. It was bright blue, the same shade of *The Blue Wonder,* and he thought about Selah again and—

It hit him.

Selah was always bringing him things. Dinner, marionberries, that hedgehog sticker plastered on his phone case. Her sister, Hailey, had given him the biggest nudge of all. Selah was not indifferent, had never been indifferent. She'd loved her dad with everything, had grieved for him, but most of the time, people would never know because she'd kept herself buttoned-up. The few times one of those buttons came loose, she'd fallen apart. And now she was doing the same thing to him. It had to mean she felt more than she could allow herself to say.

And, yes, it was messy. He finally understood that in getting involved with her, it wasn't just her, but her whole family. And things could get complicated, especially when the Morenos were still struggling with loss. But the good side of this family, the things that shined through in spite of the darkness, was the very thing he'd always wanted in his life. If he loved her, he would have to accept all the different sides. Something told him it would be worth it.

"Dex? Hello, Dex? Have we lost you?"

"No. Sorry. I just lost my train of thought for a minute." He tried to focus.

"Now you've recently received a lot of attention because of a certain partnership with a local hot-air balloon business. But this wasn't just a simple collaboration, was it? We're told there's an interesting story behind it all. Can you tell us a little bit about that?"

He grew wary, but tried not to show it. "Well, I, uh, booked a hot-air balloon ride for me and my girlfriend at the time, and that's when I met *Captain* Moreno." He smiled at the camera as he emphasized the title. If she was watching, he wasn't going to let her return to being "just" anything. "She's the hot-air balloon pilot at High Desert Tours and, though the proposal I planned for my ex-girlfriend didn't end as expected, Selah and I became really close. I guess you can say her friendship fell into my lap, literally—"

"So you broke up with your girlfriend and are now with the pilot, who was flying the hot-air balloon?"

God, these people were nosy.

But, in a moment of inspiration, he decided to switch tactics and use it to his advantage. Because maybe he'd only have one shot to fight for her, to show he saw right through her indifference, and he didn't believe it.

Chapter Twenty-Four

"MOM, CAN WE talk to you?" Hailey asked once Selah and Naomi arrived at the farmhouse that day.

The Moreno sisters had already had a conversation about this amongst themselves, with Hailey agreeing to take the lead. Selah realized she didn't need to take on everything herself. Her sisters were capable and strong, too, when given a little push.

Her mother turned from where she stood at the kitchen counter, kneading some kind of dough. "What is it, mija?" When she noticed her other two daughters as well, her eyes grew wide with worry. "What's wrong?"

"Nothing," Hailey said, going to her mother's side. "I . . . or, rather, we want to discuss Dad's ashes."

Elena automatically went sparkly eyed with tears at this. "His ashes? Do we have to talk about this right now? I'm really very busy. Maybe we can talk about this—"

"Mom," the youngest sister interrupted gently. "Dad wouldn't want to just sit on a dresser, collecting dust."

"Oh, no, you don't understand. I cover it with things so that it won't get dusty. You can check—"

"That's not really what I mean. He was a pilot. He wanted to fly. He wanted to be free." Her sister's voice cracked, but remained strong. "You know I'm right. It's what he always wanted. This is important, and we need to honor him."

Her mother's focus shifted between each daughter, finding a united front between them. She swiped away a tear, her shoulders dropping. "I know. I know that's what your father wanted. But I loved him and I don't . . . I don't know how to live without him."

"I know it's hard, but we're ready to do this for him. And if you're not ready, that's okay. You can keep some of the ashes, but let us have the rest. Can you do that? Selah said we can take him up on *The Blue Wonder* one final time and let him go," Hailey said. "We need our last flight with Dad."

Elena looked to Selah, who gave her mother a small smile and nod of encouragement, knowing they were all in this difficult situation together, but it needed to be done. "And I can keep some of him?" she asked.

When Hailey had discussed this with Selah, there hadn't been any mention of letting their mother keep a portion of his ashes, but, she had to admit, it was a good compromise. She was proud of her younger sister for not only tackling a tough situation but also thinking quickly on her feet. It was a moment where she could see her sister growing into the adult she was destined to be.

A few days later, their mother decided to take all of Robert's ashes on one last final balloon ride. Selah met her family in the launch field with *The Blue Wonder*. Boone was there as part of the chase crew, but he also brought along his friend, Alan, to help since Naomi would be going up.

Elena stood nearby as everyone prepped for liftoff, clutching the simple metal black box to her chest and crying silent tears.

Then it was time to go.

The family climbed into the gondola after the envelope was fully inflated and ready, and Selah ignited the burner, lifting them from the ground. There was that same familiar prick in her chest, but this one was bittersweet, feeling glad it was finally happening, knowing Robert would have liked this—all his favorite people together in one basket.

As a soft breeze brushed across her skin, she removed her aviators, closing her eyes and immersing herself in the feeling of flight. She realized a person didn't get this while piloting a plane, at least not in normal circumstances. They may have had the height and the speed, but they didn't get to feel the wind. They didn't get bright sunbeams dancing across each molecule of their face that didn't come through a laminated windscreen first. They didn't get to feel like a cloud without the constant roar of engines in their ears. There was no experience like a hot-air balloon flight.

"Your dad used to do the same thing," her mother said. "This is why he loved it so much. Why, in the end, he was happy things worked out the way it did. Every night when we would go to bed, I'd ask him how his day was, and he'd always answer the same way—*No regrets*." Elena wiped another tear away. "Oh, Robert. All your daughters are so amazing. Selah does such a good job flying your balloon. Naomi is so creative and comes up with great ideas. And our Hailey has so much spirit and tenacity. You'd be so proud. I am so proud. I couldn't have done this without any of them.

They are my heart."

Her mother hugged Selah before pulling the other two girls into the hug as well. "I love each of you so much," she told them, before looking to Selah and asking, "Is it time?"

They were about as high as Selah wanted to go. Checking the landscape beneath them, she confirmed it was the wild, untamed land of the High Desert in the farthest corner of the Moreno farmland. She dropped a handful of the bark chunks she'd collected earlier from beneath her mother's marionberry plant, testing the wind direction. "Do it on that side," Selah informed them. "That way, it won't blow back on us."

Hailey helped her mother open the urn, removing the plastic bag containing the white, brittle flakes of Robert's remains. They undid the metal tie at the top. "Are you sure you don't want to keep any of it? It's okay if you do," Hailey said.

Her mother lifted her chin in a show of strength. "No. You're right. This is what he would have wanted."

Tipping the bag over the side, the wind took Robert away. He was flying, he was free and, in a way, Selah was free too.

There was something odd in letting go. One always assumed it would be the hardest thing in the world, but when the time was right, it was also easy. The weirdest part was that Selah didn't feel that way about the business. Earlier that week, she had talked to another potential pilot and he hadn't felt right, either, but maybe it was because she was looking for another Robert and there wasn't another one. He was one of a kind. She was trying to have it both ways in getting someone else to take over because she was afraid she'd never live up to her dad, while also finding no one worthy enough to take over his legacy because they wouldn't love *The Blue Wonder* and the business as much as she and her dad did.

Yes, she'd made mistakes and she might make a few more in her career. There was an old piloting joke that, technically, every landing was a crash landing . . . the only difference was if anyone noticed or not. Truth be told, she knew her father wasn't perfect, but as much as she pondered the idea that roadblocks had been thrown at him, it was also true he had picked his ultimate path. He hadn't given up. He'd chosen this. He'd chosen her. And that wasn't fate. That was love.

They were all his legacy.

She sniffed away her emotion and cleared her throat. "I think . . . I'm going to stay."

Her mother whipped around from her spot at the side of the basket, touching her chest with a gasp.

"What do you mean by that?" Naomi asked, since no one else was taking the initiative.

"I think I want to continue flying for High Desert Tours, if I can count on Naomi and Hailey to help—"

Her sisters screamed before wrapping their arms around her in a wild hug.

"You can count on us! I'm going to be so on top of it. I promise," Hailey cried.

"Okay, okay. Everyone needs to calm down, as we're still a thousand feet in the air." Selah slid on her aviators. "If I'm going to be captain, I'm in charge up here. When it comes to the balloon or flights or anything relating to them, I have the final say. You will listen to me. The other particulars surrounding the business on the ground, we can talk about who will be in charge of what. Is that a deal?"

Her sisters exchanged glances with each other and grinned. "Yes, Captain," they said in unison.

"Oh, Selah," her mother said. "This would make your dad so happy."

"You have to call her 'Captain.' Didn't you just hear her?" Hailey said, her eyes sparkling with happiness.

"Ay, mija, you watch yourself. I'm still your mother and I can call you what I want. But your sister will make a very good captain. She will always be as strong and sturdy as a rock."

"Only when I'm in the air. On the ground, maybe I don't have to be a rock all the time."

"Yes, okay," Elena replied. "On the ground, we will be your rock. Okay?"

"Yeah, sounds good." Selah smiled through tears.

With the balloon sinking to a lower altitude and the return trip in progress, she took a deep breath and looked at the far landscape toward the Three Sisters Mountain Range. This was her home. She felt connected to it like never before, even to the rugged, rocky landscape of Smith Rock. She wondered about Dex, hoping he was okay, wishing more than anything she could talk to him again.

"Are you going to tell him?" Hailey asked, seeming to read her mind. "I mean, you have to now."

"Because I'm staying?"

"Well that, and because of the interview—Wait a minute? Ma? Ma!" Hailey called, trying to get her mother's attention away from a conversation she was having with Naomi.

"What? God, Hailey, stop shouting—"

"You didn't tell Selah about Dex's interview?"

"No, I thought you did."

"Why would I tell her? You always tell her everything."

"Mija, I asked you, *Are you telling your sister about this?* And you said *Uh-huh* and you were doing this . . ." Her mother mimicked her sister frantically typing on an invisible phone with great exaggeration.

"I don't remember that. I wasn't listening. I was busy talking to someone."

"And who were you talking to that was more important than your own sister?" her mother asked.

"I don't know . . . someone."

"Okay, stop. Stop!" Selah said, cutting in. "I don't care about any of this. As far as communication goes, this family is the worst. Now, what interview are you talking about?"

"The *Wake Up, USA* interview!" her mother said.

"Oh my God! I can't believe you haven't seen this. No wait, let me show you," her youngest sister said, pulling her cell phone from her pocket. "Ugh, why don't I have any reception? Can't we get Wi-Fi on this balloon?"

"He loves you, mija!" Elena said, jumping in, her eyes glittering with excitement.

"What?" Her family had lost their ever-loving minds. "Do you know anything about this?" Selah asked her calmer sister, Naomi.

She shook her head. "This is the first I'm hearing about

it. I wasn't there."

"Can't we go down any faster?" Hailey asked.

"No," Selah responded. "Why can't you just tell me?"

"I already did, mija. He loves you."

"Okay, so Dex is there doing the interview and that crow of his just flies out of nowhere, landing right onto his arm. Maybe that guy is some kind of wizard or something . . . it was pretty badass—"

"Get to the important part, Hailey."

"Oh, yeah. So, Wanda—you know, the one with the big blond hair—she's asking him about you and the whole proposal thing, blah blah blah." Hailey rolls her eyes. "And Dex just says, yes, you're friends and you really mean a lot to him and he admires you, and something about your piloting voice. I don't know, he was kind of rambling. That part was a little weird."

Selah covered the smile spreading across her face with a hand. The whole thing made her want to burst out laughing.

"Anyway, and that guy host . . . What's his name? Jim something? He's a real old man bitch. He just makes some kind of bad joke about sometimes you just need to get back on the hot-air balloon again and something about a rebound. If I was him, I'd be embarrassed because, for real, it was so awkward. And Dex, who has this serious look on his face, kind of stern, says, no, his relationship with you would never be a rebound for him. In fact, he says, if he actually believed in that stuff, then, technically, his last ex would be the rebound because they started seeing each other three weeks after his live-in girlfriend left. It was just supposed to be a casual thing, but it went on for too long and his ex was right to turn down his proposal. They didn't belong together. With you, he's removing the 're' in 'rebound' and he's just bound. This is one hundred percent grade-A truth, no lie. And then he said that if it was possible, he wanted to take you on a date. But he understood if, like Harper, you needed to spread your wings, and he fully supported you in finding your dream wherever that took you."

Selah was in full disbelief, staring at her family as though this would help to make things clearer.

"I swear to God, Selah, that's what happened. He said he was *bound* to you," Hailey said.

"And no one thought to tell me?" Selah was overwhelmed by this information. After all the things she had said to him, it wasn't fair he should still want to be there for her. She'd hurt him terribly, and since she didn't know how many days it had been since he'd given the interview, he probably assumed her silence was an answer. She wanted nothing more than to see him and tell him she was switching off autopilot, and she wanted the full experience with him. Unfortunately, she was stuck up here until they reached a coordinated landing spot.

"God. This is so romantic," Naomi said, bringing a hand to her chest. "I mean, it was pretty obvious he fell hard for you, but to tell everyone on national TV? You need to do something for him too."

"Like what?" she asked.

"Oh, how about we take this balloon to his house or Smith Rock? Which one do you think is the best place to find him? We can land there, and then you find him and grab him and kiss."

Selah gave her romantic sister a flat look. "Are you kidding? We'd have no chase crew—"

"This is your time to do some special grand gesture, like in the movies."

"If they ever do a movie based on my love life, they can land the balloon wherever their movie magic ass wants. But in real life, that's not practical. We're staying on course. Besides, when I do see him, I don't want my whole family there."

"Ooh, Captain Selah wants Ranger Dex all to herself." Hailey pumped her eyebrows suggestively.

Hell, yeah, she did. She wanted him all to herself because she was bound to him as well, and needed to show him in all the ways possible.

Chapter Twenty-Five

THE PUZZLE PIECE was waiting for him in front of his door when he got home from work. It stood out against the dusty brown wood of his porch. "Thank you, Harper. But I hope you're not stealing my puzzle pieces and bringing them outside," he said, reaching to retrieve it.

The thought of finishing a whole puzzle and discovering pieces missing was some kind of crime against him personally. He didn't need this kind of grief, especially right now.

In response to his thank you, Harper tippity-tapped across the railing, cawing twice, similar to her greeting when Selah would bring the bird a treat. Did the crow have her own signature greeting for people, like individualized handshakes? Usually, with him, she'd bob her head and flap her wings a few times. He didn't think about it for long, as the bird returned to playing with some broken peanut shell she'd found.

He sighed as he entered his house. Dex hadn't worked on the coffee table puzzle since the evening Selah had departed his home, and there'd been no word from her. He'd been hoping, after his *Wake Up, USA* interview, she'd reach out. But after several days of silence, hope had faded away.

Dex should have accepted the invitation to go out with

some of his fellow rangers after work today, but he was worn out and depressed. Going home and being by himself was a more ideal plan.

He went to the coffee table, where his in-progress jigsaw puzzle was located, and started to toss the piece into the box to join the others, but stopped. The piece in his hand didn't belong. It was larger. The colors didn't match. It was the odd man out, the weird one, the one that didn't fit in. He knew how it felt.

Although it was impressive Harper figured out he liked jigsaw puzzles and brought a piece she'd found. Except, he wasn't quite sure what to do with it. He didn't want to throw it away, so he tossed it, along with his keys, into the small bowl on the entryway table.

The next day, there was another puzzle piece waiting by his door. He became less amused and more annoyed. "Stop bringing me someone else's puzzle," he said to Harper, who cocked her head in different directions and wasn't the least bit bothered by Dex's irritation. If anything, the crow's reaction made him think she found it hilarious. The second piece went into the key bowl, along with the first one.

The next day, there were more. A lot more.

"What the hell?" he said to a small pile of puzzle pieces placed at his door. He carefully gathered them while Harper landed on his shoulder and beaked through his hair. "Why are you doing this? Some other puzzler is going to be very unhappy."

He let himself into his home and dumped the pieces on the entryway table. Fingering through them, the pieces were of similar size and coloring, all bright colors. There weren't many of them, maybe fifty pieces.

A couple of pieces seemed to match, and he fit them together with a snap. Placing all the pieces right side up, Dex clicked them together, making more matches. The picture emerging motivated him to finish it until he got to the end of the small puzzle with two pieces missing. It was a natural landscape picture, with mountains and lush, green pine trees. The sky was the rose-gold hue of sunrise.

The two empty spots were in the middle of the puzzle, in the sky, one right beside the other. He fished the pieces from the key bowl, fitting them together.

A hot-air balloon.

They fit within the empty spot, and the puzzle was complete. Harper cawed and hop-flapped away, but he remained standing in front of the entryway table, his finger running over the smooth glossy image before him.

Was this some kind of message? It couldn't be a coincidence... not with a hot-air balloon. Harper was an intelligent bird, but this had to be Selah and—

The hope that had previously faded reignited, growing brighter by the second. Did she change her mind? Was she finally reaching out? He was afraid of reading too much into it. It was a puzzle, that's all, and Dex was done trying to read between the lines.

He couldn't let it go, taking a picture of the puzzle and sending it in a text to Selah along with a message of *???*. She was the only one who could pull him from his misery or plunge him deeper into it. He hoped for the former.

In reply, there were dots and then no dots and then dots again. What kind of sick weirdo created this type of cruel torture? He was sure his body was growing old and turning into dust as he waited, which was why he made the decision to call her. Before he could, a message appeared from Selah.

Flip it over.

Okay, this at least confirmed the puzzle was from her. He put his hand in the center of the puzzle and twisted it until the image was upside down, expecting something obvious to jump out, as if the secrets of his romantic universe would be revealed.

Except it remained an upside down hot-air balloon image. Whatever secrets the puzzle held, they remained unknown. He looked closer, wishing he had a magnifying glass to search it, like an old-timey detective. Was there a heart hidden among the pine trees? Was it one of those Magic Eye things? He crossed his eyes. Nothing. He was going to be here all day, and Harper was no help at all. He was knocking the bird's status down from "very intelligent" to "meh" which was, coincidentally, the same rating he'd give his own intelligence at the moment. Selah was obviously working at a much higher level than—

Oh, wait. She'd texted, "flip."

He carefully took the whole thing and flipped it like a pancake so the back side of the pieces were facing up. He didn't even need to cross his eyes. The message couldn't be any clearer. While he had noticed that some of the pieces had black lines on the back, he hadn't paid attention to them, focusing solely on the image side. With all the pieces put together, it revealed a note in large, scripty handwriting.

Ranger—

I also want to go on a date with you.

—Your Captain

His heart stopped.

He needed to see her now.

Picking up his phone, he hit the dial button. "Did you know about this?" he asked Harper as it rang. Maybe she'd been trying to tell him the whole time. He'd likely believe anything at this point, even something ridiculous like a calendar year in the High Desert was nothing but sunny days.

"Hello?" Selah answered, her phone voice similar to that of an angel.

"Hey—"

"Oh, shit." In the background, there were angry car horns blaring.

"Oh, God! Are you driving right now? You shouldn't be talking on your phone and driving at the same time. Is everything okay? Are you hurt? I love you, but we don't need to talk right—"

"Dex," she replied calmly. "I'm fine. It was another driver who suddenly pulled out in front of a car going too fast on Highland. It was a close call for them, but no one crashed. I wasn't in any danger."

"Are you sure?"

She laughed. "Yes, I'm sure. I'm almost at your place."

"Oh, good. I just wanted to ask you to come over because I think Harper is missing you."

"Is that so? Even though she's seen me for the last three days."

"Wait. Harper got to see you. How is this fair?" Dex walked outside to his porch, taking one of the Adirondack chairs as he waited for her arrival, he bounced one of his knees nervously in anticipation.

"It could be worse. I was going to leave you one puzzle piece a day, but the thing was like sixty pieces and, after a couple of days, I decided there was no way I was going to wait two months. I'm not that patient."

"Three days was still too long, Selah."

Her truck pulled along his curb and the phone call disconnected as she grabbed it from the phone holder on her dashboard. She stepped out, her skin glistening in the September sun. She wore a tight white tank top, little navy shorts, and her aviators. With her dark curls framing her face, the whole package made her look the epitome of cool and sexy as she strolled over to him.

He shot to his feet, almost stumbling down the steps as he approached her, wanting to drag that petite, curvy body to his, to remind himself what every inch of her felt like. "Illinois Beach," he blurted when he stood close enough.

She slid the aviators to her hairline, confusion shooting from those beautiful, black eyes. "What?"

"I was talking to Chris about Chicago, and she said the closest state park to the city is Illinois Beach. I looked it up and it looks pretty nice."

"Is it as nice as Smith Rock?"

"I don't know, but I'm sure there are a lot of great things I can learn about it. And I've moved states before. It's not that big of a deal."

"Dex," she said with a sigh, shaking her head. He was squandering his chances to crack a window between them, to show her how their future could look together.

Except, then she shrugged and smiled, before saying, "Okay. If that's what you want, and you have your heart set on it, then I guess we can work it out. Of course, you being at Illinois Beach would still make this a long-distance relationship since I'll be here but—"

He snatched her into his arms, holding her to him, breathing in the lovely sage scent that was uniquely her. "What the hell, Selah? What are you trying to do to me?"

"I'm sorry," she said, taking his face between her hands and pulling him lower so she could press kisses to his temple, eyelids, cheeks. "I'm so sorry. Things have been a little awkward for me, and I'm still trying to figure things out, figure me out. And it just took some time to see that I wasn't being forced to overcome some kind of roadblock—that things could just be different."

"And you're staying here? At High Desert Tours?"

"Mm-hmm."

The joy was immediate and immeasurable. "In that case, I guess I can tell you that I'm in love with you, *Captain* Selah Moreno." He punctuated this by melding his lips to hers, drawing out the deepest kiss, his tongue sliding along hers. Turns out when he was truly in love, saying the words was the easiest thing in the world.

"And I love you," she replied the moment they broke the kiss.

"Good, so do you want to get going, then?"

"Going where? I just got here."

"I'm going to take you out on a date."

"Right now?"

"I thought that's what we were doing," he said. "You're not hungry?"

"No, I can eat but . . . You know that brewery where I went for my last date—"

At the mention of that place, his hackles rose in response to being reminded of the other man who got to date her before him. "Are you kidding me? I'm not taking you back to the same place where that dump truck took you. I can do better than him. A lot better."

"It's not that, but there's a fish and chip food truck in the lot behind it, and I've always wanted to try—"

"We're finally going on a date, and you want me to take you to a food truck? I wanted to shower you with steak and flowers." He wanted to give her a lot more. He was going to woo her so much, she'd never forget this was a real relationship, and he wasn't planning on ever stopping.

Her hand slipped along the button placket of his shirt, her eyes turning soft and alluring, her beautiful lips becoming pouty and irresistible. "But I don't want steak and flowers, Ranger Dex. I want fish and chips. And I'm not really dressed for some place fancy. I'm still wearing my work clothes and feeling a little grubby."

He couldn't argue, as this was the same status for him. "Yeah, I guess I could use a shower too."

"You're a park ranger, so you already know this," she said, as she pressed a kiss to his collarbone, "but water conservation is very important in the High Desert. We should probably share."

"Someone is being responsible again and you know I find that trait very sexy."

"Mm-hmm. How about this? We take a shower, get fish and chips to-go, and then maybe we can stream *Galaxy Quest*?"

"Are you sure that's what you want?"

"Yeah, but mostly, I just want you."

Dex pulled her into his house, but they didn't get very far past the front door and nowhere close to the shower, at least not yet.

"God, I missed this house," Selah said, pushing off her shoes and helping him get his off too.

"You did?"

"Yes, it's just so lived-in. And it's wonderfully comfortable and familiar, sort of like you."

"And also weird because of the whole crow thing," he said, nodding toward Harper, who was busy tearing some junk mail on his desk.

"I think it's very sweet."

He pulled off her tank top because he couldn't wait any longer. In doing so, the aviators on her hairline fell to the ground. He retrieved the glasses, setting them carefully on his entry table. One of these days, he'd let her take him while wearing only the aviators, but at the moment, he missed her too much to not look into her eyes.

Selah, a woman on a mission, roughly undid the buttons of his uniform shirt, pressing hot, open-mouthed kisses across his chest, as she yanked it off and shoved a hand down the front of his pants to fondle him.

His heart thudded against his chest, his breath catching. "Seriously, honey, I'm kind of gross from work still." Dex didn't want her to stop, but a warning was the polite thing to do.

"Dex, honey, I love you, so I don't find you gross. What's the point of a shower if you can't get a little dirty beforehand?"

That snapped him from all his concerns. Grabbing his wallet from the key bowl, he lifted her with one arm, carrying her to his sturdy wooden kitchen table and plopping her on the edge of it. From there, he quickly pulled off the rest of their clothes, giving himself a few moments to appreciate her nakedness while he located the condom in his wallet and rolled it on himself. As frenzied as he felt, he slid into her slowly, helping to support her upright position by wrapping his arms around her frame as he pressed his face into her neck. He couldn't wait, establishing a rhythm quickly as he slid in and out. She moaned, scratching her nails along his neck, and it was the sexiest thing he'd ever heard.

As he continued rocking against her, he took her jaw in hand, tilting it upward. "I want to hear you say it," he said, his breath short and his tone rough and stern.

Her gaze on him was soft and hazy, but after a moment, she gave a small whimper and replied, "Ooooh, Dex, honey. Your dick feels so good."

He paused. "What? I mean, thank you, but what I want to hear is that we're . . ." He gestured with a hand to fill in the blank.

"Dating?" she guessed.

"Well, yes, but I mean that I'm your . . ." he continued

prompting.

"Park Ranger?"

"*Boyfriend.*"

"Really? That's what you want me to say during sex?"

He huffed a laugh. "I know it's odd, but I just want everything to be upfront and clear between us. It would be nice to know exactly where I stand for once in my life."

Selah's lips tipped in amusement. "Okay, if that's what you want."

He gave her face careful consideration. "But I am your boyfriend, right? I don't want to push you into anything—"

"Dex—"

"Because I do want you as my girlfriend . . . you know, for now."

Now it was her turn to pause as she leaned back on her arms to give him a good look. "Excuse me? What do you mean *for now*?" Her brows pressed together, but her body shook with light laughter. The rippling sensations vibrating around his dick were amazing.

He wasn't sure how this whole thing got off track, but laughing while having sex with a woman he was in love with was a whole new experience, one he really liked. "It's not a rebound thing," he assured her. "I just mean that it's no secret I want to get married someday. So, yeah, that's all I meant by it."

"God, Dex. Can you just kiss me, please?"

That he could do, and soon he was driving into her hard as he gripped her thighs. She moaned about how good her boyfriend's dick felt, and it was everything he wanted it to be, even while being a bit ridiculous. He didn't care. After she cried out and he grunted his own release, he held her sweat-beaded body to his as they both attempted to catch their breaths.

"Who knew when you tipped that basket over and landed on me, we'd end up here?" His heart was so full of her, he couldn't imagine a different life for himself. This was it. All he ever wanted. He grinned as he joked, "You didn't tip it over on purpose, right?"

"Of course not," she said with a beautifully sated smile. "I'm pretty sure it was fate."

Epilogue

Loop Video posted by @HaileyTeaTime

"HAILEY HERE. HASHTAG Moreno sisters. It's too early. But, look who I have with me. Harper! We're hanging out this morning for a very special reason, which I'll get to in a minute.

"So, yeah, I still get asked all the time for an update on the whole thing with my sister and the park ranger guy. Gah, why are you guys so obsessed with them? You're supposed to be obsessed with *me*. And, no, I'm not talking anymore about R. I haven't said anything, even after that interview Dex did because, no lie, but that video I made like a year ago, got me in so much trouble. I'm not even kidding.

"But this is the problem with being a visionary, like me. People get mad just for pointing out the truth. Like my other sis . . . wait, a minute, let me turn the camera around. Okay, so over there is my other sister, Naomi, and she's constantly annoyed by that guy, Boone—like there are lasers shooting from her eyes all the time for him. Who exactly does she think she's trying to fool here? Like, please, be for real with us but also with yourself, Naomi, because we know you're lying about how much you hate him. Just kiss already. Seriously."

"Who are you talking to over there, Hailey?"

"No one! Te quiero, hermana."

"Anyway, back to me, or rather the other tea. So, yeah, my other sister, Selah, finally realized she's in love with Dex. And I know, I know, about what I said about him before, but he's actually great. It kind of feels like having a big brother around. Like sometimes, he's a little nerdy but, I don't know, he's just really nice, and he's perfect for my sister, so they've been together for a while now. My sister practically lives at his place. Okay? Like just move in, Selah. It's not like we all don't know what's going on—What are you trying to prove?

"They got together officially soon after he did *Wake Up, USA*, so, yeah, that interview was kind of cringe, but apparently, that's what my sister likes. Ha! Even better news, at least for Harper, but some rich old lady in Wisconsin saw the interview and said that her husband, who had died a few years earlier, had a pet crow he loved too. And she sent a bunch of money, so Dex's wildlife thing can be built. They haven't started yet, but Dex is totally geeking out over the 'specs' or whatever, so I think that's going to happen soon.

"But today is very important. Dex had reached out to me because he said he wants to ask Selah to marry him and he wants my help. Me! And first I was like 'Really? You're going to do the hot-air balloon thing again? What exactly are you doing here, Dex?' Because we all know how it worked out the first time around. And he said, this is different because this time they've already talked about marriage, so he's not going in blind. Plus, he knows how much my sister loves the balloon and he wants one amazing memory to take the place of the not-so-great memory.

"Oh? Let me show you real quick. See? It's the new envelope or balloon or whatever. We decided to retire *The Blue Wonder* because we wanted to feel like we're starting a new chapter for the business now that Selah is captain, and this is what my dad wanted. She decided to name the balloon *The Engage*, which Naomi thinks is so romantic and perfect for some new business idea she has, but Selah told her that it's actually some geeky thing from *Star Trek*. So nerdy. Anyway, I think it's hilarious because she doesn't know she's about to get engaged on *The Engage*.

"So, yeah, Dex and my sister are up in the balloon right now, not very high, actually, because he told her he just wanted to get some selfies of them for their future Christmas card, in the balloon, with Smith Rock in the background. I honestly don't know how anyone would fall for such a story, but maybe she's like the rest of us and thinks there's no way he's going to try for another proposal in a hot-air balloon. And I'm waiting here with Harper for the signal. Dex told me he's been working with her to come when he whistles and, look, here's a fake ring she's supposed to bring with her. I said, why aren't you giving my sister a real ring? My sister and I don't always get along, but we're still sisters, and there's no way I'm going to let her get engaged with a cheap, fake-ass ring. And then he said 'You really think I'm going to trust Harper with something expensive?' so I guess he'll give Selah the real thing later and—

"That's the whistle! Okay, Harper, here's the ring. You're up. Oh my God, she's flying right up to him. I think I might actually cry, for real. Let me see if I can zoom in on this. I can't see him. Maybe he's kneeled down. Oh, I think he kneeled down. AHHHHHH! It's happening. Ma! Ma! Did you bring the champagne?"

"Mija! Did you see? Oh, I'm so excited!"

"Okay, so more hugging and kissing, and Dex just dumped a bag of rose petals off the side of the basket. Like what? How is this happening? Oh my God. Okay, I have to turn this off before my sister comes down and catches me, and you nosy people don't need every detail. Hailey Tea Time is out, besties, and as my dad used to say, 'No regrets.'"

The End.

Want to read a bonus chapter from Selah's point of view? Sign up for Janine's newsletter at www.janineamesta.com

Acknowledgements

Recently, I read a social media post that said, on average, most authors don't write more than three books. Like the whole three hundred days of sunshine in Central Oregon affirmation, I don't know if this is actually true. But because this is my fourth romance book being published, I'm using it to boost myself up. Woohoo! You did it, Janine!

I wouldn't be surprised, though, because writing can be a lonely, long, and, at times, frustrating process. Even though I like to joke that I'm motivated by spite, the truth of the matter is my support system, the people who surround me during my writing journey, have helped push me through every single time. This spot is dedicated to them.

First, I'd like to thank my publisher, Jane Porter, for her unending support and believing in my abilities as a storyteller. She also put together a great team at Tule. Thanks to my agent Kelly, my editor Sinclair, my copy editor, my proofreader, and everyone else who helped me make my words the best version they could be. Wrapping my words in the most beautiful cover is a dream, so I also want to thank Lee and my cover artist, Sugam Thakur. I'm forever grateful I get to use such talent for my books.

I always believe that one should surround oneself with

writer friends. In fact, I have no idea what I would do without them. Special thanks to Denise Williams and Sarah Smith for not only listening to me vent but also helping me when I need advice or find myself stuck in a tricky plot point of my own making. To both of you: your wisdom and talent continue to inspire me.

My wonderful Pen Pal friends who make the writing journey bearable and also often funny. Katy, Colleen, Abigail, and Natalia—you are my ladies, and I'm so lucky to be included in your group. This can be a wild journey, but I'm so glad that we're doing it together.

Romance Fight Club—Did we ever make a plan to meet? I don't know because I wrote this in the past. Thank you for giving me my turtle power: B, Allie, Janel, and Denise. You make the book world delightful and always give the best advice.

Special thanks to my fellow Tule authors who have been helpful and supportive to someone who still feels like a newbie author. I feel so proud to be in your company. Big hugs!

To all my readers who have picked up my books, know that you have my gratitude. I want to give a special thanks to those who have personally reached out to let me know that you've enjoyed my words. Never doubt that you keep the fires going in my creative heart, and your kind words have meant so much to me. If you're ever in doubt about reaching out to an author, do it. You could be making someone's day.

And, lastly, I'm very lucky because I'm married to my biggest supporter. Who knew that when we went on our first date and you bragged about how the seats in your Element folded into a bed, we'd eventually get married and be exactly here? It's funny how life works, and I'm glad it didn't work out any other way. Thanks to my husband for never wavering in his support of my writing and always being my biggest cheerleader. If it weren't for you, I'm sure I would have given up by now. Love you.

More Books by Janine Amesta

Love in El Dorado series

Book 1: *Striking Gold*

Book 2: *A Poinsettia Paradise Christmas*

Book 3: *Lucky Strike*

Available now at your favorite online retailer!

About the Author

Janine Amesta has loved reading kissing stories most of her life. She currently resides in Oregon with her husband and their pets, Hitchcock and Pippin. She studied screenwriting in college and her banter is influenced by the screwball romantic comedies of the 1930's. She's always on the lookout for the perfect line.

Thank you for reading

Love at First Flight

If you enjoyed this book, you can find more from all our great authors at TulePublishing.com, or from your favorite online retailer.

TULE
PUBLISHING

THE WORLD OF LAVENDER SMOKE

Character Name Pronunciations

Cordelia Halloway (Kor-dee-lee-uh Hal-oh-way)

Lilith Ravenscroft (Lil-ith Ray-vens-croft)

Thane Lycus (Thayne Lie-cuss)

Talin Nightveil (Tah-lyn Night-vayl)

Sage Ashcraft (Sayge Ash-crahft)

Lydia Halloway (Lid-ee-ah Hal-oh-way)

Nolen Lycus (No-lyn Lie-cuss)

Rosemary Lycus (Rohse-mare-ee Lie-cuss)

Asmond Calderon (As-mund Call-der-on)

The Celestials

The Celestials are the Goddesses who created the world, and each Goddess created a species of Magical. The Magical are the various species that inhabit the world.

It's important to remember that all Goddesses are each referred to by their honorific in addition to their name. For example, when referring to Hecate, you would refer to her as the Goddess Hecate. As a group, the Goddesses are referred to as the Goddesses or the Celestials—either is acceptable.

Below are the Goddesses mentioned in *Lavender Smoke*:

the Goddess Hecate (Heh-cah-tay)—Goddess of magic and witchcraft, created the witches

the Goddess Artemis (Ar-teh-miss)—Goddess of the hunt, created the Artemisian (Ar-teh-miss-ee-an) wolves

the Goddess Theia (Thay-uh)—Goddess of light, created the Theian (Thay-uhn) wolves

the Goddess Selene (Sell-een)—Goddess of the moon, created the fae

the Goddess Atlas (At-luhs)—Goddess of the sky and heavens, created the dragons

the Goddess Hades (Hay-dee-z)—Goddess of the underworld and the hidden wealth of the world, created the demons

Locations

Ilyndria (Ih-lyn-dree-uh)—country where *Lavender Smoke* takes place

Elysea (Eh-lee-see-ah)—city where *Lavender Smoke* takes place

Witchhaven (Witch-hay-ven)—district of Elysea where the witches live

Lunegrove (Loon-growv)—territory on the outskirts of Elysea where the wolven live

Olysan (Oh-ly-sahn)—territory in the Elysean Mountains where the dragon shifters live, outside of Elysea

Elysean Mountains (Eh-lee-see-an Mountains)—mountain range outside of Elysea

To everyone who's ever wondered what life looks like outside of your bedroom window, to everyone who's ever dreamed of finding star-flecked peace in the open night sky. There's a special corner of the world tucked away just for you, and you'll find it one day.

One day, your life won't be filled with heart-aching tears and soul-wrenching longing for escape. You will find solace. You will find people who lift you up, see you as you are, and offer a hand. You will find yourself laughing and smiling more than hiding under the blankets from the weight of life. You were made for happiness, and you were made for the life you crave. Don't let anyone take it from you. Because you are worthy, and you are lovely just the way you are.

CHAPTER ONE

CORDELIA

C ordelia's steps maintained a steady beat against the damp cobblestone walkway as she tried to let the rhythm of the movement calm her racing mind.

"You've had your fun, dear, but it's time for you to accept your responsibilities." Lydia's clipped tone was growing more and more agitated as the conversation progressed.

If you could even call it a conversation. They'd been having this argument for years now, neither of them willing to concede.

Cordelia groaned as she came to a stop, squeezing her eyes shut in an attempt to protect herself from the onslaught of anger that coursed through her. Not here, she couldn't get into this here and now. Lydia Halloway needed to learn some Goddess-damned boundaries, and starting Cordelia's day with this same tired speech was something that had to stop.

"No, I've had enough. I can't even begin to count how many times I've made myself clear, Mother. I will not be the heir to the Halloway coven. I will not be working at Halloway Spells. And I will not have this conversation again. I'm not the little girl you could control and manipulate anymore."

And with that, Cordelia hung up and slipped her phone into her pocket, willing the weight of her anxiety to tumble out of her fingers with it.

A cool, early spring breeze whispered down the sidewalk, pressing against Cordelia's cheeks in a soft kiss. She hummed along to it, letting her eyes flutter closed briefly. The cold had always stabilized her, helped her find peace and comfort. With the season changing to spring, she was holding on to every last drop of chilly air she could get.

Taking a deep breath, she continued on her way to Quartz Coffee, her favorite coffee shop in Elysea. Her muscles relaxed with every step she took, as if she were physically walking away from her mother's call, every inch of distance unclenching the cage around her battered heart.

For as long as she could trace the history back, her family had been involved in dark magic and everything that came with it. Her mother, Lydia Halloway, was just the most recent in a long line of witches to head the family business and had her sights set on Cordelia as the heir to the family legacy. The only problem was that Cordelia had no interest in taking that position.

Her gifts lay elsewhere. She wanted to work with her plants, her spells. That was her calling, it brought her true happiness—and happiness was something she'd been desperate for her whole life. It was a constant battle with Lydia, but one Cordelia wasn't willing to give up on.

Finally, she made her way into the coffee shop. She zeroed in on her favorite spot in a corner alcove and made a beeline for it, rushing past the other customers shuffling about for their caffeine fix. Once she scattered her belongings on the table to ward off anyone looking to steal her treasured seat, she strode to the counter to place her usual order: an iced lavender latte with oat milk.

She pulled out her phone as she stood at the end of the counter, waiting on her order. A slew of text messages from her mother had already come through in the minutes since the call, urging Cordelia to rethink her decisions, as per usual. She exited out and checked her calendar for the day. She had a few client meetings this morning, but otherwise, she wouldn't be too busy. Good. She could use a break from life, and a relaxing afternoon was just what she needed.

"Iced lavender latte for Cordelia!"

Her gazed darted up, and she grabbed her coffee with a quick "Thanks!" to the barista before returning to her tucked-away corner. Usually this corner of the store was quiet enough for her to hold her client calls, while the noise of the shop also kept the rest of her brain busy so she didn't fidget or wander off in her thoughts too much.

She flipped open her computer, got everything she needed ready for her client meetings, and plopped her headphones on her head. She loved her clients, but she had been working a lot lately, her body and brain slowly and silently screaming their protests. The rest she needed was just around the corner, and she was desperate for it.

A few hours later, Cordelia finished her last call of the day. They had all gone fairly well, and she was happy with the work she had done. Her clients were the best, and working with them gave her so much joy. But social interaction, especially for extended periods of time, was hard on her and she already felt exhausted. She eyed her now-empty coffee cup and decided she would go for one more before heading home to Merlin.

After placing her order, she gathered her things and waited for her coffee to come up, absentmindedly tapping her fingers and feet in time with her racing thoughts.

"To-go order for Cordelia!" the white-haired barista called.

She couldn't lie, part of the reason she came here so often was for the beautiful barista who usually made her orders. She couldn't help the flutter in her chest or the pounding in her ears whenever she got close to her, or when she caught a glimpse of her moonlight hair and flushed cheeks. The name tag on her apron read *Lilith*, and Cordelia knew she wanted to breathe her name as many times as she could. Just attempting to talk to Lilith always left Cordelia feeling a little out of sorts and words tended to fail her.

Cordelia realized she had been staring, lost in her thoughts, when Lilith chuckled and called her name again. She scurried up to the counter, muttered "Thank you" while trying to hide her flushed face, and attempted to exit the store without embarrassing herself any further.

Rushing back out into the chilled spring air, Cordelia's eyes quickly darted around, trying to find purchase on something of interest. Something to get her mind off the encounter she just had with Lilith—if you could even call it that. It was something more akin to a train wreck with how worked up she felt.

This was her problem. She picked apart every interaction she had, let it run her thoughts and consume her emotions. Trying to clear her head, Cordelia took a deep breath and focused on walking in the right direction. She tried to calm herself, counting her steps on the pavement, gripping the strap of her bag, and listening to the wind fluttering through the new leaves above her and the groaning of the tree branches.

Remembering the drink in her hand, she brought the straw to her lips, delighting in the cool refresh of lavender mixed with the bittersweet taste of coffee. She hummed, satisfaction flowing through her as she picked up her pace toward home.

Once she made it to her driveway, she immediately spotted her black cat familiar, Merlin, lounging on the front porch. Rolling her eyes, she dipped down to scratch between his ears, and his head perked up as she bounded across the porch.

Cordelia threw her things across the entryway without a care beyond the sweet satisfaction of finally being in her own home. Plopping down on the couch and discarding her cup on the side table, she let her head roll back on the couch cushion and her eyes close.

Today had been a good one, which was much appreciated as she'd been struggling to find joy lately. With her mother breathing down her neck more and more, she felt so suffocated and anxious, and it was starting to bleed into every facet of her life. She found herself fumbling over simple spells for her clients, forgetting to water some of her plants, aimlessly wandering around while lost in her chaotic, jumbled thoughts, and struggling with work.

Hearing the tap of tiny paws on the floor, she peeked through her lashes to see Merlin strolling toward her before he jumped onto her lap and made himself comfortable.

"Hey, Mer. I missed you, buddy." She repositioned to lie across the couch, bringing Merlin with her as she continued running her hands over his back. The soothing purrs coming from him mixed with the comfortable couch and the coolness of the house slowly lulled her to sleep, and she drifted off into lavender-coated dreams.

She was in her old bedroom in her childhood home. It was dark, the wood beneath her pacing feet creaking and groaning. The only light was from the candles her mother had lit before she locked her in and the peeks of moonlight from between the heavy curtains covering the large windows. She could hear chanting and the angry swirling of the wind outside as it howled for release. Howled for destruction, longed for the violence her mother's magic often created. Coaxing the meek to settle for her mother's depraved spells. Cordelia felt for the doorknob, finally catching the cool glass beneath her fingers and twisting, twisting so hard she felt her wrist might snap. But she kept twisting, kept hoping that the lock would give, would break and let her out of this nightmare. The nightmare she lived every day as a child.

She heard footsteps in the hallway beyond her room, heard them stop right in front of her door.

"Cordelia, we're ready for you dear." It was her mother's voice. Cold and hollow, promising to rope her into some sort of spell that she inevitably wanted nothing to do with. Cordelia scratched at the bedding that was suddenly beneath her. She was strapped to the bed, her hands and feet bound in ropes tied to the four-poster frame. As if her mother had somehow magicked her there. She screamed and screamed until her throat felt raw. She

screamed for help, screamed for freedom. She screamed for the reprieve she knew wasn't coming.

The lock clicked. The door creaked.

Cordelia woke with a jolt and a gasp on her lips, frantically searching the room with her eyes. It was a dream. Placing her clammy hand over her heart, she tried to steady her breathing. Her throat was sore and raw, as if she had indeed been screaming in her sleep. Tears pricking her eyes, she whispered, "It's not real. You're safe. She can't get to you." A soft meow jerked her attention to her lap. Merlin had woken her up, pawing at her and flicking his tail. Sighing, she wrapped him in her arms and whispered, "I'm alright, Mer. Just a dream is all."

After a few minutes, enough time to calm her breaths, Cordelia stood, grabbing the forgotten cup from the coffee table and heading to the kitchen, Merlin in tow right behind her. The cool tile beneath her feet helped steady her, helped ground and remind her that she wasn't in that stuffy old manor anymore. She flicked a switch and felt better when the flood of light surrounded her. After dumping the coffee in the sink, right before tossing it in the bin, she noticed something on the side of the cup. It was a little smudged from her fingers, but there was something scrawled along the side. She gasped, and the cup fell out of her hands, softly crashing to the floor. Scrambling, she picked it up and read it again and again and again. A phone number. Lilith's phone number.

CHAPTER TWO

CORDELIA

Had Cordelia cast some sort of spell she didn't remember? Or, shockingly, have any sort of game when it came to flirting? She couldn't remember a time where she ever had, but maybe she blacked out and was actually normal enough for someone to want to give her their phone number.

Either way, she wasn't going to question it. The universe was sending her a sign in big red letters that said, *Things are looking up and maybe you're not as socially hopeless as you thought you were.*

She rifled through her discarded bag before coming up with her phone. Quickly entering the number on the cup, Cordelia started to draft a text. And that was where she stalled out.

What did one even say to Lilith? To the girl she'd been shamelessly and terribly flirting with for who knows how long? After several moments of panic, she finally was able to string together a few coherent words.

Cordelia: Hey Lilith, it's Cordelia!

Could she have put more effort into it? Sure. But she didn't want to make assumptions and virtually stick her foot in her mouth.

She stared at the screen for a solid two minutes before telling herself she didn't need to obsess. Heading upstairs to get ready for bed, she called Merlin after her and tried to push the thought of Lilith's impending text out of her head.

After successfully readying herself for bed and pacing around the house several times to get her energy out, Cordelia finally picked up her phone. Upon seeing the tiny notification on her text messages, she let out a little nervous squeal. Which quickly deflated and dropped off into split emotions when she saw both a text from Lilith and a text from her mother. Ah, so tonight she would be getting a little bitter with her sweet. Lovely.

She contemplated dismissing her mother's text until the morning, but then realized that would mean fretting about it all night and getting next to no sleep. So, instead, she opened it.

> Mother: Cordelia, dear, could you please call me in the morning? We must finish our conversation. And this time, please do try not to rudely hang up.

Why her mother insisted on writing texts like a formal letter was beyond her. Why she insisted on Cordelia calling her was beyond her too. Her mother knew better than to expect everything to be OK between them.

Cordelia had left home as soon as she could and made it clear that she wasn't interested in having a close relationship. She only dealt with her mother when absolutely necessary. Everything else was just a waste of her time and sanity.

Deleting that, she moved onto Lilith's text.

> Lilith: Hey Cordelia! I was wondering when I would hear from you. I didn't imagine it would be so late ;)

The warmth of a blush bloomed across her cheeks. Was Lilith

implying that Cordelia was seeking out something tonight? A flood of worry stormed through her thoughts, stealing her breath. Oh no, she hadn't thought this through before she texted her, had she?

> Cordelia: Ha, sorry, I lost track of time

> Cordelia: And maybe didn't see your number on my cup until right before I texted you . . .

She was so embarrassed. She wanted to crawl in a hole and never come back up. Her phone dinged again.

> Lilith: Don't worry, I was only joking haha

> Lilith: Any chance you're free for coffee or dinner sometime?

Staring at her screen, Cordelia was pretty sure her mouth was hanging open. Reading and rereading the text over, she kept coming to the same conclusion. Lilith was asking her out. On a date.

She still wasn't sure that was right, so she reread it another three times for good measure.

Yep. Lilith was totally asking her out. Her heart started to race, and her body fluttered with excitement and anxiety. There was no way she was going to sleep again any time soon. She had too much adrenaline to work off. Too many things to think about.

> Cordelia: I would love that! I have a pretty flexible schedule, but did you have a day in mind?

She wasn't going to let herself fret over her words right now. She wanted to ride this high as long as she could before the true dread and anxiety set in. She wanted to bask in the glow of something actually going right for once.

> Lilith: If you're free Friday, I'll pick you up at 8

> Cordelia: Perfect! Here's my address. See you soon!

A heart emoji was too much, too soon, right? She thought probably, so she left that off. She wasn't going to let herself worry about it anymore tonight. Hopefully. She needed to go to bed and try to calm her racing thoughts enough to sleep.

Shuffling to her nightstand, she plugged in her phone to charge and climbed into her cool, soft bed. Merlin hopped in with her, curling up next to her head and nudging her with his nose. Her little familiar was always her grounding force, the best part of any day, and her best friend. He had been with her through the best and worst times, and she always knew he could calm her down when she needed it. She fell asleep to the sound of a dozing Merlin with her hand over his tail.

The sound of her alarm clock was going to be her undoing. Every morning, she hated its loud drone, and every morning, she cursed it for waking her.

Merlin decided at that moment to make himself at home right on top of her chest. With an *oof*, Cordelia flicked open her eyes and glared at him. She picked him up and let him jump to the floor so she could get ready. Coffee was her saving grace, her routine start to the day, and she needed it *stat*.

She gathered her iced coffee, milk, and homemade lavender syrup to ready her morning brew. Watching the swirl of the milk in the cold, bittersweet beverage was as much a ritual and meditation as anything else. She found it so soothing and always made sure to stir her day's intentions into her cup. As the mixture settled into a delightful, creamy brown, she took a deep breath to ground herself. This was her bliss every day. These were the small joys she clung to when she was sodden with anxiety and couldn't seem to find a way out.

Carrying her cup into the living room, Cordelia grabbed her

laptop and plopped into her tall-backed, tufted gold chair to check her emails. She sipped her coffee as she went, listening to her soothing morning playlist. Nothing, *nothing* could beat these moments. These moments of peace and reprieve. Her moments of normalcy. The dream she had clung to for so long as a child, trapped in her family's manor.

While she'd huddled away in the darkness of that dreary, cold house, she'd dreamed of the sunny breezes she would one day feel. She'd lost herself in the thought of the sunlight pouring in through frothy curtains and bathing her in its warmth and potential. In the possibilities and blissful daydreaming. Let herself believe in the whimsy and wonder of the world she'd so longed for. The world she'd known had to exist, she'd just needed to get out of that horrid place and find it for herself.

And she had. She had when she'd left that miserable, dark manor and said goodbye to the expectations she had been chained to her whole life. The life that'd drained her of her imagination and will. The life that had been slowly trying to claim her, pull her under and never let her return to the surface. The one that Lydia Halloway was still trying to pull her into.

Closing her laptop, she couldn't help but feel heartbroken for that cowering little girl. The one who'd dared to dream of sunshine, for the light of freedom, the light of joy, the light of love, passion, and laughter. The light that would eventually lead her to the life she'd built for herself.

As if on cue, Cordelia's phone rang, startling her from her reverie. Glancing at the screen, she let out a long groan. She might as well answer and avoid the inevitable barrage of texts and calls she would get if she didn't pick up.

"Mother."

"Cordelia, dear, I asked you to call me this morning," her mother quipped at her, immediately stealing away the last vestiges of any sort of good mood.

"It's still the morning, isn't it?" She didn't have the patience for this tête-à-tête today.

"Cordelia, I don't have time to argue about your forgetfulness. We need to discuss your role here at Halloway Spells."

Cordelia groaned. Again?! How many times would they have this conversation? "Yes, well, as you know, Mother, I don't have a role there. That was kind of a big point of me leaving and why I renounced my title."

"You can't be serious about that. Dear, I don't think you understand what that means. And I would think you'd realize by now that you can't make it on your own. It's best that you come back. Train for the day you take over the business and the family. It's your responsibility as a Halloway, as my heir, and it's what I raised you to do." She was definitely already up on her high horse. Huh. Lydia Halloway must not have had a very good morning to be starting in on Cordelia like this so early in their conversation.

"Yeah, well, like I've told you time and time again, Mother, I don't want anything to do with Halloway Spells. You can kiss that dream and the dream of me taking over the family name goodbye. I don't know how many times we have to have this conversation before you listen to and respect my decision. I'm happy with what I'm doing, and I would appreciate if you would just leave me the fuck alone about it." Cordelia had snapped.

Her patience had always worn thin with her mother, but once she'd left Halloway Manor, she had finally had the freedom to let her thoughts loose and stand her ground.

"Cordelia Halloway. I did not raise you to be a rude, selfish brat. It's high time you take me seriously. You'll understand soon what your priorities should be, and you'll realize that I'm right." Her tone was clipped, leaving no room for argument.

That didn't mean Cordelia agreed with her or would give in to her ridiculous demands. She was her own person, her own witch. She had made that very clear the day she left the manor and had continued to work toward proving that to her mother, to making her see that she was serious about her magic, her business, her control over her own life. The Halloway family just didn't see it that way. They saw it as a personal affront to their way of life, the insane traditions and ideals they clung to like children to this day.

Losing the last shred of her patience and unwilling to lose any more of her sanity to her mother this early in the morning, Cordelia hung up. Goddess, how she wished she still had a landline that she could slam down to drive home her point. But really, nothing would ever get through to her. She had a feeling she would be fighting with her mother the rest of her life. Goddess did that sound exhausting. A five-minute conversation with the woman drained her enough.

Running her hands over her face, Cordelia tried to collect herself, pull herself out of the dreary mood her mother tried to put her in.

The "responsibility" her mother loved to rant about was Cordelia's to take the position as heir to the Halloway family and magic line and then promptly marry another prominent witch coven heir and produce beautiful, powerful, bratty witches that would become their heirs in turn. Continuing on the line of bitchiness, really. This was the way of all the Halloway women. It was what her mother did, and her mother's mother, and so on.

Of course, not all of the witch covens were dreadful like the Halloway family. It was just the circles her mother ran in that were terrible. The covens Cordelia worked and socialized with weren't acceptable to Lydia. Of course they weren't. Their goals weren't centered around taking as much control as possible with hidden agendas and dark magic.

Cordelia wasn't interested in following in her family's footsteps. Wasn't interested in performing the magic that made her skin crawl. The magic that was the featured guest in all of her nightmares. That was so often used against her whenever her mother was feeling particularly cruel.

The Halloway family specialized in dark magic, the kind that crossed the line into villainous. Sure, there were plenty of families that dealt in shadow magic or various other types of "dark magic" and had perfectly respectable practices. The Halloway family harbored no such title. They catered their gifts to the desperate, the mad, or those with an inclination toward malice. Those seeking revenge, dark deeds, disreputable practices, the disappearance of anything they needed swept under the rug, the list goes on. And the Halloway family was more than eager to provide. Her mother, especially, was driven to expand the family business. To gain more power and more influence among the covens and with the Hecatean Guild that oversaw the witches.

That was why Cordelia was so happy to leave. So happy to find her freedom. To breathe in the air she had been starving for, gasping for, gazing out of her windows and dreaming of, desperate for the light that shone everywhere but that manor.

She straightened in her chair as a tear tracked down her cheek. She hadn't realized she was crying, hadn't felt the hot burn of her cheeks and the catch in her throat until now.

No way was she going to let her mother sink her dark claws into her again. She had done enough to Cordelia in the years she'd lived in that manor.

The years she'd spent listening to the screeches and screams, the scrapes and tinkling zings of a knife, the creaks and groans of the storied floorboards, the walls that held unspeakable secrets. Candles shoved in every corner of the house to create the illusion of safety in the dimmed firelight. But no safety would a patron of the Halloways find. Only pain and terror, or worse—greed and desperation for more.

Cordelia had seen a lot of things happen inside that manor. Had seen and heard her fair share of dark rituals and spells. Had been forced to participate in more than she could count. Had always worried what sort of stain it left on her soul. On her subconscious. But more than that, she wished she could get the images out of her head of the ceremonies she accidentally stumbled upon. The people and things she had seen. She would never forget.

CHAPTER THREE

CORDELIA

The next few days had been a blur. It was like Cordelia's life had flown past her after that phone call. She kept swearing she wouldn't let her mother gain control over her again. But every time she called, she inevitably left her mark. She would haunt Cordelia's thoughts and actions. Plague her with the memories she wished she could stop recalling. By the time Friday morning rolled around, she finally felt like she could pull air down her lungs again without the burn of guilt. The burn of shame. The burn of her past.

That was part of her mother's magic—she was an energy manipulation witch. Able to control and energetically drain people. When the Goddess Hecate created the witches, she gave them the ability to wield all sorts of "basic" magics to cast various spells and also gifted each witch with a special magic—energy manipulation, divination, illusion, or enchantment. Usually, a witch's gift was something passed down by a parent, but sometimes the magic intervened and gave them something else entirely.

Cordelia was never sure if her mother was using her energy magic to get her to cave, or if talking to Lydia was energy magic of its own. Draining Cordelia of all will to fight.

To try to regain her energy, she hadn't done much the last few days, simply surrounded herself with various crystals and herbs to aid in her recovery.

Now though, Cordelia walked through the house, throwing open every window. She took a deep breath, closing her eyes in bliss as she let the fresh energy soak through her and into the space, chill her to the point of refresh. The air felt stale and stagnant, so a good cleansing was in order.

She cleared out her kitchen, flitting around as she did so. After giving her living room the same treatment, she gathered her favorite crystals, carefully scattering them around various surfaces in the house. The incense she lit burned away any negative energy and flooded her home with warmth, the rich scent conjuring her imagination and intentions. Freeing her from the last bit of tightness in her chest.

More and more of Cordelia's energy soaked back into her very bones, uplifting her and restoring her own magic.

Energy manipulation didn't take away a witch's magic, but it did take away the energy needed to wield it. And Cordelia's was flooding back to her, zinging under her skin in a soft kiss of familiarity.

She wheeled around, taking in the space. She felt infinitely better, and it looked like Merlin agreed. He had perched himself on top of her favorite chair, lounging in the sunbeams falling over the surface.

"Oh, fuck." It hit her like a ton of bricks. "Shit, shit, shit, shit, shit . . ." she mumbled to herself as she flitted around the house, trying to get her thoughts in order.

She had completely forgotten today was her date with Lilith. No big deal. Just the girl Cordelia had been shamelessly flirting with and hopelessly lusting after for months now.

She looked at the clock. Good. She had plenty of time before she had to get ready for her date.

The doubt started creeping in, digging its claws deep and stealing her breath. Why did she ever agree to go out with Lilith? Why did she ever agree to do anything with anyone? Socializing was stressful enough, dating was a whole other beast. She just hoped she didn't make a complete fool of herself tonight.

She needed to force herself to keep busy until she could focus her energy on freaking out about this date. So a walk it was. Good. This would help her process some of her nervous energy and clear her head.

After getting herself changed and lacing up her running shoes, she grabbed her keys and phone, bounded out the door, and took off down the street. Her thoughts were still racing as she set a brisk pace, hoping the faster she went, the faster she could slow down her thoughts.

Everything would be fine. Tonight would go great, she told herself. And if it didn't, then maybe she could panic about finding a new coffee shop. But she could not let herself starting sweating that right now. Even though the pit in her stomach grew at the thought of it, she knew she had to keep a level head for tonight. Or else she would miss the whole date while letting her thoughts consume her, instead. And no way was she going to zone out on a date with Lilith.

Taking a deep breath, Cordelia let herself get lost in her surroundings as she found her way onto her favorite hiking trail. Let herself get swept away in the magic all around her. It was in the breeze floating past her, sweeping her hair off her shoulders. It was in the tinkling of the leaves bouncing off each other, swaying in the air. In the groaning of the flexing tree branches overhead. In the zip of a bee as it zoomed past her, a butterfly floating in the opposite direction. In the bubbling of the creek close by the trail. It was in the soft beat of her shoes on the stones underfoot as her steps slowed and she took another deep breath to calm herself.

She loved these moments when she could be alone and let herself melt into the magic-charged nature around her. The wildflowers dotted among the greenery growing alongside the path were always so delightful. Pale pinks, creamy whites, and faded blues greeted her from the rich, damp soil they inhabited. The trees that engulfed the trail were tall and spindly, the rough bark creating such a beautiful texture and contrast against the luxuriant green moss. Squirrels skittered and branches snapped under their tiny paws as they darted off in search of food and shelter. Birds flittered about, their feathered wings softly fluttering. Bright life playing among the slumbering earth. How anyone couldn't enjoy this, couldn't see and feel the crackle of the raw magic here, was beyond her.

She always left these woods feeling so much better, so much brighter, recharged afterward. It was as much part of her practice as the cleansing rituals she loved, as the beautiful spell jars she was so passionate about. Life and the creation energy that charged it all was so potent and so important in her enchantment magic.

Suddenly, a branch snapped, much closer and louder. Something heavier than a squirrel was nearby, and her breath caught in her throat. On alert, Cordelia looked for the source of the sound, and her eyes fell on a figure among the trees.

Two figures, actually. They were far off the trail, obviously not wanting to be seen. She wouldn't have noticed them if she hadn't been listening. They were leaning close together, almost conspiratorially.

Cordelia felt like this wasn't a conversation she should be witnessing. Quietly, she snuck behind a tree just off the path, trying to steady her breaths before looking back.

After gathering herself, she peeked around the tree. The pair were still in the same position, not having noticed her presence. Thank the Goddess.

Suddenly, she heard a growl coming from them, loud and angry, and her heart picked up its pace, startled by the sudden aggression.

How long would she have to hide here? Would she have to wait for them to go before she could leave? If she tried to make her way back down the trail toward her house, would they notice her? They hadn't seemed to before, but the chance of them not noticing a second time seemed lower.

She turned and planted her palms flat against the tree on either side of her hips, the bark digging into her back as she leaned her head back and took a deep breath. It would be fine. Everything would be OK. She had her phone with her in case of an emergency, and she knew how to get out of these woods. Knew the trail like the back of her hand and had explored enough off-trail to know her way around.

The voices were getting closer, and her ears perked up. It sounded like this little clandestine meeting was over. Cordelia desperately wanted to peek around the tree again, get a better look at who it was, but she didn't want to risk them seeing her. The crunch of leaves under their feet grew louder until they reached the trail, their shoes padding along the packed-dirt path. Once their voices turned, she peeked around the tree trunk, catching the backs of the two secreting away their meeting. A man and a woman.

There was nothing particularly odd about them apart from the woman's choice of clothing—an airy white blouse, gray trousers, and a pair of bright pink flats. Not exactly hiking attire, but she could chalk it up to a midday work break.

Cordelia realized they had stopped again, the man pulling the woman to the edge of the trail on the side opposite Cordelia. Looking around, he didn't bother to hush his voice this time.

"The alpha will be paying close attention, and he'll be expecting this to move faster. He feels like too much time has been wasted waiting for progress," he said with a raise of his eyebrow.

"Madam is very powerful and trying her best. Do you think she doesn't want this to move faster? Trust me, we don't want to be working with you shifters any more than you want to work with us. But it's for the good of both our causes. We expect another delivery this week." Her voice was dripping with impatience, like she had to keep her anger on a leash.

A shifter? By the rugged looks of him, he most likely belonged to a wolven pack. But who was the alpha he was talking about? And who was she? She referred to a madam, but that could mean a number of things. Shaking her head, Cordelia tried not to worry. This might be some sort of out-of-control wolven frat party business, and Goddess knew she couldn't care less about that. The wolven frats could get rowdy and out of hand quickly, and everyone knew what kind of havoc they regularly caused.

Snorting, the shifter narrowed his eyes, anger sparking in them.

"We'll get it to you Sunday night. You know what we've asked. We'll be in touch." With that, he turned on his heel and headed back down the trail, not bothering to wait for her.

She took off after him, her flats scuffling in the dirt as she tried to keep up with his long strides.

After they had been out of her sight for a few minutes, Cordelia gathered herself, pushing off the tree and stepping onto the trail to head back out. Once she crossed the bridge at the trail's entrance, she scanned the perimeter for any cars or people hanging around the mouth of the trail. When she didn't see anyone, she breathed a sigh of relief and headed across the street and back home.

But she couldn't ignore the feeling of unrest, of something lurking in the shadows. Chalking it up to the odd exchange she just witnessed, she shook it off and continued on her way, letting her thoughts cloud with all the possibilities of the night ahead of her.

CHAPTER FOUR

CORDELIA

Pacing the length of her bedroom, Cordelia kept staring into her open closet. Clothes were strewn about her bed, and she was getting more and more frustrated by the second. How was she supposed to figure out what to wear? On a date with Lilith! She was sure Lilith would show up looking absolutely stunning, and Cordelia would end up feeling like an inadequate sack of potatoes next to her if she didn't hurry up and pick out an outfit. The right one, preferably.

After sorting through everything she owned a couple more times and what felt like a small eternity later, she settled on a black satin slip skirt with a slit, a lavender velvet tank top, and a cropped, black cardigan with lavender stitched onto the hem.

Her curled hair was half-up in a clip, and she completed her makeup with winged eyeliner. Her round, tortoiseshell glasses complemented her face shape and full cheeks beautifully. She turned in front of the mirror, eyeing her reflection as she went. She actually felt beautiful, incredible in her own skin.

Finishing everything off, she added her star-shaped dangling earrings and a few gold rings, tossed on a pair of black strappy heels, and officially felt like she was ready for Lilith. She felt like absolute sex walking, in fact, and hopefully Lilith agreed.

Cordelia studied the way her curves showed in this outfit. Her full, large breasts pushed against the fabric of her top, creating swells like the rising waves of the ocean. The dips where her waist met her hips, the way her hips and full apron belly pushed against the satin skirt, screamed for attention—it was beautiful. Turning, she raked her eyes over every inch of herself. Her tummy was round and prominent, but it looked so cute, so soft and pretty. She couldn't help but stare at herself and feel nothing but adoration. With a smile on her face, Cordelia made her way out of the bedroom, feeling the confidence spread through her like the glow of a star.

A car door shut outside. Perfect timing. Racing down the stairs, Merlin hot on her heels, she grabbed her purse as she tried, and failed, to steady her nerves.

She stopped, closed her eyes, and took a deep breath. There was nothing to be nervous about. If things went great, then great. If not, she had a pint of her favorite ice cream in the freezer and a long list of go-to movies in case of emergencies.

She could hear the squeak of the floorboards of her front porch, setting the butterflies in Cordelia's stomach into frenzied flight.

As Lilith's knock sounded on the door, Cordelia let out a tiny squeal. Swinging the door open wide, she beamed at Lilith before her smile faltered and her breath caught.

Holy. Hell.

If she was hot, Lilith was on a whole new level.

She took a long, slow perusal of Lilith tonight. She was wearing a dark, oxblood-colored dress that hugged her and felt like an extension of her personality at the same time. Her hair was wavy, creating a curtain of sparkling moonlight that Cordelia wanted to run her fingers through. There was a silver comb crusted with shimmering stars that pulled one side of her hair back and out of her face. Her indigo eyes were absolutely breathtaking. They seemed to be glittering with starlight as Cordelia raised her eyes to meet them.

"L-Lilith, wow. Hi." She could barely squeak out the half-assed greeting she came up with.

Lilith chuckled, but also seemed to be captivated by the sight before her. Cordelia realized Lilith had also been looking her over before their eyes met, and Lilith was looking similarly starstruck.

"Hi." The word ghosted past Lilith's lips just loud enough for Cordelia to hear. She took one step forward, her hand slowly reaching for Cordelia.

"You're absolutely stunning," Lilith breathed, her eyes sparkling and pupils blown wide open.

Cordelia felt the stain of red splash across her cheeks, deep and hot. "I was just going to say the same thing about you." She bit her lip, feeling like nothing was coming out right, and she'd barely spoken a full sentence so far.

Trying to hide her blush and maybe save some of her pride, Cordelia turned, locking the front door before spinning back around with a smile plastered on to hide her awkwardness. Could Lilith tell she was nervous? Oh, Goddess, she hoped not.

As they pulled up to the restaurant and parked, Cordelia stared at the red brick building before them. She had been dying to visit this restaurant, but never had a good excuse to go.

Lilith opened her door and helped her out of the car, and Cordelia felt like she was floating on a cloud with their hands joined, basking in the glory of Lilith's smiles directed at her.

"I've been wanting to come here. Have you been before? I've heard so many good things." Cordelia felt like she was talking a million miles a minute.

"No, actually, but I had a feeling you might like it." Lilith smiled at her, fidgeting with her keys.

Was Lilith nervous? The idea of that startled Cordelia and didn't make sense all at the same time. No way. Lilith was the picture of confidence. She had always seemed like an outgoing, take-no-shit person. Cordelia wished she could stop caring what other people thought or said about her. She was working on it, slowly but surely.

But Lilith never struck her as someone to get nervous. Especially on a date. Especially when that date was with Cordelia—ungraceful, silly, anxious Cordelia.

As they walked through the front doors of the restaurant, the cool, slightly perfumed air wafted over them. It smelled like fresh flowers and warm bread. Absolute heaven.

The restaurant was busy and bursting with chatter and life. After being seated at their table, Lilith gave the waiter her most charming smile and ordered a bottle of wine to share, then set down her menu and turned her attention back on Cordelia.

Goosebumps erupted over Cordelia's body under Lilith's searing gaze. She shuddered slightly at her scrutiny before giving Lilith a nervous smile.

"So tell me," Lilith drawled, "what made you decide to come out with me tonight?" She took a quick sip of her water, her eyes only briefly leaving Cordelia before returning.

Fidgeting with her fingers under the table, Cordelia took a breath. "Honestly? I've always admired you. Not just because of how beautiful you are, but your attitude. The way you carry yourself. You just have such an easygoing personality, and I've always admired that in people. But you especially." She rattled on until her lungs ran out of air.

Lilith seemed to visibly relax at Cordelia's words. She cast her eyes down as she said, "Well, I'm very honored that you agreed, Cordelia. Although, I think you have a much rosier picture of me painted in your head than I do of myself. I'm glad to hear not everyone thinks I'm a bitch." She seemed to stall for a moment, taking another sip of water before she raised her eyes again with a soft smile. It flickered away before Cordelia could confirm what she'd seen on her face, though it looked an awful lot like self-doubt, and then Lilith brightened back to her charming self.

Just then, the waiter came back with their bottle of red wine. With a nod of approval from Lilith, he poured a glass for each of the women before taking their orders and disappearing back into the crowd.

A smile tugged at the corners of Cordelia's mouth as she slouched in her seat slightly, both hands cradling the delicate glass. "This is *so good*, Lilith," she practically moaned after she tasted it.

Lilith chuckled, her eyes burning into Cordelia.

"I'm glad you like it. It's one of my favorites." With her eyes still on Cordelia, softly assessing, she took a sip of her own glass and hummed her approval.

"I want to be honest with you." Lilith began smoothing the fabric of the tablecloth in front of her. "I really do like you. Admittedly, I've been wanting to ask you to dinner for a while"—she chuckled—"but couldn't get the nerve up to do it. You're just so bubbly, so full of life, so adorable. I love that you stick to a routine every day, an iced lavender latte with oat milk and your usual corner table. And you light up the day of anyone you meet. You've always seemed like magic itself."

Lilith's eyes held such admiration, such warmth and kindness.

"Doesn't hurt that you're drop-dead gorgeous and look like sin incarnate tonight." Picking up her glass and tipping it at Cordelia conspiratorially, Lilith winked over the rim.

Cordelia's breath hitched and her face flamed. It was like the air had been sucked out of the room, but it also felt like she'd been swept up in a warm wind. She felt so much lighter, like a band constricting her chest had been cut. Relief.

She hadn't realized how tense she'd been until Lilith's words. She needed to muster up some charm of her own before she seemed like a blubbering fool.

"Well, I've always thought you were hot, I can't seem to get you out of my head." Her eyes widened, and she quickly clamped her hand over her mouth. Did she actually just say that?! She might as well start burrowing as far into the earth as possible.

Lilith laughed, deep and true. It was so rich and throaty. So damn hot she couldn't stand it. Cordelia traced the outline of Lilith's lips with her eyes, wanting desperately to taste the red staining them and find out if they were as soft as she imagined.

"Excuse me for a minute, I just need to pop into the restroom and I'll be right back." Lilith stood from the table, grazing Cordelia's arms with the tips of her fingers as she headed toward the back of the restaurant.

Cordelia sat back in her chair, crossing one arm over the other and reaching for her wine glass with her free hand. Blowing out a breath, she tried to calm her heart rate.

It was hard to tell in the moment how flustered she got when she was around others, her excitement levels making her heart rate pick up a bit, her mind racing right alongside it. Now that she was alone again—as alone as she could be in the middle of a busy restaurant—her mind immediately pulled the conversation to the forefront. Picking apart every word and syllable uttered, mocking everything she'd said.

After waving a mental hand through the flurry of thoughts in her head, she settled down and took a deep breath, focusing on telling herself she was fine.

Calming down, she set down her wine glass and picked up her water, the cool condensation sliding down the glass and onto her fingers. Taking a soothing drink, she rattled the ice around before taking a look around the room. Having the glass in her hand settled her. Gave her hands something to do as she organized her thoughts.

There were a lot of couples out tonight, but it was also a weeknight, so there were plenty of groups out for a drink after work. With so many smiling faces and laughs being shared around the room, she felt more relaxed and at ease. She should be having a good time too. She was on a date with one of the hottest women she'd ever met, for Goddess's sake.

She let her eyes wander over the room. Sometimes it was just nice to people watch to pass the time and keep her thoughts occupied. And Lilith would be back soon, anyway, so she was glad she had a moment to clear her head a bit. Maybe now she could really focus instead of worrying. Taking one last look around, she snagged on a pair of obsidian eyes.

A man sitting across the room had caught her attention. Her gaze swept over him. He had a lean but powerful body. His chest and shoulders were muscled and broad. Continuing up, he had a sweep of dark scruff across his face. A slim nose, classically beautiful features in his cheekbones and jaw, full lips, and short black hair that was slightly messy and disheveled, swept across his forehead like he had been running his hands through it. His glinting onyx eyes were so deep, they seemed molten. Like she could dive in and drown in them.

She couldn't tear herself away from his eyes, which were locked on her own. Her breath caught in her throat as her chest tightened. Not with the grip of anxiety, but like it was being filled with a deep warmth. Radiating from the inside out—from a deep, molecular level inside her.

Her body straightened and angled itself toward him instinctively. Almost like she was being pulled to him. Her skin prickled and goosebumps erupted all over her body as the breath *whooshed* back into her lungs, so forcefully it felt like she was pushed back against the chair.

She hadn't even realized she'd stopped breathing.

CHAPTER FIVE

CORDELIA

The stranger's eyes widened, locking onto Cordelia entirely. The hand that was clutching her glass loosened, the water glass tumbling down and falling to the table, spilling water. Even as it dripped onto her lap—icy cold seeping through her skirt and onto her skin—she didn't care, couldn't care. Not when she was so enraptured by this stranger.

Standing, the man never took his eyes off her. Just then, she felt someone approach the table and sit in front of her.

"So sorry. The line in the bathroom was so long." The person's voice seemed so far off, so familiar, but so far off. Cordelia just couldn't bring herself to look away from this stranger.

"Cordelia, are you OK? What are you staring at?"

The stranger didn't pay attention to the person at her table either. In fact, he was getting closer, taking large, sweeping steps across the room toward her. Cordelia seemed to no longer be in control of her own body. She barely even registered that she had stood until she, too, was starting to take a step toward this approaching stranger.

Before she knew it, he was in front of her. She could feel the warmth and power radiating off him in waves. It felt so right, like this is where she was meant to be. Who she was meant to be standing with. How could it not be right? Everything inside her was screaming, wrapped in the comfort his presence offered.

His scent hit her then. He smelled deeply of pine trees, cool autumn breezes and leaves, and a hint of pepper. The scent wrapped itself around her and tugged against something deep inside. His nostrils flared, the fire in his eyes burning bright and igniting itself further.

"You," he breathed.

It didn't match the intensity in his eyes, the softness of his voice. But Cordelia was absolutely lost in the sound of it, hypnotized by the power this male seemed to have over her.

"I can't believe it. I found you." His voice was louder this time, throaty and hoarse, as if he'd been screaming her name for years, searching. "You're my fated," he said on a growl, still staring into Cordelia's eyes, into her eyes but also somehow deeper.

She felt her breath catch, a wave of astonishment flowing over her. *He was her fated.* The thought itself was absurd. A fated was never something she'd expected and hadn't really hoped for. It just wasn't something that ever crossed her mind. But hearing the proclamation sparked something inside her. Something that said he was absolutely right.

Now that those three words had left his lips, she understood why she was feeling so drawn to him. She knew it was true. Knew intrinsically, deep in her *soul* that it was absolutely true. How had she lived before? How had she breathed without his scent wrapping itself around her like a protective cloak?

"Um, excuse me?! You think you have some sort of wolf claim on her with that little growl of yours? Who are you, anyway?" There was that voice again.

The man ripped his eyes away from Cordelia, zeroing in on the person at her table. It was only then that Cordelia could move her eyes from his.

Lilith. How could she have forgotten about her date? It all came rushing back to her in a wave of horror.

"Oh Goddess, Lilith! I'm so sorry, I didn't realize you were back." Cordelia couldn't make eye contact with her.

Cordelia's eyes were darting around the table, looking for anything to latch onto while her mind raced. This was terrible. How was she going to explain this to Lilith, the woman taking her on this date right now? Especially when Cordelia didn't even know what was happening? How would she react? What would happen? Was she still on a date with Lilith? Or was she on one with this stranger now? Of course not—why would she ditch a date with Lilith for him? What was his name anyway? She hadn't even said anything to him yet. Everything was happening so fast, and she wasn't sure which thought to land on first.

"I'm Thane, and you are?" His eyes were still on Lilith, scrutinizing and tense.

His hands were clenched in fists at his sides, his jaw tight. As if he could barely contain himself enough to ask her name.

Standing from the table and crossing her arms, Lilith leveled a poisonous gaze on him. "Lilith. The woman taking *her* on a date." Her thumb jabbed toward Cordelia.

Thane. What a beautiful, mesmerizing name. Thane. *Thane*. It felt like a prayer she wanted to slip past her lips again and again. She could get lost in this feeling. The feeling that was overwhelming and overtaking her whole body, all of her senses.

"Ah, you mean the woman who *was* taking her on a date." Thane was smirking now. "I think we both know the date is over. Unless you'd like me to join you? Under the circumstances, I think it would be more than appropriate." He crossed his arms in challenge to Lilith, never letting the smirk leave his lips. *Goddess* those lips.

Cordelia felt her cheeks redden and warmth overtake her body. Oh she liked that, the possessiveness. She liked it *a lot*.

She didn't know how to make sense of everything—the warring of her body's reaction to Thane and the nerve-racking guilt she felt about Lilith. It was all so much, too much.

"And you just assume you get her time, now? Automatically?" Lilith quirked an eyebrow at Thane, stock-still and not budging. Cordelia's eyes darted between the two as they stared each other down. She felt frozen, unsure what her next move should be.

Thane took a step farther, fingers flexing wide before forming a fist again. Controlled rage. For now.

"I do," he practically growled. "We're bound to one another. And you can challenge that all you want, but it won't change a damn thing, and I won't take your shitty attitude."

Cordelia's eyes widened. This situation was quickly spinning out of control, and she needed to de-escalate it. Before it got worse.

She put a hand on Thane's arm and his head snapped to her, his muscles relaxing slightly under her touch. His gaze was like a brand on her soul. So hot it burned, but in a way she didn't want to end. Her knees felt weak all of a sudden, but she kept her composure as best as she could.

"First of all, my name is Cordelia. Second of all, I *am* on a date with her." Her eyes went to Lilith. "I'm so sorry. This all happened so quickly, it took me by surprise, and I wasn't even sure what this was. It was absolutely not my intent to interrupt our date or do anything to hurt your feelings." She pleaded with her words and eyes for Lilith to understand. She didn't want Lilith angry with her, and she didn't want to burn a bridge she was just starting to build.

Lilith's shoulders sagged, a breath rushing from her lips. "It's fine. I understand. I think it's probably best if we call it a night anyway."

Lilith started to lean toward the table to grab her things, and Cordelia's eyes fell to the floor. She'd simultaneously blown her chances with Lilith while also having such an unexpected, life-altering thing happen to her. She had a fated. How had that happened?

Without another word, Lilith took a few steps from the table before turning toward Cordelia, giving her a sad sort of soft smile, then turning quickly and leaving.

CHAPTER SIX

CORDELIA

"Cordelia," Thane said.

The edge in his voice sent a shiver down her spine. *Oh yes*, she definitely liked his possessiveness. It radiated off every word that left his lips. Something about being around him just felt right.

OK, who even was this guy? And why was she thinking of him like she knew him already? She knew his name and that they were fateds. And the list ended there. She needed to know more about him before diving into this, before making any sort of binding decision.

It was then she realized he was rubbing soothing circles into her hand with his thumb. As if he could sense her nerves and racing thoughts.

"I know this is a lot to take in, but I know two things right now. That you are my fated and that I am yours. And that's all that matters to me." Thane smiled down at her, gentle and reassuring, yet strong and powerful.

This whole night had been something out of a dream, or some sort of alternate reality. It felt like Lilith had picked her up so long ago, so much had happened since then.

Slowly, the gravity and reality of her situation started to set in. Then it hit her all at once. She had a fated?! This morning she'd had nothing but a glimmer of hope that something could happen between Lilith and her. Now that dream was gone and someone else was standing in front of her, vowing his life to hers.

This was all happening so fast. Too fast. She suddenly felt like she was running out of air. She needed to take a deep breath but couldn't seem to make her lungs work.

Flinging her arm out, stumbling, grabbing for anything to balance herself, she made her way out the door and toward fresh air. She caught the brick wall of the restaurant and sucked in a deep breath, bending over to try to relieve some of the pressure in her chest. Clear her head and make some sense out of what was happening. Figure it out.

"Are you OK?" Thane's concerned voice cut through the blood pounding in her ears.

But it didn't matter. She was too far gone already, down the rabbit hole of her anxiety. Gripping her chest and seizing her muscles. Her eyes shot to his, then to her surroundings. A deep knot formed in her gut and took root, unrelenting and growing stronger.

How could she figure out her situation? How did she land here, anyway? How would this work, and how was her life going to change?

It was already so serious, and it was like there was no way out. Not that she necessarily wanted an out from Thane. But now she'd lost her sense of choice, and choices were something that brought her comfort. Were part of the freedom she had fought to have for so long. Without a choice, she felt powerless.

"I-I'm fine. I think. I don't know, but this all feels like it's happening so fast. I started tonight not knowing what would happen, but the possibility of *this*"—she gestured between them with her hand —"never even crossed my mind. It's just a lot to take in. It's not every day you just randomly meet a stranger that you happen to be bound to for the rest of eternity. How do I even process this?" She was rambling and out of breath, but she couldn't stop the absolute avalanche of words and thoughts forming in her head and immediately spilling out of her mouth.

She just couldn't stop. As if letting it out would somehow lead her to stumble upon a solution or make her feel better.

Thane reached out an arm to steady her, to comfort her. But all it did was make it worse.

She quickly shrugged it off. "Sorry, I just need you to not touch me right now. It's too overstimulating and overwhelming, and I need to think. Can we talk?"

"Sure, where did you park?" Thane asked calmly, scanning the parking lot beyond them.

She blinked. She'd forgotten she hadn't even driven here.

"Well, Lilith actually drove me. So I guess I'm calling a cab home." Her mind raced as she fiddled with her purse, pulling her phone out of her bag. She tried to still her thoughts and hands long enough to focus and find a number for a car service.

"I'll drive you home," Thane said.

She looked up into his eyes. So strong, so sure, so confident. It wasn't a question. He was already willing to do this for her, she could see it in his unwavering expression.

Startled, she sputtered, "O-OK. Sure. As long as you don't mind? I don't want to be a bother. I mean, I'm just some girl you just met, right? I don't want to get in your way or—"

"I'm driving you home. It's not a problem, Cordelia, and I want to. I want to make sure you make it home safely. That's my job now." He was so firm in his tone, so firm in his stance.

She had half a mind to tell him that it, in fact, wasn't his job, but she kept that to herself for now.

She smiled softly. "Thank you."

He nodded and helped her straighten herself from where she was still leaning against the wall. His fingers ghosted against her back before he seemed to think better of it, dropping his hand and leading her through the parking lot to a sleek, black sedan. After opening the front passenger door for her, he helped her in before rounding his way to the driver's side. "I need your address."

She rattled it off to him to punch into his GPS, and they set off.

Settling into the seat, trying to relax her body and ease herself down from the anxiety, she took a breath, inhaling the smell of leather mixed with Thane's scent. It was intoxicating and so soothing.

With her head back, she said, "You know, this isn't actually your job. I know you said it is, but it isn't."

Thane's gaze slowly slid over to hers. "That right?" She sat up, opening her mouth to say something but he cut her off. "I know you said it's not, but let me assure you, little witch, this *is* my job now. I know this is all happening fast, but I need you to know that you're taken care of. From here on out, I will take care of you. That's my job and it's what I want." The firmness in his tone and the set of his jaw said that he was done discussing this. That it hadn't been up for discussion in the first place.

She just stared at him. She couldn't understand what he would want with her. She had never truly felt worthy of anyone, which was why she'd always struggled with dating. But now here was this strong, confident, sexy man who was telling her in no uncertain terms that he belonged to her. Not the other way around. That his life was now hers and that she was his priority. It was *a lot* to take in, especially all at once, especially in one night. And most especially in the same night she met him.

"If I let you," she let out, regaining a semblance of control. Her eyes darted to his, focused and trained on the road ahead of them. Protectively.

"If you let me?" He quirked a brow at her. "Cordelia, let's get something straight. This isn't a choice. You can tell me to back off all you want, but I'm not going away. I'll give you the space you want, but make no mistake—I want this. Nothing, and I mean *nothing*, will keep me from you. This is all going too fast for you? That's fine, and you can take all the time you need to process it. But understand me when I tell you, I'm. Not. Going. Anywhere." His hands gripped the steering wheel even tighter, the last words coming out in a growl, his eyes blown wide and almost glowing.

But it didn't scare her, didn't intimidate her. In fact, a strange calmness radiated all through her body and soothed her racing thoughts. Like a balm for her worries.

She was still hesitant and didn't want to jump into something so quickly. While she may feel calm and safe around him, there was still a part of her, a very vital part of her, that was screaming for control. Screaming to hit the brakes and protect herself at all costs.

She may have a fated, but she was still a person. Her own person. A person who needed to take her time and adjust at her own pace. And damn it if she wasn't intent on doing just that.

Crossing her arms and steeling herself, she huffed an amused breath. "Well, fine, but you're going to date me. I mean it—like real dating. I want to get to know you, everything that makes you who you are, and we can go from there. Just because we have some sort of fated bond between us doesn't mean you're entitled to me. I'm still my own person and free to make my own decisions." Letting her gaze drift out the passenger window, she tried to appear casual and as if there was no room for argument. Hoped he got the message that she was too afraid to jump in headfirst, without having to actually admit her fear.

He chuckled. "I like you feisty."

"I'm serious, Thane. This isn't a joke, and I'd appreciate it if you took me seriously. Because we can have a much different conversation if you're not." She tacked on a look that said, *Fuck with me and suffer the consequences.*

"Alright, little witch. I'll happily agree to date you. Any time I can spend with you is time that I want. I won't deny you your desires." He seemed content with the compromise. Content that Cordelia wasn't giving him an outright no.

But she wasn't giving him an outright yes either. She relaxed at that. At least she had some sort of grip on the situation now. She could get to know him, everything about him, feel normal for once. Maybe even feel like she had control over her life.

She was still a person, damn it, and she wanted to feel like it. Sure, fated bonds weren't super rare, but they were rare enough to be treasured. And you truly never knew when one would pop up, or when the bond would snap into place.

For some people, it happened instantaneously—case in point, what happened tonight. But for others, it happened at random times. You could know someone for years, be married to them or friends with them for years, before the bond snapped into place. No one could predict it, but everyone wanted it. Chased after it.

Cordelia never really bothered with it since her path had always been laid out for her as a Halloway. She'd been raised to expect an advantageous match, most likely orchestrated by her mother. And since she'd gotten away from that life, she had been more focused on her own freedom, on building the life she loved so fiercely. So tonight took her by surprise.

She felt so bad about Lilith. How would she ever face her again at the coffee shop? Would things be weird? Would Cordelia have to bring it up, or would Lilith? A million thoughts raced through her head as she tried to mentally prepare herself for that conversation.

A hand gripped hers from across the center console. "Hey, where'd you go?" Thane's touch was firm but reassuring. It was amazing how one touch from him could do so much. Maybe this fated bond was a good thing.

"Oh, nothing. Just thinking too much." She stared out the window ahead of her.

Suddenly the weight of the entire evening fell on her. The whirlwind it was and everything that had happened. All the thinking she was going to be doing in the foreseeable future. She was already exhausted by it.

"Thank you. For driving me home. And for understanding that I need some time. I just need to work it out in my head, and I need to feel a little normal here. I can't just jump in."

He nodded. "I understand, and I'll respect your wishes, Cordelia. I'm not leaving, and I'm not going to push you to do anything you're not comfortable with. Anything you want is yours." The look in his eyes was so firm and affectionate. "Plus, this gives me the chance to learn as much as I can about you, little witch." He smirked.

"Jumping the gun a bit, aren't we? I'm not your little anything." She chuckled, finding it so easy to be playful with him. Usually it took a while for her to fully open up to people, but she felt it so quickly, so naturally, with Thane.

"Maybe, but I am yours. Completely. Whether that happens all at once or a little at a time, you pick." His voice was soft, his eyes still on the road.

CHAPTER SEVEN

CORDELIA

Before she knew it, they were pulling into her driveway. Thane parked the car and shut off the engine, reclining in his seat for a second, as if hesitating. Then he was out of the car and opening her door, gesturing for her.

Cordelia took his outstretched hand and let Thane close the door for her before heading up the stairs of her porch. She heard him trailing behind her, his steps quiet even in the crunchy gravel. She had half a mind to tell him she could walk herself to the door, but she knew it would only be met with an insanely hot growl and him walking her there anyway.

Before she could turn to face him, he grabbed her waist, spinning her and then lifting her chin to meet his gaze. His eyes were somehow so bright and molten, a deep, glinting obsidian—like pools of endless night.

He let out a breath, stepping just slightly closer to her when she didn't pull away. Her breath hitched in her throat as Thane's arm tightened around her waist while the other cradled her cheek. Her head was screaming at her to push him away and preserve whatever piece of herself she still had left.

But the rest of her didn't feel any sort of apprehension. Only a deep calm spreading through her like the warmth of a fire on a bitterly cold night, chasing away any of the doubts floating around her head. Her eyes fluttered closed for a moment and he hummed softly.

"I meant what I said in the car, Cordelia." Thane's voice was just above a whisper, and her breath stuttered at the sound of her name on his lips. "I know this is moving quickly, but I need you to know who I am and that I don't intend to leave you unguarded. You can take all the time you need, but I will make sure I am always there to protect you."

"I just need time to wrap my head around things. I need to clear my mind and not let myself get caught up in all of it. Can you understand that?" She breathed out, not letting her gaze break from his.

"I understand. I may be fighting my instincts, but I understand." Thane reached up to twirl a lock of her hair, softly running it through his fingers. "I will do anything you want, Cordelia. You want me to date you? Done. You want me to take my time, get to know you? I will happily lay everything down at your feet. All you have to do is ask the questions." He looked into her eyes then, his own sparkling with hope and excitement.

How could she deny him? Sure, she didn't know him twelve hours ago. Sure, things could go horribly wrong. But no one ever said Cordelia wasn't impulsive, and no one ever said she made the wisest decisions. She was a hopeless romantic.

That was the very moment Merlin decided to jump through the living room windows in his ghost form and perch on Cordelia's shoulders, wobbling a bit as he balanced himself.

Thane stumbled back a step.

"What the fuck?" He stared wide-eyed at Merlin, who seemed to be rather proud of himself right now.

"This is Merlin. He's my familiar. He just has a lot of issues with clinging to me." She chuckled, gingerly plucking him off her shoulders and setting him down on the floorboards.

Merlin looked up at her, almost rolling his eyes as if offended that she would refer to him simply as a familiar.

"I've never seen a cat jump through a wall," Thane deadpanned, staring at Merlin like he was a puzzle to solve.

"Uh, yeah." She laughed a little nervously. "He has a ghost form. He's a special boy." Rubbing the back of her neck, she hoped he wouldn't freak out like people tended to.

Merlin wasn't your run-of-the-mill familiar. Some familiars were able to take on ghost forms, but not many. It didn't come genetically, and it tended to bounce around and choose a worthy familiar at their birth. It had to do with the kind of power they were attuned to. It didn't always correspond to their bonded witch, sometimes it just complemented their witch's magic, but sometimes it had nothing to do with their destined witch at all. There was no rhyme or reason, it just showed up. But not often enough to be commonplace, which was why it usually scared new guests. Not that she had many.

Thane just nodded his head, softening his gaze toward Merlin, who, in turn, trotted over to rub against Thane's legs. Merlin's purrs floated through the air between them like rumbling thunder. Thane just chuckled as he shoved his hands in his pockets and turned his attention back to Cordelia.

Her eyes grew wide. "Wow, he doesn't do that with just anyone. Don't get me wrong, he loves people. But he's usually pretty stingy with his unabashed love. That's high praise, my friend."

"I'm just shocked he's even giving me the time of day, what with me being a wolf shifter." He chuckled, glancing down at Merlin, who was still giving Thane a rubdown.

Huh. At least one of them was.

"Ah, that explains the possessiveness." Cordelia rolled her eyes. Thane's gaze shot back up to hers.

"And what's wrong with that?"

"Oh, nothing. I didn't have any proof that you were some sort of Magical, but I noticed you got pretty possessive when you were talking to Lilith. And then again when you tried to stake your claim on me outside the restaurant. It makes sense now that you tell me you're a shifter." With a shrug and a quirked eyebrow, she challenged him to contradict her.

"That's my girl. So observant." He gave her a wicked grin and a wink.

"No one said I was *your* anything, Thane." Crossing her arms, she smirked. "You'll have to earn that right. I hope for your sake you bring your A game. It would be a shame if I had to find another date."

He snarled at that. "Like hell you will."

Thane took two big, hard steps toward her, crowding her against the door, his arms on either side of her head like a cage. Her heart rate picked up, eyes wide, excitement coursing through her.

She wasn't scared, no. She could see his fire, and she met it with her own. Oh this was fun. She liked this.

"I'm the only one you'll even think about dating, Cordelia. I am your fated, and I will prove to you however you need me to that I will be the only one for you. I will take care of and protect you. I don't care how long it takes, little witch. You. Are. Mine." He practically growled the last words.

"And see, there you are jumping the gun again." She tsked. "We'll see about that, Thane."

He laughed a little, darkly, promisingly. "Yes, we will, sweetheart."

Just then, he swooped in. Cordelia reared her head back until it met the door behind her, her eyes wide in shock.

She thought he was moving in to kiss her, but instead he chuckled against her cheek, his hot breath causing electricity to erupt across her body. Pulling back, he stared into her eyes again, the fire from earlier gone, replaced with molten affection. Promise. Longing.

"Give me your phone. I'll give you my number." He held out his hand. He sure was a cocky bastard, with his soft, lopsided grin.

She fumbled for her phone before handing it over. He quickly typed in his contact info and handed it back.

"Well, don't you want me to give you mine?"

"Nope. I told you, you call the shots here, Cordelia. If this is truly what you want, you can decide to text or call me, and I'll happily give you anything you ask for."

He didn't say what would happen if she didn't contact him, but Cordelia thought they both pretty much knew she wouldn't be making that decision. Still, she liked that Thane gave *her* the power.

"OK. Deal." She gazed up at him, hoping the promise of her excitement shone in her eyes.

"Good night, little witch." He smiled softly before turning around, heading toward his car, and speeding off into the night.

She let out a deep sigh, staring at the darkened road, letting herself get lost in an endless night sky, glittering with hope and promise. Longing and comfort.

CHAPTER EIGHT

THANE

BEEP, BEEP, BEEP, BEEP, BE— Thane slammed his hand down on the droning alarm clock next to his bed. Did they have to make them that fucking annoying? Grumbling, he turned over and sat up, swinging his legs over the side of the bed. *Fuck, it's early.*

He sat there for a moment, letting the sleep clear from his head. Immediately, thoughts of last night came flooding back to him. The restaurant, those beautiful, bright lavender eyes across the room, the fated bond, so brilliant and golden shining between them, and hearing her voice for the first time.

It was like a weight had been lifted off his chest, one he hadn't known was compressing him for so long. Those eyes, that voice, her soft hands in his. *Fuck.* His cock stood at attention at that.

"Goddess, help me," he mumbled before adjusting himself and standing up, heading for the shower. He needed a cold one to calm his body.

He turned the water on, letting it run for a second before stripping off his black boxer briefs, tossing them aside, and stepping into the shower. Thane hissed for a second at the initial sting of the cold water before tipping his head back and letting it run down his neck, chest, and stomach. He couldn't stop thinking about her eyes, her laugh, the fire he could see in her. *Cordelia*. The most beautiful sound, the most beautiful name he'd ever heard.

He had a fated. Alive and well and out there somewhere.

Thane couldn't push past the thought of her, and his cock was unrelenting. Groaning, he palmed himself before fully gripping his painfully hard length and giving himself a rough pump.

Tipping his head back against the wall, Thane groaned long and loud, settling in. He started off slowly, getting himself worked up to the thought of her. Those captivating eyes he couldn't tear his own away from, those luscious curves and rolls he couldn't wait to get his hands on, to grip like his life depended on it. Was it weird to fuck himself to the thought of her the morning after he met her? He didn't give a shit. She was beautiful beyond words, feisty and fiery hot, soft and sweet, and unimaginably perfect. Thane was in awe of everything about her.

He set a punishing rhythm, gripping himself hard. His breathing stuttered as he looked down at his fist, stroking himself faster and harder, flicking his thumb over the head of his cock, and gathering the precum that was leaking out of the tip. The memories of last night flooded his brain. Her eyelashes fluttering at him, making him bite back groan after groan. Her fiery attitude, taking charge and not holding back. Thane loved her getting an attitude with him and fighting back, taking what *she* wanted. But oh, soon enough, his little witch would learn that he was in charge too.

Leaning forward and slapping his hand on the tiled wall in front of him, he kept up his pace, feeling the telltale sign of his impending orgasm. Thane couldn't help but thrust his hips in time with his hand, couldn't resist closing his eyes and falling into the blissful fantasy his mind was conjuring, out of control in his thoughts and desire for his little fated.

Just the thought of her being his fated sent a guttural moan up his throat, his cock swelling even further. He was a moaning, out-of-control mess, but he'd stopped caring at that point. Didn't care how crazed he may have sounded, the tiles of the bathroom echoing his heart's desires like an incanted prayer. His legs tensed, the warm, lightning-sharp pleasure gathering down his spine and drawing his balls up.

A vision of her eyes flashed in his mind, the light lavender color dancing in the light. His knot swelled, tightening with his lower back before his release finally pounded through him, his hand continuing its hard and fast pace. The ribbons of color dancing behind his eyelids flowed in time with the tension that released from his body. Waves of black, gold, lavender curling in his vision. His orgasm splashed the wall in front of him as his breathing quickened for a second then slowed. His eyes closed, chest heaving. Thane hung his head down, chin meeting his chest, and took a deep breath.

After settling down, he leaned back into the icy spray, cleaning himself and the wall before turning the water off and stepping out of the shower. He blew out a long breath, staring into the space ahead of him, dazed out of his mind.

And only from the thought of her, only from the fresh memories he harbored like treasured trinkets in the most sacred parts of his mind. Thane couldn't even imagine how it would feel when he finally got his hands on her. Was able to worship on his knees in front of her. She was like a goddess made especially for him, beautiful and radiant.

Snapping out of his haze, he snagged the towel off the rack next to the shower. *Pull it together, asshole. It's been less than one day.*

After toweling off, Thane got ready and headed back into the bedroom to get dressed. It was a Saturday, so he didn't have to work. He didn't have many plans today, but he did want to head to the gym and get a workout in. It always helped him clear his head, and right now, he needed all the clarity he could get.

Thane needed to be able to approach this situation with Cordelia in the best way possible, and he wasn't entirely sure what that looked like right now. Regardless, he needed to get a grip. He'd hardly recognized himself last night.

She'd said that she wanted to take things slow, to get to know him before she made any commitments. He wasn't feeling particularly patient right now, but he would do whatever it took to make sure Cordelia remained a permanent part of his life. She was the most important thing, his top priority from now on. And damn it did he know how insane that sounded this soon, but when a wolf found their fated, there wasn't anything that stood in their way. The witch he had found himself fated to would get whatever it was she desired.

Oh yes, Thane knew she was a witch. He could scent the magic on her as soon as he met her. It intertwined with his own scent and created an intoxicating blend that made his instincts *wild*, like it was made just to drive him out of his mind.

Her own scent was like lavender in a bonfire, so woodsy and smoky—fiery, but with the lightest thread of floral woven into it like smoke on a breeze. It was heady and tantalizing, especially with the scent of her magic, which was like fresh-turned earth and rain. It was addicting, and Thane needed to smell it again. Soon.

He rifled through a few drawers before grabbing a pair of black athletic shorts with neon green stripes down the side, a black T-shirt, and his favorite pair of running shoes.

On his way out the door, he grabbed a black baseball cap, turned it backward, and then headed to the car.

Thane had seen Talin, his best friend, shortly after he got to the gym. They'd locked eyes and waved to one another, and Talin seemed to understand immediately that Thane needed a solo session today.

Usually Thane would be down to spot each other and shoot the shit while they got their routines in. But today, he just didn't have it in him. So, instead, he went through the motions on his own, running through the workout with efficiency and barely a thought. Practiced. Everyday routine. He just had too much clouding his mind to focus on . . . anything, really. Anything short of the witch that had him enraptured in a lavender haze.

Within twenty-four hours of meeting her. How pathetic of him.

He'd been thinking of her his entire workout. Replaying everything from last night. Every second, every breath, every look into her eyes. And he couldn't believe himself. He'd never gotten caught up in someone like that. He had to get it together and reassess. He sure as hell still wanted her, wanted to be with her, but he didn't need to let his instincts drive his entire existence toward her. He didn't need to let it force his thoughts in her direction. Didn't need to let it consume him.

After a minute, he blew out a breath, shook his head clear, and grabbed his things from the locker. He didn't see Talin in the locker room or on his walk to the front door but didn't pay it much mind.

He got outside and into his car, then stopped. What did he do now? He had been stuck in a haze, his mind cluttered the entire time he was in the gym. That had been the point of the workout, but clearly it failed miserably. At least he was able to get a workout in alone, which didn't happen often.

Alone. That was what he'd been for a while now. Ever since the incident with the pack, he'd been on his own. Entirely. Sure he had Talin, but did that really count as not being alone? As the sign of a life not wasted? He had been hiding himself away for so long now.

He tossed his preworkout bottle into the passenger seat a little more aggressively than needed, then reached down and grabbed the bottle with his still-cold protein shake. After giving it a bit of a shake to remix it, he popped the cap open and downed it. He had to do something to clear his thoughts. He didn't want to think about his fucking issues anymore.

He threw the car in gear and raced off back home. He wasn't sure what he would do with himself, but damn it, he wasn't going to sulk. He could get himself out of this funk. Out of this hold Cordelia seemed to have on him. He could behave like a normal fucking person without needing to attach himself to her just because his instincts drove him to do just that. He had control, plenty of it.

He tried not to notice how his eyes kept catching on everything lavender. Tried not to notice how it made his lips twitch up. Tried not to notice the fluttering in his chest.

CHAPTER NINE

THANE

The entire drive home and walk into his house was a blur. A blur of lavenders, soft gazes, and a husky voice that drove him to the brink of insanity. He snapped out of his haze when his gym bag thudded on the floor of his living room.

Rubbing his hands down his face, he sighed and walked into the kitchen. The buzzing of his phone pulled him out of his reverie.

> Talin: Hey, dude. You seemed distracted today. Everything OK?

Talin was great at reading emotions, so it shouldn't surprise Thane that he would notice something was up.

> Thane: Yeah. Just a lot going on right now.

> Talin: You need me to come over?

> Thane: You want to come talk? Or you want the beer in my fridge?

Talin: Haha, got me. Be there in 20.

Thane chuckled to himself as he strode into the bathroom adjoined to his bedroom, needing another shower and to slap some sense into himself. Talking things through with Talin would help. And Talin was always in for drinking Thane's booze.

After finishing up and changing, he plopped on the couch in the living room, letting himself close his eyes and have a moment of quiet. A moment where he wasn't worried about lavender eyes, a desire to reach out, or controlling his instincts.

The knock at the door had him up and letting his friend in. Talin stood there, beaming with that crooked grin of his, and threw his arms in the air. "Thane! What's up?" Talin clapped him on the shoulder and let himself in.

Thane just shook his head. "Please, by all means, make yourself at home."

"Aw, c'mon now. I'm here at least once a week, and same with you at my place. What do you think I'm gonna do, wreck it?" He threw himself down on the couch, still grinning.

"Well, if you pull those wings out again, yeah, I do. And by the way, please never do that again. Goddess knows I don't want to clean up the aftermath of you drunkenly half shifting." He shook his head, making his way to the fridge and grabbing a couple beers as Talin's laugh boomed in the living room. Thane threw one to Talin and joined him on the couch.

"That was *one time*. Are you ever going to let it go?" Talin popped open the bottle and took a swig.

Thane just rolled his eyes in response, taking a drink from his own bottle.

"So what's up? You seem off today." Talin settled his gaze on Thane, his take-no-bullshit look.

Thane rubbed the back of his neck, not sure how to explain it. "Ah, I kind of fated bonded with someone last night?"

"You *kind of* did? Or *actually* did, Thane?" Talin stared at him, looking incredulous.

"Yeah, I did. And I'm freaking out. I don't know what to do, and I don't know how to act." Thane ran his fingers through his hair with frustration. "It's like I'm in someone else's fucking body, and I don't know how to handle it."

"Fuck, man. That's . . . *fuck*. I mean, are you not happy about it? That's big news!" Talin was beaming, his voice growing louder with his excitement.

"I mean, yeah, it's great. But I feel, like, this intense need to claim her, ya know? But at the same time, I know that's just my wolf instincts, and in my head, I'm freaking out. I don't know how to handle this." Thane had done so much thinking in the past day that he felt like his head might explode.

There were so many things to consider, so many directions he could take. He also needed to talk to Cordelia. And soon.

"Well, who is she? What does she think?" Talin took a sip of his beer, his eyes still dancing with delight.

Thane instantly relaxed the slightest bit at the thought of her name, her eyes, seeing her for the first time. He felt his lips twitch.

"Cordelia. Her name is Cordelia." He glanced away, trying to gather his thoughts and not let his emotions betray him. "She seemed pretty caught up in it and overwhelmed. Said she wants to take things slow, get to know me first." He took another drink, willing his heart to stop racing. To stop the panic that instinctually coursed through him every moment he didn't listen to the screaming drive to claim, take, make her *his*.

"I mean, that's good, right? I think that's the best idea—just take it easy. Have you talked to her since then?"

Thane shook his head, a lump of anxiety in his throat at the thought. His excitement mixed with apprehension and twisted in his gut.

"Well, you gotta do that first. I'm assuming you got her number, so just text her. Meet her for coffee or something, keep it casual. *Not* a date, OK? That might put too much pressure on it. Talk with her first and get on the same page before you do anything else." Talin pointed his bottle at Thane, giving him a stern look.

Thane's chest felt lighter at that. At the thought of not having to rush into dating *right now*. They were both a little rattled by what happened, and both of them seemed to be treading lightly.

Thane wondered how Cordelia was processing this, how she was dealing with the aftermath today. What she was feeling. What she was thinking.

He let out a hard breath. "Yeah, you're right."

Talin chuckled. "Aren't I always? That is why you came to me, right?" He leaned back, one hand behind his head and grinned.

"Nice memory you got in that rock you call a head, lizard boy. You came over here. Actually, you *insisted* you come over. For my beer. I think me being here was just something you had to deal with to get to it." He snorted, laughing at Talin's feigned hurt expression.

"I'm offended you would even insinuate that." Talin gasped in exaggerated shock. "And to insult me and call me a lizard? That's low. Even for you, wolfy."

"Sure it is." Thane rolled his eyes, laughing. He felt the band that'd been tightening around his chest all day suddenly snap, loosening its grip on his breathing, his heart, the knots in his stomach. Fucking around with Talin helped get his mind off things, and now he felt like he could actually approach everything from a sane perspective.

"So, you talked to your dad, lately?"

And just like that, the tension was back.

Groaning, Thane scrubbed his free hand down his face. "Why did you have to bring that up?"

Talin threw his free hand in the air in mock surrender. "Hey, I'm just checking in. You haven't talked about him in a while."

Thane had been avoiding his father. Ever since the incident with Thane's pack, he hadn't felt fully comfortable around his dad, or his entire family for that matter. Thane was ashamed, embarrassed. His father had never failed, was a successful pack alpha.

The whole Lycus lineage was made up of a long line of alphas— Thane was just the latest in the family. The thought of what'd happened all those years ago forced a lump in his throat. Caused his breath to quicken and his stomach to turn leaden. It trapped him and forced his attention entirely to the anxiety coiling everywhere. In his muscles, his head, the set of his jaw.

"He called the other day." Thane wanted to leave it at that. Wanted Talin to drop it.

"And?" Talin pressed. At Thane's refusal to meet his question with more than a grunt, Talin pushed. "You fucking ignored it, didn't you? Again? Thane, you gotta stop beating yourself up."

"I don't want to talk about it. End of." Thane cut him a sharp look, effectively shutting down the conversation.

"Fine. But you can't let everything take the back seat and just stew on it. You're gonna kill yourself doing that." Talin sounded hurt, serious.

Talin rarely did, and when he was being sincere, it hit Thane hard. He knew Talin meant business when all the laughs and jokes vanished.

"I know." Thane stared down at his hands, the bottle in them.

How long was he going to sit in the guilt? The shame? His father was someone he'd always looked up to, always admired. Now Thane couldn't even talk to him on the phone, never mind look him in the eye.

"At least start with texting Cordelia. Today. Figure out what you're going to do, and go from there."

Thane looked up to see Talin leaning forward, his elbows resting on his knees, the beer bottle hanging from the tips of his fingers.

Talin's eyes were pinning Thane with a serious expression that he'd rarely seen sketched across Talin's face.

Thane winced. Rubbing the back of his neck, he avoided Talin's gaze. "Yeah, so about that . . ."

"Spit it out, Thane."

"I, uh, kind of didn't get her number." Thane blew out a breath, bracing himself for Talin's reaction.

He erupted with booming laughter, making Thane's head snap up.

"What's so fucking funny?" He narrowed his eyes, waiting for the ridiculous laughing to end.

Doubled over and gasping for air, Talin wheezed out "You're so fucked" in between bouts of laughter.

"Wow, so glad I invited you over to talk. What a great support system you are, asshole." Thane rolled his eyes, leaning back against the couch.

Finally starting to calm down, Talin made a show of wiping his eyes and straightening himself out, the last laughs dying out from his lungs. Leaning back in his seat, he draped his arm over the top of the couch, pinning Thane with a curious look, eyebrow quirked. "So what even happened? Are you just expecting that you'll bump into each other on the street like this is some sort of fairy-tale bullshit?" Talin couldn't keep the grin off his lips.

"Of course not. I gave her my number and told her she was in charge. You know, since she was freaking out about being *out* of control?" Thane was growing frustrated with the conversation. Or maybe with himself. He wasn't sure anymore.

"Ah well, how noble of you. The wolf in shining armor." Talin puffed out his chest, posing with exaggerated, mocking grandeur. "Lot of good that did you. Now you're sitting here talking to me instead of texting her and putting yourself out of your misery." He leaned back, taking another drink from his bottle and chuckling.

"Well if you're such a genius, what should I do?" Thane snapped.

"Nothing. You can't do anything. You just gotta wait for her to text you, I guess."

Pinching the bridge of his nose, Thane closed his eyes as the racing thoughts flooded back in. He *was* fucked. What was he going to do? Just sit and pace the house and flinch at every sound that came from his phone? Pathetic. He wasn't that person. He had no idea how to contact her. No clue where she went so he could "run into" her. But that was insane.

"Well, I do know where she lives," Thane offered up, pointing his bottle at Talin across from him.

"Oh *no*. No, no, no. Absolutely not, Thane Lycus. You will not act like an insane person and go to her house. If you thought she was panicking last night, just imagine the level of panic she'd feel if you showed up on her doorstep out of nowhere." Talin was sitting straight up, his gaze completely sobered and void of his earlier amusement.

Thane raised his hands in surrender. "I know, I know. I don't know why I said that. I just feel so weird, you know?"

The look on Talin's face remained wary as he relaxed a little, like he was still assessing Thane's level of sanity. "Um, no, I don't know, actually. I'm still living the blissful bachelor life, so this is a foreign language to me." Talin smirked, and Thane thought he saw a flash of sadness on his friend's face before it disappeared completely. He shook it off, thinking he must have imagined it.

"It's like my instincts are roaring at me, telling me to focus on one thing: Cordelia, and Cordelia alone. But my brain is telling me to calm the fuck down and take it easy. I don't want to let this take over my ability to reason. But fuck, man, it's like a battle inside me, pulling me in two different directions." Thane groaned, running a hand down his face.

"Well, the only advice I have is to stay *the fuck* away from her and just wait for her to text you. Anything else makes you a crazy person, and you don't need that on top of all the other terrible qualities you possess." He snickered, clearly proud of himself for that one. "Why don't you just keep yourself busy, do something with yourself. Oh! You could just rub one out, that might calm you the fuck down." Talin quirked his brow at him, pointing his bottle at Thane like he was completely serious. And knowing Talin, he probably was.

Thane just stared at him, not even dignifying that with a response.

Talin perked up at that, his eyes blowing wide as a laugh escaped him again. "You already did, didn't you? You totally did, you little slut." Talin barked a loud laugh this time, his eyes dancing.

"OK, I think we're done talking about this." Thane stood up, taking one last swig from his bottle before snatching Talin's out of his hand and carrying both to the kitchen to dump them in the trash.

"Hey! I wasn't finished with that!" Talin whined, jumping up from the couch.

"Do I look like I give a shit?" Thane crossed his arms and leveled him with a look that said *fuck off.*

Talin shoved his hands into the pockets of his navy athletic shorts, a grin still plastered to his face. "I just don't want to see you fuck this up, Thane. You deserve happiness."

With a sigh, Thane uncrossed his arms and ran a hand through his hair. "Yeah, well, I'm trying. I promise I won't do anything crazy. I want this to work."

Talin smiled at that, a genuine smile. "Good. I'm tired of dealing with your mopey bullshit. You need to seriously get some sunshine up your ass before you wither away from that permanent frown on your face."

Thane cut him a look. "Is that supposed to be helpful?"

Talin shrugged as he turned toward the front door. "Dunno. But there it is. Take my sage wisdom and marinate on it, wolfy." Talin laughed at his own joke as he opened the door, making his way out. "And seriously, stop ignoring your dad's calls. He just wants to talk, Thane." This was the same speech Talin always gave him. Talin know how hard a time Thane had with his dad, and always reminded him that he needed to patch it up.

"One thing at a time, Talin." Thane gave a quick wave goodbye as he shut the door.

Thane knew he was a stubborn asshole. Knew he had to get out of his rut, his old habits. But there would be no changing him overnight. He could take this one step at a time, but they would be reluctant ones. He wasn't sure when he would be able to face his father again. Not after everything that'd happened. And that was years ago, years that had gone by not seeing his mother, his father. Not knowing their love and laughter in his life. He hadn't been back to his childhood home since that day either.

Would he ever go back?

As he was trying not to let the dread of that thought win, his phone lit up with a message from Talin.

> Talin: And hey, congratulations you psycho :)

Taking a deep breath Thane typed back.

Thane: Yeah, I sure hope so.

CHAPTER TEN

CORDELIA

Oh, fuck. It just kept replaying over and over in Cordelia's head.

Oh Goddess. That had actually happened.

Her head was swimming, struggling to keep up with the series of events from the night before.

She had recapped it to herself repeatedly. She had gone on a date with Lilith and walked out of it without Lilith but, instead, with a fated. A wolf shifter fated named Thane. Who was very possessive, growly, and ready to jump into this headfirst.

Cordelia, however, was not. And she desperately needed a cup of tea.

Standing in the moonlight filtering in from the arched window above the sink, she stared into the night sky. The stars that framed the moon twinkled like little beacons. As the stars blinked in and out of sight, their lights creating a soft glow around her, she couldn't help but let her mind wander.

She wondered if some of the exhaustion she felt was a lingering aftereffect of her mother's magic. Lydia Halloway's magic had always been powerful, and it usually left Cordelia feeling drained, exhausted beyond reason, when she was the lucky recipient of that magic's attention.

Interacting with Lydia Halloway was a feat in and of itself. And after talking with her mother just the other day, Cordelia was left feeling like a husk of herself. Numbly drifting through her days and hoping for some reprieve from the void where her energy should be. She always felt better after plenty of rest and the help of some spells she'd found over the years.

But the dream she'd had right before her mother called her felt ominous and pulled her right back into the reality she didn't want to acknowledge. She tried not to think of Halloway Manor. The vivid memories of her time there tucked away in the furthest corners of her mind. They had a way of pulling her under, trapping her in their depths.

Shivering from the thought, she started filling the kettle, looking into the face of the moon above her. She could feel the magic it radiated, the sweet siren song it called out each night. The upcoming full moon would be a powerful one. One filled with change, creativity, and powerful manifestation.

Cordelia would need to make a trip to Sage's shop. Her various supplies had been dwindling for a little while now, and it was time for a big trip again. She needed some restocks for her spell work, but she also needed some things for her own personal practice.

Plus, she hadn't seen Sage in a while. It would be nice to see a friendly face again, someone she could confide in and someone who brought her great comfort. Someone she could always lean on.

Sage had taken her in when she was a young witch seeking refuge from Halloway Manor. And for that, Cordelia would always be grateful.

Once Cordelia made it to Sage's shop the next morning, she pushed open the old door, the dark, rich wood heavy under her hands. As she entered, the bell above the door rang out a light tinkling sound above her. She was so excited to be back at Mystic Moon Apothecary. Sage was always the person she could trust and go to for anything, and she never failed to put Cordelia in a good mood.

The shop smelled like incense smoke and damp earth. The dark wood paneling of the walls and ever-present candlelight threw deep shadows and set the shop's offerings aglow.

Old wood tables and pedestals scattered across the floor of the shop offered space for the various items and treasures to present themselves to customers. Handwoven tapestries and various prints and paintings littered the walls around the shop, adding such unique character, energy, and designs to the riot of muted colors surrounding Cordelia.

Crystals were stacked on tables left and right. Candles both for sale and in use were littered around the various surfaces, anywhere Sage could tuck them away. Bundles of incense sticks, cones, and pots of loose incense were displayed on the shelves on the left side of the shop. You could find just about any scent you were looking for, any energy that you were looking to channel, to cleanse your home with. Altar tools and decorations were scattered around the right side of the shop. Baskets full of altar cloths, stacks of carefully curated tarot and oracle decks, dried and fresh herbs, salt, cauldrons, matches, bells, and chalices all greeted her.

Sage sat bundled in her colorful shawl next to the counter at the front of the store. Her dark brown hair was loose, the golden streaks that ran through it shining in the candlelight. She was a short, spindly woman that was so full of life and love. Cordelia felt her admiration for the strong, kind woman grow every day. To know Sage, to have Sage in her life—it was something Cordelia would always hold dear.

Sitting back in a squeaky wooden rocking chair, Sage had her feet propped on a red, padded stool in front of her, a romance book in her hands, and not a care in the world. Sage looked up from her book, letting her eyes adjust to the light now streaming in behind Cordelia.

Sage kept the windows tinted so the sun wasn't so bright. She always said she loved the soft atmosphere and the way the shadows from the candles cast a cozy glow across the space. Cordelia had to admit that it added a certain charm to the storied shop.

"Cordelia, my girl! I was beginning to wonder if you'd forgotten me. Cast me away now that you're a big, bad witch who doesn't need a little old shop owner like me." Sage had a taste for dramatics and was constantly reminding everyone of it. Cordelia rolled her eyes and chuckled.

"Of course not. First of all, I am *not* a 'big, bad witch.' And second of all, I could never forget you, Sage. Who else can I practically steal candles from with the discount you give me?" Cordelia laughed.

"Ah, but you see, it keeps you coming back and spending more money at my shop. So really, in the long run, I'm still profiting off you, girl." She winked, the usual glimmer of amusement in her vibrant green eyes. "So what can I help you with today, Cordelia?" Sage stood from her spot on the chair, letting her book thud against the surface of the front counter.

"I'm just here to pick up some things for my customers. Plus I need a few things of my own, especially with the full moon tomorrow."

"Anything special you need?"

Cordelia always knew whatever she needed, she could either find it in Sage's shop or Sage could find it elsewhere for her. She was like a second mother to Cordelia, the one she'd always wanted.

"Not today, I just need some of the essentials."

"Well, you know where to find me if you need anything." She waved Cordelia off as she returned to her chair, picking up her book again.

Cordelia wandered around the little shop, basket in hand, grabbing things left and right as she spotted what she'd come for, and a couple things she didn't *necessarily* need.

A handful of new crystals for her altar, some incense to cleanse her space with, and a few other odds and ends. Once she had everything for her customers and herself, she headed to the front counter, lugging the heavy basket alongside her.

Swinging it up onto the worn, wooden counter, she sighed in

relief. Hearing Sage pull herself from her cozy corner, she glanced around at the shop she'd been in countless times.

The ornate carvings in the counter were always so captivating. She felt like she saw something new every time she looked at it. The candles scattered around the surface of the counter and the windowsill were candles of all different shapes, colors, and heights. Some dripped candle wax on top of old drips, some were fresh, ready to give all the life they could. Some were placed in salt-filled jars, some were held in antique candleholders. Some were just placed randomly on plates, in bowls, or various other random surfaces Sage could find.

Sage smiled brightly at the array of items Cordelia had spread over the counter, ready to be sorted and totaled.

"Quite the basket load today, girl." Sage chuckled.

"I swear you know when I'm coming and put out all of your good stuff." Cordelia waggled a finger at Sage, amusement dancing across both of the women's faces.

"And you'll never be able to prove it. It's best you just let the universe guide you, especially if it guides you into my shop. You know I love to see you, not just as a customer."

"I promise I'll stop in more often. The past couple days have just been a whirlwind. And I've been dealing with the infamous attitude of Lydia Halloway." Cordelia rolled her eyes at the last part.

Sage knew all too well what Cordelia's mother was like. She scoffed, "You can handle her, Cordelia. Just remember who *you* are and don't let her mess with that."

Cordelia shrugged at that. "You're always right, Sage."

Leaning against the counter, Sage narrowed her eyes and said, "Something else is bothering you. C'mon, out with it. I can smell the indecision brewing in that head of yours."

CHAPTER ELEVEN

CORDELIA

Sometimes Sage was just too observant. Cordelia both loved and hated it, it just depended on if that observance was aimed at her or not. And whether it was something she wanted to keep to herself.

Sighing, Cordelia knew it was a lost cause to try to brush this subject off. Sage would just pry it out of her.

"It's complicated," she started, not knowing where to go. Not knowing how Sage would react.

The entire situation with Thane and Lilith was still so fresh, so confusing, and Cordelia had barely been able to work it all out for herself, let alone get ready to explain it to someone else.

"Darling, life itself is complicated. Now out with it, you know I won't let you blow this off, whatever it is." She quirked a brow, leveling Cordelia with a look that she recognized. Sage was serious about this, she wasn't going to let it go.

"Alright, alright. Can we at least take a seat?" Cordelia couldn't meet Sage's eyes. She was already sweating from the discomfort of the long story she was about to tell.

Sage swept out from behind the counter, quickly snapping her fingers to flip the Open sign on the front door to Closed and throw the lock. With another flick of her wrist, she put wards in place, wards to keep them safe from prying eyes and ears. It wasn't likely anyone was truly listening in, but Sage liked to toss in just-in-case measures any time they had their serious conversations.

"Sit, sit, while I make us some tea!" Sage threw over her shoulder as she rushed past Cordelia, making her way to the back of her store.

Sage kept a little office tucked away in the corner of her storage room. The dust motes and spiders made a home for themselves there among her cluttered desk. On top of the old spell jars, half-burned incense, and all sorts of knickknacks, she also happened to keep a kettle and cabinet of teas back there. One could always count on Sage to have tea nearby and ready.

A few minutes later, Sage emerged with two teacups floating on a phantom wind beside her and an enchanted teapot pouring the tea, waves of steam floating around the entire display of magic.

She was always a flurry of soft, billowing skirts and rich laughter, floating through rooms and showing off her little tricks with the enchantment magic she loved so dearly. It was part of her charm, part of what drew everyone to her so innately. Sage loved her magic, loved the whimsy and joy she got from it. So the floating teacups were more for Sage's own enjoyment than anything else.

The teacups settled on the table between them, both women sitting in the old, carved wooden chairs on either end. Cordelia fiddled with her hands in her lap, twisted her moonstone bracelet around her wrist as she lost herself in thought. The curling tendrils of peppermint-scented steam rose above the cups, creating a warm cocoon of comfort around the two witches.

"Now, dear Cordelia, tell me what's bothering you."

Cordelia lifted her head, meeting Sage's gentle eyes. "Well, I guess we can start with the fact that I finally went on a date with Lilith." The breath whooshed out of Cordelia as she started to let this weight off her chest.

She'd told Sage about Lilith so many times now, and every

conversation about Lilith ended with Sage pestering Cordelia to ask her out already.

Sage let out a high squeal. "Oh, Cordelia, my girl! That's wonderful!" Hands clasped together, she beamed. "And how did it go?"

"Not good. Not at all." Glancing away, she wasn't sure where to begin explaining.

"Oh?" Sage tilted her head, confusion spreading over her features. "How so?"

With a deep breath, Cordelia launched into the story. Telling Sage all about how wonderfully the date had started, how entranced she was with Lilith, and then diving into how it all changed when she met those obsidian eyes across the room. Being pulled toward one another, losing sight of everything around them, because nothing else mattered any longer. Meeting Thane. Then the inevitable breakdown she'd had once he'd left and she'd woken up confused and anxious. The reality of her situation crashing down around her, suffocating her in a decision she felt wasn't hers. A decision to be with someone not of her own choosing.

"Darling girl." Sage's eyes softened, her hands reaching across the table for Cordelia's. Cordelia instinctively raised them and met Sage's hands halfway, seeking the comfort her embrace offered.

"It sounds like you've been a busy little witch." Sage gave her a gentle smile. "And I can see how this weighs on you. Have you consulted your cards?"

"No. My mind felt too cluttered, too scattered to touch my cards. I wanted to clear my head a bit before I even touched them. I didn't want my desperation to come out in my reading."

"Ah, well, let me give you some advice, then. Trust yourself. Trust your magic. How did you feel when you met Thane? Fated bonds can be very powerful, but our magic as witches can often guide us in the right direction." Sage leaned back, waiting for Cordelia's response as she took a long sip of her tea.

Cordelia didn't know much about how shifter and witch magic interacted, and especially when it came to a fated bond between the two. She did know, though, that witches had magic running through their bodies at all times. And that they were closely attuned to it and had a much more precise grasp of it because they regularly practiced a very potent form through their spells. Magic was woven into their very beings—always protecting and guiding them. Apparently, it applied to navigating fated bonds too.

She might not know a lot about shifters, but she did know they were a lot more intense when it came to fated bonds. Or really just their existence in general. And it came down to them being more passionate—in life, love, the depth of their emotions. Cordelia could relate to that, to feeling everything so damned deeply.

"Well, I was mostly conflicted and confused. I don't really kn—"

"No, no, dear. What did you *feel*? Right here." Sage let go of Cordelia's hands to let her own point to her heart and rest on her stomach. "Dig deep. Follow your instincts."

Cordelia took a moment, blinking at the realization that came to her. "Well, I suppose I felt content. Drawn, even. Drawn to him, drawn to the feeling in my gut. Almost like comfort, but more than that." Cordelia struggled to find the right words, to describe that intense feeling.

"Home." Sage smiled, true joy written across her face. "You felt home, my girl. Your magic felt it too."

Cordelia paused at that. "So what does that mean?"

"Well, for starters, it means that you can probably stop being so damned dramatic about it. I can feel the exhaustion pouring out of you. You need to rest and restore your magic." Sage tsked at her, waving her hand and pouring Cordelia another cup of tea. "Now drink up, don't let it get cold."

Cordelia laughed, picking up the refilled teacup.

"Then, you can pull yourself together and think about what you want. I know it's heartbreaking that Lilith isn't your future. I was so excited about the two of you. But the Goddesses are leading you elsewhere. I can feel the energy thrumming from you, from the story you've told. I think this will be a good thing, my girl." Sage's eyes were alight with wonder, delight. Cordelia couldn't help but feel comforted by that.

"But what if this isn't what I want? What if it's something I have to leave behind?" Cordelia asked quietly, terrified of finally voicing the thought that had been haunting her all day yesterday and into this morning. What if this didn't bring her the happiness she hoped it would?

"Then you leave it behind. You come back to me and we work it out. You know I'll stand behind you no matter what. Your happiness should always come first. You won't allow anyone to take that from you, fated or not. Not with the strength I see in you, that I know you possess."

Cordelia swelled with pride. Sage's belief in her was dripping with love, adoration, absolutely potent with it. It made Cordelia feel those things within herself, deeply rooted.

"You're right." She stood, rushing to Sage around the table. Sage pushed out of her chair and met Cordelia's embrace with one just as big.

"My darling girl. You have such immense power and strength, don't let a little doubt and worry cloud that brilliant mind of yours," Sage whispered against Cordelia's head as she stroked her hair, providing Cordelia with the comfort she'd come to know and love from Sage, a deep settling within her soul.

Sage pulled back. "Now, go. Make sure you speak with him, and soon, Cordelia. Put that poor little wolf out of his misery." She pouted playfully, her bottom lip jutting out in mock sadness.

"How did you know he's a shifter?" Cordelia stared at her in awe and confusion.

"Oh, give me more credit, my girl. I'm an old witch with many tricks." She winked as she floated past to the counter, gathering Cordelia's purchases and shuffling her out the door.

Cordelia chuckled at Sage, grabbing her things as she went.

"And I can smell his scent on you. I've been around enough shifters to know the difference, and I can smell his scent trying to merge with yours. It's part of the shifter fated bond."

Cordelia stared at Sage, at a complete loss for words. She had no idea how Sage knew so much about the shifters, especially the shifter's fated bonds. But that felt like a longer conversation for another time.

"I promise I'll talk to him. Wouldn't want him to miss me too much, huh?"

Sage laughed, full and deep. "You sound more and more like me every day."

Cordelia beamed at that. Good. She wanted to be an Ashcraft far more than she wanted to be a Halloway.

CHAPTER TWELVE

CORDELIA

Taking a deep breath and closing her eyes, Cordelia stood at the back door leading out to her garden the next night. She let the sunlight bathe her skin in pools of gold, pulling her magic up, right under the surface of her skin where it practically crackled with excitement.

The full moon was close, and with it she would welcome in new energy. This full moon, the Pink Moon, would be powerful, and it signaled a time of reflection. Cordelia had already mapped out tonight's rituals and knew what she would seek from the Moon Goddess, Selene.

With all of the items she'd picked so intentionally, she headed outside. Passing through the carefully curated rows of her garden, she wove her way around her various herbs and flowers until she found the spot calling to her magic.

She laid out a pale linen blanket, her oracle deck directly in front of her, a few candles surrounding the blanket, and a notebook for her intentions. The pen she'd brought had been charged with her moon water from the last full moon and infused with lavender oil, ready to help her bring her intentions to fruition.

As the soft breeze full of the smell of fresh pollen floated through her hair, caressing her cheeks and arms, she let her eyes close. The cool days had slowly been warming, and with it, Cordelia's magic was sparking even brighter. She always did love this season, even though she felt more content and calm in the cold, and her magic seemed to agree. Still, the spring brought a surge of renewal to her magic, brought so much beauty to the world around her. It set her heart on fire.

Once the moon was high enough in the sky for Cordelia's liking and the light from the sun had been thoroughly chased away by darkness, Cordelia stood before her garden.

She'd spent her time inside preparing for the full moon, bathing in a salt blend made specifically for tonight, cleansing her home with incense, sweet and fragrant, and lighting a few candles Sage had crafted.

She wore nothing on her feet, nothing between her and the earth of her home. As she took her first step into the garden, she was immediately grounded by the soft soil beneath her skin.

Slowly making her way toward her makeshift altar, Cordelia let herself soak up the light of the moon. Though it was still hidden behind smoky clouds, the glow bounced off the sky and reflected onto the world around her, bright and warm. The sheer sleeves of her robe draped at her sides, sweeping across the clovers and grass beneath her feet as she basked in the magic radiating everywhere.

The opulent robe was long, trailing behind her in frothy waves. Sheer, black fabric poured off her skin like shadows, pooling at her feet and leaving a wake behind her. The moonlight bounced off the delicate, deep gold stitching on the edges and seemed to illuminate it, like little rivers of starlight.

Underneath the robe, Cordelia wore nothing at all. It accentuated the raw beauty of the curves, rolls, and dips that made up the alluring witch she was.

Feeling so close and connected with her magic, so potent and rich with her pale skin reflecting the moonlight, was like nothing else.

As she reached the blanket, now silvery under the night sky, Cordelia gently fell to her knees, thighs resting against her feet and hands on her thighs. She started with centering herself.

Inhale, hold, exhale, hold. Repeat.

Over and over until her body relaxed, loosening the tension from her shoulders to her toes, grounding herself. Once she felt centered, she raised her left hand, snapping her fingers as she glanced at the moon above her.

All at once, the candles surrounding her lit, the flames casting flickering light over the garden floor. Smiling to herself, Cordelia got to work on her cards. She lowered her hand, held out two fingers, and flicked them up. The cards lifted and floated to her on a cool, dark breeze before they settled into her now-upturned palm.

While she loved using her magic like this, in short little tricks, she preferred shuffling the cards in her hands. Feeling the magic seep into the cards themselves and vibrate with purpose, energy, and intent. And every reading was different. Sometimes her intended card popped out of the deck, sometimes it felt like flames licking against her fingers as she shuffled, and sometimes her intuition just told her to stop shuffling and draw.

A calmness settled into her body, signaling it was time to draw. She'd brought her first question to the forefront of her mind as soon as she'd started shuffling, and now she knew the cards were ready to answer.

Lilith. How would her relationship with Lilith survive?

Settling her hand on top of the deck, she drew, flipping the card over onto the blanket.

A great egg butterfly faced Cordelia, greeting her with sweet reassurance.

Transformation. She knew immediately that it was a transformation of love. Not romantic, but instead, platonic. And powerful. She would have a relationship with Lilith, a beautiful one, at that. Just something different than either of them had initially pictured.

A deep satisfaction took root. She set the card aside, quickly journaling the intuitive message.

Picking the deck back up, she repeated the process, shuffling with one intention in mind.

Thane. Would she be safe with him? Would they work together?

Cordelia hadn't had the heart to voice the questions swirling inside of her. Not even to herself. She'd barely been able to admit it to Sage, and even then, she'd skirted around the depth of her doubts. Cordelia felt that calmness overcome her again. She stopped her shuffling and drew the top card, flipping it over.

A bright lavender sprig smiled up at her. Another card of love, but this one sweeter, deeper, more connected to her soul.

Her life was cluttered with lavender. In her coffee, in her dreams, in her favorite things, in her magic. It was simply woven into who she was. And now, she felt Thane was meant to be the same. Meant to be with her on the deepest level. An equal part of her that she could no longer deny. Woven into her.

A powerful warmth flooded her senses, her hand flying to grip her chest above her heart. She caught her breath, hearing a soft laugh escape her lips. The rightness she felt was so endless, so filled with love. She could hardly believe that she'd had any doubts. Could barely believe it, even though they had been very real just moments before. It was as if she were wrapped in a lavender smoke. Drifting and caressing, holding her heart and soul in its safe embrace.

As she was falling into the embrace of the lavender pull, everything around her lit with a bright, glowing light. The moon had emerged from the clouds, casting the world in an ethereal glow and bathing her in its magic. Her body seemed to hum under the rejuvenating charge.

Cordelia felt like her soul might burst from her body as pure, raw magic flowed through her. The magic of the cards, her intuition set on fire, and the allure of the ritual all worked in tandem to create a euphoria within her. Reaching for the cards again, Cordelia snatched her hand back when she noticed she was actually *glowing*.

Brighter than she had ever seen it before, her magic was a thing to behold as it set her alight. Her magic always had a way of making her glow when it rose up, but never like this.

Like silver was forged and writhing under her skin, rivers of bright, thrumming light danced along her body, seeming to live within her. But she couldn't bring herself to feel unsettled. In fact, she felt as if it was right. Like that was where it belonged.

Grabbing the deck one last time, Cordelia shuffled with her final intention. This one sinking in her stomach like a stone. A stone heavy enough to crush her under the weight of the dread it inspired.

My mother. How can I rid myself of her cruelty and malice?

She didn't shuffle long before she felt the hot press of her intended card, stopping her movements. Drawing the card, she flipped it quickly, wanting to get this over with.

Facing her was the mustard seed card. Courage.

It offered courage, yes, but also protection and endurance. The courage to stand up to her mother wasn't anything new. She had been working on that for years now. But endurance? Protection? For what?

She didn't have an immediate reaction inside of her beyond the sense of something ominous. She shivered, hoping she could shake it off. Whatever it was, she could think about it later. For now, she wanted to continue to bask in the glow of her lavender card.

As if a phantom hand reached out and offered her comfort, a cool breeze caressed her cheek. She leaned into it instinctively, relishing the strength she found there.

She flicked her wrist, and the flames immediately extinguished, wisps of smoke curling into the darkness around her. Standing, she stepped off the linen blanket, her feet softly pressing into the earth beneath her.

With another flick of her wrist, she motioned toward the open back door, commanding everything to float back into the house.

The last oracle card floated in front of her, the rest already in her hand. She plucked it out of the air and returned it to the deck. To disperse the energy of her reading, Cordelia reshuffled the cards, preferring to do so after each use. As she shuffled, she started walking toward the house. The energy of the moon and the ritual had charged her but brought exhaustion in their wake. She would need plenty of sleep to restore the balance of energy her magic had drained.

As she finished shuffling, a card popped out of the deck, fluttering to the ground in front of her.

"Oh!" She bent to collect it and found the flame card face up. Something rooted itself inside of her. Deep. Something profound, but she couldn't put her finger on it.

A different, but equally welcome warmth blazed inside of her, bringing a wave of calm, of steady strength and reassurance. Shaking her head, she tried to dispel it from her thoughts. It was just an errant card from not paying close attention to her shuffling, from letting her mind wander.

She made her way inside, her head filled with images of a soft, blazing fire and lavender smoke.

CHAPTER THIRTEEN

CORDELIA

Hands sweating, gripping her keys in one hand and the shoulder strap of her bag in the other, Cordelia stared at the front door of Quartz Coffee. She could do this. She could definitely do this. And she had to do this.

Cordelia felt like she might just turn into a statue, standing there until she actually petrified and haunted the doorstep, forever warning others of her sad tale. Warning them to avoid the same fate. The fate of a pathetic, socially uncomfortable witch who couldn't face her own fears. Or, at least, warn them to handle their problems and maybe not be nearly as dramatic as she was.

Pushing herself from where she was frozen to the ground, Cordelia pulled some of her magic to the surface, bringing herself comfort from its presence and gathering some courage, almost like it was armor.

The air of the coffee shop whooshed around her as she pulled open the door. The aroma of fresh coffee grounds and roses, the sound of the machines whirring, and the chatter of customers surrounded her instantly.

She instinctively relaxed, the familiarity of the space conjuring feelings of ease and comfort. Just as suddenly, she remembered why she was there, and the dread settled into her stomach like a brick again.

It was like she wasn't even aware of what she was doing, automatically making her way to the counter to order her usual. She searched for a glimpse of Lilith's moonlit hair and found it almost instantly, the brilliant white gleaming in the sunlight streaming through the shop windows.

Cordelia's breath caught in her throat. This was someone she'd been so excited to see every day, someone she'd been so hoping for a future with. But those dreams had been dashed, and Cordelia couldn't help but mourn what could have been.

"Iced lavender latte with oat milk for Cordelia!" one of the baristas called out.

She made her way to the counter and mumbled her thanks before making her way over to her usual table, her head down. If Lilith hadn't already known Cordelia was there, she definitely did now.

Cordelia slipped into one of the chairs at the corner table. She couldn't calm her racing thoughts, her heart that felt like it was going to beat out of her chest, and the anxiety that was quickly spiraling out of control with the amount of what-ifs floating around in her head.

Suddenly, she heard her name, and very close.

"Cordelia," the voice called again.

Snapping her head up, she stared blankly at Lilith. She hadn't even heard her come over, hadn't heard her pull out a chair and sit down.

"You OK? You look like you've seen a ghost." Lilith furrowed her brow, looking at Cordelia like she was a puzzle Lilith was trying to solve.

"Uh, yeah, hi, Lilith. So sorry, I didn't realize you were there." Cordelia chuckled, tucking her hair behind her ear, trying to ease the tension and get her thoughts in working order.

"Yeah, you looked like you were deep in thought over here.

Thought I'd come see if you were alright. I haven't seen you here in a little while. Not since . . ." Lilith trailed off, not finishing the sentence that both of them were filling in in their heads.

Not since the disastrous date they had the other night. Not since Thane. Not since Lilith spared Cordelia a sad parting glance before she darted out of the restaurant. Not since Cordelia's entire world had been turned upside down.

"Yeah, about that. I wanted to talk. Do you have time to meet sometime this week?" Cordelia was so hopeful they could work it out.

"I have time now. My shift just ended, so I'm all yours." Lilith leaned back in her chair, looking expectant. The seemingly innocent statement made her heart clench.

But you aren't mine, are you?

Cordelia felt like her heart might leap out of her chest at any moment. This was it.

"I just wanted to apologize. For everything that happened the other night. None of it was fair to you, and I honestly wasn't sure how to react." She tried not to let her voice waver.

"Oh, Cordelia. I know it's not your fault." Lilith gave her such a soft, affectionate but sad smile.

Cordelia could see the adoration and heartbreak all at once in her expression. Could see the possibilities of what could have been and the deep sadness of losing it. All in that one look from Lilith.

But she didn't feel like she was deserving of that affection. Not after what'd happened. Not when she had amends to make.

"That doesn't make it OK. I feel so guilty for all of this happening, and I don't know what to do. With myself, with us, anything. I don't know how to make this right." Cordelia couldn't help the sadness that laced every word.

And that was the truth. While she had gained so much clarity from her reading under the full moon, felt so much excitement at the messages the cards had given her about Thane and Lilith, she also knew that it all hinged on her own actions. On actually carrying out what needed to be done to make those readings come true.

And regardless of that reading, Cordelia still harbored guilt. Over the fated bond, over it not being with Lilith, over the heartbroken look on Lilith's face as she left Cordelia standing in that busy restaurant. As she left behind the remnants of their what-ifs.

They may have gone on a total of one date, and they didn't even finish it. But Cordelia knew that she had fantasized so many times about what being with Lilith would be like. Knew those same thoughts had clouded Lilith's head when she'd looked into her eyes that night. Cordelia had seen the excitement and the sparkle of hope in her eyes.

She couldn't bring herself to be sorry she met Thane. Couldn't bring herself to regret what linked them. But she could be sorry that she and Lilith would never be what they both had hoped. She could still mourn the lost potential. The heartbreak she'd caused both of them.

"There's nothing to feel guilty about. What could you have possibly done differently, Cordelia?" Lilith leaned forward. "I picked the restaurant, not you. You didn't ask for this fated bond, the Goddesses gave it to you. Fate brought Thane there that night. There's nothing you could've done to prevent it." Lilith gave her a soft smile.

"But—"

"Cordelia, that's what was supposed to happen. It's what the Goddesses wanted, and it's not something we can change. It was meant to be."

"I suppose you're right." She hadn't thought of it that way.

In all of her sulking the past few days, she hadn't thought about the fact that it was actually fate. Everything had aligned just so, so that Cordelia would meet Thane. And she supposed she could be grateful for that, knew she would be one day. Her only regret, only hesitation, was that it came at the cost of another's happiness.

Cordelia returned Lilith's soft, bittersweet smile. "You're right."

She took a deep breath, feeling her body settle. Feeling herself accept what happened and let it root inside of her.

"As long as it's something you want and it's something you're choosing." Lilith paused. "Is this something that you want? With Thane?" She looked into Cordelia's eyes, searching for that reassurance that she was certain, that she wasn't being pressured. It softened something in Cordelia, knowing that Lilith cared.

"Yes, I think so," Cordelia breathed out, certainty flooding her at the thought of Thane. "It's something I want to explore. I want to see if this can work, and I think it will." She smiled at that, at the confidence she felt in her intuition.

The same intuition that was pulling her toward Thane, toward the possibilities a future with him might hold.

"At the risk of sounding cliché, can we still be friends?" Cordelia asked, hope sparking in her chest.

She didn't want to lose Lilith, as selfish as that might sound. They may not be a fated match, but she felt so connected to her. She couldn't just let her go.

Lilith beamed. "I hoped you would ask that."

Cordelia laughed, feeling her chest loosen, her body relaxing and releasing the tension it had been holding on to all day. She was relieved, to say the least.

Relief of her own shone in Lilith's indigo eyes. Cordelia took a sip of her coffee, letting herself settle into the joy overtaking her body.

"I guess no more flirting with you every day, huh?" Lilith chuckled. "Now that you have that possessive fated of yours."

"Well, he's not officially my fated. I haven't even spoken to him since that night."

"Really?" Lilith stared, a little shocked. "I would think he'd be going crazy over you by now. He's a wolf shifter, right? The wolven don't seem to be a particularly patient bunch."

"How did you know he was wolven?" Cordelia was a little surprised. She knew she'd clocked it, but she chalked it up to being his fated and being tapped into him through the bond, somehow.

"Well, I guessed. That man went from zero to possessive in point five seconds." Lilith laughed, and Cordelia couldn't help but join in. It was so nice to just laugh together, to feel so weightless with Lilith after all they'd gone through the past several days.

"Uh, yeah. He was intense, to say the least." Cordelia scratched the back of her neck, not sure what to do about that.

She knew she'd told Thane they needed to take things slow, but she also knew how impatient the wolven were known for being. How possessive they could be. She had a feeling nothing about their relationship would be normal. But she would be damned if she didn't try to rein him in. She deserved a little time to adjust, to take it all in.

"I don't think *intense* is quite the word to describe it, but we can start there." Lilith laughed, leaning back in her chair again. "You two need to talk. Unless, of course, you're afraid to?" Lilith crossed her arms, quirking her brow at Cordelia like she was genuinely concerned.

"Oh, no. I'm not afraid of Thane. I just haven't talked to him, yet." Cordelia shrugged, trying to keep the nerves at bay, to let herself soak up this happiness for a little while longer.

"You haven't talked? Didn't you two exchange numbers?"

"Well, kind of. He gave me his, but he didn't get mine, and I haven't worked up the courage to text him yet." Cordelia was nervous. She wasn't entirely sure why, but she felt like talking to Thane again would solidify things, make them more real. And that thought scared her a little.

"Oh, please put that poor boy out of his misery, Cordelia. I'm sure he's about to drive himself up the walls worried about you. His poor little puppy hormones are probably driving him insane." Lilith mockingly pouted.

Cordelia laughed and agreed. She would need to text Thane, but that could wait. She wanted to soak up some time with Lilith, her newfound friend.

It was bittersweet to lose their what-ifs, but she was so looking forward to the friendship she could feel forming between them. Was practically bubbling over with excitement about the deep feeling of *right* settling deep inside her.

CHAPTER FOURTEEN

THANE

I t had been days. *Days* of waiting for Cordelia to make any sort of contact. The first day he'd thought he might go insane from the sheer number of times he'd checked his phone. Then he'd forced himself to put it down and eventually turn it off.

It had felt like a small eternity. Every day chipping away at his patience.

He just needed to escape the constant cycle of wondering where she was, what she was doing, when he would see her again. It was nauseating, even to himself.

"Eyes up here, Lycus!" Talin shouted.

Talin had unilaterally decided that Thane needed to get his stagnant energy out, in the form of an intense workout. They'd been here for close to two hours, and at this point, it felt like Talin would never tire.

"Can you please chill the fuck out for one second?" Thane shot him a glare.

His temper had an especially short fuse lately. Ever since he'd found his fated.

Cordelia.

Goddess, he needed to get a hold of himself. He felt like a pup chasing after a crush. Except, this was far more than just a crush.

He had a chance of regaining sanity if he could just hear *something* from her. And soon, he hoped.

"Oh, stop whining and get back to your reps, Thane. I didn't bring you here to listen to you whine. Now give me fifteen." Talin wasn't having any of Thane's warnings.

Fated bonded wolves could be incredibly volatile, aggressive even, which Talin well knew. They were vicious when it came to defending and protecting their fated, in their drive to claim their fated. It was an instinctual need.

Thane was pretty sure he was a strong, smart enough man to resist those urges, but only time would tell at this point. His patience was already wearing thin, and desperation was taking over.

That desperation meant his temper had slipped a few times in the past couple days. Talin had seen Thane's temper enough to know it was something to behold, but Talin had never given a shit about it before, why would he start now?

Thane huffed a laugh at the thought, rolling his eyes and grabbing the bar above him. Hefting the weight off the rack, Thane pushed himself into another set of bench presses.

With every rep, every push of the bar, Thane let out a deep grunt, his concentration zeroed in on the steel in his hands. The rough texture on the grips rubbed against his calluses.

The heavy weights Talin had loaded onto each side were a little more than Thane usually attempted, but his blood ran hot today. His strength was more than he could make sense of, larger than even himself. It had to be the fated bond.

Not only was his strength heightened right now, but so was his sense of his wolf. He could feel the shift pulling at him, had since the fated bond made itself known. His wolf was prowling just beneath the surface of his skin, growling and desperate to be let out. Desperate to run, for his own freedom.

"Fuck," Thane cursed, pushing the bar back up as Talin kept count of each rep.

Thane and his wolf were one and the same, but he was much stronger as a wolf, in more ways than one. Everything was heightened, all of his senses, his strength, and his clarity. Clarity about who he was and his purpose in the world. Except, Thane didn't like shifting anymore. Didn't like the ache in his bones that came with it.

Because every time, he could feel the call of the pack he'd lost, the life he lost. It hurt to know that he had failed, to know that he had lost the one thing he was born to do as a Lycus alpha.

When Thane finally was old and strong enough to take on his own pack, everything had seemed to click into place. His purpose, his passion, his drive, it was all there. It wasn't something his father had ever pressured him into. Wasn't something expected of him.

Deep down, he knew that. His father had told him as much countless times, and his mother echoed the same sentiment. Thane had wanted it on his own. He'd felt the call to it, his very blood sang at the idea of becoming an alpha and leading a pack of his own.

But a few years into actually leading his own pack, disaster had sent it all tumbling down. He'd lost his pack in the chaos, and with it, a key piece of himself was lost too.

He lost his sense of purpose, his sense of pride. And what did he do? Retreated into the shadows like the coward he truly was. That was the sickening part, the part that pissed him off the most. He'd let the fight be ripped out of him and slinked away to lick his wounds. Alone. That was the fate he'd assigned himself.

"Keep it up! I want five more—now!" Talin shouted, pushing Thane. And today, Thane could take it.

And now, here was this new hope, this new piece of Thane locking into place. With one look into those enchanting, lavender eyes, Thane found a home. Found a part of himself that he hadn't known even existed. He was having a hard time reconciling it, and reconciling with the part of himself that howled at the thought, howled for the claiming. It was a lot to take in.

Cut to the reason why Talin dragged Thane from his pathetic

wallowing. Thane had been holed up in his house since their talk days ago, working out in his basement until his body gave out, going on long, unrelenting runs, and sulking in his own misery when he wasn't doing either of the former. He'd had to take off work the entire time. Had to get himself under control before he could get back to normal. Whatever that even meant anymore.

Talin had come to check in on him and was immediately disappointed.

"You need to get your shit together, Lycus," he'd said, his arms crossed, glaring down at Thane on his spot on the couch.

And here they were, Talin pushing Thane harder and harder on the bench press in an attempt to calm him the fuck down.

Growling, Thane pushed hard, finishing his last rep and practically throwing the bar back on the rack.

He sat up, running his hands through his hair before reaching for his water bottle. Hoping the chilled water would cool him down, he took a long, deep drink, letting the ice water burn down his throat, a stark contrast to his heated skin.

He was dripping with sweat at this point, and he glanced over at Talin, who had the most outrageously smug look on his face.

"What?" Thane bit out.

"It's just so fun to see how hard I can push you right now." Talin chuckled. "You're so fucking strong, and you're hitting so many PRs, dude. It's insane and I love it." Talin pulled the weights off the bar, reracking them.

"Are you done trying to order me around, Talin?" Thane stood from the bench, stretching his arms.

"Yeah, for now. But no sulking anymore, got it? I don't want to see you that pathetic ever again. Seriously." Talin leveled Thane with a stern look.

"Got it. It's just—" Thane was cut off by a buzz in his pocket. Reaching in, he grabbed his phone and unlocked it.

His heart skipped a beat.

Unknown: Hey! I was wondering if you were free for dinner?
Unknown: Oh right, it's Cordelia

"What is it?" Talin whined. Celestials knew Talin was the most impatient person.

Thane didn't even have the time to roll his eyes at him.

"Cordelia. She texted me. She wants to get dinner." He couldn't pull his eyes away from the screen.

He was transfixed by those simple little words. By the way she acted so casual, like she knew him. He smiled to himself.

"Well, get in there, Lycus!" Talin whooped, playfully punching his shoulder. "Now you can stop being such a miserable bastard."

Thane couldn't stop smiling. Couldn't even think of a response. It felt like his blood cooled, his pulse stopped racing, his muscles relaxed. Everything inside him calmed at those two messages. Those few little sentences set him right again.

Holy shit. I'm going on a date with Cordelia.

CHAPTER FIFTEEN

THANE

Thane stared in the mirror in front of him, securing the buttons on the charcoal-gray sleeves of his button-down shirt.

He was wearing a pair of black cotton slacks, the black so deep it felt endless. Finishing off the moody look was a pair of sleek, black boots and a leather harness over his shoulders.

The harness was his favorite part. He loved it, loved the control and the sense of safety the harness gave him. He had them custom made and wore them whenever possible. Smirking to himself, he could only imagine the look on Cordelia's face when she saw it.

This particular harness was a soft, black leather that looped over his shoulders and converged into a Y shape at his back, connected to a strap that wrapped the entire way around his torso. He had a pretty large collection at this point, and they were a key piece of his style. He had them all outfitted with slots for various types of blades. Some were equipped for daggers, others for hunting knives, but every harness had several slots for throwing knives.

Thane liked the reassurance of knowing he was prepared at all times. Knowing that he could defend and protect those he loved. He'd had to do it before, and he'd been underprepared. But now he knew better. Now he was ready.

Tonight, though, Thane was going without his blades. He didn't want Cordelia feeling uncomfortable and didn't want to imagine the kind of impression it would give to be armed to the teeth on their first date. Still, the weight of the leather was a grounding comfort.

Taking a deep breath, Thane closed his eyes. Releasing the breath, he found his peace. His resolve. This is what he was meant to be doing. Everything was clicking into place now.

He pushed past every doubt and trepidation. All he could think about were those soft lavender eyes.

Before he knew it, Thane found himself knocking on Cordelia's front door.

"Oh, fuck!" she shouted inside.

He chuckled, apparently he had gotten here a little too on time.

"Merlin, Goddess damn it! Where are you? I need to make sure you know I love you before I leave!" She was yelling, apparently looking for the small ghost cat he'd met the last time he was here.

He grinned, remembering the amusement on her face when the little cat had scared him.

A minute later the door opened, and Cordelia stood in the doorway, practically glowing. The surprise of it stole his breath.

Wow. Thane could decipher it now, the force of her presence. It was her magic. He could feel it radiating off her in waves. Like she was *made* of it. This little witch was powerful. And he liked that.

"Thane! You're here!" She seemed distracted, and he could tell now that she was out of breath, her chest heaving a bit.

"You OK?" Thane quirked a brow at her, a smile tugging at the corners of his lips.

She was adorable like this. Trying to steady her breathing, clutching onto the door, her cheeks flushed and pink. An unbidden image of her underneath him with the same flush popped into his head.

Oh, I'd like to see that for myself. I'd like that a lot.

"Yeah, I just was running a little behind." She laughed, stepping over the threshold and pulling the door shut behind her.

She looked at him properly for the first time this evening and froze, then slowly traced a path from his feet to his eyes, locking her gaze with his, her eyes wide and cheeks flushing a deeper shade of pink.

"O-oh, you look s-so handsome tonight, Thane." She flushed again, her cheeks flaming red now.

He reached a hand out, gesturing for hers. He couldn't help the smirk that pulled at his lips. She was absolutely checking him out, and he didn't mind one bit.

"And you, Cordelia, are absolutely stunning." Taking her hand in his, he pulled her closer, letting his eyes run down her body as he did.

Stunning didn't even begin to describe her on an ordinary day, Thane suspected. But tonight, it really didn't apply. Tonight he was awestruck, mesmerized.

Her legs were covered in sheer black tights and black leather boots. She wore a deep burgundy satin slip dress, or at least skirt, as she had a loose black sweater layered on top. The gold around her neck and adorning her ears sparkled against her dark honey hair.

But the second he met Cordelia's eyes, everything around him disappeared. The wind stopped ruffling his hair, the world around him went silent. All he could see, all he could focus on, were those soft lavender eyes. The rivers of silver he now noticed that flowed through them like little lightning strikes that sparkled in the light.

A gasp came from his mouth, his jaw dropped, the tension he always held in his body melted away. Everything fell away except for her.

"Should we get going?" He could hear the gravel in his voice, could feel it swelling in his throat, constricting his air and sanity at the same time.

"So what do you have planned for us tonight, Thane?" She beamed.

He couldn't help the smile that grew on him. Couldn't help the eruption of relief, excitement he felt at her proximity. "I guess you'll just have to be patient." Keeping hold of her hand, Thane led her to the car and helped her inside.

Once they were on their way, she said, "Well, you're not kidnapping me, right? I'd hate to have to use my magic against you if you were." He could tell she was joking. She trusted him enough to get into his car, to agree to this date. To agree to speak to him at all.

He let out a snort. "I can assure you, I'm not. But I guess I can give you a hint. On a scale of one to ten, how OK are you with nature?"

When he glanced at her, his heart skipped a beat at the absolutely electric excitement in her expression.

CHAPTER SIXTEEN

CORDELIA

T hane had brought Cordelia to some sort of park, it seemed. It was already getting dark, but she could see there were walkways spread around the area they were in, illuminated by wrought iron lampposts. The golden glow from the lights cast warmth across the paths, setting the park aglow.

"Well now I'm really not convinced you're not kidnapping me." She laughed.

She turned, meeting his gaze in the dark. Thane's eyes were like pools of obsidian, the light catching and glinting off them, creating ethereal, glittering depths of endless night. She could bathe in them forever. Get so lost and wrapped up in him that she forgot who or where they were. Only remembering that they simply *were*.

He chuckled. "I promise you, Cordelia, you're safe with me. You're always safe with me."

His tone turned serious on the last part, his gaze now piercing, conveying the importance of the statement. The importance that she understand that he meant it.

And, surprisingly, she felt it. She felt it in his stare, felt it in his presence.

Her mind kept flashing back to the full moon. The potency of the magic that night. The lavender oracle card flipping up. The immediate rush of safety, warmth, and comfort. Cordelia knew it was true. Knew that the cards weren't wrong.

They were fated. Regardless of her hesitation to jump into anything with Thane. She'd been easing herself into it and found it surprisingly easy to do so now. But that didn't mean she wouldn't still guard her heart.

She had worked too hard for her freedom, for the happiness she'd always longed for. She wouldn't chance throwing it away over anyone else. But she would let herself lean into the comfort she felt, the safety and sense of right that pulled at her.

But, there was also something so deep within her that called out to Thane. That pulled her to him like the moon and the tides. *The fated bond.*

She hadn't realized she'd drifted off, forgetting where they were. Looking up at him, she grabbed his hand. His eyes flared, his shock at the gesture showing. She felt a flutter in her heart at that. Felt the flare of life between them.

"Take me on an adventure, Thane."

He'd led her down one of the wooded trails in the park, and they'd long since left the warm glow of the lampposts dotting the paved walkways.

Now, the trees thinned out and opened up to a small clearing. As Thane stepped into the meadow, her view was no longer obstructed, and she gasped at what she saw before her.

It wasn't anything grand, but it was still breathtaking. The ground was covered in a mix of grasses, clover, and patches of moss. Little budding wildflowers were scattered throughout the grass here and there but were mostly concentrated in a ring surrounding the meadow, at the edge of the tree line. It was like a little fairy tale come to life.

"Goddess," Cordelia breathed out, taking in the sight of the meadow, the sight of what Thane had done for her.

In the middle, there was an array of blankets and pillows strewn about, creating a little nest of sorts. Surrounding the blankets were candles, so many candles. They dotted the perimeter of the blankets, creating a ring of warm light, the little flickers casting a dreamy, cozy glow.

"Y-you made this?" She whipped her head to Thane, looking at him expectantly. Her heart was swollen with affection. She was shocked he would go to the trouble. Would create this little piece of wonderland nestled into this serene hideaway.

"Just for you, Cordelia."

"Thank you," she murmured, looking over the scene before grabbing his hand again. "What are you waiting for?"

She tugged him toward the blankets, heading straight for the middle as he let out a chuckle. The blanket was so soft beneath her boots, the grass crunching softly underneath.

The air around them was cool, but not unpleasantly so. With Beltane coming soon, the depths of spring had started to pull the bitter chill of winter from the air. Still, she was glad she'd worn a sweater. The weather could be fickle this time of year.

She was still holding on to his hand when she collapsed into the pile of pillows at the center of the blanket nest, so she pulled him with her. His eyes widened as he went down, and he threw his arms out as he landed on top of her, his hands on either side of her head. She giggled, the look on his face too funny not to laugh at. Even he huffed a little chuckle under his breath, a grin pulling at the corners of his mouth.

"Cheeky little witch, aren't you?" He quirked a brow at her, the expression teasing and playful. She blushed profusely at that.

Why? She didn't know. But she knew she liked this side of Thane.

She felt content, safe here with him. And maybe that was fast, but damn it if she didn't care right now. The lavender card kept popping into her head, the card that brought her clarity and grounding. She no longer felt anxious when she thought about Thane. Seeing him today had just further cemented that.

When she'd opened her front door and had seen him standing there, that smooth grin on his face, it'd felt like everything cooled around her into blissful peace.

"I'm sorry I took so long to reach out to you," she blurted out suddenly.

She searched his eyes for any signs of apprehension, any sign that he was upset. Instead, she just saw reassuring warmth reflecting back.

"That's alright, little witch."

She rolled her eyes at the name, but let it slide for the moment.

"You're here now." He smiled at that.

"Did it make you regret not getting my number?" she asked playfully. Poking fun at the chivalry he'd displayed when they met. That Thane very well may have regretted after she took her sweet time using the power he'd handed her in that moment.

He moved away from her, reminding Cordelia that she was still caught between the blanket beneath her and the wolf shifter above.

"No. But I may have had a hard time practicing my patience." He scratched the back of his neck, looking a little sheepish at the admission. She blushed, which prompted his quick follow-up. "Eventually, Talin had to keep me occupied. I was fine, just crawling out of my skin a little bit. Needed to get my energy out."

She blushed even further at that. *Needed to get my energy out* conjured thoughts of where else he could have directed that energy. Had she been ready to accept the bond sooner. She ducked her head, hoping to hide the deepening blush, tamping down the rising heat in her very blood.

But something else he said caught her attention too.

Talin. The name flashed in her head, repeating itself over and over. As if she were turning it over in her mind a few times. Hm. Odd. She felt a shivering sense of interest.

"Who's Talin?"

"Oh, he's my best friend. I've known him forever. And he uses that to his advantage to be a giant pain in my ass." He rolled his eyes and she laughed.

But she couldn't shake the feeling Talin's name had conjured. Cordelia couldn't quite put her finger on it, but she shrugged it off as interest in Thane's personal life. In the life that, maybe soon, she'd get more insight into.

The thought of being ingrained into, being part of, that personal life was a stark realization, and it conjured a wave of excitement that flooded her.

The butterflies in her stomach were a riot, taking flight all at once and battering against the confines of her tummy.

Pushing herself up, she took another look around.

"This is so beautiful, so peaceful. How did you know about this place? It's not even on the trail."

"I actually patrol these woods as part of my pack duties. This is a spot I found years ago. I like to come here sometimes."

She hadn't realized they were so close to pack territory. She knew the park he'd taken her to was right next to the wolven border but hadn't known they were connected. She'd assumed he brought her here since it was so close to where she presumed he lived, assumed that it was probably someplace familiar to him. She didn't realize just how familiar.

"What do you do for the pack?"

She didn't miss how he briefly stiffened, the rigid set of his shoulders before he visibly forced himself to relax.

"That is a very long story," he said, his voice thrumming with a riot of emotion. She could feel the darkened energy simmering beneath the surface.

A glimmer of red sparked in his eyes, bright and beautiful like the flash of a crystal. She gasped at that, the surprise of the new color in his gaze. It was like turning over labradorite and seeing the shimmering blues and greens. But instead, it was the deep onyx of

Thane's eyes mixing with a blood-red flash, a shimmer of . . . something. She couldn't quite put her finger on it. And it surprised her to see it.

What was that?

CHAPTER SEVENTEEN

THANE

Thane felt the shift pulling at him, screaming to be released. He hadn't expected Cordelia to ask about the pack, hadn't expected to be pulled right back under that tidal wave of memories at the simple question.

It was like Cordelia pulled the deepest emotions from him. He wasn't sure why. He had been asked about the pack so many times, reminded of it so many times before. Years had passed since those events, time had weathered him. Smoothed out the jagged, rocky pain of it all.

He had worked so hard to smooth it out, so he could endure the bitter regret for the rest of his sorry life. But here Cordelia was, this little witch that pulled at his heart and tugged out the rawest version of him.

"I'm sorry if I said something wrong," she said, her voice dripping with hesitation.

"It's fine. I just . . . have a lot of history there." He was avoiding telling her everything. At least for now. "I volunteered for my duty. I patrol this corner of our borders and make sure everything is in line."

After everything had happened all those years ago, he'd been lost. Lost in the storm of his heart, the storm of losing himself. The path to reaching his dreams had been steep, but so rewarding. So richly satisfying. But the fall from grace was just as steep. It felt like the air had been ripped from his lungs, his heart ripped from his chest. Like he had been slashed open and left to bleed.

When he'd finally picked himself up enough to function again, he knew he had to do something with himself. Knew he couldn't just sit in his misery, turning everything over and over again. So he'd volunteered for patrol duty. The duty no one wanted because it was so isolating.

It gave him purpose. Gave him a way to contribute without having to face his shame every day. Without having to see the pity in some of the other wolves' eyes. That was what he hated the most. The pity and the sadness.

The duty also gave him some peace. In the forest he really felt alive and truly free. He loved breathing in the rich scent of pine on the wind, the sound of the rustling leaves in the trees above him, the feel of the breeze flowing over his skin.

He explained this to Cordelia. Well, at least the part about what the job entailed and the love he had for the forest. He left out the rest, the parts he was too afraid to voice.

"That sounds so beautiful." She closed her eyes, a hum on her lips. "I love nature, love the woods and the sounds of life all around you. It's just magical." The smile plastered to Cordelia's lips was so endearing, so lovely.

He couldn't help but smile at it, letting himself get swept up in her, soothing and sweet. "I take it your magic is connected to that?"

"It's probably pretty obvious, huh?" She chuckled. "But yes. My magic is fueled by and entwined with who I am, so I mostly derive it from plants, nature, the life all around me, since I'm so drawn to all of it."

"That fits you," he observed.

She beamed, the soft glow of her magic pulling to the surface of her skin, subtly illuminating her from the inside. It was striking. He was full of wonder at her.

The conversation between them flowed so easily. Thane was amazed by it, amazed by Cordelia. Her laughter, her smile, her easy nature. It drew him in like a fluttering moth to a bright, blazing flame.

They chatted about her practice, the magic she so deeply loved. He was in awe of her enchantment magic. The ability to manipulate everything around you—plants, objects, people even, if an enchantment witch was strong enough. Which Cordelia was.

Thane told her about Talin a little more. Told her about how they'd met when they were just kids and had been friends since. How Talin had to keep him from climbing the walls while she left him desperate for a call, a text. She laughed at that, found it hilarious, actually. He just smiled, tucking away the beautiful trill of the sound to treasure.

After a while, they fell into an easy silence. The world around them was completely dark now, the candles casting a soft glow against the blanket and across their faces. His gaze narrowed in on her hands, fiddling in her lap as she seemed to contemplate something. Before he realized what was happening, she was grabbing him, pulling him down to the blanket with her.

His eyes widened, surprised at the sudden contact. Surprised that Cordelia initiated it.

She must have caught that look, too, as her eyes glittered and she laughed, bright and clear, before she lay down beside him on the blanket, leaning her head in to rest against his.

"I've always loved stargazing," she said wistfully, her words coming out breathy and ethereal. Like she herself was made of stardust.

And, he supposed, maybe she was, for all that she was made for him. That they were made for each other. Destined by the Goddesses themselves. Stardust, indeed.

He guessed that made him the same. And he'd happily grind himself to stardust, to absolute ashes, to sprinkle himself across her galaxy, lighting up his beautiful witch for all eternity.

"It's almost Beltane," she mused. "Which means we're closer to the sun now. It kind of feels like we're closer to the stars too, doesn't it?

Like they shine a little brighter for us. Like a little show of magic and light to celebrate life returning to the world." She sounded far off, dreamy, wistful. "It's so beautiful."

She was staring intently at the stars above them. He was staring intently at her. "So beautiful." He reached for her, turning her face, her chin between his thumb and forefinger.

She followed the turn, her eyes meeting his. Her soft lavender eyes, sparkling with rivers of shimmering silver, were filled with adoration, and it set his blood on fire.

He didn't realize he was leaning forward until her eyes fluttered close, his following suit, as their lips met.

CHAPTER EIGHTEEN

CORDELIA

T he kiss was so soft, so gentle at first. Her magic stirred inside her, swirling around in a riot of excitement. She hummed into the kiss, leaning in and pushing against Thane with fervor.

He groaned into her mouth and it set her on fire, heated her blood to boiling and set her into motion.

She parted her lips, deepening the kiss as he let her tongue sweep into his mouth. The gentle motion didn't match the intensity of their lips crushing together, but it kindled the fire between them further. The difference between the two sensations spurring her on.

Swinging her legs over to straddle him, she pushed her hands against his chest. His hands moved to her hips, squeezing and firmly holding her in place as he moaned.

She ate the sound up, absorbing it through the kiss as they fought for dominance. Suddenly, Thane ripped his mouth away from hers, his lips trailing down her jaw, then her neck. He nipped her skin just below her ear, then soothed it with his tongue.

His lips blazed across her skin, and her hips began to move against his, setting her body on fire. Fast. So fast this was all happening. But she didn't care—didn't care how much time had passed or how little they actually knew each other before now.

She could feel the threads of their golden bond between them, bright and clear tonight. Could feel them strengthening, glowing brighter and brighter the longer she was with him.

She didn't care about anything as he groaned, his hips snapping and jolting beneath her, grinding his now very present erection against her.

She squealed in surprise, the yelp trailing into a deep moan as she reached down and grabbed his hands where they were still gripping her hips. Threading her fingers with his, she shoved his hands above his head, pressing them into the blanket.

Thane grunted, his hips still grinding against her as he squeezed her hands a little harder, encouraging her.

She pulled back a little, catching her breath and Thane's gaze. His eyes were practically on fire, the red glimmer she saw earlier now molten streams dashed across the endless night of his black eyes.

He looked feral, his chest heaving, his lips already swollen, and his eyes crazed with the fire burning brightly in them.

"Don't tease, little witch," he growled and leaned up, nipping her bottom lip with his teeth before enveloping her in another kiss, this one deeper, more carnal than before. His tongue swept in, staking claim and dominion over her, setting a river of need alight in her lower belly.

She whimpered, her hold on his hands briefly easing. Enough for Thane to take control and flip them, his hands now pinning her wrists above her head.

"What a pretty witch, desperate for her fated," he said, his voice gravelly and laced with desire.

"Now who's the one teasing?" She tried to sound lighthearted, but she couldn't hide the slight bite in her tone, wanting, no, *needing* his lips again.

"Need something?" He ground his hips against hers, eliciting a long, pleading moan.

She jolted forward, trying to reach his lips, but he jerked away, his movements following hers. He tsked at her, mirth lighting his eyes ablaze.

"You're going to need to find some patience, Cordelia. Especially if you want me to show you just how much fun we can have." His voice was so dark, sinister.

It only made the want within her deepen until it was seemingly endless.

He gently released her hands, leaning down and giving her a soft, quick kiss. "I think that's about enough for tonight, my pretty witch." As Thane stood, he held out his hand, helping her up beside him. "Let's get you home so you can rest."

Thane made his way around the blankets, blowing out each candle, then setting them back down.

He tucked her into his side and guided her out of the little blanket nest, back toward the trail they came from.

Turning her head back, she said, "But what about the blankets and everything? You can't just leave it all here."

"Oh, I'll just grab it tomorrow on my patrols," he said simply, apparently not worried at all.

Her head was still spinning, still reeling from the depth of desire she felt, from the electricity of the kisses they'd shared. And she was still a little annoyed at the level of teasing Thane had just exhibited as he left her desperate for more.

So maybe that was what spurred her little display of attitude. She snapped her fingers, and everything Thane had set up vanished behind them. He turned, his eyes darting around.

"And what was that?" he said, his brow quirked at her.

"I cleaned it up for you. You shouldn't litter, you know."

"Thanks. Saves me the trouble of cleaning it up and putting it all away." He chuckled, and it set her blood on fire again. For him, for the smirk on his face.

"What are you laughing at? How do you know I didn't just incinerate all of it and drop it on your doorstep?"

CHAPTER NINETEEN

THANE

Fucking hell.

Thane had been in a daze since the night before, wafts of bonfire and lavender drifting to him and filling his senses with serene warmth.

The scene of his evening with Cordelia just played on repeat in his head. The deep, beautiful sound of her laughter, the glimmer of excitement and happiness in her sparkling pale-orchid eyes, the feel of her soft, full lips against his.

But the second he'd drifted off to sleep that night and became vulnerable to his subconscious, he'd fallen into something further from bliss. The fitful bouts of sleep he'd managed to get were riddled with nightmares, glaring reminders of how deeply he'd failed himself and his pack. How he'd failed his father.

It had been enough to drag him out of sleep several times, and was enough to have him up, wide awake at three a.m., rest a lost cause now.

It was like he couldn't get his brain to stop, couldn't get his nerves to calm. His heart was racing as he thought of all the things he'd left unresolved, of all the dreams he'd left dashed on the forest floor all those years ago.

His focus kept flashing to what Talin had told him the other day. That he needed to just do it, just talk to his dad. He was right, annoyingly so.

Thane had been wondering for a long time now why he continued to do this, continued to torture himself and shut everyone out. The longer he went without his family, the weaker he felt. The less he recognized himself.

There were so many reasons to break his silence, to make things right. And it felt like Cordelia was just the straw that broke the camel's back. The prospect of opening up to her about everything, admitting to her that he had isolated himself, admitting his cowardice, it all left him unsettled.

Today would be the day. Today he would finally just get his shit together and face it. The thought alone had his stomach turning. The anxiety that surged inside him was unpleasant and had him on the edge of being sick. Like a storm of unease and discomfort that stirred inside him, desperate to be let out.

He stood in his kitchen, staring at the sink in front of him, willing himself to move. To not let this fear keep him frozen forever.

He'd known for a while now, even if in just some small part of himself, that the way he'd been living was unsustainable. If you could even call it living.

His thoughts immediately flashed to Cordelia, and the idea of denying himself a full connection with her twisted his gut. No. He wouldn't deny himself that, wouldn't deny her her own happiness, if she found that in him.

Goddess, he hoped she would. He would make it his sole mission to bring her all the happiness in the world. To give her everything. Even if it meant cracking his chest open and giving her the bloody offering of his still-beating heart.

But in order for that to happen, he needed to change his shitty attitude. And fast.

The pale, watery light of the moon filtered in through the kitchen windows, throwing sharp shadows in its wake. The full moon had been a couple days ago now, and he basked in its eerie, beautiful light as it soaked his home, coated his skin in its reassuring caress.

Closing his eyes and taking a deep breath, Thane steadied himself and started making the first coffee of the day. Because, yes, there would be several since he had a three a.m. wake-up call.

As he waited for the coffee to brew, he stared at the old, chipped mug on the marble counter in front of him. The mug was ivory, the color of the moon, with small gray speckles spattered across the outside. He smiled to himself.

He'd made it with his mother when he was a boy. She had always been a soft, gentle woman, had always loved creating art. But she especially loved pottery—loved making things with her hands, creating beauty and joy in her artwork.

He had begged several times to help her, and sometimes she let him, but then other times she kindly declined so she could actually create pieces to sell. He chuckled at that, at the memory of all the pottery he'd destroyed when he was allowed to join her.

This was one of the few pieces to survive.

His mother loved tea, loved the act of making and drinking it. So he'd wanted to make her a mug, one she could always use. He supposed it was his small way of taking care of her, even from a young age. A small action that pointed to his desire to take care of everyone around him.

Thane let himself get lost in the memory as the smell of brewing coffee perfumed the air, the steam from the coffee maker swirling around him.

When he'd made the mug, he had just learned about the moon cycles and their significance the week before, so it was his inspiration in the design. He'd painted it a bright, pale ivory. The speckles representing those curious little craters in the moon.

He could remember making it so clearly, so vividly. He'd flung the paintbrush left and right, letting the paint splatter across the surface of the mug. His mother had laughed, bright and full, at his display of enthusiasm.

He could practically hear her laugh now, could feel the warmth of her at his back as she guided his small hands in forming the lump of wet clay into something that resembled a mug. It was full of craggy dents and imperfect curves.

But he'd been so proud of the creation and the fact that it'd survived, fully intact. And he'd always insisted that his mother drink from it when they had tea together. Always loved knowing that he'd made that, he'd given her a piece of himself.

After everything with the pack happened, Thane had shut out both of his parents. He'd been terrified of their reactions, terrified of letting them down. He'd always admired and adored them, modeled his dreams after them. And when those dreams came crashing down, he couldn't bear the thought of facing them with his shame. The shame that clung to him, thick and heavy like a set of cold, iron chains.

A few weeks after the incident, he had left the house for a run and found the mug sitting on his front porch, a little note taped to it that simply said, *I love you, Thane. Never forget who you are.*

He poured his brewed coffee, getting lost in the swirling liquid, the memories of his childhood taking root in his heart and clogging his throat.

Seeing his mother's handwriting taped to that little chipped mug had brought him down, completely wrecked him. He had turned around and rushed back inside, the mug gripped tightly in his hand, and hadn't left the house for another week after that, cycling between bouts of tears and streaks of anger.

He had used that mug every single morning since then. He had made it for his mother, sure, but now he had a piece of her through it.

He had also taped that little note to the inside of the cabinet that housed the mug. It was his daily reminder.

Of what, he wasn't certain—maybe of the unending pain he'd inflicted on himself by pulling away from his family. Maybe it was a reminder that he had lost himself, and still couldn't find a way back. Or maybe it was a reminder of the warmth of his mother. The love he could still feel from her every day.

Grabbing the mug, now filled with steaming-hot coffee, Thane made his way to the kitchen table, plopped into a chair, and set the cup down.

How many times had he sat here the past few years, with this mug in front of him, dreaming about his mother, reciting the conversation he would finally have with his father?

He hadn't heard either of their voices since he'd abandoned them three long years ago. Not for lack of them trying. Neither of them had given up on him.

He blew out a breath and, with a shaking hand, pulled his phone out of his pocket and brought up his father's phone number. Staring at the screen, he felt a knot form in his throat, felt his chest constrict.

It was early, sure, but his father would be up. He was a chronic insomniac, like Thane, and always liked to get his day started early. He'd been that way all of Thane's life. Nolen Lycus was nothing if not a man of routine.

Thane clicked the green Call button.

His dad picked up on the second ring.

"Thane?" His broken voice came from the other end, setting Thane's nerves at ease, his tears now flowing freely.

CHAPTER TWENTY

THANE

"Dad?" Thane's voice broke too. He was on the edge of ruin at finally hearing his dad's voice all these years later.

He missed his parents so deeply, so completely. It was his own fears and doubts that had kept him from them for so long.

"Is everything alright?" His father's tone hardened, immediately shifting into protector mode, bracing himself for whatever Thane needed. It made Thane's heart swell with pride.

Nolen Lycus was well respected and known to be one of the strongest alphas of any of the wolven packs. Thane had always been proud to be his son, always revered and adored his father.

"Yeah, I just . . . I just think we need to talk. It's been long enough," Thane said, blowing out a breath and resting his head in his free hand.

"You have no idea how long I've waited for this call, son. And before you start your grumbling, I already know what you're going to say. Your mother and I are *not* disappointed in you, we are not ashamed of you. We just worry about you. So cut it with your bullshit." His voice was pleading, hurt, but still edged with stern declaration.

Thane knew he'd hurt them when he'd unceremoniously cut ties. It had been more for their benefit than his.

He wasn't shocked it was what his father led the conversation with. He was only picking up where they'd left off in the last conversation they ever had. When Thane had broken down in front of them, baring his broken heart and admitting his guilt and his shame.

He could still remember their desperate pleas for him to stay, to let them help. But the guilt had overridden everything else. Even the desire to cling to his family, his greatest support.

Thane had only been an alpha for a couple years, but he had decided from a young age that it was what he wanted—to be just like his dad. He wanted to lead a pack of his own, to take care of the wolves he was charged with, take care of those in need.

The purpose of the packs was to provide protection for all wolven and to protect the land. That included the other Magical and the land they all lived on. The Magical were any Goddess-created species: both wolf and dragon shifters, vampires, fae, demons, witches, and those of the sea. The wolven were protectors of the land, appointed by the Goddesses Theia and Artemis, and his father embodied that in his leadership, in his position as an alpha. Thane had done his best to do the same when he stepped up to the role.

"But Dad, I let down the Lycus family. I let down your legacy. I let down *myself*." He was on the verge of tears again, breaking down as the memories of that night came flooding back, fresh as ever.

He'd had a small, but proud pack appointed to him. They were all relatively young, Thane being the oldest and most experienced of the group at twenty-five. He had known them all his life, some were even close friends.

Those years as alpha were blissful, Celestial blessed, even, like the Goddesses themselves smiled upon him.

Two years in, there was a late-night distress call that his pack answered. Another pack had a run-in with some other Magical and was in trouble.

When they arrived, his pack jumped right into the thick of it. There was a small group of vampires and a couple demons attacking the other wolf pack. It was obvious why they'd called for help, their three wolves facing the group of seven.

Time seemed to move in slow motion after that. One second they were gaining control, Thane himself taking down a couple of the vamps, and then the next, one of the other wolves attacked one of Thane's pack members. Lila. He couldn't believe what he was seeing.

Before he could react, one of the demons grabbed him, hooking his arm around Thane's neck and yanking hard, crushing him to his chest. They grappled, and eventually, Thane managed to get his hands around the demon's neck and twist until he felt a sharp snap.

He dropped the now-dead demon, limp and heavy, to the forest floor below them. The leaves rustled beneath his feet as he turned around to launch back toward Lila.

Lila. Who now lay on the forest floor herself, her eyes open, but lifeless. *Thane surveyed the rest of the horrifying scene before him.* All of them. *They'd killed damn-near all of his pack.*

The vamps and the demons had been taken care of, no problem. But he knew it wasn't them that had gotten to his pack. It was the other wolven. The other wolven who he now paid more attention to, identifying them instantly by their scent. They were Artemisian wolven.

He snapped his head in the direction of a small whimper. One of them had the last living member of Thane's pack in their arms. It was Vale.

He grabbed ahold of the wolf attacking Vale, tried to pull him away, tried to pry his claws out of Vale's throat. But just as Thane knocked Vale's attacker loose, another Artemisian wolf leaped out of the trees, one hand slashing Vale's throat while the other carved deep gashes in his stomach.

Vale's eyes met Thane's in his final seconds, the fear and pain in his pleading expression striking Thane to his very core.

He saw the split second when Vale's eyes went vacant, now forever out of Thane's reach.

He howled, deep and piercing, and lunged, aiming to return the favor, but he was hauled back by another wolf and thrown to the ground.

As he was held down, the wolf who killed Vale approached slowly, a grin spreading across his lips. He chuckled, dark and steely. "Well, well, well, looks like all that's left is the pathetic alpha." He spit on Thane's chest.

As Thane opened his mouth, the Artemisian wolf kicked his side, stealing his breath.

"Just finish it off, already. I don't want to waste any more of my time on these mutts," one of other wolves growled.

The one standing in front of Thane sneered, malice and cruelty lining every inch of his expression, before lunging and slashing across Thane's chest, deep gashes cutting into skin and muscle. The pain was blinding, searing.

"Let him bleed out, for all I care. Let him suffer a little while longer before he kicks it."

Thane couldn't see them anymore, he was too busy focusing on the white-hot pain coursing through his body to see where they went. But he'd heard them go, the leaves crunching underfoot until it'd faded into nothing.

"Thane, where'd you go?" He heard his dad's voice on the other end of the call again, pulling him out of the memories he'd shoved deep.

He could feel the weight of his heart, feel those gashes in his chest all over again. It stole his breath, crumbled his strength.

That asshole Artemisian wolf hadn't cut deep enough to kill him, but he had cut deep enough to fuck him up for a couple months. Left him to lie in bed, healing and reliving that night over and over again. Trying to put the pieces together and figure out what the fuck had happened.

Thane's whole pack had been slaughtered. He was the only remaining survivor. He'd been questioned for days by the elders, the ones who oversaw all Harmonious wolven.

He'd told them everything, every possible detail he could recall. But it led nowhere. Nowhere but Thane's demise. He'd lost his pack, and because of it, he'd lost himself.

"Sorry, Dad, it's just hard to think about that night." Thane pinched the bridge of his nose, trying to regain some composure. "They never found that pack. Never found those assholes that fucking slaughtered my wolves. My best friends.

"They told me I was fucking crazy! Those fucking Artemisian wolves wanted me dead. I *watched* them murder Vale. Watched as they ripped them all away from me. It was *my* job to protect them, and I failed."

His father sighed on the other end. "Thane, I know what happened was terrible, was so traumatic for you. But you have to come to peace with it eventually. You can't let it eat at you forever." His voice softened, took on the tone that said he was attempting to calm Thane down. "It's not your fault, none of it is. You did the best you could, you did protect them, you were just blindsided."

Some of the tension released from Thane's shoulders. "I know, Dad. I know that. I know I need to . . . not isolate myself. I know you and Mom miss me. I miss you both. It's just . . . hard." He couldn't describe it to his father.

How he felt like he might drown in the guilt and the anger always simmering under the surface. How he felt like he was the one that should have died that night, not them. He'd wished so badly so many times that he could trade places with Vale, at least save one of them. How was it fair that he was still here and they weren't?

"How about you come visit her? It'll be good for both of you."

There was a soft smile in his father's voice. Thane had always had a strong bond with his mother. His father had been at home as much as he could when Thane was growing up, but Nolen Lycus led a large pack and had a lot of duties that kept him away.

So Thane had been around his soft, fierce, mother most of the time. They'd been the best of friends Thane's whole life.

Ripping himself away from his parents had been hard, but ripping himself away from his mother had been the hardest. He hadn't depended on her, but he did admire her. He admired her spirit, admired her fairness, admired her strength. And when he'd lost that, he'd lost his foundations. Like the earth had been ripped out from beneath him, leaving him suspended and lost.

"OK," he said softly, barely hearing himself. "We've got a lot to catch up on, anyway."

His father laughed. "That's my boy. I can practically hear your mother scrambling for the teacups and filling the kettle now."

Thane laughed at that, rich and deep. And he surprised himself with the sound.

His heart clenched, pride and warmth filling his chest.
He was finally going home.

CHAPTER TWENTY-ONE

THANE

T hane stood before the front door of his childhood home. The stairs leading to the porch still creaked in the same spots, the same worn footpath led to the door where a wreath of sunflowers hung, ivy and foraged tree leaves scattered through twisted branches.

It was reassuring, comforting, the familiarity of the home he'd always known. The home that hadn't changed, no matter how much he had.

He raised his fist and knocked on the door. The anticipation of seeing his mother again had twisted a knot in his stomach throughout the entire car ride here. And it still hadn't eased. Sweat collected in his palms, and he could practically feel his heartbeat in his throat.

"Surely, no son of mine is knocking on a Lycus door instead of barging on in," his mother shouted from inside the house.

The windows were open, the curtains framing them blowing in the soft spring breeze. The sound of his mother's voice dissipated all of his earlier apprehension, like it held the power and authority to make everything better. Chuckling, he turned the handle and pushed open the door, finally stepping foot in the house he had hadn't seen in three long years.

He took in the home around him, the same furniture scattered through the living room, his dad's worn boots next to the front door, an old, tattered book open and face down on the coffee table.

Beyond the living room, he instantly spotted his mother at the kitchen table, a book in her hands and a smile on her face as their gazes met.

Her face was still the same, if aged slightly since he last saw her. She broke out in a smile, wide and bright, the corners of her eyes crinkling and a laugh escaping her lips. Pushing the chair back quickly, she stood and rushed to him.

He ate up half the distance between them to envelop his mother in a warm, tight embrace, her arms squeezing him as hard as she could. Their bodies were shaking, and he soon realized that it was him that was shaking them, his body racked with sobs.

His mother was here, she was in front of him and in his arms again. He was *home*.

He pulled back, grabbing his mother's shoulders and taking a closer look at her. She had tears she was holding back, but her deep emerald eyes were glimmering with love and warmth too.

"My son, my sweet boy," she breathed, before pulling him in for another hug.

Rosemary Lycus always smelled of tea leaves and mint, and it engulfed Thane now as he embraced her.

She gave him another once-over before patting him on the shoulder and looping her arm in his, the other hand resting on his forearm as she led him to the kitchen.

"It's so nice to have you home, Thane. Nothing has been the same without you." Her soft voice inspired a fresh wave of emotion in him.

"It's good to be home, Mom," he said, fighting back the urge to cry.

Goddess, what the fuck was happening to him? He had cried more in the last twelve hours than he had in well over a year.

"Before you ask, your father isn't home. He's out on pack business.

But I still wanted to see you." She looked up, beaming at him, then pointed to the table. "Sit. I'll make us some tea."

He chuckled, obeying and taking his usual seat at the table. It felt so odd to be back here, to be sitting in the seat that was always his growing up. Directly across from Mom, his dad's seat to the left of Thane's.

Since they didn't have a formal dining room, the small, round table sat in the kitchen, worn down and covered with tiny wolf scratch marks from the many years he spent trying, and failing, to control his budding shifting abilities.

After a couple minutes, his mother carried two steaming mugs to the table, setting one in front of him before taking her usual seat.

"My love, you're home," she said, a soft smile lighting up her face.

His affection for her, his adoration and love, was an ache in his heart, so deep and unbearable. He had missed her dearly for three long years, and now, here he finally was. Sitting in the rickety old chair across from her at the kitchen table, looking into her warm, familiar emerald eyes.

Her hair was still the same, a deep warm brown with soft waves, flowing around her shoulders and down her back, half of it pulled back to keep it out of her slender face. Just like she preferred it.

Celestials, he'd missed his mother. Missed her warmth and her wit and her laughter.

The kitchen was almost completely unchanged save for the art on the walls. His mother was constantly creating, in every medium imaginable, and with that came her tendency to constantly change the artwork she displayed.

Today there was an abstract painting on the wall to his right, the strokes were quick slashes and flecks of paint as if she had splattered it quickly and aggressively. The colors were mostly warm with bright pinks, burnt oranges, pale yellows, and rich, vibrant reds. Scattered among the bright colors were a few thick splotches of blues of varying shades. Some pale robin's egg blue, some gray blues, and a couple deep royal blues. It was captivating, breathtaking.

He felt a rush of adrenaline and sadness just looking at it. He couldn't place that twinge of sadness, couldn't place what might have inspired it in the painting. But he could feel it so deeply, so tangibly.

His mother must have caught him staring, because she cleared her throat and said, "That one I made not long after you left."

He snapped his head back to her at that. Startled and a bit lost for words, he just stared at her, his lips parted and breath catching.

"I just couldn't keep it all in, Thane. I missed you so much. It killed me to know that there was nothing I could do to ease your pain, my pup." The sadness laced in her voice threatened to choke him up again.

Goddess, what he wouldn't give to do it all over again. He regretted leaving his parents like that, regretted everything he had missed over the years.

At the time, he'd thought it was the right thing to do. But looking back, he knew it wasn't what was best. For him or for anyone.

"I'm so sorry, Mama." He reached across the table, taking her hands in his and squeezing them before letting go again. "But I'm here now. And I promise I'm not leaving you again." He smiled, bittersweet and full of feeling. But the dominant one was excitement. For so many things.

One of those things came front and center as his mother said, "Well, my love, tell me what's happened? What has my Thane been up to?" She sipped her tea, watching him over the lip of her mug.

The tendrils of steam from her tea swirled around her, creating a soft halo as it reflected the light streaming in from the window behind her.

The excitement of finally being home combined with the swelling riot of emotions from the night before mixed together, creating an intoxicating level of bliss within him.

"I met my fated," he blurted out, shocking even himself.

That was . . . one way to break the news to his mother.

Her eyes widened, too, a bright smile blooming across her face, lighting up her features.

"You what?!" Her voice was breathless. "What is their name? Who are they? Tell me everything!" She was practically bouncing in her seat now, the glow of her happiness growing brighter and brighter.

She had always told him stories growing up. Stories of the adventures he might have one day, of the people he may meet, of the things he might do, and she especially loved telling him stories of love.

True love, deep love, and stories of fateds. His mother had always been a hopeless romantic, and it was something that had rubbed off on him a bit. Though, he kept that tucked away to himself, his own little secret wish for the love he hoped he would one day deserve.

His parents were fateds, blessed by the Celestials and destined for one another, and he had always dreamed he would find the same one day.

So he looked his mother in the eyes, excitement lighting him up from the inside, and said, "Cordelia. Her name is Cordelia."

CHAPTER TWENTY-TWO

THANE

By the time Thane had finished telling her about Cordelia, giving her every detail he could bear to give her, he had to stop to catch his breath. To soak in the bliss of finally confiding in his mother.

The accompanying joy that was rolling off her in waves was infectious, her delight soaking into him and settling deep. And the smile on her face had never waned. In fact, it had only continued to grow the more he spoke.

"Cordelia. A beautiful name, and I'm sure, an even more beautiful witch for my handsome wolf." She reached across the small table, her hand cupping his cheek.

"She's really something, Mama. You'll love her," he said, a little breathlessly.

Goddess, he needed to get his feelings for Cordelia under control. It was as if every time he thought of her or spoke her name, he turned to jelly. His whole body lit up, as if already attuned to her.

"What does Talin think of her?" She chuckled and lifted her eyebrow. He rolled his eyes at that, laughing right alongside her.

"He hasn't met her, yet. But don't worry, he's all for her already."
He thought back to the conversation he had with Talin just the
other day.

Thought of how Talin had pushed him to not only pull himself
together with Cordelia but also to talk to his father again.

Talin had constantly been saying, for the past three years, that
Thane was out of his mind. That it was ridiculous to shut everyone
out. Thane had even tried to shut Talin out along with everyone else,
but that stubborn reptilian asshole had other plans and shoved his
way back into his life. There would be no getting rid of him.

But something about that conversation with Talin mixed with
Cordelia asking Thane about his past had done the trick. It had all
culminated in finally pushing Thane to call his dad. And now here he
was, having tea with his mother as if no time had passed at all.

He had realized the night before, as he'd lain in bed replaying the
conversation over and over, that he had to make a change. He knew
that he had to grant himself the happiness he desired, make himself
happy, before he could give Cordelia any sort of happiness with him.
Before he could give her the happiness he so desperately wanted to.

Not only that, but Thane knew—deep down as the realization was
—that he deserved happiness. He deserved to know the soft touch of
familiarity, of love and joy. So he was making an effort. For Cordelia,
yes.

But mostly, and more importantly, for himself.

"Well, I'm sure he'll find a way to sneak himself into meeting her
sooner than you plan. And I'm sure those two will get along famously
if you already like her."

"I can only hope," he said wistfully, letting himself get caught up in
hopes for what his future with Cordelia would hold. Fucking hell,
what was happening to him?

After spending the afternoon with his mother, Thane left his childhood home, hugged her goodbye, and swore that he would call soon. That he wouldn't isolate himself again.

It all felt like a dream. The fact that he visited that old house, one of the few places he could truly feel at ease and held so much love.

The fact that he spoke to his mother and father, got to hear his mother's laugh again, drank tea with her at that old kitchen table, let himself get lost in conversation with her. It felt like a big part of him had mended, at least a little bit, after today. Like breathing was a little easier and his head was a little lighter.

Driving home, Thane thought back on Talin. Thought about everything that had happened lately and how his best friend had always been there for him.

Soon he found himself parked in front of Talin's apartment building, the keys still in the ignition but the engine off. He stared at the building in front of him, the old, faded brick that he was so familiar with.

He didn't really remember making the decision to drive here, didn't really remember getting here. But he felt a want inside himself, a want that was inexplicably pulling him toward Talin. Toward the laughter of his best friend, the comfort of being around him.

He got out of his car and hurried into the building, taking the steps two at a time. He wasn't sure where this knotted feeling in his stomach was coming from, he just knew it was pushing him to Talin's home. Pushing him to Talin himself. He made it to the top floor, bounded down the hallway, and finally stopped in front of Talin's door. He knocked quickly and waited with an anxious energy roiling in his stomach.

It felt like a small eternity passed before Talin was swinging the door open.

"Thane! What are you doing here, man?" Talin boomed, flinging the door the rest of the way open and throwing his arm out, gesturing for Thane to come inside.

Thane stepped inside the apartment, greeted by the plush gray carpet under his shoes. The space was open, airy. The kitchen and the living room were basically one space divided by the island in the middle.

The living room had two loveseats, both a rich, deep brown leather, and a small, dark wood coffee table just in front of them. Beyond that was a TV mounted to the wall and a cabinet underneath to house Talin's various pieces of tech equipment. For movies, games, anything. The rest of the space was just shelves and shelves and cabinets and surfaces of trinkets and treasures that Talin had collected over his life.

It always amused Thane to no end—Talin's dragon tendencies running rampant in his home. And Thane always noticed something new when he looked around the space. It was impossible to have everything memorized. All of Talin's glinting and mysterious treasures were a wonder.

"Can I get you anything, man?" Talin called from the kitchen where he was rooting around in the fridge.

"Nah, I'm good," Thane said as he plopped himself down on the couch, his mind still racing from the memories of the night before, the conversation with his mother earlier, and finding himself at Talin's apartment.

"So what's up?" Talin said as he sat down in the couch diagonal from Thane.

"I finally called my dad this morning."

"Really?" Talin perked up at that. "And I suppose I'm the one responsible?" He looked pretty proud of himself. Not that that was unusual. He was the picture of pride at all times, and now was no exception.

"Yeah, sure." Thane snorted. "Actually . . . I went out with Cordelia last night."

The series of events the past couple days was a whirlwind, leaving Thane in its wake of blissful chaos and restorative peace.

"And?" Talin quirked his brow, taking a drink from the bottle of water in his hand.

"And she asked about the pack, asked about what I do. It really got me thinking." Thane still had a hard time thinking about the events that led to his self-imposed exile, but he was pushing past it. Trying to, at least.

He knew he needed to come to terms with it, to let go of the guilt that ate at him every day. It was just way harder than it seemed.

"Thinking about what?" He could tell Talin was really going to make him open up today. Bastard.

"About what you said the other day. Don't get a big head about it," he warned, already feeling Talin's ego swelling past the point of no return. "So, I called my dad this morning. And . . . I . . . *may* have gone to see my mom today." It still all felt so surreal, like it was a dream Thane was waking up from.

"*May* have?" Talin stared in shock, mouth hanging open in disbelief. "Or did you actually go see your fucking mom, you shit?"

"I saw her." Thane smiled at that, at the lingering warmth within him.

It had changed something fundamental in him to be without his support system, the two people he had always adored, for three long years. And it was just as healing to speak to both of them again.

Talin reached over, clapping Thane on the knee. "You finally did it, asshole." He laughed, raising his water bottle in the air in a mock toast. "To you finally crawling out of your hole of misery."

Thane shook his head fondly at Talin. It felt like a giant weight had eased off his chest. How had he gotten here? To this point of finally freeing himself of his misery, even if only in a small way.

"And how is the lovely Cordelia?" Talin asked, taking another swig of water.

"She's . . ." Goddess, he didn't even have the words. Rubbing the back of his neck, he attempted to come up with at least a few. "She's . . . everything. It was incredible. I just still can't fully wrap my head around it all, ya know?"

Talin chuckled. "Well, not really, but I can imagine. So, she's really your fated?"

"Yeah, she really is." There was just too much in Thane's head, too many thoughts and things flying around his mind. He didn't know how to voice any of them.

"I'm happy for you, man." A mischievous grin spread across Talin's face. "So when do I get to meet her?"

"Oh, fuck off. Not any time soon, if I have anything to say about it."

"Ah, c'mon. You afraid she'll like me more than you?" Talin winked at Thane, clearly trying to incite him.

"Watch it, Talin."

"Ooo, is wolfy coming out to play today?" Talin teased. He knew Thane hadn't shifted in a while, surely knew that the fated bond would be bothering him, urging him to shift.

Thane just leveled him with a look.

"Oh calm down, you know I'm only teasing." Talin kicked Thane's leg, laughing the entire time.

Thane rolled his eyes at that, at how casually Talin loved to rile him up.

"It's not like I'm going to bond her," Talin said with a grin, taking another smooth sip of water.

Thane's eyes tracked him the entire time, a growl rising in his throat.

CHAPTER TWENTY-THREE

CORDELIA

Cordelia sat in her garden, her eyes closed and face tipped to the sun-soaked sky above her.

Once her annoyance at Thane's teasing had waned, it was replaced with unending affection, deep and warm. It clung to her all day, igniting hope and sparks of thrilling anticipation along her skin every time she thought of him.

She opened her eyes, looking down at Merlin where he lay at her side, dozing among the lavender patch with the soft breeze blowing through his rich, black fur.

She lay down, looking back to the sky and absently twiddling the moonstone beads at her wrist. Twisting and rolling the smooth, pale stones between her fingers as she meditated, contemplated things.

Soon, her mind drifted, her brain rushing from one topic to the next. And then she wasn't thinking about Thane at all. Somehow, her thoughts landed on the storm cloud that was Lydia Halloway.

She hadn't heard from her mother in a few days, which was odd. She'd been so adamant the last time they spoke, so insistent. Cordelia had expected to hear more from her in the following days, but instead, nothing. Radio silence.

A sick feeling turned over in her stomach, souring the good mood she'd been in. The inky claws of doubt and worry started to seep their way into her. Strung tension in her muscles, ached in her bones, sowed anxiety deep inside her heart.

She couldn't avoid the idea that her mother was planning something, scheming and hiding away until she revealed her master plan. It wouldn't be surprising. Lydia Halloway always had something in her back pocket—another plan to enact, another goal to achieve. And Cordelia felt like she was right in Lydia's crosshairs.

Turning her head to the side, she closed her eyes, inhaling deep the scent of fresh lavender. She tried to let the stone-solid comfort of these sorts of simple magics stand guard for her. And it worked, to a certain degree.

Until those inky-black thoughts curled at the edges, wormed their way into her again, relentless and cruel. She opened her eyes, trying to let the light of the day flood back into her senses, hoping it would calm her down. She heard Merlin rustling next to her, felt his warm, wet nose nudging at her arm, giving her some semblance of comfort.

Turning her head back to the sky, she fluttered her eyes closed again and began practicing the breathing techniques Sage had taught her.

Breathe in, hold. Breathe out, hold. Breathe in, hold. Breathe out, hold.

Over and over again, she repeated the exercise, trying to only let her mind focus on the words, on the act of breathing. Tried not to let her mind wander to lingering doubts and anxieties. She couldn't, *wouldn't*, let her mother control her anymore. Not in any way, shape, or form.

It was time she took matters into her own hands. She couldn't sit around waiting for something to happen, for things to get better on their own. And she had an idea of how she could get her mother off her back. Hopefully.

After a long while, she realized she'd stopped focusing on her breathing and was just thinking aimlessly. Those inky claws had retracted, the tendrils of shadow that had crept in had now disappeared, replaced by soft, warming light and peace.

She let herself daydream of glittering flashes of red, the warmth of blazing fires, and searing touches of lips.

That night, Cordelia sat in her bed with her notebook in her lap and laptop in front of her. She was doing a little research, some planning of her own, to get her mother untangled from her life.

Lydia Halloway was desperate for Cordelia to take her place as the heir to the Halloway coven. As a Halloway, Cordelia was perfectly poised to take that place, and that gave her mother too much of an advantage.

The Hecatean Guild oversaw the witches, and their law dictated that the heir to a coven must possess the surname of said coven.

And Cordelia was going to use that.

Smiling to herself, Cordelia closed her laptop, her plan in place. She was content with the decision and had the perfect name in mind. She just hoped the person that the name came from would be on board. Cordelia would ask tomorrow.

It had started to rain earlier that evening, and the sound of it pattering against the roof and the windows of her bedroom was soft and soothing. She loved times like this, safely tucked away in her home, warm and dry, listening to the rain as the world around her rested and relaxed with the storm. She especially loved the smell of the earth after it rained. How as soon as she stepped outside after a storm, everything smelled of damp earth and humid, rich air.

Even the soft, rolling thunder outside was a comfort. She smiled, humming to herself as she reveled in the cozy ambience.

She had texted Thane earlier in the day, but he hadn't answered yet. Which was fine. She didn't want to seem like she was hinging everything on him.

Since the night before, she just couldn't get him out of her mind. Every thought she had somehow ended up drifting back to him. He'd entangled himself into her life without even trying. Had woven his shimmering red threads among her moonlit lavender ones, weaving a dark and beautiful connection between them. The start of a story still yet to unfold.

Cordelia's mind kept wandering back to how Thane's eyes had flashed that iridescent blood red—little sparks that caught her eye every so often. But they had mostly remained their usual deep black. She still wasn't sure what that was, but it was captivating. Beautiful.

And that kiss? It had destroyed her. One touch of Thane's lips against hers had set her whole body aflame. She could barely contain herself after that, couldn't contain the fire that blazed within her, and had ended up taking the kiss even further than she'd planned.

The thought of Thane's lips hot against her skin, her throat, the little sounds he'd made, the way he'd let her take over and pin his hands down. It was all enough to set that flame anew again. Cordelia felt like she might crawl out of her skin just at the thought of it all.

She could practically feel his lips blazing a path down her neck, could hear his groans in her ears, filling her with a brightness she hadn't known existed before now.

Her whole body felt like it was on fire, unquenchable and blazing. She pressed her hand to her heart, a flush rising in her cheeks.

Reaching into her nightstand drawer, she grabbed one of her favorite vibrators: a long silicone toy, pale blue in color and shaped phallically without outright looking like a cock. It had sleek lines and a bulbous head that vibrated. Her cheeks flushed even hotter.

She had no shame in her positive attitude toward her sexuality and her sex drive, but what set her skin aflame was the idea of masturbating to the man that she had only just met and gone on one date with, even if that man was her fated.

Was that ridiculous? She wasn't sure, but she figured being fated gave her a pass, so she brushed those thoughts away. Besides, being with him, even just being near him, felt so inherently right. Like an aching truth hidden deep within her, woven into her very being, into her bones.

Settling into the bed, Cordelia closed her eyes and ran her free hand up her thigh, the tips of her fingers gently stroking. She trailed her fingers up over her hips, her soft, round belly. She could already feel the arousal swirling within her, like a sparkling flame.

The vibrator quietly buzzed in her hand when she powered it on. A little zap of electric excitement raced over her skin, bringing a fresh wave of heat through her body.

Outside, the rain picked up—fat, heavy water drops beating a little harder against the windowpanes as she closed her eyes and leaned back into the pillows on her bed, the soft linen warm beneath her.

Humming, she moved the vibrator over her body, starting on her arms and running it up over her clavicle, down her chest, before swirling around her nipples. A little gasp escaped her lips, and a chill shivered down her spine. Heat pooled between her legs. She was already absolutely dripping.

The vibrations from the toy sent more and more sparks flying across her skin as she continued her path down, down, down. At the same time, she heard a long, rolling bout of thunder, the sound of it mixing with the vibrations of the toy and creating an intoxicating combination of cozy solace and thrilling excitement.

As she reached her pussy, she stopped, moving the toy slowly around her vulva, teasing herself. She wasn't sure why she did it, she was already out of her mind, but it was like something came over her. Like she could hear Thane's voice in her head, urging her to go slowly.

She groaned at the thought of Thane's deep, growling voice commanding her body and her pleasure.

Goddess, how she wanted that so badly. Felt so desperate for his touch, his sounds, his taste. *That* thought set off a new riot of heady thoughts. Goddess, how would he taste? How would he react to her kneeling before him, ready to give him the pleasure he craved? The pleasure she was so desperate to give to him.

Her hand drifted with her thoughts, and the vibrator grazed her clit, startling her and pulling a moan from deep in her throat at the same time. Goddess, it felt so good. She toyed with her clit, softly caressing it in rolling strokes as she worked herself higher and higher, feeling desperate for more, more, more.

Her legs opened wider on instinct, and she moved the vibrator lower. Just barely pushing it against her opening, she teased herself a little further.

As she relaxed even more, she pushed in the head of the vibrator, eliciting a soft whimper from her lips. Celestials, she wanted—no, *needed*—to be filled. Finally, she pushed the vibrator in all the way, letting out a sigh of relief as she let herself take it.

She paused for just a moment, getting used to the thick toy, before slowly pulling it out and pushing it back in again.

The fullness of the toy mixed with the vibrations of the head were an explosion of pleasure, racking her body with another deep shiver. As she pushed the toy back in again, the head brushed against her G-spot, pulling a louder gasp from her at the same time as a booming crack of thunder sounded outside.

Her orgasm shimmered in the corners of her vision as she climbed higher and higher. But she needed more, needed something else to push her past that threshold.

With barely a second thought, she conjured her magic. Cordelia moaned deeply as wisps of soft but firm magic brushed against her clit. She let out a breathy laugh, the pleasure taking over all of her senses, overriding all sanity.

"Ah, Goddess," she breathed as another wisp of magic pressed against her clit, harder this time.

With half a thought, she had the magic focused, swirling against her clit as she pumped the vibrator in and out of her pussy. The stimulation of her clit combined with the fullness and vibrations against her G-spot was too much—she was so close and knew she was about to explode.

Stars were already dancing across her vision, her eyes squeezed tight. Then, with a final thought, her magic flicked harder against her clit, swirling still as it pressed down, setting off her orgasm. She whined loudly, bordering on a scream, as her release tore through her entire body, and her hips bucked against the toy, desperately seeking to prolong her orgasm.

With a choked sob and erratic breathing, she finally started to calm down after what was probably only a minute or two, but felt like a small eternity. Her body was boneless and limp, and she slumped even further against her bedding as she let out a little whimper as she pulled the vibrator from her.

She heard another crack of thunder, softer now than it had been just minutes before. The rain was still pattering against the house, pulling her further into the lull of safety and comfort.

After cleaning herself up, she plopped back into bed, pulling the blankets snuggly around her and against her face. The soft scratch of the linen against her cheeks was gentle and familiar as Merlin curled up next to her, purring quietly as he dozed off.

She fell asleep that night with her skin buzzing in anticipation and desire, thoughts of growling voices and flashing black eyes dancing in her dreams.

CHAPTER TWENTY-FOUR

CORDELIA

T he next day, the rain was still pouring, and even stronger than the night before. Cordelia fumbled with the keys in her pocket, standing under the small awning over the door to Mystic Moon Apothecary.

Trying to balance the bag on her shoulder, the coffee in her hand, and her keys was precarious and difficult. But as soon as the lock clicked, she pushed open the heavy, wooden door and breathed a sigh of relief as the ringing of the door's bells filled her ears.

Finally stepping into the warm, dry shop was a blessing. She kicked the door closed, the lock clicking back into place as she rushed to the counter, haphazardly throwing her belongings down.

Sage had called that morning to ask her to mind the shop today. She had some business out of town, and Cordelia was happy to help. She loved just being in the shop and always loved helping out around the place whenever she could.

Taking a deep breath, she let the earthy aroma of the shop fill her senses. Like patchouli and damp earth, it was her favorite scent in her favorite place, the dark cozy shop offering refuge and safety.

She unpacked her bag, pulling out a notebook and pen, her phone, and her laptop. She could get some work of her own done while she watched the shop.

The chiming of the large, old grandmother clock on the wall to her right boomed through the small shop. Without a second glance, Cordelia flicked her pointer finger, and the deep thunk of the front door's deadbolt met her ears. Without hearing it, she knew the small Open sign had turned itself over as well.

After what felt like only minutes, the front door opened, the small bells above it tinkling with the movement.

"Welcome to Mystic Moon Apothecary. Sage is away today, but let me know if you need anything," she said into her paper, still frantically scribbling some notes.

Lifting her head, she started to smile as she faced the customer. But as soon as her eyes met theirs, the smile faded from her face.

"Cordelia, darling. I didn't know you were a shop clerk now." Lydia Halloway's voice was melodic and smooth, but Cordelia knew how to spot the vitriol her mother tried to hide.

Lydia sneered at Cordelia as she looked over what little she could see of her over the counter.

Her mother was wearing a long, black cotton coat with matching black gloves over her hands. Her jet-black hair was pulled back in a smooth bun that lay at the nape of her neck, everything perfectly neat and in place. The angular features of her face didn't match Cordelia's soft cheeks and youthful appearance. It was a wonder they were mother and daughter. They looked nothing alike.

The rigid set of Lydia's lips was a permanent fixture on her face. Just being in the presence of her mother had Cordelia on edge, anticipating a fight at any second. That was all they seemed to do now, all they had done since Cordelia took her fate into her own hands many years ago.

"Ms. Halloway, how can I help you?" Cordelia hoped that maybe if she just ignored her mother's existence, she would go away.

"Ms. Halloway?" Lydia quirked a brow.

Nope, it wasn't going to work. Goddess damn it.

"Is there anything in particular you're looking for today? I can check in the back, but I'm pretty sure we're all out of toxic-bitch incense. Do you know if there's anything you can substitute it with? It would be a shame for you to run out."

This was how it always was between them, and Cordelia knew she had to be on the defense whenever her mother was present.

"Now, darling, there's no need to get an attitude." Her mother waved her hand before pulling her gloves off.

Cordelia's throat tightened, the anxiety coursing through her running thicker, quickening her pulse.

"I'm here to have a discussion with you. One that we've danced around for long enough."

Cordelia blew out a breath, laughing incredulously as she did. "Well, I'm honestly impressed with how long you've held on to this. And I already know what this 'discussion'"—she put air quotes around the word, letting her temper take the reins for a second—"is about. I don't have any interest in talking about it anymore."

"Cordelia Halloway, you have a Goddess-damned responsibility. Not just to the Halloway coven, but to *me*. And I will not stand by and watch you throw that away or ignore it any longer. You've had your fun and games with your plants and playing shopkeeper, but that ends *now*."

Cordelia could see the glow overcoming her mother. It was a sign of Lydia's magic rising to the surface. The energy manipulation magic Lydia possessed.

Cordelia had enchantment magic flowing through her.

Witches that held such magic could enchant anything—objects, shadows, nature, the elements, even animals and people. Each enchantment witch was different, and there were different classes of strength. Cordelia happened to be a very powerful enchantress.

Those with weaker magic couldn't enchant people or animals. But those with stronger enchantment magic could do much, much more. It was a power that Cordelia feared, even though she possessed it in spades. She knew that, in the wrong hands, that magic could do great harm. And she also knew that her mother was very interested in taking advantage of that.

Since Cordelia's magic worked differently than her mother's, she was still vulnerable to Lydia's attempts to drain her energy or control her emotions.

Cordelia rolled her eyes. "I'm not entertaining this idea. These ridiculous notions in your head have got to stop. I *am not* your property."

"You are as long as you are part of the Halloway coven," Lydia seethed.

Cordelia smirked, the ace up her sleeve just itching to be revealed. "Well, thank you for the reminder. I've been meaning to notify you, I am no longer a Halloway." Her tone was strong, firm.

Lydia seemed to deflate before Cordelia's eyes. Her anger seeping away to be replaced by confusion. She cocked her head. "And what, exactly, does that mean?"

"It means, Lydia Halloway, that my name is Cordelia Ashcraft, and I am no longer a member of the Halloway coven." Cordelia stood straighter, pride swelling inside her.

She'd asked Sage that morning what she thought of the idea. Sage had cried and graciously welcomed her to the newly formed Ashcraft coven of two.

"Excuse me?" The anger flooded right back into Lydia, her eyes burning with a fire Cordelia had never seen before. "If you think I'm going to let you do this, you are out of your mind, daughter. *I* am your *mother*, your coven leader."

Cordelia let her magic seep into her skin. Whenever her emotions ran high, she could feel it pulling at her, begging to her to let go.

The lights crackled with steady pulses of Cordelia's energy. The candles all around the shop rose, dotting the air. Her hair floated as she hovered from the floor. The groan of the wood beneath her feet as her weight lifted was an eerie sound, a sign of the rage that flowed freely through her now. She didn't let this sort of magic out often, but she needed to send a message that her mother would understand.

The fury that flowed through Cordelia was like a crackling of electricity, humming along her skin and fueling her. Outside, the cracks of thunder and lightning were picking up, as if sensing her flare of magic and echoing it.

Lydia's eyes reflected the same sentiment, sparking with anger and frustration as she let out a sound akin to a snarl, her features contorting to crack the carefully constructed mask she always had in place.

She stalked forward and slapped her hands on the counter, the sound reverberating through the shop.

"*Enough*, Cordelia," Lydia seethed. "If you don't come willingly, I'll have to take matters into my own hands."

Cordelia's magic flickered, faltering at that haunting promise. Her brows furrowed, a drop of anxiety finding its way back into her senses. She knew what her mother was capable of. Just the statement alone triggered fleeting images of her past, of her years in Halloway Manor. Years of nightmares and torment, screaming and crying. It sent a shiver racing up her spine as she lowered to the floor, the glow of enchantment magic waning from her skin.

But she kept her shoulders back, setting her body rigid and firm against the onslaught of violent promises. She would not look weak in front of her mother.

"I don't take kindly to threats. Especially not in my family's shop. Now, please leave. And be sure to remember that you are not welcome here, Ms. Halloway."

Cordelia didn't even have to move, her magic just followed her thoughts and flung open the front door with a loud bang. A gust of wind blew in, curling around Lydia and pulling her toward the door. She grunted against the force, eyes flaring with anger at Cordelia's defiance.

"We're not finished here, Cordelia. I'll be seeing you soon."

The door slammed shut behind her, the sound reverberating around Cordelia in a swirl of emotions.

What did her mother mean that she would be seeing her soon? What exactly did she mean when she said she'd take matters into her own hands?

Cordelia needed to find a way out of her mother's line of fire. She had fought too long and too hard for the freedom, the bliss, that she had found in this life.

Standing behind that counter, feeling lost, she focused on the sound of the rain outside and desperately tried to push away the dread creeping in from her mother's words.

She wouldn't go back to that manor. She wouldn't let those haunting walls pull her in again. The shadows that lined every wall and corner of Halloway Manor were filled with terror. Her whole life, she'd hated living there and had always been desperate for a way out. One day, she'd found a spell to cloak herself, keep herself from being detected by the house or her mother.

Lydia had been busy in the cellar with a new client, and Cordelia had overheard her tell one of the other witches that it would most likely take all day and well into the night. Cordelia had seen the opportunity hanging in front of her and had taken it.

When she'd gotten out that night, she'd never looked back. She'd run and run and run. Had run all the way into the heart of town, stumbling around in the rain, lost for hours. She remembered the cold fear that'd chilled her down to her bones. Remembered wondering where she would stay, how she would eat, take care of herself, stay out of her mother's grasp.

That was when she'd found Sage. Cordelia had somehow stumbled down the same street as Mystic Moon Apothecary, and Sage had seen her wandering in the rain. The same kind of rain that poured outside now, hard and unforgiving. Blanketing the world in tepid gray.

Sage had called to her from the doorway, ushering her inside the warm safety of the shop. A cup of steaming peppermint tea had floated to her across the room, and Sage had grabbed a towel and blanket from the back office.

As if sensing her memories, Cordelia's magic summoned a steaming cup of peppermint tea from the back of the shop. She smiled softly as she took it, her magic's comfort a welcome reprieve.

That night, Sage had taken Cordelia home with her and offered her a place to stay, not even pushing for a story or explanation. Sage's home had quickly become Cordelia's home.

Sage was like the mother Cordelia had always dreamed of, had always needed. She'd helped Cordelia learn her magic—let her grow, flourish. As far as Cordelia was concerned, she'd always been an Ashcraft in spirit, though a Halloway in name. But the spirit was what mattered more. The warmth of Sage's smile, the patchouli and damp earth smell of the old shop, the laugher they shared, the days they spent together. It was all Cordelia had ever wanted.

And now she could finally call herself an Ashcraft in name too. The thought alone brought her to tears. She was home in so many ways, and for that, she was forever grateful.

Lydia Halloway was not going to get in the way of that. Cordelia would do anything to make sure.

CHAPTER TWENTY-FIVE

CORDELIA

By the time Cordelia trudged home, the rain had stopped. The trees and plants and greenery all around her had gotten a thorough soaking, and with it, she could feel the relief and buzzing of life. She had always been tuned into the balance and energy of nature. Could feel the shifts and differences in that energy every day. It was always reassuring, a comfort among the emotional storms she tended to weather.

Thane had texted her earlier in the day, asking her to grab drinks with him. She had texted an enthusiastic yes, though she didn't feel it in her body.

The interaction with her mother had drained her mentally—she was exhausted both from the expenditure of her own magic and from the effect of her mother's.

Stepping into her house, she immediately heard a soft meow from the kitchen as she watched Merlin float through the wall into the living room. She laughed, rolling her eyes as she bent down to scoop him up. He purred contentedly and leaned into her other hand stroking his head.

"You silly little ghost. I missed you, Mer."

Once she finally made it to her bed, she let Merlin jump from her arms before face planting into the bedding, the familiar lavender smell in the linen soothing her. Before she knew it, she was drifting off.

Cordelia was racing to get ready. She hadn't meant to fall asleep so quickly, certainly not before she set an alarm. Sure, she'd wanted a quick power nap when she got home so she could actually stay awake when she went out with Thane tonight. But a three-hour nap wasn't what she'd had in mind. So now, she was hauling ass to get herself dressed and ready for drinks.

Cordelia threw on a black velvet dress that hugged her curves and hit midthigh, then draped a shawl over her shoulders. It was black and sheer, with intricate patterns swirling around the entire piece. The fringe on the edges fell just past the hem of her dress to brush against the exposed skin on her thighs.

She pulled her hair into a half-up twist with a moonstone hair fork and kept her makeup simple as usual with her standard sharp, black winged eyeliner, mascara, and soft pink blush. After grabbing a pair of black kitten heels, she looked in the mirror. Celestials, even she had to admit that she looked hot. She smirked at that, picturing the look on Thane's face when he saw her. Her body heated at the promise of what tonight might hold.

A few minutes later she was swinging open her front door to Thane. They both looked each other up and down for a long minute before finally meeting each other's eyes, the heat blazing in his gaze surely a mirror of her own.

"Goddess, you're stunning," he breathed, holding out a hand to her as she pulled the front door shut.

She could say the same about him. He was dressed very similarly to their last date, pressed black pants and a black button-down collared shirt with a leather harness on top. This one was a dark brown leather with gold stitching. It was gorgeous. The slots along each strap that were clearly meant to hold blades were empty, but Cordelia thought she'd like to see them filled. Would love to see this dangerous man strapped down with steel. He was deadly on his own, but armed? Well, it wouldn't be a terrible sight.

As Cordelia walked into Hell's Spells with Thane, she was immediately hit with the overwhelming and welcoming atmosphere. The lighting was dimmed, but not too dark. She could definitely still see everything around her, it was just toned down and intimate enough for everyone to have their privacy. The walls were lined with trailing string lights and floating candles, casting a soft glow around the space. She knew the candles had been spelled to never run out, to never go out, and to not catch fire to anything surrounding them. It all added to the magic of the space.

Across the room, Cordelia spotted the famous bar top that everyone chattered about. It was a long, solid slab of labradorite that glittered and flashed blue and green under the candlelight. It was awe inspiring, and she was desperate to know how the owners had gotten ahold of such a big piece.

There were spelled candles of varying sizes and heights, clumped in groups and forever burning, littering the bar too. It was like being in an enchanted forest, even more so because of the plants scattered throughout, hanging from hooks in the ceiling, climbing trellises on the wall, and crowded in front of windows and around the bar. It all culminated in an inviting decadence that drew her in.

The place was famously run by two best friends, a witch and a demon, and the bar was a wild success from the day they opened. It was a place where no one was judged, no one was unwelcome, and everyone had a good time.

Thane took Cordelia's hand and led her through a maze of tables and patrons, tracking down a table of their own. After sitting at one of the few empty spots, Cordelia peered at everything surrounding them. There were so many people, so much chatter, so many laughs and smiles. She could feel the buzzing of the energy around them, could feel the joy, elation, and excitement thrumming in the air.

Their table matched the others in the bar, a dark mahogany with crystals inlaid in a circular pattern over the entire surface. Colorful rings of rose quartz, lapis lazuli, citrine, green malachite, tiffany jasper, moonstone, red jasper, and pyrite glittered in the light. It was stunning, so beautiful. Cordelia pressed her palms to the table, closing her eyes and taking it in.

"You feel something, my pretty witch?" Thane's deep voice pulled her out of her reverie. She opened her eyes and was greeted by the smirk on his lips and the wonder in his glinting obsidian eyes.

"This place is just so magical. I mean, makes sense. The co-owner, Rhea, probably designed a lot of it. It just feels so serene, so welcoming. Like I want to bathe in the energy they imbued this place with." Cordelia closed her eyes again briefly, humming, soaking it all in.

"It really is something." He looked around them, a soft smile pulling at the corner of his mouth. "I'll grab drinks. What would you like?"

"Mm, I'll take a Hexpresso Martini, please!" she chirped, excited for her favorite drink.

She supposed she might drink too much coffee on a regular basis, but she didn't care. Thane just chuckled and turned, weaving his way toward the bar.

As he walked away, Cordelia suddenly felt very aware of herself, as if someone was watching her. She scanned the room, looking for anything out of the ordinary. All she saw was a sea of Magical.

There were a few groups of wolf shifters, a couple of them looking a little leery, peering around the room, but otherwise fairly normal for wolven. There was also a group of vampires and demons cackling in the corner, swaying with the music. She smiled at that, at the carefree spirit.

She took in everything around her again and considered the events of the past couple weeks. She couldn't believe the turn her life had taken, couldn't believe the path that had been forged for her,

Celestial blessed for her. Sure, things had been stressful at first, and they had gotten off to a bit of a weird start. But Cordelia was so confident in this path with Thane, in her decision to pursue a relationship with him. The fated bond was an added bonus but wasn't the entire reason they were together. Cordelia had made sure of it. Had made sure there was a real connection there before she dove in headfirst, before she got herself too lost in him.

The booming music in the bar was upbeat and flowing through her. She was practically drunk on the energy around her already, without even a drop of alcohol passing her lips. She was excited to be here, excited to be sharing in this with Thane, to be moving forward with him.

Peering around what felt like a sea of people, she finally spotted Thane. He had his back turned to the bar and was staring directly at her.

It made her cheeks burn, the flush hot and surely bright. His eyes held such intensity, such depth of emotion. And she felt like she could read those emotions like poetry from his lips. Like they called out to her, like *he* called out to her.

Thane smirked, no doubt his heightened shifter vision made it abundantly clear just how much he affected her.

She gave him a little wave, and he flashed her a small smile before turning back to the bar.

She could tell that he had a lot he was working through, a lot that held him back. But she knew Thane was strong enough to make it through, to pull himself through it. And she would make sure she was there with him, giving him whatever support he needed.

It wasn't until she felt a light burning sensation prickling at her skin, like someone was looking at her, that Cordelia realized her thoughts had drifted. It was like a gentle caress—like a lick of flames, but softer, almost familiar. She looked toward Thane, expecting him to be staring at her again, but he was still facing the bar. Waiting on their drinks, she assumed.

Looking around, she could still feel that humming within her, the featherlight caress of flames dancing on her skin. She just couldn't pinpoint where it was coming from.

Then, her intuition pulled her gaze toward the door. Like her body was suddenly attuned to where it needed to turn. And Cordelia was instantly met with golden eyes. They felt like staring into rivers of gold set alight, like the very heart of a flame.

She suddenly felt like she had been consumed by a wildfire.

CHAPTER TWENTY-SIX

TALIN

Today had fucking *sucked*, and Talin was ready for a drink. Or a few. Between the long days he'd had and his general dreary attitude lately, he needed a break.

So he'd decided to ride the bike down to Hell's Spells tonight to try to get his mind off things, to try to find some sort of fun. Not fun in a one-night stand, nothing like that. He had given up on that lately.

No, the fun he was looking for was a drink in a dark bar, feeling the excited energy around him. It made him feel less alone, helped him forget the stresses plaguing him.

But as soon as he stepped foot in the bar that night, he felt a charged energy that hadn't been there before. Felt something in him pushing, pulling him toward a tempting intrigue. He instinctively looked around, trying to find something different in the space today. Whatever could be calling to him.

As he scanned across the crowd, his gaze snagged on a pair of lavender eyes, glittering and cool. Talin felt a tightening in his chest, felt a bubbling deep inside him. It felt like it was almost . . .

glimmering. Like it was taking over, taking control and replacing his body with a star-filled wonder.

This woman was *magic*. She was like a siren calling to him, like a secret on a chill-kissed breeze, her magic gently brushing against his cheeks.

He realized he was closing the space between them, taking long strides to eat up the distance. He needed to get to her, needed to hear her voice, know her name. He needed—

Suddenly, Thane stepped into his line of sight. It made Talin stumble a bit, stopped him in his tracks.

"Hey man, what are you doing here?" Thane's eyes held a mix of surprise and excitement. Whether it was for him, he wasn't sure, but Talin knew his own face was filled with confusion. He desperately tried to shift gears away from the beautiful woman he was drawn to and toward his best friend.

"Ah, just here to grab a drink, man. What are you up to tonight?" Now that Talin was thinking about it, he was shocked to find Thane out of his routine. Not only was he outside of his house, but he was at a bar?

Then it all started to click into place, seemingly in slow motion. As Thane started to turn, gesturing toward someone behind him, Talin realized several things in quick succession.

One, that Thane was holding two drinks in his hands. Two, that he was now pointing one of those drinks toward the woman behind him. Third, he wasn't just pointing, he was *handing* her the drink. And fourth, that the woman was, in fact, the one that Talin had been making a beeline for just a minute ago.

Everything started to crash down around him as the grim reality settled into his bones. This was Cordelia.

Oh, fuck me sideways.

Everything started rushing back to Talin—time sped up, the sounds around him flooded his hearing.

"Talin, this is Cordelia Ashcraft. My fated and my beautiful date tonight." Thane flashed her a grin, earning a blush and a chuckle.

Goddess, the sound was like a warm caress against his skin. He wanted to close his eyes and bathe in it.

"Uh, hey, Cordelia. Nice to meet you, heard a lot about you from Thane." Talin stumbled across his words, stuck in a trance between world-crushing bliss and a nightmare straight from the pits of hell.

Cordelia seemed to be stuck in the same place, the torn look of confusion as she tried to keep a smile on her face was heartbreaking. Talin offered his hand to her in greeting, but he also just desperately needed to feel her skin on his. To feel the connection between them come to life.

She hesitated before taking hold of his offering. Her small hand was engulfed in his, and the absolute fire that broke out across his skin where it touched hers was nothing short of magical. He knew she felt it, too, when her breath caught, her gaze snagging on their hands.

He wanted nothing more than to pull her to him, to hold her in his arms and never let her go. But then he remembered Thane. His best friend. Cordelia's fated. Celestials, he couldn't wrap his head around it. If this was Cordelia, Thane's fated, then what was this connection between them? What was this incessant pull he felt deep within him? The pull that demanded he never leave her side.

"It's so nice to meet Thane's best friend, and apparently the man to kick his ass into gear." Cordelia laughed, the sound dancing across Talin's senses, filling him with a euphoria that was completely novel to him.

He loved the way her eyes crinkled in the corners when she laughed, the beautiful smile that etched its way across her lips, lighting up her entire being.

He faintly registered Thane laughing right alongside her. Talin needed to snap out of this. What the fuck would Thane do if he realized what Talin suspected was happening right now? He didn't care to find out.

"Well, unfortunately for him, I jump at any opportunity to kick his ass. So thanks for giving me the latest reason." Talin forced a smile across his face.

A smile to cover up the chasm he felt forming inside him, cracks threatening to break him as the realization of who—what—Cordelia was to him set in.

"Oh fuck off, Talin. You know I would stop you if I wanted to." Thane rolled his eyes, the broody bastard pulling Cordelia's attention away from Talin. She smiled up at Thane, amusement dancing in those gorgeous lavender eyes.

"Talin, would you like to join us for a drink?" Cordelia offered, her voice cutting through his daze.

"Ah, no thanks. Don't want to crash your date." He flashed her a grin, desperately hoping it came off as casual as he was aiming for. "I'll let you two be. I'm just gonna . . ." He hitched his thumb toward the bar, an awkward laugh leaving his lips before he quickly turned on his heel and hightailed it toward the alcohol. Turning his head back quickly, he shot behind him, "Nice to meet you, Cordelia!" That part he actually meant.

Once he finally pushed his way to the front, Talin pressed his palms to the labradorite bar top, letting the chill of the crystal seep into his hands, flood his senses. Goddess, he needed to get a fucking grip. How the hell was he going to get through tonight?

Being in the same room as Cordelia, being so close to her. He could feel the pull under his skin, desperately searching for her. It was a damn good thing he turned down joining them. Thane would rip his head right off if he caught wind of what was happening.

His mind was still swirling as he ordered his drink. Taking a seat at one of the stools at the end of the bar, he found he could still see Thane and Cordelia from this angle. Goddess, she was gorgeous. That luminous, honeyed hair, almost stuck between blond and brown. The sparkling lavender eyes, rivers of silver coursing through them. And her scent. *Celestials.* Like lavender in a bonfire. So warm, so sweet, and so earthy.

He felt like he could chant Cordelia's name for all of eternity and never tire of it. It was the sweetest, most exquisite name he had ever heard. He wanted to taste it on his tongue, wanted to hear her say his over and over again.

It was like all the air had been sucked out of the room. The reality of what was happening between them hit him like a ton of bricks. Sure, he was pretty certain before, but the full weight of it settled in now. Settled deep inside him, chilling him to his bones, to his very core.

Fucking Celestials. How the fuck was Cordelia his fated?

CHAPTER TWENTY-SEVEN

CORDELIA

S *tay calm. Everything is fine. You're fine. Just breathe and don't let on*
like anything is happening.

Cordelia chanted to herself over and over in her head after
Talin walked away. She couldn't help but track him as he'd made his
way to the bar where he was now sitting, his head hanging down.

Goddess, he was gorgeous. His tousled, dark brown hair. Like the
color of a fresh, rich cup of coffee. She wanted to run her fingers
through it, to see if it felt as soft as it looked. And he was tall, so tall
compared to her, and even taller than Thane.

And those *eyes*.

Fiery rivers of gold, gleaming with so many emotions. She felt like
they were probably the same emotions filtering through her eyes.
Surprise, wonder, curiosity, excitement, and a little bit of fear. Fear of
what this meant, fear that what they were feeling was right.

When Cordelia had heard Talin's voice, she'd felt like her soul left
her body for a second. It was a sound she wanted to hear for eternity.
Rich and deep, but also somehow holding a hint of playfulness, as if it
lived in his tone permanently.

But as the reality of what was happening sank in, her attention turned toward Thane again. Goddess, Thane. Her fated. The man that she had just gotten far more comfortable with.

She was at ease around him now, like everything was just so right between them. And now here was this curveball thrown her way. Great.

Focusing back on the man in front of her, Cordelia smiled softly at Thane, staring into those eyes like pools of endless night.

Celestials, he was beautiful. Tonight was far from the exception—he looked about as dangerously gorgeous as he had the other night. But she felt guilty tonight. Because she couldn't focus on Thane and Thane alone, and that made her stomach turn over.

"Something on your mind, Cordelia?" He hummed as he sipped his drink, his eyes never leaving hers.

She waved her hand, hoping it would dissipate her racing thoughts. "Ah, nothing. I feel like I never remember just how beautiful this place is until I'm back here."

Thane chuckled. "It really is. I thought you'd like the place. It feels very you."

She felt like she might as well address the elephant in the room. Thane had been a little quiet since Talin had shown up at their table.

"So, that's your friend Talin? He seems nice." Her voice had gone up in pitch, and her cheeks heated a little at the use of his name. It felt like fire erupting across her skin.

"Uh, yeah. That was him. The one and only." Thane scratched the back of his neck, visibly uncomfortable. "He can be a bit much, but he's been my best friend for as long as I can remember. Hope it didn't make things weird with him showing up. I didn't know he would be here tonight."

Cordelia frowned at that, hoping his discomfort wasn't her fault. "No! I don't mind. It was nice to meet him after you mentioned him the other night." Trying desperately to reassure him, she offered him a small smile. He seemed to soften a little at that.

"I'm not sure you'll be happy to meet him once you get to know him more. He can be a giant pain in the ass."

Her heart warmed at that, at how definitive Thane was in his statement. That she *would* be getting to know Talin. Because she was part of Thane's life now, and he a part of hers.

"Speaking of the other night, you actually inspired me." He blushed a little, and Cordelia couldn't help but delight in how absolutely adorable it was.

"Oh yeah?" She beamed at him, taking a sip of the cold drink in her hand. She hummed around the rim of the glass, enjoying the sweet and bitter of the drink. Thane's eyes narrowed at the sound, a glint of red flashing in them again. Something that looked a little like desire. Her body warmed under his gaze, rising to meet that desire.

His eyes slowly moved from her lips to her eyes, the expression softening back to something she couldn't quite place. Something close to affection, but mixed with heartbreak.

"Yeah, I, uh, actually hadn't spoken to my parents in a long time. It's a long story, but after we talked the other night, I couldn't stop thinking about them. So, I decided to reach out and called my dad." Thane's voice was hoarse, like he was overwhelmed with emotion and it spilled into his words.

"Oh, Thane. That's . . . that's amazing! You don't have to tell me anything you're not comfortable with, but how was it?" She reached across the table for his hand, to show him that she was here, and she wasn't going anywhere.

He blew out a breath that mixed with a gentle laugh. "It was amazing. I actually ended up seeing my mom when I got off the phone with him and—" His voice caught for a second. "And I got to see her, right in front of me. I got to hold her, hug her, hear her laugh again. Goddess."

She could see the tears in his eyes. Could see the relief and unending affection for his mother in his expression alone.

"It was a dream. So, while you may not have known it, I wanted to thank you for inspiring me." Warmth filled his gaze as he smiled at her.

"Inspiring you?"

"Yeah, I mean, talking with you about my past, even if I didn't get into it. I don't know"—Thane shook his head—"it just got me thinking."

She didn't press when he paused. She knew he was finding the words, finding the strength, and she would give him as much time as he needed.

"I want to be better. Better for you, for my family, but especially better for myself. You deserve a fated that can open up to you, that can give you everything. And how can I do that if I don't even give my family or myself what we need?"

Grief, regret, love, pain, relief. She saw it all in those beautiful, glinting dark eyes of his. She wanted to reach out and put the stars back in them. To let that light shine through him again.

And in a way, she supposed she had, if what Thane was saying was true. That she had inspired him. It filled her with unending joy.

"Thane, you are enough as you are. I want you to know that." She squeezed his hand, as if tethering him to the physical present. "And you don't have to shoulder the burden of everything in life on your own. You have your family, you have Talin, and most of all, you have me." She smiled, tears welling in her own eyes now.

Goddess, how did she get so lucky to be fated to Thane? This person sitting in front of her, calling her his heart, his inspiration, and give, give, giving all of himself to her. She couldn't think of anything to do but give the same right back to him.

"You, Cordelia, are a wonder." Thane smiled fondly, and the creases that formed around his eyes when he returned her smile were something of beauty. She loved it, she thought. Loved the look of happiness on him.

Finally, a date in a public place that didn't end in disaster.

Cordelia and Thane had been sitting in the bar for a couple hours at this point, and nothing catastrophic had happened.

Not that she'd expected something to. But a girl could only

wonder what was up with her luck when the last public date she'd had was very dramatically interrupted and abruptly ended.

Though, she supposed that was due to Thane waltzing his way into her life. It would be a hard one to match.

At that, her mind drifted off to Talin again. She peered over Thane's shoulder and saw Talin still sitting at the bar, sulking and staring into the empty glass in front of him. She wasn't sure how to handle the situation. Should she tell Thane?

She glanced back to Thane, taking him in. Broad shoulders, defined muscles, that face that always seemed to have a resting scowl etched into it. Yeah, she didn't think he would take it very well. But she also couldn't ignore what she suspected was between her and Talin.

This was a fucking mess.

"Talin, hey man! You heading out?" The sound of Thane's voice snapped Cordelia out of her thoughts.

Looking up, she met Talin's eyes. Goddess, the expression on his face was torture to her. It looked like torture to him too. He was looking right at her, staring into her eyes.

Celestials, those eyes. So bright and gleaming with their almost-iridescent gold coloring. But they looked on edge. His whole face looked like he had been punched in the gut. She felt the same, felt that undeniable pull that she was powerless to do anything about.

"Ah . . . yeah, man." Talin scratched the back of his neck with one hand, hitching his thumb toward the front door with the other. "I figured I would just go home. Just tired, ya know? Long week."

Talin's sentences were short, clipped. Like he couldn't even bear to talk for very long. It tore Cordelia's heart in two.

She could sense a panic rising in her, but why? Because Talin was leaving? Some instinct inside her was screaming to not let him go.

"Well, I'm glad you two finally got to meet, if only briefly." Thane tipped his head toward Cordelia before turning and meeting her eyes, pride and joy sparkling in his, those beautiful depths of black.

Talin turned slightly to her, giving her a soft, sad smile. And that was when she saw it—the flash in his eyes. Almost like streaks of bronze, bold and gleaming. It made her breath catch. It was brilliant, beautiful, like something made of magic itself.

"Well, good night," Thane said gruffly, bluntly dismissing Talin and redirecting his attention to her. His whole demeanor had changed in a split second.

Talin startled, giving them a quick wave before dashing for the door, weaving through the thick crowd.

"Everything alright?" she asked softly, inclining her head toward him. "You seem like something's off."

She reached for Thane's hand, and he quickly retreated, pushing back in his seat before standing. He ripped his jacket off the chair as he dug into his pocket and threw money on their table. "Let's go," Thane almost mumbled as Cordelia stood. He placed his hand on her back, firm and unrelenting, as he led her out of the loud bar.

CHAPTER TWENTY-EIGHT

THANE

The entire drive to Cordelia's was tense, quiet. Thane knew she was a little on edge, especially with how rigid she was in the passenger seat.

But Goddess fucking damn it if he didn't notice the flash in Talin's eyes.

Talin looked right at Cordelia and Thane saw it, subtle as it was. The shift in Talin's eyes between their regular gold and that glinting bronze. And Thane knew, he fucking *knew*.

That motherfucker had somehow gotten a fated bond with Cordelia. How, Thane wasn't sure. But he intended to find out.

He gripped the steering wheel tighter, the rage flowing through him like an inferno. His blood was running fiery hot—his jaw set and his breathing deep.

As a wolf, he knew what that flash of a shifter's eye color meant. It meant that they needed to shift, something in them was triggering that instinct.

Now, a number of things could pull at that—shifters needed to regularly shift into their beast forms for their own sanity and to keep balance. They also needed to shift if they sensed distress, mostly for members of their own pack of wolves or flight of dragons, or someone they loved or cared about. Sometimes exercise helped with the need to shift too. And Goddess knew Talin was always at the gym or moving in some way. The man couldn't sit still.

There was one more reason the need to shift pulled. *Fated bonds.*

"Are you sure you're alright? You seem like something is wrong," Cordelia asked tentatively.

He took a deep breath, blowing it out slowly. He wasn't angry with her. He was mostly angry at the things he couldn't control. And Talin motherfucking Nightveil.

The urge to shift was pulling at him right now—it was intense and insistent. Pulling against him so hard he could barely stand it. Thane hadn't shifted in years. Not since that night. Add in the fated bond with Cordelia and now this with Talin, and it was driving him fucking insane. He felt like he could lose control at any moment.

"It's nothing." He hated lying to her, it soured something in him.

But the rage he felt was so volatile, he didn't know how to get it out without scaring her.

"It's not nothing. Talk, Thane." Cordelia's voice wavered, and he wasn't sure if it was from fear or something else.

How did he tell her that he could sense a bond between her and Talin? How did he explain that to her when he didn't understand it himself? He hadn't even known fated bonds with multiple partners was a real thing. Apparently, tonight was proof enough.

The thought of it sent an electric shock of possessiveness through him. There was no other way to describe it. The steering wheel creaked under the force of his tightening grip. His need for Cordelia was riding him hard.

A slight growl rose up his throat. "Cordelia. Do you know what I learned tonight?" He didn't even glance over at her.

Her emotions shifted. He could scent it. Not quite fear, but something else. Something akin to anticipation.

"What is it?" She was breathless, and that was interesting.

What did his pretty witch know?

"I learned that Talin has a fated." Her breath hitched at that, and he took it as his cue to keep going. "I saw it in his eyes. His body was pulling at him to shift. Did you know he's a shifter?" He chuckled, dark and ominous.

He didn't even wait for her response before continuing.

"He's a dragon shifter, not a wolven like me. But it all works the same. And I saw the need to shift, saw it in his eyes. I know Talin, and there's only one thing that could force that in him tonight."

Cordelia was silent next to him. Thane peered over at her from the corner of his eye to find her tense, unmoving. He could barely tell she was breathing. She looked over, a mixture of fear and sadness in her eyes.

"Talin has a fated. One that I'm willing to bet he met tonight." He pulled into her driveway, smoothly putting the car in park. The engine idled softly below them, the only sound in the car.

"Oh?" She looked like she was afraid of setting Thane off. Like she *knew something*.

"Mmm. And I think I know who it is. Do you, little one?" Thane was fully looking at her now, still gripping the wheel with intense force.

"Me."

It was barely a whisper, but he heard it all the same. He already knew, but hearing her acknowledge it sent a snarl ripping from his throat. She startled and turned toward him, pleading with her eyes.

"I-I didn't know. Not until after I met him and he walked away. Oh Goddess, Thane, are you mad?" He could hear the fear running thick in her voice, and it broke his heart, made him falter a bit to hear it.

He didn't want her afraid, not of him. But he sure as fuck could be pissed with the man who was trying to take her away. Take what was his.

"I could never be angry with you." His voice was still dark, laced with a growl. "But I am feeling very possessive of what is mine tonight. *You* are *mine*, Cordelia. And that little shit Talin isn't going to change that."

He saw a shiver run down her spine, her eyes closing. He scented something different on her now. The fear had dissipated, and in its place was something heady and laced with desire. *Fuck.*

Thane was rock hard already. The need to shift, the drive of the shifters, was intense and could alter your emotions in a split second. Much like now.

"Are you afraid, Cordelia?" His tone echoed with a dark desire.

"No." Cordelia opened her eyes, looking directly into his.

He understood two things in that moment. That she was not afraid of him, in any way, and that she wanted this just as much as he did.

"Good. Now, I need you to get out of the car, and I need you to go inside your house. The second you close that door, you have ten seconds to run and hide. Understand?" His voice felt like the rumble of thunder, like the storm brewing inside him was starting to spill over.

"Yes. I understand, Thane." She was breathless again.

He could hear her heart racing, and he could practically taste the excitement and desire coursing through her, it hung so thick in the air.

"That's a good girl. Now . . ." He leaned in, his lips ghosting over hers. Her eyes closed as she leaned into him a little farther. "Run."

Cordelia's eyes snapped open, and she floundered trying to get out of the car. Once she was out, she raced up the front steps, fumbling with the door before finally swinging it open and slamming it shut. Thane chuckled, counting to himself mentally now that she was inside.

Once ten seconds had passed, he smoothly pulled himself out of the car, stalking for the house.

Let the fun begin.

CHAPTER TWENTY-NINE

CORDELIA

Cordelia's heart was racing, her eyes darting around, as she desperately tried to think of what to do, where to go as the seconds ticked by. She felt like her heart might beat right out of her chest.

But she wasn't afraid. She was *thrilled* by the chase.

She'd been afraid of Thane's reaction to the fated bond with Talin. Was both surprised and not that Thane had figured it out so quickly.

But when she heard the rumble of dark promise in his voice, saw the desire and hunger flashing in his gaze, she melted. Goddess, she wanted him. And when he told her to run, it was like lightning coursing through her.

She'd only gotten her shoes kicked off in the front doorway, her shawl and purse hurriedly tossed aside as she darted into the kitchen.

Before she could do anything more, the front door swung open. She froze, listening to the sound of Thane's calm, measured steps as he strode into the house, closing the door behind him gently.

"Oh, pretty witch. Did I not give you enough time?" He clicked his tongue teasingly. "I suppose I'll just have to chase you if you won't hide."

The growl that rumbled through his words was a fan to the flames inside her. She slowly turned toward him.

The man who stood before her was like a dark god—she could feel the power, the strength radiating off him. The cool authority in his tone could command mountains to crumble. And Cordelia wanted to kneel before it.

Thane was cast in shadows, nothing but the moonlight streaming through the windows to illuminate the dark house. But the glint in his eyes was unmistakable. As he took a small step forward, the silvery light flowed over him. It caught on the shining stitching and leather of his harness, creating a savage air of power and control.

He was about twenty feet from her, and from where she was standing in the threshold of the kitchen she had a straight shot to the staircase. If she hurried, she could rush to the stairs and miss his grasp if he tried to lunge for her.

Her eyes flicked over to the stairs in question, and he tracked that, a smirk pulling at his lips.

"Go on, Cordelia. Let's see how you run." The dark promise in his voice almost made her moan. The thrill of the chase, the thrill of *being* chased, was something she'd never expected.

Without a second thought, Cordelia dashed for the stairs, her bare feet pounding against the hardwood. As she passed in front of Thane, he lunged after her.

She was excited, her heart beating wildly as she closed in on the stairs. She was so desperate, needy, and so badly wanted to be caught.

A snarl ripped the air behind her, and she shivered at the sound. Celestials, she loved this side of Thane. Insane with need, his feral desire, and the force of his shifter personality. It was potent, and she was drunk with lust.

His steps thundered closer and closer on the hardwood floors. Halfway up the stairs, she gasped when a pair of arms gripped her hips, looping around her waist and pulling her down. Her heart stuttered as her knees fell to the unforgiving wood of the stairs.

Cordelia whimpered, but not from pain. She was flooded with a mixture of adrenaline and relief from Thane catching her. Goddess, the feeling of his hands on her, gripping her, was so fucking good.

"*Fuck*, Cordelia," he growled, his mouth against her ear as he pressed his whole body against her, grinding his very present erection against her ass. "You've been a very good girl, running for me," he rasped into her ear, his hips still grinding against her.

She felt like she might combust, felt the wet heat pooling between her legs. She could hardly respond to him beyond whimpers and moans. She was a chaotic mess, but she hardly cared at that moment.

"I need to hear you, little witch. Whose are you?" The rough gravel of his voice rippled through her like electric currents.

"Goddess, I'm yours, Thane. Yours, only yours," she chanted, pushing back against him in a rocking motion.

He chuckled, and the sound was positively wicked. "That's right, baby. And I'm yours. And I'm about to claim what's mine." He nipped at her ear before pushing her down to her hands on the stairs.

She caught herself against one of the steps, her knees balancing on one farther down. Thane ran his hands from her hips up along her sides, gently caressing. His touch felt like a claiming of its own, possessive and curious. He ventured up Cordelia's shoulders, briefly clasping the back of her neck before his fingers threaded through her hair, gripped it, and pulled her head back.

Leaning into her neck, he inhaled deeply before his lips started to devour her throat, trailing up and down and over her jaw. She let out a sound, garbled as it was from this angle, but she hoped he realized it was a desperate plea for more.

Thane's lips against the sensitive skin of Cordelia's neck drove her wild with need, the sensation left her squirming and moaning. Goddess, if he already had her so worked up from this, how would she survive the rest of what he had planned?

His voice rumbled against her neck, the vibrations rolling right into her. Her body happily absorbed it all, deliriously blissful to get any sort of stimulation from this man.

"You like that, hmm?" he said against her neck, his one hand still twined in her hair while the other roamed to her breasts.

She was still wearing her dress, and she was desperate to get it off, needed to feel his hands against her skin.

Cordelia bit her lip, lifting one hand to fumble with her dress. She wanted it gone.

"Ah, I see what you want, little one." His hand moved from her breast slowly, so slowly down to the hem of her dress. He toyed with it a minute, letting her squirm, letting her restlessness grow. "Can you use your words, baby?"

"Goddess, Thane, just take off my dress!" she shrieked, not caring that her impatience was clear. He just laughed, the sound deep and intoxicating.

He let go, straightening as he pulled her up with him before making quick work of taking off the dress. She hadn't worn a bra, so she was left in just her panties now, bare before him.

He groaned, long and pained. "Are you fucking kidding me, Cordelia?"

Before she knew it, his hands were on her again, roaming. Only hungrier this time, more hurried and needy.

His mouth latched onto the side of her throat again as his hands shot to her breasts. The two movements didn't match, his mouth was hot and quick against her skin as his hands were gentle, lightly toying with the area around her nipples. The combination had her pushing against him, into his hands, seeking more friction.

Finally, *blessedly finally*, he plucked her nipples with his fingers and something inside of her caught fire. The inferno was rising, blazing a trail through Cordelia's body. She pressed her legs together, the need growing more and more each second. If she didn't get some sort of pressure, some sort of stimulation, she was going to crawl out of her skin.

He must have felt the movement, because he groaned against her, grinding his cock into her again.

"Does my pretty witch need something?" Thane whispered in her ear, one of his hands still playing with her nipple, while the other trailed down, down, down, over her hips and ass, getting achingly closer to where she needed him.

"Please, Thane," she whimpered, rocking her hips, encouraging him to move.

"Please, what?" he whispered, still teasing and toying with her neck.

"Please, please, please, Thane, play with my pussy," Cordelia gasped, her fingers curling against the wood under her palms.

He chuckled but said nothing more. Suddenly, he was pulling away from her and standing up. She started to turn around and opened her mouth to protest when she heard a loud thunk followed by a whisper of fabric on the stairs behind her.

Before she could react, his hands gripped her thighs, spreading her legs, and she felt his hot breath against her ass. She moaned, a surge of heat racing to her already soaked pussy.

She yelped, startled as he bit into her ass. Not too hard, but enough to surprise her. Her breath caught as she turned her head, leveling him with a stern look. Thane laughed before smacking her ass.

"Be a good girl and turn around. Let me take care of you, baby."

She wasn't going to argue with that, snapping her head back around.

Immediately, Thane's fingers were gliding through her wet folds, the action followed by a growl. "*Fuck*, Cordelia, you're fucking drenched." He pulled his fingers back before slowly, so fucking slowly pushing them back through. "Oh, baby, you need some relief, don't you?"

She nodded fervently, even though he couldn't see it.

"Words, Cordelia."

"Yes, Goddess, yes. Please eat my pussy, Thane." She needed him on her, and fast.

"As you wish," he murmured into the skin of her thighs.

He ran his flattened tongue up her pussy, groaning as he did. He gave it one, two, three more licks before he started teasing her, lazily licking up and down the sides of her vulva. Gently, playfully stroking her, amping up her sensitivity. As he did, his hands gripped both of her thighs, fingers digging in and leaving their marks. Suddenly, she felt small, sharp pricks of his claws against her skin. A little squeal mixed in with her moans.

"Celestials, you taste like mine," Thane groaned into her, the vibrations clinging to her pussy, another wave of euphoria washing over her.

He flattened his tongue, swiping it side to side over her clit. It was perfect, and Cordelia could feel herself climbing higher and higher already. It was so fucking good.

But she wanted—no *needed*—more from him, more *of* him.

"Please, Thane," she whimpered, hardly able to grasp the ability to speak. "I need you." She was practically panting at this point, but she didn't care.

He ignored her, instead pulling her tighter against him as he loosened the tether on his control a little further. He growled into her, eating her like these were his last breaths.

He moved lower, down her pussy, licking and stroking with his tongue as he went. Experimenting between long, firm licks and gentle, teasing ones. She was breathless, the wood under her palms and knees ached but somehow added to the pleasure. The inability to see Thane, to touch him, was driving her wild. But she just couldn't get enough of this.

He licked around her opening, swirling his tongue and applying more pressure in random spots as he went. As he did that, his hand snaked over her thigh, his fingers slowly inching toward her pussy. Finally, they were running through her wetness, dragging, teasing. She bucked against him, trying desperately to guide his hand exactly where she needed it. He just laughed against her.

"Don't get too eager, little witch." He moved his slow cadence up toward her clit and gave her a couple more licks.

"Now, I want you to give in to me, baby. Give me an orgasm, and then maybe you can have my cock. Mmm?" He didn't give her time to respond before he set back in, diving into her pussy with a renewed fervor, his fingers still idly stroking just above her clit.

She couldn't respond with anything other than a moan and a

further push back against him, in dire need of more—more friction, more pressure, more everything.

Finally, blessedly, he started rubbing her clit. Hard and slow, he swirled his fingers in a circle, throwing her right toward the edge. The pleasure was borderline torture at this point. She was only getting more and more wet by the second, and now she was desperate to be thrown into the glittering dark of her orgasm.

"Ah, Thane! Fuck, I-I'm . . ." She trailed off, biting her lip and squeezing her eyes closed before she exploded, letting go with a scream that quickly turned into a long moan. Stars danced in her head as her orgasm rolled through her, wave after wave of pure bliss.

He just kept lapping, not stopping until her orgasm had fully faded and she was starting to fall limp.

"That's my girl." He gave her one more long lick before pulling back, his arms looping around her waist and pulling her to stand.

She felt boneless, in a dreamy, cloudy state as she looked up at Thane and smiled, pressing her cheek against his chest. One arm was banded around her, holding her steady, while the other stroked her hair.

"Now, let's see how well you can take my cock."

CHAPTER THIRTY

CORDELIA

Cordelia felt a chill run down her spine at Thane's words. Her eyes fluttered shut for a second before they shot back open, surprise lighting her up when he threw her over his shoulder.

As he bounded up the stairs, he gave her ass a hard slap. A squeak burst from her lips. He chuckled, dark and promising as he strode into her bedroom and threw her onto the bed where her body bounced for a second as she settled. His eyes narrowed in on her, his stare hungry and all-consuming.

She took a good, long look at him. His hair was still so perfect, as put together as it had been when he had picked her up that evening. The short, inky-black strands were gleaming in the moonlight streaming in from the bedroom window. His eyes were sparkling with the heat of desire, and she kept gleaning small flashes of blood red in the depths of his onyx irises. Like mischievous, colored stars lighting up his gaze.

His jaw was sharp with the force of his clenched teeth, a sign that he was holding himself back right now. His broad shoulders and muscled chest were rapidly rising and falling, his breaths deep and fast as he silently devoured her with his gaze.

And Goddess, those fucking pants. Molded to his legs, and still frustratingly clinging to him. She wanted them off. Wanted him bare before her just as she was to him.

She smirked, her magic crackling under her skin as a fun idea popped into her head. "Thane, baby, this is a rather uneven circumstance. Don't you think?"

She didn't give him time to respond before she snapped her fingers. His pants disappeared, reappearing on the floor across the room. Thane now stood before her wearing only his black boxer briefs.

"Ah, there we go." She hummed, giving him her most winning smile.

The smile that quirked at the corner of his lips heated her blood, setting her very soul on fire.

"Clever, little witch. What other tricks do you have up your sleeves, I wonder?" He tilted his head, his eyes boring into her as he crept forward.

"Mm, I'm not sure." She bit her lip, glancing over him again. "But I would be interested in seeing what you can do." She lifted her hand, twirling her fingers in a *spin for me* motion.

He shook his head, coaxing a laugh from Cordelia's lips. "Oh, my pretty witch. I think you're sorely mistaken about who is in charge here."

He stalked forward until his legs met the end of the bed. Her breath caught as he kept his eyes on her and pulled his boxer briefs down, down, down until he was kicking them across the room. His cock slapped against his lower abdomen as he stood there, gloriously naked before her.

Wet heat coursed through her, down to her pussy as she stared. He was fucking huge, and she was both a little nervous and very excited at the same time, the thrill of being with Thane running through her veins. His cock was long and thick, thicker than she'd thought, but she imagined it would be a delicious stretch to take him completely.

And at the base of that glorious cock was a thick bulge. Cordelia knew enough about shifters to know what it was. Both wolf and dragon shifters had knots—big and bulbous at the base of their cocks —that were made for breeding. They were also known to increase the pleasure in a shifter's partner, and she couldn't fucking wait to take Thane's. Eventually. Taking a partner's knot was a big moment for a couple, and neither of them were ready for that just yet. And besides, Cordelia knew she couldn't take Thane's knot all in one go. She would definitely need some prep to work her way up to it.

She would start with that beast of a cock first.

Climbing on the soft linen sheets, inching closer to her, he said, "Your magic is fun, darling. But I'll show you what being mine looks like."

He grabbed her hips, pulling her toward him and ripping a squeal from her throat. She couldn't help but giggle as Thane settled himself between her legs.

He kept his eyes on her, kissing the inside of her thighs as his hands pushed them wider. His path led him higher and higher until he placed a soft kiss just above her pussy, his tongue briefly flicking out against her clit and forcing a moan from her, breathy as it was. But too soon, he was rising, pulling himself away from her, only to drag his body fully over hers. She was completely enveloped in him, and she reveled in it.

"Mmm, are you ready for me, little witch?" He leaned in close, his lips ghosting over her own.

Cordelia could only moan in response, her chest rising to meet his.

"Do you want me to use a condom?"

"No. I'm protected. I use a contraceptive spell," she breathed.

Thane growled in response, leaning into her again.

His lips brushed against hers oh so gently before moving to her cheeks, his hot breath further igniting the fire within her. He moved to her jaw and then her neck where his lips finally pressed into her skin, firm and insistent. He trailed openmouthed kisses up and down her neck before settling in just under her ear, the sensitivity of her skin leaving her mewling and moaning.

She was out of control, unable to hold herself back. She had always had sensitive skin, which was both a curse and a blessing. But right now, it was a blessing. The intense sensitivity just set her alight, heightening her pleasure to the point of insanity.

Both of her hands clutched his biceps, and her nails dug in. The pain of it made him grunt, his hips canting into hers, which just set off a chain of frenzied pulling between them. Cordelia pulling at Thane, Thane pulling her closer, his mouth growing more fevered against her.

Finally, he pulled away, both of them trying to catch their breath for a split second before his mouth descended on hers. It was the first time they'd kissed that night, she realized suddenly. The heat of everything had gotten to them, had pulled them into its hazy, lustful spell. And Cordelia was blissfully trapped in it, in this world of heated desire.

She ripped her mouth away, desperate as she pleaded, "Please, Thane. Goddess, *please*." It was all she could muster, and she trusted that he knew what she wanted, what she *needed*.

And she thanked every fucking Goddess of the Celestials as he reached down between them, gripping his cock and guiding it to her pussy. She was only getting wetter with anticipation. And neither of them said anything before he pushed in, so slowly.

A sound halfway between a groan and a plea was pulled from her lips, her hands clamoring for his hips, her nails digging into his silky, hard muscles. Her legs fell wider, her knees bending slightly. She was ready to push herself onto him if he didn't pick it the fuck up.

Only the head of his cock was in, and she was already ravenous. He was so fucking hard, she could already tell, and the wide, hot expanse of his tip was a welcomed burn.

Thane even seemed at a loss for words as he groaned, his expression pained as he pushed in farther, but still only feeding a couple inches into her.

"Fuck, baby, please," she whined.

"Goddess damn it, Cordelia," he gritted out before thrusting in the rest of the way.

The burn and stretch flared to pain for a split second before melting into the most mind-numbing pleasure she had ever felt.

Her vision flashed with threads and stars of the most brilliant gold. Her grip on Thane was her only lifeline, a tether in the chaotic storm that was their world. And his grip on her felt like a branding, like a claiming. Like the deepest ocean of affection. She could drown in it.

He held still like that for a second, letting her adjust, letting her body melt into the pleasure he was offering. And as soon as she did, he must have felt it, because he pulled back, withdrawing to just the tip of his cock, before plunging in again. And they both screamed as he did. Her hands scrabbled for purchase, one to wrap into his hair at the back of his neck and the other to his back, and she held on for dear life as his pace continued to pick up.

The hard, slick feel of his cock pounding into her was like coming home.

Cordelia's feet were still propped up on the bed, giving her the perfect leverage to thrust into him, to match his pace, perfectly in sync.

Thane leaned down, his head resting in the crook of her neck and his hand holding her hip down, forcing her to take it.

"*Fuck*," he breathed before his head tilted and his tongue ran over her neck. "Oh fucking *fuck*, Cordelia."

Grabbing hold of her hips, he sat back on his heels and pulled her onto his cock, sliding her farther toward him on the bed. The wet slap of her pussy on him sent a new wave of heat through her.

His cock was deeper in her now, so blessedly deep she felt his knot bump against her. The feeling of it alone sent her into a frenzy as she moaned and bucked against him.

His thumb found her clit, rubbing slow, sloppy circles as he continued to fuck the life out of her, his hips snapping in the most delicious rhythm.

"Is this what you want, little witch? Is this how you like it?" He grinned down at her, his entire demeanor all power and domination. It lit her up and made her pleasure fucking soar.

"Yes, baby, please don't stop." She could hardly get the words out between pants, her body like a live wire.

She shook her head from side to side, hardly able to control her motions. She had heard of shifter heats, but every single thought had already emptied out of her mind, so she couldn't quite make sense of it right then.

Thane slowed his tempo, dragging his cock in and out of her so fucking slowly it drove her out of her mind. She pushed back against him, her hips desperately trying to up the pace.

Then he stopped thrusting, now only grinding his thumb into her clit in those big, hard circles. She whimpered, her lips parting, ready to start begging. Because he was right, she absolutely *needed* to come. But he spoke before she could.

"Tell me, darling. Tell me what you are, and I'll let you come." He pulled out even slower before thrusting in *hard*. "Tell me," he growled, the sound reverberating through her body so deliciously.

"I'm yours. I'm fucking yours, Thane!"

He chuckled, his grin growing, his elongated canines showing now. "That's my good girl."

Then he let the final tether on his control snap, falling back on top of her. One hand braced above her, the other still working her clit as his hips snapped hard into her, his pace getting faster and faster until she was a moaning, sloppy mess beneath him.

"Fuck, I'm fucking coming," Cordelia groaned, a scream forming and dying on her lips before she could release it.

"Fuck, fuck, fuck," Thane chanted, his orgasm crashing into him at the same time.

They rode that wave together, his thrusts softening, but not stopping. He stretched their pleasure as far as he could before he collapsed next to her, a whimper falling from Cordelia's lips as he pulled out.

While they both caught their breaths, he wrapped her in his arms, holding her tight as he kissed her forehead.

"That's my girl," he murmured. And it was the last thing she heard before she dozed off, unable to keep sleep from taking her away.

Cordelia woke up dazed and bleary eyed. It took her a second to get her bearings, but once she did, it was only to find herself wrapped in an explosion of sensations.

Thane was awake beside her, kissing her neck and running his hands down her body so softly, just the tips of his fingers gently trailing the length of her chest, her breasts, over her belly.

Once he finally made his way to her hips, he hesitated before moving down to her legs, caressing her thighs and rubbing slow circles with his thumbs. The sigh that escaped her was breathy and content, a slow, soft smile blooming across her lips.

When his touches turned more insistent, she scrunched her eyebrows together. His hand worked its way to her exposed pussy, her body still naked from their earlier activities.

She couldn't fathom his ability to keep going. They had been at it for hours, touching, exploring, and pulling so many orgasms from one another. She had fallen asleep after their last round almost immediately, her body so heavy with satisfaction she could only be dragged down to the depths of sleep. But now it was like it was reluctantly lighting up again, the sore ache of her muscles screaming

His fingers worked against her clit, the sharp stimulation forcing a pained moan to rise from her throat. Too much, it was all too much. She writhed against him, his other hand lifting to brush against her cheek. Desperate to distract herself from the sharp sting of pleasure, she leaned into the touch.

"C'mon, pretty girl. You can give me one more." His voice was a low murmur, encouraging and deep. "I know you've given me so many tonight, but you can give me more. You *will* give me one more."

He shifted so he was braced above her, still so gloriously naked and powerful. She knew she could never get tired of this sight. Of the power of knowing he was hers.

His fingers were still swirling circles against her clit, pulling uncontrollable sounds from deep within her. Whimpers and pleas and moans. Begging for it to stop, begging for more, begging for something she wasn't sure of. All she knew was that he was addictive, and she didn't know how to stop. She needed him to be the one holding the reins, to be the one controlling and manipulating her body, her pleasure.

She hadn't realized her eyes were closed until she fluttered them open, a combination of exhaustion and blessed bliss making them heavy. She was so suddenly full as Thane sank his hard cock into her, and it was both a sore stretch of every aching part of her and a fucking heavenly, silken euphoria. She wanted to disappear into it and let go.

"There you go, darling, nice and full. Now, give me one more like I know you can, baby. One more and you can rest." His voice was so soft and encouraging, and his eyes held a mocking sweetness that glittered like dark jewels. Cordelia loved it and it spurred her on, her hips now moving on their own accord.

As Thane slowly dragged his cock out and just as slowly pushed back in, she thought she couldn't stand it, she would have to die like this. She was so fucking full of pleasure it was like that delicious ecstasy had invaded every nerve ending, every sensitive inch of her skin, every single part of her and was pulsing through her from the inside out.

And suddenly, she was exploding. Her eyes squeezed shut as a riot of colors exploded in her mind. She felt like she had left this plane of existence and entered another as she rode that exquisite pleasure for all it was worth. She was vaguely aware of a growl above her as Thane found his own release.

A small eternity had passed by the time she came back to reality, and she found herself wrapped up in Thane. He had pulled them under the covers, his arms wrapped around her and her legs tangled with his.

And that was how she drifted off, her breathing even and matching his as golden threads danced in her dreams, tying them together and sparkling like stars.

CHAPTER THIRTY-ONE

TALIN

Fire. All-consuming fire licked up Talin's skin, seemingly unending and unquenchable.

Fuck.

He took that back. He knew what would quench it. But he needed to get this shit under control. There was no way he was going to be able to get what he needed.

Get *her.*

He groaned, squeezing his still-closed eyes. A streak of sunlight streamed in from the bedroom window, warming his bare skin in the morning light.

He could hardly believe last night had actually happened. And if he kept his eyes closed, maybe he could keep thinking it was a dream. A beautiful, lovely, panic-riddled dream. He could still see those soft lavender eyes, captivating and entrancing. Could still feel the pull to her, that bone-deep *need* to be near her.

Finally opening his eyes, Talin stared at the ceiling above him. How the fuck was he supposed to act like everything was normal, like he didn't have this wonderful and terrifying new horizon? And how the fuck was he going to tell Thane?

He groaned again, loud and long, as he rolled over and shoved his face into his pillows. He hoped the bed would swallow him whole, drown him in soft blankets and fluffy pillows until everything else disappeared.

He pulled himself out of bed and trudged to the kitchen, his nerves on fire. He was so strung out on the high of utter joy and the brain-frying anxiety of this situation he found himself in.

A Goddess-damned fated. Not only that, but his best friend's fucking fated.

But holy fuck was she gorgeous. He had never seen someone as beautiful as Cordelia. With that honey-blond hair, shining lavender eyes, those fucking delicious curves everywhere.

He just wanted to sink into her and never return. Wanted to swim in the beautiful, light-filled pools of her eyes. He had gotten close enough last night to see the twinkling lights above them illuminate her irises, highlighting the sparkling rivers of silver that flashed in them. *Celestials*, he was fucked.

Running a hand over his face, he tipped his head back, standing in front of his kitchen sink. He straightened before slumping over, flipping on the cold tap on the faucet and plunging his head under the icy stream of water. He gasped, momentarily shocked by the temperature, before he shivered and settled into the clarity of the cold.

It also helped to calm down the raging fucking erection he'd been desperately trying, and failing, to ignore. Sure, what man didn't wake up with morning wood? But today it was a fucking nightmare. He'd momentarily thought he'd woken up with a fucking tactical missile in his boxer briefs.

Yeah, today was going to be a long-ass day.

Talin's breaths were coming out in stuttering pants at this point as he pushed himself further and further. He just couldn't stop running.

After he'd pulled himself somewhat together this morning, he realized that part of the fire burning hot in him was the urge to shift, demanding and relentless. He could feel his wings threatening to pop out of his back at any moment. So, he'd panicked and started running.

It usually kept his mind off the shift, and any other shit that he was trying to avoid. But today was different, today was a special circumstance. A special kind of hell.

His mind was a racing whorl of chaotic thoughts.

What is Cordelia doing right now? Did she feel the bond like he did? Is she wondering about him? Do her eyes change color in the light? What's her favorite food?

And then a shift in direction.

How will Thane react? How will he even tell Thane? Will Thane kill him? Will he have to run away, change his name, grow a mustache to try to keep up a secret identity?

Goddess, he sounded just like Thane not so long ago. When Thane had been out of his mind waiting on a text from Cordelia. Talin had needed to beat some sense into him, and the only way he could was through training.

Which was a thought that'd popped into Talin's head this morning. He could always take his tension out on some weights. But then he might run into Thane at the gym, and Goddess knew he wasn't fucking ready for that conversation yet.

He was sure Thane would start poking around eventually, and then he would realize something was up. Talin wasn't the quiet type. And his silence would definitely be noticed.

It was fine. He just needed some time to figure out how to explain himself, how to strategize. And how to make sure he came out of it alive.

A hand wrapped around Talin from behind, slowly making its way toward his aching cock. He was so fucking hard, he might explode just from the slightest of touches. He groaned, pushing himself back into the presence behind him.

"Fuck, please," he begged, unable to care about how desperate he sounded. He needed relief, needed connection, needed something.

A small, husky chuckle sent a shiver through him. His cock leaked at the sound.

Their hand traveled lower, lower, before soft fingers ran over the hot skin of his cock. He was so painfully hard and needed an escape, a release.

Finally, Goddess finally, they wrapped their hand around Talin's cock and gave it a rough pump, nice and hard just like he liked it. He threw his head back, breathing out a long "Fuck."

They kept pumping, slow and hard, teasing him. His cock just leaked more and more as he wound higher into his ecstasy.

"Are you going to come in my hand, baby?" the voice behind him murmured.

It was a feminine voice, one that he didn't know very well but was familiar. Something tickled at the back of his mind, nagging to identify the voice.

"Yes, Goddess, yes," Talin breathed, his hips bucking into the hand wrapped around him. The hand holding him at their mercy.

"That's right, my love. My beautiful boy. My fated."

It rushed to him at that last word. Cordelia. It was Cordelia.

Fuck, he couldn't hold back now. His control snapped. He bucked harder, desperate for more friction, more pleasure—just more. He was racing toward his orgasm, Cordelia's hand hot and insistent against him.

Talin woke with a jolt, his eyes snapping open in the dark of his bedroom. He was panting, sweat beading on his forehead.

Did he just have a fucking wet dream about Cordelia? Shit. He needed to get ahold of himself and snap out of this.

Eyes closed, his head still resting against his pillow, he groaned. Then he became very aware of the raging erection he was sporting.

His skin felt hot and tight, and his blood pumped faster in the wake of his dream. There was no way he'd be able to go to sleep now. Not until he got some relief.

Eyes still closed, Talin reached down and gripped his cock, a moan immediately ripping from his throat. He could still feel the ghost of Cordelia's hands on him, could feel the hard, slow rhythm against his cock.

The shift pulled under his skin as he pumped himself, his dragon insisting to be let out.

Then the memory of Cordelia's eyes, that hair, those delicious curves of hers flashed into his head. He could just imagine being able to grip her, grip those fucking incredible hips as he feasted on her. Could imagine that belly in his hands as he squeezed her, fucking her from behind as she screamed into the bed beneath her. Or the couch, or the grass, or the kitchen countertop. Anything he could fuck her against, really.

"*Fuuuuucking* hell."

Ecstasy pulsed beneath his skin, rolling over him in waves. He ran his thumb over his tip, and he hardened further beneath his palm. The ribbed texture of his cock burned hot, his knot tightening.

He wondered what it would feel like, his knot bumping against that sweet pussy as he fucked Cordelia for all he was worth. Wondered what it would feel like to actually knot her.

"Shit." His breath stuttered as his orgasm rose to the surface.

"Shit, shit, shit," Talin chanted as he came, his cum splashing hot against his stomach. He kept pumping in shallow strokes, trying to wring out every bit of pleasure.

Talin could imagine his hand replaced with Cordelia's, could imagine the look of satisfaction and hunger on her face as she witnessed the sight before her. Could imagine the squeal that would burst from her lips as he pounced, toppling her over to devour her pussy.

Talin ran his cum-free hand down his face. "Fuck, I'm screwed."

CHAPTER THIRTY-TWO

CORDELIA

Cordelia's entire body was sore. Even her soul felt sore at this point.

She and Thane hadn't stopped touching or fucking one another since that night after the bar. It had been amazing, but she was exhausted, and the thought of being touched or entered or brought to release made her cringe. She wasn't sure she would ever be able to orgasm again.

Leaning back where she sat in the garden, she stretched her legs out in front of her as she faced the warming light of the sun. The rosemary and lavender plants surrounding her tickled her arms.

She'd needed to be out here, to be among her life-filled garden. Nestled in the herbs and flowers. All mostly used for spells or some sort of magic, but all a grounding force for her, as well. Her magic was drawn to the life of plants, and it bloomed under their buzzing energy.

Thane wasn't far behind her, lazily strewn in one of her lounge chairs closer to the house with Merlin sprawled across his lap, clearly already enamored with the wolven.

Thane hadn't left Cordelia's side since they'd gotten back from their date a few nights ago. And while she usually preferred her alone time, his presence was welcome, comforting even.

How had two days already passed since then? Celestials, had they been that wrapped up in each other? To not know how much time had passed?

She sighed, contentment settling into her very bones. Yeah, she was fine with that.

But now her thoughts were converging , swirling and brewing a storm inside her. The weight of the reality of everything else surrounded her, threatening to choke and control her.

She had so many things to focus on now that she and Thane had sated themselves.

Lydia needed to be dealt with. Cordelia had been content for so long to just try to exist peacefully, the occasional nuisance of her mother's incessant orders just a pest. But after their encounter at Mystic Moon the other day, she knew something had to be done.

And then there was the matter of Talin.

Sure, Thane had said he wasn't upset with her. But that didn't mean he wasn't upset with the situation. And she wasn't going to just ignore it, try to will it away. That wasn't fair to her, and it certainly wasn't fair to Talin.

Goddess, she had two fateds? How that was true, she wasn't sure. There had been accounts of multiple fated partners before, but not in recent history, and they were so very rare. To have so many threads bound together in the fated bond was something of a mystery—and a wonder, she thought.

She could still see Talin's beautiful golden eyes, the way they'd flashed bronze, the way they'd focused on her and nothing else. It was like fire consuming her from the inside out, and it was addictive. Even after experiencing it only once, she already knew she wanted more.

But how would this work with Thane? How would she have this conversation with him, how could she explain this? She didn't want Thane to think she didn't want him. But she also wanted to be clear that she and Talin both deserved to know one another, at the very least.

Thane had sounded so sure of her getting to know Talin before. But that was before he'd realized what had rooted between her and his friend. Before he'd felt the rage that fueled their claiming.

Cordelia's cheeks burned at that, at the memory of how absolutely feral Thane had been that night. The wild look in his eyes, the way he'd chased her. It was enough to send heat flowing through her body to pool lower, lower, lower. She groaned, the feeling of her arousal both welcome and not. She pressed her legs together, trying to dissipate it somehow.

Behind her, she heard a low growl. The perks of having a shifter fated meant that he could smell *everything*.

"Rein it in, wolf boy. If you touch me, I might scream. And not in a good way," she called to him, not even bothering to spare him a glance.

Thane laughed, the sound a balm to her aching soul. "You sure you don't need me to lick that sore little pussy better?" His voice was low, needy.

She wasn't sure how he was so unfazed by their literal marathon of sex, but she was going to be the voice of reason here.

"I think that falls under the definition of *touching me*, so no. Keep your mouth to yourself, Thane." She gently shook her head to herself, a faint smile blooming on her lips.

Cordelia stepped into the blessedly cool house hours later, her skin buzzing with the energy of organic life and her magic all at once. She was so refreshed, so recharged. It was a blissful feeling, one that inspired and fueled her.

Grabbing her water bottle, she made her way to the kitchen table where Thane was looking at his laptop and writing in a notebook. He'd left earlier to grab a few things, he'd said. He'd also showered and changed, and a few strands of his wet hair hung in his eyes. She smiled at that, at how soft he looked like this.

"What's that?" she asked.

"Just some pack stuff. I just feel like I'm running in circles on it." He ran his fingers through his hair, frustration and confusion lining his features.

"What's going on?" She hoped she wasn't pressing him too hard on this, hoped she wasn't overstepping.

But they'd had a discussion between rounds of sex a couple days ago about what this all meant. What it meant to have taken this step between them, to have claimed each other as fateds.

The agreement was that they were together, fully and completely, and that they would be much more involved in each other's lives, including the everyday things.

Cordelia was excited to take him to her favorite places, to introduce him to Sage and show him the shop. To show him what her blissful peace looked like, what her spells looked like, her rituals. Share her walks with him, play with Merlin together, have their coffee together, laugh until it stole their breath. To let him in.

"There's been a string of kidnappings. All Harmonious wolves, but there's no pattern about which packs they come from, and we can't pin down a single person who might be behind it. Though, I have my guesses." Thane's eyebrows were scrunched together, his eyes moving across the screen as he spoke. Like he was poring over a puzzle he couldn't quite solve.

"The Harmonious wolven are where you come from, right? They're the blend of Theian and Artemisian?" Cordelia had been trying to brush up on her wolven knowledge.

She hadn't met many, as they tended to keep to themselves, preferring the company of other wolves.

"Yes, that's right." Thane looked up at her now, those beautiful pitch-black eyes shining in the midday light as he gazed at her affectionately. "Harmonious wolves came about with the Harmony Treaty, hence our name. Part of the treaty included an agreement that

Theian and Artemisian wolves would breed together, mixing their bloodlines and sealing the peace they had negotiated. It was also an offering to the Goddesses to appease them, since they were the ones who made the treaty happen. But there were factions of the Theian and Artemisian wolven that refused to mix with one another. 'Keep the bloodlines clean' as they say." Thane rolled his eyes, and Cordelia couldn't help but agree with the sentiment.

It was ridiculous, the notion that they didn't want to "dirty" their bloodlines. It disgusted her.

"And, naturally, because of that, there's always been tension between the 'purebred' wolven and the Harmonious wolven. They don't like our very existence, and they don't like each other. So there's always some sort of horrible rhetoric being spewed on either side. And the Harmonious wolven tend to get caught in the middle, because we're the scapegoat for their hate." His voice was low and dangerous, a sign of the misery he had most likely endured his whole life as a Harmonious wolf.

She couldn't imagine it, why the very existence of someone would cause such hatred, just because of what they were born as. Her heart ached at the thought, ached for the peace she so wished Thane could have known growing up.

"So, even though I run border patrol as my regular responsibility for the Harmonious wolven, I'm also usually pulled into these sorts of things. Since I used to be an alpha." His voice softened at the end, and Cordelia couldn't help but reach to grasp his hand in hers. To give him some sort of reassurance.

"Anyway, so that's what I'm looking at right now. The details of those missing wolves, to try to figure out what happened and where the pattern is that I'm not seeing." Thane sounded tired and ragged just talking about it, like it was something that had been weighing him down for a while. From the sound of it, it had.

He closed his laptop, leaning back in the chair and blowing out a breath. "I just need to clear my head, think about something else so I can come back to it with, hopefully, new eyes." His gaze returned to hers, a slight smile pulling at the corner of his lips. "What are you thinking, little witch?"

Cordelia laughed, the sound nervous and riddled with anxiety. "Well, I don't know that you'll like why I came in here. Especially not after dealing with that." She pointed to his laptop and notebook, stalling and trying to think of something else to discuss.

Her mind was clouded with Talin and Lydia Halloway. And the latter was not something she really wanted to think about right now.

"Oh?" Thane leaned against the table, his brow quirked and his smile growing. "Try me."

"I wanted to talk about Talin."

His smile dropped instantly, his gaze hardening. "What about him?"

She immediately felt defensive of Talin, her eyes narrowing. "Don't be cute with me, Thane. We need to talk about what happened the other night." Her tone was firm, leaving no room for argument.

"We already did." He leaned back in the chair again, crossing his arms. He seemed to want to shut down the conversation, to pretend what was between her and Talin was nothing.

But it wasn't nothing, and Cordelia was going to make this hardheaded man see that. "You telling me you're not angry with me and then chasing me down and fucking the life out of me doesn't count as having a conversation."

He just chuckled, the dark sound shooting straight to her traitorous pussy. "Well, you didn't seem to have a problem with it at the time, if I remember correctly." His eyes glittered as he said, "I actually seem to recall you begging me for it. I can still hear you pleading, desperate for my co—"

"Shut it, Lycus. You're not going to distract me or change the subject." She stood firm, intensity coursing through her. "I'll beg and scream and moan for you, call your name, and let you fuck me however you want, however *I* want. But I'm not begging right now, Thane. We're not fucking. We're talking, and you're listening. We have to talk about Talin, as hard as that may be for you. I understand it's not an ideal situation—"

He scoffed and rolled his eyes, but she just kept talking.

"But ignoring it won't make it go away. And it's not fair to Talin and it's not fair to *me* to ignore it."

Thane stared at her, his eyes still hard, but she could see them softening. "You think I'm OK with the thought of him fucking you? Of anyone but me fucking you? Of anyone else touching or kissing you? Getting your smiles, your laughs, your touches? No fucking way, little witch. Not when I just got you. I won't lose you."

"Oh, Thane." Her throat constricted. "You won't lose me."

Cordelia wanted so badly to hold him, to reassure him that everything was OK. But she knew she needed to give him space. Give him time.

"I'm not saying I'm going to jump into bed with him. But I have to talk to you, as my partner, about it, and then I have to talk to him about it. Just because Talin is my fated doesn't mean he automatically has a right to me or vice versa. But it does mean that he deserves a conversation with me—that he and I both deserve to discuss it, at the very least. I can reject him just the same as he can reject me. We don't have to be together just because of the bond. And you, as my partner, as my fated, get a say in the situation. But you have to be rational instead of acting like a possessive bonehead." She needed to stand firm on the subject, but that didn't change Thane's position in her life.

His position as her fated, her partner, the one she had chosen and claimed.

Thane stared at her for a long few minutes, silence the only thing filling the room.

Cordelia refused to back down, holding her stance and not flinching. He may be an alpha wolf, but she was a powerful witch and his partner, his equal. He would listen to her just as she would listen to him. There was no telling one another what to do. There was only room for equal discussions and agreements.

"Fine." His body relaxed as he conceded and uncrossed his arms. "It doesn't mean I'm thrilled about the situation. But you make a good point and I agree. If I were in Talin's position, I would want you to give me the time of day too," he grumbled.

He sounded a little defeated and haughty, but his body language and words reassured her that he was calming down, seeing her point, and trying.

She smiled, her heart suddenly so full. She was overwhelmed with so many things at that moment. Affection, deep and adoring, joy, anticipation, and soothing calm. Like the cards were all falling into place.

CHAPTER THIRTY-THREE

CORDELIA

Walking down to the coffee shop the next day, Cordelia was still a little worried about Talin. Worried about how things would go between them and what would ensue after their impending conversation.

As she rounded the corner onto the street Quartz Coffee sat on, a prickling sensation bloomed across her skin. Her steps faltered, slowed a bit. It felt like someone was watching her, observing her. She casually glanced around, taking in her surroundings to try to find the source of the sensation.

She was always on alert, always watching everything she could around her. It was just natural, an instinctual urge. But today it felt like she'd missed something as that feeling nagged at her, pulled at her every thought.

As she opened the shop door and stepped inside, she swung her gaze wide, still searching but coming up short.

She hoped the door closing behind her would dissipate the eerie feeling, help her release the tension so she could calm down to focus.

The smell of the coffee shop immediately flooded her senses, the aroma wrapping around her like a blanket. The scent of freshly ground coffee and roses met her like an old friend. She smiled, hiking her bag up higher on her shoulder as she wove through the coffee shop, finally setting her things on her usual table.

It was a comfort, being back in her routine. So many things had changed lately, her life was like a whirlwind of unrest. But the dust was finally starting to settle on everything with Thane, becoming easy and beautiful. Weaving this new piece of her soul into her everyday life was as easy as breathing air, she found. Sure, things would be different still. And fitting two people together wasn't necessarily a piece of cake, but it felt natural, right. And she had found ease in it so far.

Before Cordelia even made it to the counter, she heard her name and order called out.

"Iced lavender latte with oat milk for Cordelia!" Lilith's voice rang out to her, another soothing presence.

She was glad to not feel the twist of anxiety in her stomach as she spotted Lilith, bounding to the counter radiating only joy.

"Thanks! I feel like I'm predictable to a fault at this point. Do you have some sort of divination magic to know when I'll be here?" Cordelia laughed, taking the cup.

"Well, predictable? Maybe, but not in a bad way. But I also saw you coming down the street." Lilith smiled, and it was soft and friendly, familiar and easy.

Cordelia was relieved that they were able to work things out and not have any sort of weird, awkward tension between them after everything with Thane.

"Honestly, I'm a little disappointed it wasn't divination magic." Cordelia chuckled, giving a small wave as Lilith did the same before she darted back to her station behind the counter. Cordelia settled herself into her seat, delighting in the chill of the slightly sweet, slightly bitter coffee. The lavender exploded across her tongue, coating her in a buzzing, soft happiness.

But her reverie was soon interrupted as that nagging feeling of being watched returned. She stiffened in her chair, going completely still for a moment before setting down her cup and glancing around the shop. No one in here was watching her, the other patrons minding their own business and happily sipping and working away. The baristas were all chattering with customers and each other.

She turned and looked toward the front of the shop, through the windows that made up the front wall. And that was when she saw it, a pair of eyes in an alley across the street, narrowing in directly on her. She couldn't see much beyond just those eyes, but they were piercing, scrutinizing. She froze.

If this was someone who had ill intentions, as she suspected, then leaving was a terrible idea. Talking to the shop staff would only alert them that she had noticed their presence. And an immediate phone call might scare them off, or into action. So she continued to look outside, moving her eyes away from the alley as if she just briefly passed over it and continued to gaze at the spring morning. Then, slowly, casually, she turned to a fresh page in her notebook, chewed on her pen a little, and opened up her laptop, typing for a second. She wasn't actually typing anything other than gibberish into her writing program. It was just an act.

Finally, she pulled out her phone, leaning back in her seat to appear normal, unalarmed. Made herself look like she was scrolling an app between occasional taps of her keyboard.

> Cordelia: I need you to meet me at Quartz Coffee. I felt like someone has been watching me since I got here, and I just spotted someone in the little alley across the street, next to the open storefront. Can you come check it out? I'm nervous.

She sent the text without further thought, her skin itching for Thane to be here with her.

She acted like she was scrolling and tapping for another couple seconds before putting her phone down and going back to her computer. Her elbow braced on the table next to her laptop, she leaned her chin on her hand. After a second, maybe two, her phone lit up.

> Thane: Fuck, absolutely. I'm on my way. Will check it out before I come inside.

Cordelia smiled, reassurance flooding her at the confirmation that she wouldn't be alone soon.

Sure, she could protect herself. But she'd never felt watched before, had never been in this sort of danger, and it scared the shit out of her. And she had a possessive wolf shifter fated who had been glued to her for nearly an entire week. So, yeah, she was going to be extra cautious right now.

Not even twenty minutes later, Thane was stalking through the door of the coffee shop, a hard look etched across his face. He spotted her almost immediately, then walked right up to her and dipped down to drop a kiss on her head.

"You alright?" Thane asked as he took the seat across from her. His brows were pulled together, his hands clenched into fists, resting on the tabletop.

"I feel better having you here. See anything?" she asked, reaching for his hand. Her eyes flickered to the shop counter, immediately landing on Lilith, who was staring at her and Thane. As soon as Lilith registered Cordelia's gaze, she met it with soft warmth, a smile on her face that conveyed happiness, not bitterness, not jealousy. And Cordelia was immensely grateful for that.

"No, whoever it was must have taken off right before I got there. I don't know if they finished their job or if they were spooked. But I took a look around the alley to see if they left anything behind." His eyes were hardened, his jaw ticking, shoulders coiled tight with anger.

"And?" she pressed, anxiety rising in her, twisting her stomach into knots. She thought she might throw up. She had seen the person, sure. But hearing Thane confirm it just cemented it, made it feel more real.

"It smelled like a wolf. They tried to cover their scent, but it didn't work. Not well enough, at least. I can't tell which group they're from, but I could tell it was a wolf, that I'm certain of." A low growl vibrated in Thane's throat, barely audible to anyone around them, but loud enough for Cordelia to hear. She tensed, not liking how on edge he was. Because if Thane was this upset, that didn't soothe her own anxieties at all.

Sure, Thane was a possessive baby, but she was sure that if it wasn't a big deal, he would tell her as much. But he wasn't, and she hated it all the more.

"Have you noticed anything else weird lately? Or is this the first time this has happened?" he asked, like he was trying to gather all the clues he could to piece this puzzle together.

"N-no. This is the first time. And I'm usually pretty aware of my surroundings. I don't like to be caught off guard, and I want to make sure I'm safe." She grabbed her cup, letting the cool condensation ground her. "Thank you, for coming and calming me down." She blew out a lungful of air that had been trapped in her chest, finally feeling like she could breathe.

Sure, the situation was far from resolved, but having someone to listen to her concerns, to share those concerns, and to be there for her? It was a priceless, wonderful thing.

"Always, Cordelia. I am always here for you." Thane's eyes held that strong, firm look but had also melted a little, made room for warm affection that curled its way across the table to bloom in her tummy. "By the way, I have something for you," he mumbled, digging into one of his pant pockets.

"Oh?"

"Here." He slid a piece of paper across the table.

It took a second for her to register what it was. A phone number.

"It's Talin's. Figured you needed a way to actually get ahold of him." He shrugged, his body coiled with tension at the subject.

Cordelia stared back down at the scrap of paper. He had taken the time to write it out. Taken the time to make this something important. He could've just texted her, could've just rattled it off and hoped she would miss a few numbers in his haste. But instead, he found a pen and paper and wrote it down.

As much as Thane hated the situation they found themselves in, he clearly cared for Talin. In a deep way. And Cordelia knew he cared for her. So to see him reconcile his anger with his affection was awe inspiring.

She caught his gaze again, letting her admiration of him shine through her eyes, her smile. "Thank you, Thane."

He offered her a soft, tentative smile in return. He was trying.

Later that night, Cordelia sat in a cushioned, wrought iron chair in her garden, basking in the light of the moon. She had a mug of peppermint tea on the old wood-and-wrought-iron table beside her. Merlin had poked his head out the door briefly when she walked out, but then had opted to join Thane in the bed upstairs.

She picked up her phone, unlocking the screen with shaking fingers. Why was she so nervous?

She'd saved Talin's number in her phone earlier, after Thane had given it to her. She wanted to be sure she had it before he potentially changed his mind and the paper was mysteriously lost.

To try to ease some of her anxiety, Cordelia took a deep breath, held it, blew it out. She repeated that a couple times until she felt more stable. Typing into the text conversation she pulled up, she wrote the words quickly and pressed send before she could backtrack.

> Cordelia: Hey Talin, it's Cordelia. I hope it's OK, but Thane gave me your phone number. I want to talk, soon. Whenever you're free :)

She hoped the smiley face wasn't weird. She was just trying to dispel any awkward feelings between them.

She set her phone on the table, picking up her mug of tea to take its place in her hand. Looking up at the sky, she watched the few soft, wispy clouds float among the stars, obscuring the moon only for a second.

The light was beautiful, a watery silver that gleamed and illuminated her garden. It pulled her magic to the surface of her skin, crackling and buzzing with excitement, with pure, charged energy. It reminded her of the full moon ritual she had done not so long ago. Of the cards she had pulled that night.

An unbidden image of the flame card flashed in her mind just then, conjuring a fire within her. She could practically feel the soft caress of flames dancing across her skin, gentle and loving. A warm haze of comfort soaked deep into her bones.

Her phone lit up beside her. A message.

Talin: I would love nothing more, Cordelia. How's tomorrow?

CHAPTER THIRTY-FOUR

CORDELIA

The cold reached out to her. A numbing caress Cordelia couldn't resist.

She always did love it. The way the bitter chill would seep into her bones, wrapping her in a cocoon of odd comfort. The wind swirled around her body in a lover's embrace, gently sweeping across her skin, smoothing out the chaos that flooded her mind.

The darkness met the cold in equal measure. Driving out all light in its vicious crusade. Seeking to extinguish all hope.

There was no room for joy here. No room for life. At least, not any life beyond that which filled her, kept her flickering existence sputtering along. For anything that inspired hope was beyond the patience of the darkness. Inky and thick. Like plumes of invisible smoke, choking everything else out.

With her knees pulled up to her chest, her arms wrapped around her legs, she closed her eyes. Willing away the darkness that surrounded her. Seeking comfort in the darkness within her, the darkness she controlled and created. Her safety lay within the confines of her own magic, her own will.

A prickling sensation tingled along her skin, humming with energy. Energy begging to be released. As if it wanted to chase away the darkness *that engulfed her, to replace it, to seep into the world and into the earth below her.*

She could see it clearly. Cracks of bright power spider-webbing in the damp soil she sat on. Tendrils of light stretching across the ground like veins. Flashing quickly before being replaced with a deep, consuming black.

She could see now the shape it made. Like a crown of roots, flowing around her. Reaching for everything outside of the circle. Reaching for anything cruel. For this energy had its own cruelty, cruelty so all-consuming, so hungry for power, that it felt endless. Like it would stop at nothing to fulfill its purpose.

What was that purpose, exactly? Cordelia couldn't see it. Couldn't see past the endless glittering darkness within her. Couldn't see beyond the waves of chilling comfort, lulling her into complacency. Lulling her into a sense of safety. This may be her own darkness, but it was no force of good. It was no power to create.

It was a power to destroy.

A power to conquer, a power to control. Just a different kind of control.

Yes, her mother wouldn't like it. Wouldn't like the magic vying for control. Wouldn't like its need to seek destruction. To seek redemption at any cost.

For this power was not interested in being subdued, not any longer. This power would destroy that cruel, malicious dark that was the very foundation of this manor. Would replace it with Cordelia's own shadows anew. The shadowed darkness inside her that shone, glittered. Glittered with its own cruelty.

Her mother just wouldn't like that at all. And maybe that was why Lydia was set on destroying that power. That power that she must see already.

Lydia saw it in Cordelia. And that made Cordelia . . .

A threat.

"Goddess, I slept like garbage last night," Cordelia moaned into her coffee cup, her forehead pressed to the kitchen table.

"Well, my suggestion is to stop thrashing around so much. Really contradicts the whole 'peaceful sleep' you're generally supposed to be getting every night." Thane chuckled into his own mug at the counter.

She picked up her head, leveling him with a withering glare. "Try me today, wolf boy, and we'll see how I treat that precious little cock of yours the next time you try to get it anywhere near me."

He put his hands in the air, a laugh still on his lips. "Hey, now. No need to get violent."

Head thunking against the table once more, Cordelia groaned again. She had gotten such terrible sleep because she couldn't stop having nightmares about her mother. About Halloway Manor. And a particularly eerie one about the eyes watching her from that alley. She couldn't shake the unease that accompanied that particular thought. And she had a bad feeling that it was tied to those ominous words her mother spoke to her just the other day.

"If you don't come willingly, I'll have to take matters into my own hands . . . I'll be seeing you soon."

"I can't stop having nightmares about my mother," she admitted.

She hadn't wanted him to be up with her all night trying to soothe or help her. She wanted him to get enough sleep, to rest and relax. Especially since she felt guilty enough for the whole Talin situation.

Not that she had any control over that, but she still didn't like seeing Thane struggle to come to terms with it. They would work through it, though. That would all turn out fine, the way it was meant to be.

Lydia Halloway, on the other hand, was a much less welcome presence and a much more volatile subject.

"Do you want to talk about it?" Thane asked, concern in his features and genuine curiosity and respect in his tone.

Respect for her boundaries, she recognized. If she didn't want to talk about it, he wouldn't push her.

"Actually, it might help." She let out a long sigh, slumping back in her chair. Where the fuck did she start with the entire story?

With a deep breath, Cordelia steadied herself, tried to organize her thoughts.

"I didn't have a great relationship with my mother growing up. She wasn't the most affectionate, not the most warm or welcoming. And when you grow up in a coven, the dynamic is different. Especially in the Halloway family." She rolled her eyes at that.

At the knowledge of how power hungry her family had always been. She'd never known them to be anything but.

"I grew up in Halloway Manor. The matriarch of the coven at any given time lives there, and my mother, Lydia Halloway, is the matriarch. It's this big, important estate in the witch neighborhood, Witchhaven, and a beloved relic of the Halloway line. But I've always hated it, hated how it felt to live there, to just *be in* that house." A shiver ran through her. "It's cold and unwelcoming. And so dark, full of shadows and spirits that don't belong there. And with the kind of magic my mother performs, it just—" She cut herself off to take a steadying breath.

Cordelia hated the Halloway coven, hated the magic that ran through their veins. The Halloways practiced a darker magic, peddled it to both suspecting and unsuspecting clients. Not that there were any strictly "dark" or "light" kinds of magic. That all depended on the way magical ability was wielded, the intention behind it.

The family business, Halloway Spells, served their clientele in various ways—summoning spells, hexes, curses, charms, and on and on. But the resounding theme of the intention behind their magic was revenge, cruelty, misguided mischief.

And she had never wanted any part in it. Even from a young age, her intuition had guided her away from that magic. As a result, she'd never felt like she belonged with the family with whom she shared blood. She'd even had nightmares, pleading dreams of terror, where she was desperately trying to drain the Halloway blood from her body, hoping to be born anew, hoping to rid their evil from her tearstained soul.

She explained all of this to Thane, explained how the Halloway magic worked, steeling herself to explain the rest. She couldn't help the lump that formed in her throat, or the vise that seemed to squeeze her heart the closer she got to the darkest truth of it all.

Steadying herself, Cordelia pressed her hands against the cool surface of the table.

"When my mother realized what I was, what sort of magic I would wield, I became a weapon to her, a tool, something that she could use for her own agenda. Not a daughter, a child, not her own flesh and blood to be cherished or loved." She blew out a breath, not able to meet Thane's gaze as she continued, "And she forced me to use my magic, to be there while she worked."

Unbidden images of dark hallways, white chalk circles and runes, the creaking, aching wood of the manor flooded her head. It sang a steady, eerie song of sinister magic, moaning for more, more, more. That hunger would never be sated, never cease. She could still smell the tang of iron-rich blood in the air, hear the groans and wails of the Halloway clients clattering through the twisting halls of that manor, making their way to Cordelia's bedroom door. The bedroom where she would be tied down, held captive.

"I don't remember much from when I was very little, and I'm not sure if that's a blessing or a curse. But once I was old enough to understand, to tell her no, that's when my memories start. My earliest memories of Halloway Manor are of hiding, trying to get away from the shadows in that house, and trying to get away from my mother." Cordelia hadn't realized Thane had crossed the room and grabbed her hand until she felt a squeeze.

Looking up, she met his gaze and had a second realization that tears were forming in the corners of her eyes, threatening to spill alongside her battered heart.

"I didn't want to be a pawn in her schemes, in her magic. But she always told me that it was my duty as a Halloway, that this is what she had created me for." Lydia had made that ominous statement countless times, but Cordelia had never understood it. "Who knows what that means."

She shook her head, trying not to dwell on that lifelong mystery.

"I finally got out, though. Obviously." She snorted at that, trying to find some spark of humor. "When I was eighteen, I left while my mother was busy, preoccupied with a spell that was going to take her hours upon hours to complete. And she blessedly forgot to keep me . . . contained. So I snuck out, and eventually ran into Sage." She smiled at that, at the memory of the beautiful kindness that Sage had shown her all those years ago.

"Sage found me wandering, alone, in the rain, and she took me in. Gave me a home, taught me my magic, taught me peace." She squeezed Thane's hand now, reassuring him that she was alright.

He had grown rigid beside her as she told her story, sparks of red dancing in his eyes.

"But I still have nightmares about my mother, about that house. Most of the nightmares are pretty similar to one another—I'm trapped, tied down to my bed in my old bedroom. There's barely any light, just the light from a few lit candles, and I panic because I can hardly see anything around me. Then my mother calls for me, needing me for some spell, some sacrifice. And before I see her open the door, before I can claw my way out of the ties holding me down, I wake up. And never seeing that door open, never getting out, it makes the nightmares feel like they're suspended, like they'll never end. Like I can't get any sort of relief." Unease settled low in her stomach, coiling around her heart like a venomous snake, ready to strike at her mother's command.

Her heart was racing, the visions of those dreams unwelcome as they flooded her thoughts. Those dreams felt like a tool in and of themselves.

Something she couldn't escape, something designed to keep her trapped under Lydia Halloway's control. It was just another way that she felt she would never be free of her mother's wrath.

Thane's voice broke through her thoughts, low and threatening.

"Cordelia, did you say *tied down?*"

CHAPTER THIRTY-FIVE

THANE

Rage. Pure, unending rage filled Thane's every thought. Every single inch of his body was electrified, tensed, ready to unleash his fury.

Cordelia's mother sounded like a piece of work already. But when she said *tied down* when recounting her nightmares, he had a feeling that it wasn't something her imagination had conjured up. It was something she was *remembering*. Her fucking mother had tied her up, a helpless child, and *used* her for Lydia's own gain.

"Um, yes?" She phrased it as a question, but she winced as she did. He knew it was true. And he could see that she didn't need to be pushed on it right now.

Spots of red coated his vision, the shift pulsing low and needy under his skin. He wanted to rip that woman to shreds, and he had never even met her. Had only heard anything of substance about her today.

No wonder Cordelia had a nearly nonexistent relationship with her mother. Lydia had used her, treated her like a tool at her disposal. She'd *abused* her. And he simply wouldn't let that stand.

He needed to rein in his anger, he absently thought as he stared at Cordelia. Her face had blanched, pale and stricken. Like she hadn't realized she'd said that, hadn't realized that she had admitted that to him. He couldn't stop the anger coursing through his veins, calling to his wolf like a siren song. But he did need to get it under control. Thane didn't want to scare Cordelia, didn't want her to feel uneasy or unsafe around him.

Goddess, he needed her to know that she would always be safe with him. The need to protect her clawed at him from the inside, desperate to reach her.

Thane settled for pulling her into his arms. Cordelia clung to him as he held her, as he tried to offer her comfort while needing to be physically reassured that she was here, that she was fine.

"Sweet witch, you're not there anymore. You're here, you're with me, and I won't let that happen to you ever again." He gave her another reassuring squeeze. "You are better than that, you are worth more than that. And I intend to love you so thoroughly that you'll have no choice but to stop doubting."

Cordelia smiled up at him, the picture of it so warm, so beautiful, he couldn't help but marvel at it. She was the epitome of happiness. She was *his* happiness.

"OK, well, enough trauma dumping first thing in the morning." Laughing, she pulled away from him and swiped her hands at the tears pooling on her cheeks.

She let out a rough breath, like she hadn't been breathing that whole time. And he saw the way she looked more relaxed now, more comfortable. Like letting that out was a relief to her system.

While Thane was happy to be that support system for her, *wanted* to be that support system for her, he was also heartbroken for the little girl she had been. For the little girl that'd suffered at the hands of her mother, the one person charged with protecting her. He could see that fear still gripped her, still had its claws in her, deep and unrelenting.

He also knew that it was Cordelia's decision as to how to handle her mother, both now and in the long run. But he wanted to support her, to be by her side, for whatever it was that she decided. If she wanted to unleash her vengeance, if she wanted to let her mother drift away, through her hands like the sands of time. All of it was OK. He would be there with her.

He would tell her all of this in time. But for today, for this, his presence was enough. He knew that right now wasn't about him declaring his loyalty, wasn't about anything to do with him. Right now was about Cordelia—getting this off her chest, opening up to him. This was about her seeking a safe space in him, a shoulder to lean on. And he would gladly provide it.

Without another word, Thane and Cordelia continued to sip their coffee, taking in the warm morning spent together.

Thane walked through the woods later that evening, lost in thought, so many puzzle pieces scattered in his mind. He walked a trail close to Cordelia's house, one that she had shown him when he said he needed some time to himself, some time to think. She had just smiled, understanding immediately what he meant. He was thankful for it.

And while he may not have necessarily wanted to leave her unguarded after what had happened that morning, she had assured him that her house was heavily warded. Having a witch for a fated worked out well in that regard. Plus, she was going to meet Talin shortly after Thane left the house.

He tried not to linger on the feelings that pumped in his veins at that thought, but he did feel comfort in Talin's presence with her. Whatever Thane felt about Talin right now, he still knew he could trust him to protect Cordelia.

He took in everything around him as he walked the path winding along the forest floor. The trees were tall and thin close to the trail and grew thicker, wilder the farther they grew from the trail. Tiny flowers bloomed at the edges of the worn path, their soft petals and delicate colors bold and beautiful among the rich, wet soil. Patches of moss dotted the ground beyond the flowers, clovers and grasses mingling there too.

It had rained recently, and the scent of the still-damp earth was rich and heady mixing with the tepid spring air. It hadn't gotten so warm that there was humidity, and the remnants of winter still clung to the early spring air ever so slightly. Making the breeze more refreshing than cloying. It was all so innately beautiful, and he reveled in the feeling of it. His wolf stretched and purred inside him, like a house cat resting in the sun.

But Thane's thoughts kept turning to Cordelia's recounting of her childhood this morning and whoever had been following her, watching her. He couldn't shake the unease that followed both of those thoughts. As if they were in some way . . . connected? But how?

If Cordelia's mother had wanted so badly to control her, he didn't think she would let go so easily. Thane had heard some of the higher-ranking witch covens were aggressive in their thirst for power.

The fact that any parent would treat their child that way, as a weapon or a tool rather than a living, breathing person . . . It was enough to get his blood pumping faster, his heart rate picking up, the desperation of his wolf pulling at his bones.

He pushed down the urge to shift, trying to calm himself down. Now wasn't the time. Right now, he needed to focus on Cordelia, whoever was watching her, and the wolves. He needed to piece together why it was he felt they were all somehow related.

Thane's steps slowed as he came to a worn wood-and-wrought-iron bench along the path. The moss covering it and the way the legs seemed to blend into the clovers and damp earth below gave the impression that it was as much a part of the forest as the wildflowers and the wind.

Taking a seat, he tipped his head toward the canopy of trees above him, trying to gather his thoughts.

Every single wolf that had been kidnapped in this string of cases was a Harmonious wolf. Some of the other alphas helping on the case found that odd, unsure of why there wouldn't be other wolves involved. But Thane and a few others knew that it was exactly *because* they were Harmonious. Their kind had been a target of the Theian and Artemisian wolven since the Harmonious first came into existence.

The Theian and Artemisian fancied themselves "purebred" and called the Harmonious "mutts." It always got under his skin, pissed him off to no end.

What Thane didn't understand, though, was *why* they were being taken. He had originally thought it was just to pick off the Harmonious and try to run them into extinction. That motive wouldn't be a shock. But the pattern didn't match that. They were only taking alphas, betas, and the stronger members of the packs.

Maybe they wanted to use them as leverage? To gain something over the Harmonious? But if that were the case, why didn't they ever use them for ransom, or make it known that they had the kidnapped wolves? So far, no one had stepped up to make a power play by claiming the kidnappings.

Sure, no one would intentionally take responsibility, but why weren't there attempts to stake claim, even anonymously? Why hadn't there been any sort of taunting? It didn't make sense. Once the wolves disappeared, the trail dried up. Everything after their last sighting was like they had vanished into thin air.

So what the fuck could the motive be? And why did he feel like the witches were involved?

CHAPTER THIRTY-SIX

CORDELIA

Cordelia wasn't sure why she was nervous as she walked into Hell's Spells. The nerves had been slowly building since she'd started getting ready, and especially ever since she'd stepped foot outside her front door, knowing that she would be face-to-face with Talin so soon.

She had opted to meet him at the bar instead of either of them meeting at the other's home. She knew Thane would lose his ever-loving mind if Talin picked her up. And it felt like less pressure on both Talin and Cordelia if they met here.

As soon as she opened the door to the beautiful bar, a riot of butterflies erupted inside her, unceasing and battering against the confines of her skin.

Cordelia took a quick scan of the room, trying to spot Talin in the sea of people already cluttering the bar. The air in the space thrummed with so much life, so much excitement.

After a second look, she spotted him across the room. He had already found her and was trying to force his way through the thick crowd, his eyes glued to hers. Those butterflies grew more frantic, a renewed excitement running through her as Talin drew nearer. His golden eyes were so warm, like the heart of a fire on a cold winter's night. Warm, inviting, and just so deliciously molten.

Before she knew it, he was standing in front of her, his chest heaving slightly from his scramble to get through the tightly packed crowd.

"Hi," Cordelia breathed. She couldn't tear her eyes away from his.

Instinctively, they both reached for each other as he let out a breathless "Hey" in return.

He towered over and completely enveloped her as they embraced. Wrapped in him, Cordelia took a deep breath, taking in his scent. Like wood smoke, cinnamon, and crisp mountain air. It was immediately comforting, though it shouldn't have been. Not for someone she just met. But she couldn't help but melt into it.

They both pulled back, taking one another in. Talin was wearing a pair of dark jeans, a dark blue T-shirt, and a black leather moto jacket. The cut of the jacket hugged every inch of his shoulders and arms. So well, in fact, that she might just drool at the sight of it.

Goddess, this man. His dark hair, disheveled in the most perfect, chaotic storm—the color of it like the bark on the trees of Cordelia's favorite path, deeply shaded on a stormy afternoon. It was beautiful, as if Talin himself was crafted from the very nature that she drew life and power and magic from.

He had a bright smile on his face, lighting up his eyes with a blazing fire. Crackles of white and the bright, pale shade of firelight shone in that golden gaze.

"You look absolutely stunning tonight, Cordelia." Talin's voice broke through her haze.

It was soft, reverent. Probably misplaced affection for a stranger, but she didn't feel like he was a stranger. There was a warmth burning between them. As if this was right, this was what was meant to be. She welcomed it, instinctively leaned into it.

She didn't know what came over her as she said with a wink, "Well you don't look too bad yourself."

He blinked for a heartbeat before letting out a loud, roaring laugh.

Looping his arm around her shoulders, he tucked her into his embrace and held her close. "Let's get a table. Then you can tell me all about how hot you think I am."

He gave her his own little wink, steering them toward a cluster of tables in the back of the bar as she delighted in how at ease she already felt around him.

As they made their way through the crowd, Talin smiling and greeting people as they squeezed through tight gaps, she thought about the juxtaposition between being with Thane and being with Talin. Thane was so much more reserved, much more the strong, serious alpha wolf. He was always on alert, guarding Cordelia and making sure everyone knew she was his in the most demanding way. Not that she minded, she loved how possessive he was. Loved the strength and power he exuded. It suited him, her stoic, brooding boy.

But Talin was loud, joking, and flirtatious. He soaked up the energy of the room and bounced with it in each step. Being with him was like being in the presence of happiness personified. It felt lighter, adventurous, and she reveled in it.

She didn't want to compare the two men as if they were pitted against each other. But she couldn't help but notice the differences between the two. The duality of light and dark between them. It was beautiful, poetic in a way.

She was given two fateds by the Celestials, and they were opposites in so many ways. And yet, they were best friends. Proving that they could coexist. There was harmony and balance in the two. And she felt that balance, felt it bubble inside her with peace and excitement.

Talin led Cordelia to a table in a little alcove close to the bar itself, tucked away in a private corner. There was a semicircle booth surrounding the table, both made of a dark wood.

The wood itself was rustic in shape, as if a giant tree trunk had been dropped here and they'd carved the booth and table from it. The surface of the wood was glossy, with little cracks and crags and tree rings visible in darker shades. The top of the table was inlaid with rings of labradorite, sparkling under the twinkle lights above them.

Gauzy, light blue curtains draped over the opening of the little alcove, pulled back so they could see into the bar. The space was intimate, and quieter than the rest of Hell's Spells.

"I hope this is OK. I wasn't sure how well you did with crowds, and I wanted to be able to actually hear you over the obnoxious roar of everyone else." Talin chuckled. But his eyes held hers, waiting for her permission. Waiting for her to voice any concerns she might have.

"It's perfect, and I love this little space. It's so pretty."

As Talin was getting ready to respond, a man stepped up to the curtain, a devilish smile on his face as he zeroed in on Talin. He had short, jet-black hair, meticulously styled and smoothed back. His eyes were a deep, blood red, almost an oxblood color, rimmed with smoky black. They were striking and held an air of danger and mischief. His pale skin had a golden sheen in the twinkling light. He looked effortlessly and casually elegant in his creamy button-down shirt, sleeves rolled up to his elbow, and a gray-and-gold tweed vest. Adding to his rakish effect, the top few buttons of his shirt were undone, and it suited him.

"Ah, the dragon returns." His voice was a smooth caress, almost a purr.

"Asmond! Hey man, how are you?" Talin leaned over to smack the man on the shoulder. "Wasn't sure if you'd be here tonight."

"And who is this lovely witch you've lured into your cave?" Asmond raised his eyebrow in Cordelia's direction.

"This is Cordelia, and I did not *lure* her here." Talin laughed, shaking his head as he scooted closer to her. "Cordelia, this is Asmond. Friend, bar owner, and demon."

"You love announcing that, don't you?" Asmond said with a long-suffering sigh, rolling his eyes before reaching across the table for her hand. "It's lovely to meet you, Cordelia. Please don't let Talin bother you. I'm not above accidentally mixing a fun little spell into his drink." He gave her a wink at that, a sly grin spreading across his lips.

"And I'm sure you would, As." Talin let out his own sigh. "Now, please stop bothering my date and threatening me." His eyes darted to hers at the word *date*, as if he'd caught himself saying something he shouldn't have.

But she just reached between them and brushed her fingers against his in a reassuring touch.

"Well that's no fun, now is it?" Asmond pouted a little before pulling himself out of the booth and standing at the mouth of the alcove again. "What can I create for you two this evening?"

"I'll have the Palo Santo Gimlet," Talin said.

"Mm, gin sounds good. I'll have the Quartz 75, please. Thank you!" Cordelia chirped, giving Asmond a smile as he left them. "Well he seems fun."

"I think that's an understatement, but he is." Talin chuckled.

"What did he mean about you pointing out he's a demon? I've only ever met one."

"That makes sense. Demons have just never had a big presence in this town. They're more common closer to Olysan, the dragon territory. But they never actually claimed a territory in the main part of Elysea."

"Why not?" She'd never really learned much about demons. She knew they were created by the Goddess Hades, that they had the ability to wield magic like witches, just in much smaller ways, and they didn't have the special abilities witches had received from the Goddess Hecate.

"Demons and witches haven't always gotten along. In fact, there have been a lot of disputes between the two. Mostly over magic, and really about power and authority. Some of the witches think they should be the only ones to wield magic, and the demons just want to be able to practice their magic, no matter how small it is. So, when Elysea as a town was formed and the Magicals started to claim their own territories within it, the demons stayed far away, opting for peace over tension. Of course, not all witches were of the same opinion, but the opposing witches were a loud group."

Cordelia was horrified, but not surprised. She very well knew just how nasty the witches could get, especially when it came to hierarchy and authority. How could she not? When you grew up with Lydia

Halloway as your mother, you grew up familiar with hatred and violence. Cordelia had always done everything she could to banish those things from her own life, her own power. But that didn't mean she didn't know its bitter song, didn't understand the thick, dreadful air it carried.

"So where do the demons live, then?" she asked, wondering where they would have settled. They may not even be anywhere close.

"Near Olysan for the most part. The dragons and demons have always gotten along well enough, so we don't mind sharing territory with or being near them. We live among one another peacefully. And Asmond is a good friend of mine. He's always been reliable and a good one to count on."

It sounded as if he held the demons to the utmost respect, as if he treasured Asmond's friendship dearly. It warmed Cordelia to hear the adoration and respect Talin held for Asmond. It also made her curious to visit Olysan someday. To see the infamous dragon territory.

Elysea sat at the foothills of the Elysean mountains, and Olysan resided in those mountains. It wasn't actually within Elysea, but the dragons were still part of their community, regardless. Plenty of dragons lived within Elysea's city limits, and those who didn't still visited regularly enough that seeing dragons was a frequent occurrence.

"I've never been to Olysan, but those giant, dusky blue mountains look so peaceful. Do you like living there?" Living in the shadow of the mountains, Cordelia had admired them her whole life. Those cragged, sharp peaks were like silent sentinels, always watching over Elysea, always protecting them.

"I grew up there, and it was beautiful. I love those mountains. But I actually don't live in Olysan anymore, though I do work there." His eyes had a far-off look to them, like his mind was among the tall, airy peaks.

"Oh? Why do you live here and work there?"

"Because I love what I do. I work in the Goddess Atlas's Celestial Temple. I do archival and mapping work there. When I was old enough to leave home, I knew I wanted to explore. To get away from everything I knew and find out who I was. Cliché, I know, but still something that I really wanted." He laughed, as if remembering his younger self, and it made her smile softly in return. "Don't get me wrong, I have always loved Olysan. But I knew it wasn't good for me to just stay in the same place forever. I would get too attached, and then I would never leave, never see anything new. And while those mountains are tall, there's only so much you can see from those heights."

Cordelia knew what Talin meant. Knew that itch, that need to get out. To go somewhere else and find something new. She may not have been as fond of her childhood as he was of his own, but that feeling was something she knew well. One she treasured as soon as she'd gotten that breath of fresh air she'd craved for eighteen years.

CHAPTER THIRTY-SEVEN

CORDELIA

Asmond swept into the alcove again. "For the enchanting witch," he announced as he set Cordelia's drink in front of her with a flourish. The opaque black coupe glass was crafted to look like a flower, the stem of the glass the stem of the plant, the top designed to look like petals. Inside was a sparkling, fizzing drink, garnished with a metal pick adorned with a clear quartz spearing a lemon peel and a few flower petals.

Cordelia smiled, taking a sip and letting the sweet, botanical drink coat her tongue. The bubbles of the prosecco danced in her mouth and set her senses alight.

She beamed up at Asmond. "It's delicious. Thank you."

He returned her smile, his deep red eyes dancing with delight. Then he turned and placed Talin's drink on the table, expectantly raising his eyebrow. The glass was also a coupe glass, but this one was clear, etched with swirling smoke designs. The drink itself was cloudy with citrus juice and garnished with a lime wedge studded with cloves.

Talin took a sip and swept the hand holding his drink into the air, giving a small mocking bow in his seat. "Delicious, as always, As. You've truly outdone yourself, haven't you?"

"Anything less would be unacceptable," he said with a grin before stepping out of the space and blending into the crowd like he was made of shadows.

"I understand that, though. The need for freedom, for knowing who exactly you are," Cordelia continued, picking up where they'd left off. "It's definitely cliché"—she chuckled, and Talin joined her, tipping his head back—"but it's cliché for a reason. And we all have a different reason to want to find freedom. To find the world. But it's all valid just the same."

"Ah, so you're a fellow freedom seeker yourself, I take it?"

Cordelia found herself tracking the movement as he brought his glass to his mouth. Watched his lips close around the rim of that sparkling glass, watched his eyes momentarily close as he took his sip. She felt her breath catch ever so slightly before forcing herself back into her train of thought.

"Uh, yeah, you could say that." She was a little nervous, and she definitely wasn't going to get into that tonight. But she also wasn't going to lie. "My reasons weren't as pretty as yours, I'm afraid." She lifted her own drink to stop herself from continuing, to keep herself occupied.

"Fair enough. I won't push you." Talin let it go with a wave of his hand, as if physically dissipating the subject from the very air they were breathing. "I take it you live here too?"

"Yeah, I've lived here my whole life. Not surprising considering I'm a witch. I grew up in Witchhaven and haven't ever lived anywhere but Elysea. Haven't really traveled either. Boring as that is." She had visited some neighboring towns but had never gone very far.

Growing up, her mother didn't really grant Cordelia her own freedom, unsurprisingly. And she was only allowed to leave Elysea if she were with her mother. After she left home, she never really left the town except for small, short-distance trips to those same neighboring towns.

Sure, she'd always wanted her freedom from the Halloway family.

And she'd never really imagined where exactly she would live. She just knew that she had to get away from Lydia Halloway and the manor. When she'd stumbled across Sage, who'd then taken her in, she'd known she'd found her home. It never occurred to her to leave after that.

"Well, would you like to see Olysan?"

The question caught her off guard.

Of course she wanted to see Olysan. She always had, not just since Talin brought it up tonight. Those mountains were simply stunning, and she could practically feel the magic they thrummed with just by basking in their majesty.

"So badly." She laughed a little, setting down her almost-empty glass after taking a long drink.

The bubbles of the prosecco were going to her head. She wasn't drunk by any margin, but she felt light and airy. She could practically feel the pleasure of the alcohol coursing through her already. But she supposed maybe some of that feeling was attributable to Talin.

"Then let's go." Talin downed the last of his drink, his eyes dancing with excitement and childlike wonder. She briefly thought that this was a regular look for him. She couldn't even picture any sort of dark or heavy expression on his face. He was made for joy.

Then his words hit her.

"Right now?!"

"Hell yeah, why not?" He was practically bouncing in his seat now. "It's a beautiful night, completely clear. It's perfect."

"Well . . ." She was at a loss for words. It sounded fun, adventurous. She was briefly swept away by the thought of the entire night. The magic of it all.

"C'mon, Cordelia. Be impulsive with me." His face was a thing of beauty.

The elation sketched across his face, the striking smile he was giving her, and the fire in his eyes. It was heady, and she felt like she could get drunk off that alone.

"Yes. Yes, let's do it." The butterflies in her stomach took flight, battering against the confines of her tummy. Celestials, this was so fun.

Everything else was a whirlwind after that. Talin slammed down money on the table, pulling Cordelia out of the booth and alcove with him. He gave a wave toward the bar as they passed it, presumably at Asmond.

He wound them through the tightly packed bodies in Hell's Spells before they finally broke through and raced out the front door. The chilled night air hit them suddenly, and it briefly took Cordelia's breath away. Her gasp was audible, loud even, and Talin's head snapped to her. His eyes danced with mischief and a wicked, devastating grin captured his lips.

"Don't get too caught up in my charm, Cordelia. You might just fall in love." He winked before turning back around, his hand still holding hers.

Her heart skipped a beat at his words before taking off in a run. Fall in love with Talin? That felt too easy.

CHAPTER THIRTY-EIGHT

TALIN

Talin's heart was beating so wildly he thought it might leap right out of his chest. He couldn't believe he said the words *fall in love* to Cordelia. But he didn't have time to overthink it.

"I hope you don't mind, I drove my bike tonight. You ever ridden?"

"No, but I've always wanted to." She bit her lip, taking in the bike, and it made him feel like he'd been set on fire. Goddess, she was fucking gorgeous, and he'd been doing a shit job of regaining his sanity tonight. The second he'd seen her when she walked into Hell's Spells he was a goner. Like his soul had been signed away to her, and he would happily let it go.

"Well, it's your lucky day." He laughed, grabbing the helmet from where it was hooked on the handlebars. "You can use my helmet. It just clips together, and then you can tighten the chin strap if you need." He handed the helmet over before checking to make sure the peg stands were down on both sides of the bike for her.

"Thank you. It's a gorgeous bike. I mean, I don't know anything about them, but I love yours."

Talin was proud of his bike, loved it, and had put a lot of work into it over the years.

It was a café racer, and from his favorite foreign make. Café racers weren't as big as other bikes, and not exactly like a zippy sport bike, but it was still fucking cool and compact, making it pretty fast and super fucking fun. It was mostly a satin black nearing on matte, but the gas tank was a bright mix of bronze and gold, almost as if it were gilded. Obviously he'd had to go for something eye-catching, something worthy of attention.

"Thanks! I love riding. It's almost like flying. I think you're gonna love it, Cordelia." He flashed her a winning smile, excited didn't even cover what he felt in that moment. "I'll get on first, then you can climb on the back. Don't get scared, I won't let anything happen to you. I promise. Just make sure you lean into the turns."

She nodded in response, pulling the helmet onto her head. After he swung his leg over the bike and angled it toward the road, he turned it on, the engine roaring to life under him. He loved the feeling of the bike idling beneath him, the motor purring. And the speed he knew he could reach once he hit the gas was a rush in and of itself.

Talin turned toward Cordelia, nodding at her to climb on. Once she settled in, he grabbed her hands and looped them around his waist.

He leaned back so she could hear him. "I don't mean to be forward, but you're gonna want to hold on." He laughed, and Cordelia returned the sentiment.

"Sure, Talin. Anything to get my hands on you, huh?" Her chest was pressed to his back as she leaned into him, so he felt her voice like a hum through his body, landing in his chest like vise grip around his heart. He loved it, wanted more of it.

"Hold on tight." He twisted the throttle and whipped out onto the road. The wind against his skin as he sped down the pavement was like the most delicious, untethered joy. It really was the closest you could get to flying while on solid ground.

Behind him, Cordelia squeezed her arms around his waist, but he didn't feel like it was out of fear. No, he imagined it was the excitement, the rush of adrenaline, the uninhibited, freeing feeling of it all. Soon, her grip relaxed and he felt her leaning into it. It made his heart soar. To have Cordelia on his bike, racing through the streets toward Olysan, felt like a dream he never would have thought possible.

As they neared the base of the Elysean mountains, entering Olysan, Talin slowed, taking in the forest that would always be his home. He wanted Cordelia to take it in too.

And if she thought the most adventurous part of the night was over, she had another thing coming. He choked down the wicked laugh that rose in his throat. This was going to be so fucking fun.

After pulling into one of the overlooks at the base of the mountain, Talin parked. They were only about one hundred feet up, but it was still beautiful all the same. There were rocky outcroppings scattered around the mountain that the dragons were fond of. They served as good jumping points for flying. They also made for good spots to survey the forests of Olysan and even to see all of Elysea, if you were up high enough.

They both climbed off the bike, Cordelia taking off her helmet and setting it on the handlebars as Talin toed down the kickstand.

"Goddess, this is breathtaking," she said, taking in the forest and the mountains surrounding them. The complete awe and wonder on her face was inspiring, beautiful. He felt like he could look at it forever.

"You feeling up for more adventure?" He stepped close, about ready to burst with giddiness.

"What kind of adventure?"

"I'm sure you've realized that me being a dragon shifter also means that I can shift into a dragon, right?"

She nodded, obviously confused by where this question was going.

"And that means I have wings, yes?"

Her eyebrows were raised now, obviously starting to follow his train of thought.

"And did you know that shifters can partially shift?" His grin was wicked, filled with delight as he stepped closer, brushing his hand along her fingers.

"Spit it out, dragon boy," Cordelia said, becoming impatient. Talin could tell she wasn't annoyed, and it delighted him. She wasn't shutting him down, not yet anyway.

"I say we go for a little late-night flight. Hey! That even rhymes! That must mean it's meant to happen." He laughed at his own little joke, unable to help himself.

Her breath caught in her throat, and his shifter ears could pick up the flutter of her heartbeat. It sounded like it would beat right out of her chest at this rate.

"Of course, if you don't want to, we don't have to," he corrected, afraid he'd scared her now. "I don't want you to feel like you have to do something you don't want to. It was just an idea. A ride on the bike is also fine. I at least wanted to you to see how beautiful Olysan is for yourself. And hey, you have now! And—"

She cut him off. "Calm down, Talin, it's OK."

Thank the Celestials, too, because he could feel his rambling wasn't going to end. He'd gotten nervous that her hesitation was discomfort. And this situation was tricky enough as it was with Thane in the mix. He didn't want to throw in scaring Cordelia to top it all off.

"I think that sounds fun, I just am a little nervous." Her cheeks flushed, her nerves starting to get the best of her, it seemed.

"Well I can promise you that, just like the bike, I wouldn't ever let anything happen to you. Actually, let's just go ahead and make that a blanket promise—I will never let anything happen to you under any circumstance. Sound good?" He put his hand to his heart, hoping to lighten the mood with the gesture.

Cordelia let out a laugh, half-nerves half-humor. "I believe you. You've got yourself a deal, Talin."

He whooped, throwing his hands in the air. "Oh, fuck yeah! It's going to be so fun, Cordelia, you don't even know. OK, hold on, I need to take my jacket off so I don't ruin it." He tossed it over the back of the bike before continuing. "Alright, so I'm just going to conjure my wings. They're fucking huge, so don't freak out," he said with a wink.

Cordelia rolled her eyes, letting out a little chuff. He just grinned wider at that.

Closing his eyes and concentrating, he pulled at his dragon within. The dragon was both Talin and not Talin. An innate and separate part of himself that he coexisted with. *Shift. Wings.* As soon as he thought it, the magic within him swirled, and his wings took shape, their weight heavy on his back. And, unfortunately, he heard the rip of his T-shirt. Oh well. He didn't give a shit about this one, anyway.

Opening his eyes, he was met with the face of an awestricken Cordelia. "Goddess."

"The Goddess Atlas, to be exact," he said before looking to the sky. "Thanks, Atlas! The wings are pretty sweet."

Cordelia laughed at that. "I'm sorry, did you just call the Goddess Atlas by her first name only? No honorific?"

"I like to think, as one of her children, that I get a pass." He shrugged, a smile pulling at his lips. "I'm sure she would've made her displeasure known by now if that wasn't the case."

"Wow, I like how cocky you are." Cordelia laughed, full and loud, and it made Talin's heart sing in return. Goddess, he could listen to that all day and never tire of it.

"Alright, so, I'll scoop you up into my big strong arms"—another laugh from Cordelia—"and then my only advice is to hold on tight. Keep your arms around my neck, and enjoy the ride."

"And my only advice to you is to make sure you don't drop me or let me slip and fall to my death. Otherwise, I might have to haunt you for the rest of eternity. And I'm not afraid to cockblock you." She winked, making Talin feel like he'd been set on fire. Goddess, this woman.

"Woah, fair enough. But I'd never let you fall. And if I did, I'd catch you before you hit the ground."

"Very reassur— Fuck!" She looped her arms around his neck as he gripped her under her knees and midback and scooped her up off the ground.

Talin bent down before launching into the night sky with a powerful flap of his wings. It was spring, and the nights were still chilled, so it was perfect flying weather. Flying in the summer was the worst, it felt like flying through bathwater when it was hot out. Absolutely fucking miserable.

He peered down at Cordelia, watching as she heaved a few breaths before calming herself down.

"Fuck, that is terrifying," she said, still gripping him tightly.

"Take a look around. The view is the best part."

Her eyes lit up with wonder, amazement, and something akin to affection. And it was something to behold, something beautiful and precious. He wanted to remember it forever. This feeling of being so close to her, sharing his love of flying with her. His home, his heart, his joy. And, he thought, pretty soon those things could apply to Cordelia too.

CHAPTER THIRTY-NINE

CORDELIA

After landing on one of the smaller mountain peaks, Cordelia and Talin sat, leaning back on their hands with their legs stretched out in front of them, in the quiet, chilly night. They'd found a little flat expanse of the mountain with grass and some wildflowers, and they could see over all of Elysea and just beyond as they looked over the dense forest before them. Words couldn't describe the raw beauty this place held.

The feeling of being so deep within nature was incomparable, indescribable. Her magic had been singing since they'd gotten into the forests of Olysan. As soon as she felt that fresh forest air, a deep peace washed over her.

The stars above them were twinkling so bright, so clear. There wasn't a single cloud out tonight, and Cordelia couldn't help the inescapable feeling of rightness. Ever since she saw him at the bar earlier that night, the feeling kept hitting her, coaxing her into complete contentment.

"Sooo, I guess we should address the elephant in the proverbial room?" Talin asked, looking over at Cordelia. "The elephant actually being a wolf, and that wolf's name being Thane."

She took a deep breath, trying to steady herself. She didn't want things to be weird. Between Talin and her or Thane and her. And she definitely didn't want them to be weird between Talin and Thane. They were best friends, and she didn't want that to end because of her. Because of something that wasn't definite.

"How does he feel about everything?" Talin asked, wincing a bit at the question. She could tell they'd both thought about it tonight, and they needed to address it.

"Well, he wasn't exactly pushing me out the door to come tonight, if that's what you're asking. But I calmed him down. He's not pissed off, but he's not quite rooting for you either." She gave him a halfhearted smile.

"I get that. I'd be in the same boat if the roles were reversed. But Thane can be an especially stubborn one.

"You can say that again."

"But I need you both to know that I respect your relationship. I respect the fact that you're fateds and you actively chose each other. That's not something to take lightly. And if you decide that you don't want to be with me, that's OK. I will absolutely respect that. But if you decide you do want to be with me, I'll be honored."

Cordelia met Talin's gaze, met the passion and burning desire she could see so clearly in his eyes.

"Because make no mistake, Cordelia, I do want you. I want you so badly. I want to see where this can go, and I want to be there for you. In every way. But I also want you to make your own decision. Because I can't, and don't want to, make it for you."

Emotion welled up in her. An ache in her heart, affection, respect, and a desperate longing in her bones. She needed to work things out with Thane. She needed him to see her side of things. Needed him to understand that she didn't actively seek out another fated. *The Goddesses* gave her two. That didn't take away from what she felt for Thane. What she felt for Talin was already completely its own beast. Its own part of her heart. It was just multiplied on top of what she felt for Thane. It already felt innately wrong for Cordelia to not give that to Talin, to not recognize and honor it for what it was.

"Thank you. And I need you to know that I don't expect anything from you. Even if you walked away, if you decided this isn't what you wanted, I would respect and understand that. We may be fateds, but that doesn't mean either of us has to commit to something we don't want."

Talin nodded, and it felt like that was all that was needed. They didn't need to explain or discuss it any further, because it was a choice, and they both understood that innately.

"But know, Talin, that I do want this. I have a commitment to Thane that I will honor, and I value his consent. But my intention is to keep you."

Cordelia opened her front door, to find the house completely dark and completely silent. Had Thane gone back to his house? Not even Merlin greeted her at the door. Odd. She stepped in farther, shutting the door behind her as she kicked off her shoes.

After their visit to Olysan, Talin had driven her back to Hell's Spells so she could get her car to go back home. It had been such a perfect night, and she was buzzing with anticipation, desperately wanting to see and talk to Thane.

Upon further inspection, the downstairs portion of the house was empty, so she made her way up the stairs. And what she found was a big, tired wolven asleep in her bed with an equally tired Merlin curled up in his arms. She smiled to herself at the sight.

Thane must have heard her somehow because he opened his eyes and peered at the doorway.

"And my pretty witch returns. How was your date?" he grumbled, sitting up and startling Merlin, who looked annoyed to have lost his spot in Thane's arms.

"Sassy even when sleepy, that's quite the accomplishment."

She made her way to the closet, stripping out of her black velvet dress and her underwear as she went. She directly ignored the growl of approval from Thane as she pulled on a short, olive-green satin nightgown trimmed with black lace before making her way over to the bed. As she climbed in, he reached out his arms to pull her into him.

"I've been thinking," he mumbled in his gravelly, sleepy voice.

"Yes?"

"I-I think I can be OK with the Talin situation. As long as I get to be let into everything."

She held her breath, shocked to hear him giving so much on this already. He sat up in bed, looking fully at her now.

"I was pissed when you left earlier. Not at you, just at the situation. I couldn't stand that he was out with you, he was getting what I thought was mine. But you're not mine, not in the sense of my ability to hoard you. You are your own person, Cordelia, and I was letting my pride get in the way of that." He blew out a long breath, running his hand through his hair. "None of this is your fault. Hell, our meeting was coincidence, chance. Fuck, you were on a date with someone else when I met you, for Goddess's sake! And look how far we've come. Look where we are and who we are to each other. I don't want to take that from Talin. He's my best friend, has been my whole life. And I want him to be happy so fucking bad. I want him to feel what I feel for you."

Thane's eyes were shining with so much emotion, Cordelia couldn't help but feel it all crashing over her in waves as he spoke. She'd been trying to prepare this whole discussion. To talk to him about her choice, her happiness, Talin's happiness. Their roles in each other's lives—all three of them. And here Thane was, his kind and gentle soul offered to her with a heartbreaking tenderness.

Tears pricked at the corners of her eyes, and without thinking, she lunged for Thane. She wrapped him in a crushing hug, burying her head in his neck, breathing him in as he held her just as tightly. "Thank you," she choked out, feeling the weight of everything settle over her.

He pulled back for a moment before diving back in, his lips

crushing against hers. She met him with the same fervor, the same need. Their lips worked feverishly as they tore at each other's clothes. It was fairly easy to undress one another since Cordelia was in nothing but her nightgown and Thane was clad in only his black boxer briefs.

He pulled her over top of him, one hand in her hair as he kissed her endlessly, his other hand creeping down her body to play with her nipples, flicking and teasing each one. He absorbed her strangled cry, humming into her mouth.

His fingers slowly drifted farther and farther down, ghosting over her tummy, coasting across her hips, before settling over her pussy. His middle finger immediately found and gently teased her clit, pulling a gasp from her. He broke their kiss, breathing into her mouth. "Fuck, I need you so bad, Cor."

Cordelia couldn't do anything but gasp as Thane dipped his fingers into her vulva, testing how ready she was. She was already so fucking wet, so fucking needy for him she couldn't stand it.

He moved his fingers lower before teasing her entrance, his thumb going to her clit, working it in circles as he pressed the tips of his fingers into her. She moaned, a plea on her lips. She was desperate for more.

"Fuck, Thane. Baby, please, I need you." The words came out broken and strangled.

Suddenly, he pulled his fingers away and she began to protest before he put his hands on her hips, guiding her over his hard cock. Cordelia reached down, gripping his base and giving him a pump, pulling a groan from his throat. She smiled at that.

The smile quickly left her face as Thane growled on her second pump, ripping her hand off him and pulling her down onto his cock. It was hard and fast, and she cried out as she was instantly filled. His fingers flew to her clit, rubbing in hard, messy circles.

"Fuck," Cordelia breathed as everything melted into mind-numbing pleasure, soaking into her bones, into her very soul.

She rocked back and forth, needing friction, needing movement. She rode him in a drunken, lustful haze as one of his hands gripped her hips, guiding her rhythm, the other playing with her clit, cranking her pleasure higher and higher.

"Goddess, you feel so fucking good wrapped around me, little witch." His voice was rough, husky. "I think I might just have to fuck the orgasms right out of you. How does that sound, baby?" There was a wicked grin on his face now, his hips snapping up into her, forcing deep cries from her throat.

"Fuck, yes, anything." She could barely comprehend words. Could barely understand what was coming out of her mouth as she babbled a response.

His hand left her hip to wrap around her head and pull her down into a hard kiss, crushing her to him.

Cordelia's tummy was pressed hard against Thane's, his hand a tight fit between their bodies. She started to protest, to pull away. "I don't want to crush you," she whined as Thane's fingers continued to work her clit.

He growled, "You can't crush me, Cordelia. I don't want a single inch of you away from me. I need to feel you, all of you." His hips snapped again, hard, as he pulled her back down.

"Fuck, baby, I'm going to come." Her orgasm built higher and higher. She could feel every single inch of Thane's cock, could feel as his hips shifted and suddenly he was hitting that delicious, magical spot inside her over and over on each thrust.

"Come for me, my love. I want you to come all over my cock like a good little witch."

Her body lit up at the praise and love spilling from Thane as her orgasm crashed over her.

It felt like it was endless, a sea of pleasure, and she was drowning in it. Thane tensed under her, cursing as his orgasm hit him, spilling into Cordelia for a long moment.

Their pleasure started and ended in one another in a continual, infinite loop. When their orgasms finally subsided, Thane tugged her down to lie on top of him. As she pressed her cheek into his chest, he pulled out of her, adjusting so that they were both on the bed, Cordelia safely tucked away in his arms.

She hummed in satisfaction against him, breathing in his scent, breathing in Thane. He kissed the top of her head, his arms tightening around her in an affectionate squeeze.

As she drifted to sleep, she faintly heard the word *love* fall from his lips. So softly it could have been an echo of her own thoughts.

CHAPTER FORTY

CORDELIA

A chill crept over Cordelia's skin. Almost like icy claws gently scraping. But this wasn't the comforting chill Cordelia had come to know. The one that helped set her nerves at ease and let her catch her breath.

She suddenly felt the tension strung in her body, the way her arms were stretched on either side of her. She became increasingly aware of everything all at once.

The soft bedding beneath her, the chill of the stagnant air, somehow both refreshing and stale. The hum of the house around her, the creaking of the bed as she shifted her body. And the ropes twisted around her wrists and binding her in place. The last observation sent a shudder rolling through her, her heart clenching.

No. Not again.

Her eyes flew open, staring at the canopy of frothy white surrounding her, the dark shades of the house just beyond that. Dust motes swirled in the air, catching in the faint glimmers of light cast around the room by the various candles scattered across every surface.

Some of those candles had burned to the quick, melted, and extinguished.

Some of them still had life left, life of varying degrees as some of the candles were taller than others.

How long had she been here? She couldn't remember anything leading up to now.

All she could remember anymore was the feeling of being eternally trapped. Like she had never left. Never actually gained her own freedom.

No. No, no, no, no.

The panic swelled within her, cresting and crashing over her in an unwelcome spray of anxiety. She needed to get out, needed to just get off this bed.

Pulling at the binding on her wrists, she tugged and tugged and tugged. But they wouldn't give. The soft creak of the rope only heightened her frustrations. Goddess, please.

Looking down, she noticed her feet were unbound and that she was dressed in a white linen slip dress, the frothy lace hem reaching her knees. The soft scrape of the fabric against her skin was a direct contrast to what she knew was coming.

Her heart stopped. Her blood ran cold.

Not again. Not today. She'd gotten out of this, right? She'd left. Her mother couldn't do this to her anymore.

The panic clawed through her body, clogging her throat and making her breathing stutter. She felt both numb and as if she was flooded with a wave of pins and needles all at the same time.

Suddenly, footsteps sounded outside in the hallway, measured and slow. She knew those steps. Knew it was Lydia Halloway coming to retrieve her daughter.

She closed her eyes tight, holding her breath and willing this vision away. Because surely, it was just that—a vision. She couldn't be back here. Not again. She wouldn't allow it. Wouldn't dream of it.

But when she heard the soft jingling of the old silver-and-glass doorknob, she knew this wasn't something she was imagining.

"Cordelia, darling, we're ready for you now."

Her eyes flew open to see her mother's saccharine smile in the shadows of the hallway. Lydia's features were cloaked in darkness, the harsh lines of the candlelight illuminating the malicious look on her face.

"No. N-no, I won't be part of this. You can't do this to me anymore."
Cordelia's voice was quiet and unsteady, her eyes pleading with her mother.

"But, my dear, we need you. You are the key piece to the spell. Don't you
want to help your mother? Don't you want to help the Halloway coven?" The
soft, commanding tone of her voice was tinged with poison, directly
contrasting with the smile her mother was attempting to soothe her with.

A roar sounded from outside the manor, loud enough to rattle the shutters
and windowpanes, pulling Cordelia's attention away from Lydia. Tense
anticipation coiled through her, laced with relief.

She looked back at her mother, feeling a bit more at ease, feeling strength.
But when she met her mother's eyes, it dissipated just as quickly as it had
gathered. Her mother's smile had only grown, twisting into a cruel grin.

"My, my. It seems like the sacrifice has arrived."

A tear tracked down Cordelia's cheek, the droplet hot and salty as it met
her lips.

And as she opened her mouth to protest, her arms lifting to thrash
violently against her restraints, it all went black, taking her with it.

"Fuck, fuck, fuck. Please wake up, Cordelia!"

She jerked awake, a gasp on her lips as she startled. It took a
second to get her bearings, to realize she was safe.

She could immediately see she was in her own bed, in her own
home. The soft bedding beneath her was warm, not cold. She was
covered in blankets. Merlin was sitting in her lap, gently nudging her
with his nose.

"Fuck, baby, are you OK?"

She turned her attention to the man next to her, the man lying in
her bed, holding her in his arms. *Thane.*

She threw her arms around him and held him tight. She had an
apology ready on her lips, but before she could say anything, his voice
curled around her.

"Cordelia, baby, it's OK. I'm right here, you're safe." He shushed
and soothed her, gripping her tighter to him while one hand ran
through her hair, stroking and calming.

She couldn't speak, didn't even know what to say. The dream swirled around her head like a tornado, consuming her every thought, but she still couldn't find the words. It was like they ripped themselves away from her as soon as she started to identify them. So she let Thane hold her until they fell back asleep, his soft breath in her ear as he held her tight.

Cordelia was walking through the forested trail in her neighborhood the next morning, trying to calm her thoughts, steady herself. She still hadn't recovered from the nightmare she'd had. This one was so similar to all the others she'd been plagued with for so many years, but there was one stark difference.

The sacrifice.

She kept playing it in her head over and over again. She heard a roar and felt oddly calmed by it. Then her mother seemed all too pleased, mentioning a sacrifice. And Cordelia had a feeling it wasn't her.

Ever since she'd woken up, she'd had a sinking feeling in her gut that she couldn't shake. No amount of breathing exercises, grounding work, or garden time had helped. She'd hoped a walk would do the trick. So she'd left Thane still asleep in bed, hoping not to disturb him while she was trying to dispel this worry. So far, the trail wasn't making a difference either.

She couldn't help but get lost in the swirling thoughts, handing herself over to the anxiety that took root in her, spreading out of control like a wildfire. Her breathing was quickening, her heart rate skyrocketing. It was like a sickness taking hold of her, refusing to let go.

Stopping in the middle of path, she took a minute to gather herself. She leaned against one of the trees nearby, planting her palm firmly against the bark, and took a deep breath, holding it before releasing and repeating. She let herself connect with the energy thrumming through the life surrounding her, feel the rough, craggy texture of the tree beneath her fingers. The cool spring air was a safety blanket of sorts, helping to soothe her heated skin, flushed with desperate anxiety.

Finally, some of the sick feeling eased, the tight tension in her muscles started to uncoil. Relief swept through her, deep and appreciative.

Until a pair of hands gripped her arms, pulling her against a hard chest. Cordelia's eyes flew open, and she realized she was being pulled farther into the woods, farther and farther from the trail. She twisted and kicked, trying to get out of the stranger's hold. As she screamed, a hand clamped down over her mouth, cutting her off.

"Quiet, witch," a gruff, deep voice said into her ear.

Their hot breath was on her neck, forcing her panic to rise higher and higher. Who the fuck was this?

She couldn't stop fighting, couldn't stop kicking and twisting and pulling.

"Hurry up and get on with it," another voice called from behind her. They sounded almost bored, ready to get her kidnapping over with. It sent a million questions racing through her head and horrified her all at once.

The person tugging her through the forest still had their hand clamped over her mouth, and Cordelia bit down, hard. They yelped in pain, momentarily loosening their grip on her. It was enough.

She ran forward, back toward the path. She wasn't thinking, wasn't even concerned with looking back at her captors. She was only focused on getting the hell out of there.

A loud curse and then thudding footsteps sounded behind her, leaves crunching under their feet. She let out a swear of her own before picking up the pace, numb to her body with how much adrenaline was pumping through her.

Too slow, just barely too slow.

As she broke through the trees and back onto the trail's path, her captor caught up and pulled her down. Her face was pressed into the ground, damp soil and fallen leaves crunching under her cheek.

The stranger on top of her yanked her arms back, pulling them into one of their hands while the other tangled in her hair, pushing her farther into the forest floor. She wished so desperately in that moment that the earth would just swallow her whole, let her disappear from this nightmare.

"Nice try, *little witch*," they said mockingly, "but we've got other plans." With a hard, fast motion they twisted her wrists, sending a blinding, hot pain shooting up Cordelia's arms.

"Let's see if your little spells help you now, bitch," her attacker snarled in her ear.

She cried out, everything fell to utter darkness, and then there was nothing.

CHAPTER FORTY-ONE

THANE

"*F**uck, fuck, fuck*," Thane chanted, racing down the path. Where the fuck did they take her?

He had woken up that morning to an empty bed. He'd grumbled about it as he walked downstairs and into the kitchen, expecting Cordelia to be there making her coffee. But it'd been empty. So he'd checked the garden, thinking maybe she was basking in the sunlight among her lavender plants. But no, she hadn't been there either.

He hadn't been able to find her *anywhere* in the house. No note, no texts, nothing. Which was unlike her. He knew intrinsically that she wouldn't leave him without a word. That'd been when the panic set in.

He'd tried to calm himself once he remembered she liked to take walks on her favorite trail in the neighborhood. So he'd thrown on some sneakers and done his best not to walk too fast, seem too worried, as he'd made his way to the trailhead. She would be there. She had to be there. Walking along the path and taking in the blooming wildflowers, listening to the song of the birds high above.

Instead, what he'd seen was a nightmare. He'd made his way into the thick of the forest, worry clawing back up his throat the farther and farther he went without a sign of her.

Then he'd heard crashing sounds off the trail and had finally seen Cordelia break through the trees in the distance. He'd screamed her name, trying to grab her attention, but she couldn't hear him. Either because he'd been too far away or she'd been distracted by whatever she'd been running from. He hadn't thought, he'd just run, trying to eat up the distance between them as quickly as possible.

Another figure had soon followed her, taking her to the ground and pinning her down. Rage had boiled in him, consuming his vision, his every thought.

They'd still been cloaked in the shadow of the trees, and he'd been unable to make out who it was attacking Cordelia. He'd just kept running, kept pushing himself harder and faster, desperately needing to get to her.

In a split second, he'd seen her attacker twist her wrists, a scream of pain breaking past her lips. It'd sent a shiver racing through Thane, his own whimper of pain flashing through him.

He'd closed in, closer and closer, almost to them. And then they'd disappeared. Magicked away and out of his reach.

He came to a sudden stop, staring at the space where she had just been. He blinked, and the scene before him did not change. The leaves and soil where Cordelia had been pinned down were still rumpled, showing signs of her presence. But she was not there.

Collapsing, he fell to his knees on the trail path. After what felt like an eternity, he registered the hot trails of tears tracking down his face and the hard lump that'd formed in his throat. A scream burned inside his lungs, clawing its way through him, demanding release.

He could hardly feel anything else, couldn't feel the change of his eyes, didn't notice the claws breaking through his hands. Only when he released a roar, a deep, vicious sound, did he realize he had fully shifted.

His bones and muscles ached from the strain. From the soreness of a long-refused shift. His wolf was both delighted and furious. Relieved to be let out, to be in his animalistic form. But so Goddess-damned angry about his fated. Fucking *ripped* away from him.

Without another thought, he tore into the trees, racing past them, desperately trying to track Cordelia's scent. It was even stronger in his wolf form, flooding his senses with a warm familiarity. A possessive urge overtook him.

She was *his*. And she had been taken from him. He would track these motherfuckers down and fucking destroy them.

Thane didn't know how long he had been running, he just knew his sole purpose was to find Cordelia.

Eventually, he decided he needed to gather his thoughts and get a fucking strategy in place. Because frantically tearing through every inch of Elysea would take far too long and was just sloppy, especially on his own. So he turned and took off in the direction of his own house.

He just couldn't get the image of Cordelia disappearing out of his head. It was like she'd vanished into thin air, right in front of him.

As he slowed, Thane's mind swirled with a myriad of racing thoughts, alarm creeping in and taking hold of him. Fuck.

The vanishing, almost no trace of her left behind, it was just like the kidnappings. The panic seeping into his muscles seized his lungs and stomach, twisting like a vise.

Oh fuck fuck fuck.

He took off running again, faster and faster as he tried desperately to close the distance. His initial instinct had been right, the kidnappings were connected with the person watching Cordelia. The person that he now swore he would slowly shred to pieces before happily bathing in their blood. And if he didn't find Cordelia soon, he would tear the whole world apart, rip out the throat of every person who stood between him and the woman he loved.

CHAPTER FORTY-TWO

TALIN

T alin felt an aching in his chest. One that wouldn't go away. It sent a wave of sickening anxiety through him before it finally took root in his gut. He couldn't brush it off and couldn't stop his mind from drifting to Cordelia at the same time.

He had been pacing the length of his apartment for the past ten minutes, trying to dispel the worry, to dispel the racing thoughts of the night before.

But nothing worked, nothing would pull him out of this. He had to get it out of his system, had to get out of this fucking apartment before he tore himself apart.

He found himself aimlessly wandering the streets of Elysea, stewing in the anxiety swirling in him and the incessant thoughts of Cordelia.

Fuck.

Everything seemed to halt, crashing down around him as he realized what was happening. Something was wrong, something was very wrong with Cordelia. He barely registered what he was doing until he realized he was running, running as fast as he possibly could. Toward Thane's house.

Talin stood at Thane's front door, banging his fist on it as hard as possible.

"Open the fucking door, Thane!" he shouted, impatience dripping in his tone. He was getting antsy at this point, like he was filled with a million needles prickling at him to get to Cordelia, to keep her safe.

He didn't even fucking know what was wrong, *if* anything was wrong. But his instincts wouldn't let up, wouldn't back down.

Thunderous crashing rumbled in the woods behind Thane's house. He darted off the front porch and rounded the corner of the house into the backyard. As soon as Talin cleared the house, the yard in full view, Thane barreled out of the tree line.

In full fucking wolf form.

Thane's wolf form was something to behold, something terrifyingly powerful. He was massive, one of the bigger wolves of any of the packs. Wolven looked exactly like wolves, just much, much larger. Thane towered over Talin by several feet, his fur a deep jet black, practically absorbing any and all light. His eyes glowed an intense blood red, so different from their normal obsidian.

Thane immediately marked where Talin was standing, his head swinging around before his eyes landed on him. Stopping in his tracks, a deadly stillness settled over Thane as a growl rumbled from his muzzle.

Talin threw his hands up. "Hey, man, it's just me. I need to talk to you, OK? So I need you to calm down and let regular Thane out for a sec, hmm?"

Talin wasn't afraid of Thane in either of his forms. He had grown up with him, knew him better than anyone. He knew Thane wasn't anything for him to fear, but he still wasn't going to give him a reason to try to bite his head off right now.

With a chuff, wolf Thane backed off, sitting on his hind legs before tilting his head down. And after a couple seconds, regular Thane was standing in front of him. In all his naked glory.

Talin whistled. "Didn't know I was coming over here for a strip show, Lycus."

"Shut the fuck up, Talin. I'm not in the mood." Thane barely spared him a passing glance as he darted for the back door of the house, racing inside as Talin followed close behind.

"What's wrong with Cordelia?" Talin was cutting right to the point too. Now that Thane had calmed down and returned to his normal form, he needed to get down to business.

Thane whipped his head around. "What do you mean?"

"Something is wrong. I know neither of us have accepted the fated bond, and I know you're not my biggest fan right now, but I can *feel* something is wrong with her. So tell me right fucking now, *what happened?*"

Thane's gaze hardened, narrowing in on Talin before he gave in. "She was taken." It came out mostly as a growl.

Talin could feel the anger pouring off Thane

"I watched it happen. I woke up this morning and couldn't find her. So I checked the trail by her house, she loves walking it. But when I found her, some fucking asshole was hunting her down. He took her."

Thane's hands were fists at his side, his eyes flashing red still, mixing with their usual onyx color. Talin could see that the rage was pumping through Thane so fast, riding him so hard, that he could barely control his shifting.

"She was right there. I was so fucking close, and I lost her. I didn't get there in time, and now she's Goddess knows where, and who the fuck knows what they're doing to her." Thane dropped his eyes, his voice was breaking, and Talin's heart was clenching right along with it. He knew this had to be even worse for Thane right now, after what'd happened all those years ago.

"It's not your fault, Thane. What could you have done to stop it? What could you possibly have done differently?" He paused before continuing, "And that's a rhetorical question, asshole, so don't bother trying to pity party yourself on this one. It's not your fault, end of story."

Thane looked back up at Talin, fire burning in his eyes again, but he didn't say anything.

"Now, regardless of how you feel about me and my fated bond with Cordelia, what matters right now is that we fucking find her and we make sure she's OK." Talin leveled Thane with a serious glare, urging him to let Talin in on this. Let him protect her.

"You're right," Thane said resolutely, "you're part of this now."

Talin was relieved momentarily before his mind started racing with questions. "OK, so let's think. Did you get a good look at who it was that attacked her?"

"It was too dark where they were under the trees. And before I could get to them, they disappeared. Like they magicked away somehow." Thane's brows furrowed as he contemplated that.

"Hm. I wonder if any of the illusionary witches have the ability to do that." Talin knew the illusion magic witches could do a multitude of things depending on how powerful they were. But he didn't know much, especially didn't know if they could make someone disappear like that. As if they'd been portaled somewhere else.

"I'm not sure, but I can still pick up on her scent where she disappeared. I can take you there."

"Fuck, absolutely. Let's go." Talin started for the door again. Thane followed behind him immediately.

His dragon's instinctual need to protect his fated, his own need to shift, was riding him hard now. Fuck, he needed to find her, needed to make sure she was OK.

Talin stopped in the backyard, closing his eyes and taking a deep breath. He shook out his arms and rolled his neck as he let the urge to shift take over. He knew he could get there faster in his dragon form, and his senses were much sharper too. He would be able to track her better that way.

Talin felt the shift in his eyes, forcing him to blink quickly as they turned from their normal shining gold to his dragon's deep, flashing bronze.

His claws followed next, jutting out from his hands as glimmering charcoal-colored scales stretched up his arms and over the rest of his body. Then his wings started forming, the familiar weight of them settling into his muscles as he stretched them out behind him.

It felt delicious to finally shift, an ache briefly settling into him like stretching right after you wake up from a deep sleep. His dragon purred, eager to take to the skies.

He glanced over to see Thane beside him back in his wolven form. They were of similar sizes when they were both shifted, eye to eye now. Thane nodded to Talin, and Talin dipped his chin in return before taking off with a mighty flap of his wings, shooting into the sky.

He would track Thane from above, following his path toward the hiking trail. His hide itched with desperation to be with Cordelia, to find her. It only made him move faster, fly harder as he tracked Thane's furiously fast form below.

CHAPTER FORTY-THREE

CORDELIA

Cordelia woke up groggy, her head throbbing and throat dry. She was sitting, her back propped up against a cold, hard wall behind her. She tried to take in her surroundings, but the darkness that engulfed her was total. She looked down at her hands as she lifted them, barely able to even make them out. *Where am I?*

Feeling around the cold concrete floor beneath her, Cordelia tried to get her bearings so she could stand. Maybe she could feel her way around whatever room she was in.

Bracing herself with one hand on the wall and one on the floor, Cordelia tried to stand, but it proved to be difficult. She was so extremely tired. Exhaustion weighed her down, deep and thorough, making her movements sluggish and delayed.

Finally, she pulled herself upright, leaning against the wall for support as she continued to feel her way around her immediate vicinity. She'd felt nothing so far. Heard nothing. Nothing beyond the scrape of her sneakers against the floor, the brush of her hands against the concrete walls.

The room was freezing and smelled of damp earth, dust, and stale, musty air. How big was this place? She imagined it was a room, but it could be some sort of chamber that opened into a larger maze. Slowly, ever so slowly, she made her way around the room, encountering nothing along her way but the same, seemingly endless walls.

Finally, she felt something else, something different. The rough wood grain beneath her fingers set off a small spark of joy, briefly stalling the dread that had been growing heavier and heavier in her heart. She searched for a handle. This had to be a door, had to be her way out.

To her relief, her hand closed in on a smooth, metal doorknob. She let out an involuntary yelp at her victory, quickly realizing how hoarse her voice was. But that didn't matter right now, couldn't be her main focus. Gripping the doorknob, Cordelia twisted.

Only to feel panic rise in her, faster and higher this time. The door was locked. A quick check confirmed that it was from the outside.

She was fucking trapped.

She rattled the knob, desperately trying to somehow find it unlocked, find a way to get the stubborn thing to budge. But no matter how hard she twisted, how much her wrist screamed in protest, the lock wouldn't give.

Scrambling, Cordelia tried to pick the lock with her magic. She coiled it around the internal locking mechanism and then flicked her wrist. But no matter how her magic pulled, it wouldn't budge. It must be spelled. Her magic was strong, but if a strong enough witch had spelled it, it would hold against her. At least for now, until the spell weakened.

Hot tears stung at the corners of her eyes, her throat heavy with the searing soreness of an impending sob. A physical, pained manifestation of the dread coursing through her veins.

It suddenly felt like the world was crashing down around her, a million thoughts swirling through her head unbidden. How would she get out? Who took her? Who was keeping her here? Why did they want her? When would they even come back? Would she starve to death? Could she somehow rattle the door off its hinges? Would someone eventually find her?

She couldn't get the barrage of questions, of horrifying worst-case scenarios, to leave her mind. They flooded in tidal waves, unceasing and cruel. She stumbled back, grabbing her hair and gripping it with clenched fingers as she fell to the floor. A sob finally ripped out of her throat, tearing her heart with it.

She was caught in a chaotic storm of her own making, the aching panic that rooted in her gut spreading like wildfire. Her breathing stuttered, catching itself in her throat as waves of dread coursed through her.

She didn't hear the footsteps clicking down the hallway outside the door, didn't register the slide of the key in the lock, didn't even notice the creak of the doorknob as it turned in place. But when she heard Lydia Halloway's voice break through her panicked haze, she froze.

"Cordelia, dear, it's so lovely to see you again." Lydia's greeting was so sweet. As if she wasn't looking down at her daughter, crying on the icy floor of a cell. A cell of Lydia's making.

Her stomach dropped at the sound of her mother's voice. Her body tensed, her heart skipped a beat. This couldn't be happening.

Slowly, ever so slowly, Cordelia lifted her head, looking up toward the sound of Lydia's voice. A soft, faint light came from the hallway beyond the door, illuminating Lydia's silhouette. The sight of her mother standing in front of her turned Cordelia's heart to stone, her blood to ice.

She felt no comfort in the presence of this woman. And she suddenly was intensely disappointed in herself. For not immediately knowing this all had to be Lydia's doing. For not being prepared. The vague threat she'd received from her mother came swiftly to mind.

"If you don't come willingly, I'll have to take matters into my own hands. I'll be seeing you soon, Cordelia."

Her stomach twisted, hopelessness flooding her. It was a feeling she knew well but hadn't experienced in so long. Hopelessness had clung to her like a second skin, growing up in Halloway Manor. She was a necessary tool for her mother's destructive tendencies, and feeling like an object of power rather than a person was tiring, demeaning. That exhaustion eventually wore away into loss of happiness, loss of hope. And it dredged itself back up again as Cordelia sat on that cold, stone floor staring up at Lydia Halloway. She was trapped again, and in her mother's control.

"Why am I here?" Her throat felt raw. She was weary, bone-tired, at the thought of becoming that same little girl again. The same little girl locked in her dark room, the light of the moon her only beacon toward something else, something better.

But this room held no such beacon. This room was void of all light, void of anything for Cordelia to hold on to for that dangerous word: hope.

"Dear girl, you know I need you. I've always needed you." Lydia walked forward, her eyes roaming over, surveying Cordelia's body.

It made Cordelia physically cringe. She knew that look, it was one she was familiar with from her mother. Always judging, always assessing, and usually followed by some sort of snide remark about her looks, her body.

"You are the heir to the Halloway coven, as I once was. When I die, you will take up the family business, the coven, and Halloway Manor. You've known this since you were a child, and I raised you better than to behave like you have been." Lydia's eyes were cold, demanding. "And I had so hoped to talk some sense into you when I spoke with you in that silly little shop you love so much. But it seems you're still determined to defy me. And you know what happens when you don't follow my rules."

Cordelia flinched, knowing exactly what her mother meant. Visions of her childhood flashed in her mind. Shoved in her bedroom, locked away for days without food or water or interaction with another person. Tied to her bed for more of her mother's spells and experiments.

"No, no you can't do this. You can't do this to me and expect to get your way, Mother. I'm done. I've been done with this since I left home. I said *no*." Cordelia's voice started as a plea and gradually hardened as she continued. Her resolve solidified, her anxiety easing as she spoke. It was her rage that flipped the switch, her rage at her mother's words, her mother's endless impulse to *take*.

"I know you think you did the right thing by leaving. But I can't just let you cater to your own whims and not take your responsibilities seriously. You are a great, powerful witch, Cordelia Halloway. And I won't let you waste your talents. Even if I have to force you to see." Lydia stood tall and proud, unashamed of how she'd always treated her daughter. To Lydia, this was what had to be done. This was the way of the Halloways. No one said no. No one defied their matriarch.

But Cordelia did.

"I won't waste my talents on the Halloway bullshit. You all sit in the manor, plotting and scheming, looking down on everyone else. You're so worried about appearances, about power, about *breeding* more precious little witches." The well of rage within Cordelia bubbled, her words flowing out of her like daggers.

"There's never been a Halloway like me, and there never will be again. I won't let this poisonous family continue on. You may have been able to hold me down as a child, but I'm a grown witch now. I know how to use my magic, and I know how to protect myself, Lydia."

The fire in Lydia Halloway's eyes was a raging inferno of fury. That was Lydia's weakness, her anger. She'd always let it get the best of her, let it control her words, her actions. And Cordelia knew how to play that to her advantage.

"And what, exactly, do you think you're going to do about it, Cordelia? Hm? You can't change that you're a Halloway. You can't even change your circumstances. I have you exactly where I want you, whether you like it or not. I suggest rethinking your position and getting comfortable, daughter." Lydia was practically spitting by the end, anger lacing her every word.

As Lydia turned, reaching for the door, Cordelia flicked her wrist, twisting her fingers in the same motion. The door slammed back hard against the concrete wall, the wood splintering.

Lydia wheeled around, eyes wide.

Before Lydia could do anything, Cordelia flicked her wrist again, effortlessly pulling several nails from the door before commanding them to move. In an instant, Cordelia had Lydia's throat caged by a necklace of nails, all of them pointing inward.

CHAPTER FORTY-FOUR

CORDELIA

"**O**ne more word from you, one move, and I drive them through your throat, Mother." Cordelia's words were dripping in venom as she stood, her back straight and chin held high. Power thrummed under her skin as her magic pulled to the surface, her power calling for more, more, more.

As she lifted her hand toward her mother, her magic pushing the nails forward ever so slowly, she noticed her skin. It was glowing, silvery and pulsing, illuminating the room softly. She smiled to herself, smiled at her magic and the comforting feeling of it.

"Cordelia Halloway, put your hand down right now."

Lydia was trying to appear strong, confident, but Cordelia could see through it. Could see the slight tremble in her hands, the fire banking in her eyes. There was fear there, no matter how small it was, no matter how tight of a leash Lydia held on it. It was still there.

"I'm going to walk out of here right now, Mother. And you're going to leave me the hell alone. I wasn't kidding when I told you I would show you what my magic could do. So here's a taste." Cordelia's voice was laced with so much authority and raw power. It was delicious on her tongue, dripping like the sweetest honey.

As Lydia opened her mouth, Cordelia snapped her fingers, her magic locking her mother's mouth closed.

"I've had enough of this conversation," she said, dropping her hand but leaving the nails in place. They were just barely grazing Lydia's throat now, and they would continue to until Cordelia was far enough away that she felt safe again. "Now, leave me the fuck alone."

With that, she strode through the doorway. The warm glow of the sconces along the hallway mixed with the silvery glow of her skin and created an ethereal, mysterious light. The silver of her magic thrummed stronger, the light under her skin growing brighter and brighter, almost as if trying to choke out the shadows of the villainous space.

As Cordelia wound her way through the halls, she realized where she was with stark clarity. Halloway Manor.

This was the basement, the one area that she was seldom allowed to roam growing up. That was why she hadn't recognized it until now.

The basement had been fashioned into a series of hallways and rooms. Rooms like the one she had been locked in, which served the express purpose of caging people in. People like her, and people who were to be sacrifices.

Quickly, she realized if she was in Halloway Manor, then she couldn't leave through the main house without being spotted. Surely, other Halloway coven members were in the building and, at the very least, Lydia's lackeys. They would know Cordelia was here and subsequently know she wasn't to be let out.

She turned left at the next intersecting set of hallways and made her way to the long-neglected secondary exit. It was hidden in the basement and led to the back of the estate.

She hadn't been allowed to roam the basement, but she'd had to escape from it once before. There had been a night when she'd been running from her mother as a child, trying desperately to get away from her. She'd made her way into the basement and gotten lost, until she found the old door, tucked away at the back of the maze of hallways. The back section was rarely visited or used, so no one had ever bothered with that door.

Finally, her exit came into sight. She rushed forward, her hands pressing against the old, weathered wood. Trying the doorknob, she was relieved when it turned, though the decayed old metal stuttered. Chips of coppery rust exploded into the air as she pulled the door open, her heart leaping at the knowledge that she was getting out of there.

It worked.

Night had already fallen, but Cordelia wasn't concerned about finding her way. She had lived with the darkness all her life, had observed and memorized the Halloway Estate with and without the light of the moon.

Rushing through the doorframe, Cordelia was led out into an overgrown part of the back garden. This part of the manor bumped up against the edge of the woods, and some old flower beds had been overrun by roses. The roses had long died out, but the thorny, skeletal remains of the bushes still stood.

The tangled rose bushes were too tall and crowded for her to climb over, and there was no path through. But there was a small opening near the ground. This much she remembered from her last escape through this path.

Dropping to her hands and knees, she crawled her way through the sharp, tangled mass of vines, ignoring the poking and scratching as the thorns pulled at her from every direction. She would bleed, she would cry, she would go through whatever she had to to get out of the manor and off the Halloway Estate as quickly as possible. Before someone spotted her and tried to get in her way.

As she crawled through the damp, decaying earth, and the tangled vines started thinning, she breathed a sigh of relief. She had finally made it to the forest's edge. She pulled herself off the ground and didn't waste time as she took off into a sprint. There was nothing, no sounds apart from her feet pounding against the forest floor, crunching through leaves and rocks and sticks, and the sound of her hard breathing. She couldn't force herself to stop, didn't even think about stopping. She just knew she needed to get out.

Suddenly, she heard a shout and she was pulled from her thoughts. Her heart pounded harder in her chest as the surprise of hearing a voice made her stumble.

"Cordelia!" the voice shouted again, closer now.

Panic clawed up her throat.

Fuck. They caught her.

She tried to keep running, but she wasn't paying attention and slipped on a mossy patch on the ground. As she fell, all she could think was that she would rather die than be subject to her mother's torture ever again.

Then, a pair of hands wrapped around her, wrenching her up just as she was about to hit the forest floor.

CHAPTER FORTY-FIVE

THANE

Thane couldn't think, couldn't feel anything beyond the combination of brutal rage and heart-pounding panic that was coursing through him.

Talin and Thane had tracked Cordelia down to Halloway Manor. Mostly off gut instinct. Neither of them could pick up a trail from where she'd disappeared, and there wasn't much to go off of from there.

But Thane had heard the terror and hurt in Cordelia's voice when she spoke of her mother. He knew Lydia had put her through hell, even if he didn't know what exactly it was. He knew enough to understand that Cordelia hadn't had a childhood at all. And he got the distinct impression that Lydia was far from through with using her daughter for her own advantage.

So Halloway Manor was the likeliest direction.

They both were still in their shifted forms, finding that gave them the best advantage with their heightened senses in these forms.

As they were trying to find a way into the manor, to try to find Cordelia, a crashing sound neared them in the woods. Thane prepared himself for the worst, for the potential of a fight to break out.

Then he caught the person's scent, that bewitching combination of lavender and bonfire smoke, and a shudder rolled through him. The relief of knowing that she was alive was deep. Then that relief was replaced by a bone-deep need to get to her, to make sure she was OK, and to have her back in his arms.

He caught up with her quickly, calling out for her as she booked it through the darkened forest. He didn't want to alarm her, but he was also growing more and more frantic to get to her, to soothe her. He heard the panic in her body, heard it in her heartbeat and the sharp, erratic pace of her breath.

Suddenly, he burst through the trees and saw her, terrified and running for her life. She'd gotten out. She'd made it on her own. Thane pushed himself harder, faster, even as he shifted back into his human form midstride. He didn't care that he was naked, didn't care about the tree branches and leaves whipping and scratching at his skin as he crashed through underbrush and bushes.

Just as Cordelia was in Thane's reach, she tripped, falling to the mossy forest floor. His heart jumped in his throat as he desperately grappled for her, trying to shield her from the blow of the fall.

He blessedly got to her before she hit the ground. Thanking the Celestials, Thane pulled her to him, gathering her against his chest.

She was breathing hard, her cheeks flushed, and she had enough sense to fight back against him, mistaking him for an attacker. Good. He wanted her to defend herself, wanted her to fight for her safety and her life. It meant that she wouldn't go down easily and that she could protect herself. And her protection was all that mattered to him.

He pulled back, holding Cordelia at arm's length as he met her gaze, locking on to her soft lavender irises.

"It's OK. It's just me," he gently reassured her, trying to get through to her, to calm her at least a little bit.

He saw the moment she registered his presence, registered that she wasn't in danger. Her shoulders relaxed as her eyes welled with tears. She gripped his arms tightly, crushing herself to him again like he was her anchor. It made his heart ache and his breath catch. She was shaking both of them as sobs racked her body.

"Cordelia, darling, are you OK?" He buried his nose in her honey hair, closing his eyes as he inhaled deeply, his grip on her tightening.

She was here, she was alright, and he had her in his arms. Relief pounded through him in tidal waves, cooling his blood and calming the erratic rhythm of his heart as he drank her in. Her presence, the feel of her, her smell, the sound of her breathing.

Alive. She was alive.

"Thane," she breathed.

"I've got you. You're safe. You're OK."

"You came for me. You found me." She was still gripping him like she was afraid he would disappear if she let go.

"Of course I did. I will always come for you. I will always make sure you're safe and protected," he growled into her hair, possessive need riding him hard.

He would rip apart the person who took her from him. He would make them suffer. It was a promise to himself and a silent one to Cordelia.

He was faintly aware of Talin behind them, slowly coming closer. Probably to keep from startling Thane and to make sure Cordelia was OK.

Thane loosed his grip on her, pulling his head back to look into her eyes.

"You're OK." It came out breathier than he meant, and as reverent as he felt in that moment.

She smiled, and it cracked the cage around his heart.

"I'm OK." She took a deep breath, visibly centering herself as she closed her eyes. He felt her body relax under his hands, felt her breathing slow as she continued to calm herself.

Once she opened her eyes again, a branch snapped behind him, refocusing his attention on Talin.

"What was that?" Cordelia sounded on edge again, like she was still afraid someone was after her.

"It's OK. It's just Talin. He helped me find you tonight." Thane dropped his arms, stepping aside so Talin was in her line of sight. Talin was only a couple feet behind them, his expression a combination of relieved and nervous.

He must have shifted back to his human form as Thane was racing for her. And he was just as naked as Thane, though it seemed Cordelia hadn't even noticed yet. He held back a smirk. That would be a fun little revelation for her in a minute.

"Cordelia," Talin started, his voice broken, dripping in anxious tension. He took a tentative step toward her, looking a little unsure of himself.

"Talin, I can't believe you're here. You came to help me?" Her voice was filled with awe, like she couldn't quite believe it.

Talin straightened at that, the anxiety visibly easing from his body as he stood taller.

"Abso-fucking-lutely I did. I wasn't going to let anything happen to you, and I wasn't going to let Thane go out of his mind looking for you on his own." Talin and Cordelia were standing so close to one another now they were almost touching.

As Thane watched Cordelia gaze up at Talin, their eyes locked and breathing hard in each other's presence, he had a realization. He'd been tense waiting for this moment, this moment when he would first witness them together after that night at Hell's Spells.

He'd been worried he'd be overcome with anxiety and anger, jealousy coursing through him like the blood in his veins—hot and thick.

Instead, he was calm, so at ease. Like this was normal. Like it was meant to be.

Just then, Cordelia took another step forward, reaching for Talin and pulling him into a tight hug. Talin's eyes blew wide with shock for a second before he immediately melted into it, pulling her close and wrapping her in his arms.

Thane didn't miss Talin also burying his nose in her hair, breathing deeply. Thane knew the feeling, knew how good it felt to have her close, to have her returning the affection. It was addictive. Pure bliss.

"Alright, Talin, hands off her while you're naked. That's a little fast, even for fateds." Thane chuckled, taking a couple steps toward the two and slapping Talin on the shoulder.

Cordelia went rigid and was the first to pull back as she jerkily ripped herself from Talin's arms.

"You're naked?!" she screeched, turning to Thane. "You're *both* naked! Where the fuck are your clothes?!"

Talin and Thane both broke out into raucous laughter, doubling over, the sounds rich and deep as Cordelia stared at them in horror.

CHAPTER FORTY-SIX

CORDELIA

"It's not funny! Where the fuck are your clothes?" Cordelia stared at Talin and Thane, absolutely bewildered.

She'd been relieved that it was Thane who caught her. That he had come for her, had come to make sure she was OK and to protect her. She was shocked to see that Talin was also with him, also willing to risk his own safety for her, a woman he had only just met.

Now she couldn't even form full sentences in her head as she stared at the two men, doubled over and laughing. Completely fucking naked.

Thane composed himself first as Talin was choking back laughs and trying to catch his breath, his hands braced on his knees. His very naked knees.

"We both were in our fully shifted forms looking for you. When we found you, we shifted back. I didn't think it would be a nice surprise for a giant wolf to chase you through the woods while you were escaping a kidnapping." Thane still had a cocky grin on his face, his hands braced on his hips as he stared down at her.

How the hell did this man seem so confident while he was entirely naked in the middle of the woods? She envied that arrogance, and she also hated it. Hated how hot it made him.

"And now you're just going to . . .what? Walk home naked? I think that's frowned upon, boys." Refusing to let Thane get the better of her, she crossed her arms. She sure as shit wasn't going to let the naked men make *her*, the fully clothed person, feel uncomfortable.

"Nah, we'll probably just shift back," Talin wheezed out, finally catching his breath and righting himself back to a standing position.

"Oh yeah? And I guess *I'll* just walk home? Alone?" She put on a brave face, but her gut twisted. Even though Thane and Talin were here, the thought of walking home alone right now set her on edge. She didn't trust her mother not to send someone after her.

"Of course not. You'll ride back with one of us." Thane stepped forward, a stern look on his face. She had a feeling he was on the same train of thought as her. And there was a possessive need glinting in his eyes she didn't expect he'd let go of. Especially with Talin here and near her.

"Do I get to pick?" Cordelia arched a brow, a grin pulling at her lips.

Thane relaxed a little now that she'd accepted what they were offering. Now that he knew she'd be safe with at least one of them. "If you'd like." His voice was weirdly calm. She noted that for later.

Why wasn't he acting more territorial around Talin? Why didn't he seem more on edge at the idea of her picking Talin? She would investigate that further. But for now, she needed to get the hell off the Halloway Estate and as far away as possible.

"Hmm, I think I'd like to go for a ride with you, wolf boy." She gave Thane a wink, trying to let her anxiety ease a bit. She was getting out of there, away from this cursed place. She was going home with her fateds.

He shot a cocky look at Talin, who just rolled his eyes in return.

"I know, I know. Fated privilege you've got there, Lycus." Talin chuckled.

Rolling his shoulders and neck, Talin took a few steps back, giving

Thane and Cordelia, and presumably himself, space. It looked like he was about to shift, and she immediately started to panic.

"Wait!" she shouted, halting Talin in his tracks. His golden eyes met hers, a worried look in them as he searched her expression.

"You're going to come with us, right?" Cordelia wanted him to follow them home, needed him near her.

Talin softened at that, his muscles relaxing. "Of course, if that's what you want." He offered her a sweet smile, kind and affectionate.

A lump formed in her throat at the expression on his face. All she could do was nod in return with a smile of her own.

"Talin, follow close behind me. I'll lead the way," Thane yelled out, now farther away.

She hadn't realized he'd moved away from her. But as she turned toward him, she saw it. The flash as he shifted into his wolf form right in front of her.

Her jaw dropped as she looked up and up at him. He was *big*.

Thane's wolf form was so incredibly tall, even on all four legs. And strong, judging by his muscles and build. His fur was so dark that it seemed to absorb the moonlight above them. His massive paws thudded against the ground as he approached her slowly. Most likely to be sure he didn't scare her.

But she wasn't scared. Not as she looked up his chest, over his snout, and into his blood-red eyes. They were deep and flashing like glimmering crystals. Her breath caught in her throat.

She remembered seeing his eyes flash red before, in smaller glimpses in his human form. It must have been this, his wolf pulling at him. His eyes were striking in this shade, and she stared back at him in wonder.

"Thane," Cordelia breathed, "you're so beautiful." Silently asking for permission, she stretched a hand tentatively toward him. He nudged her hand with his snout, urging her on.

She reached up and placed her palm against his chest, rubbing his impossibly soft fur. When she felt a rumble under her hand, she looked up to see him closing his eyes and leaning into the touch, his nose coming to bump against her shoulder.

Cordelia laughed a little before tucking herself against him. "Alright, let's go home, wolf boy."

Dipping his head, Thane lay down so she could climb onto his back.

She hoisted herself up, grabbing his fur for leverage but trying not to hurt him as she pulled herself into position. As soon as she was up, she settled herself in, her legs straddling his back.

As Thane lifted his head, Cordelia looked up and toward Talin standing in front of them. Except, he wasn't in his human form anymore.

A dragon about the size of Thane's wolf stood before them now, his scales a deep, almost-black gray. Talin stretched his wings as much as he could in the limited space of the forest, and what Cordelia could see of them was already mighty and grand. They were taller than her and so wide, each tipped in a sharp talon. His full wingspan had to be absolutely massive.

Each of his four feet had five huge talons that dug into the soft earth beneath them, gleaming in the moonlight.

Her eyes traveled up his scaled body and chest, his serpentine neck, and to his snout and eyes. Talin let out a huff of hot breath, the steam from it fogging in the chilled night air. His eyes were now a deep, glinting bronze. Her mind went back to the night she'd met him. Seeing that beautiful flashing of bronze in his captivating gold eyes. How it had made her breath catch.

She smiled at the memory and at the dragon proudly towering before her as Thane stood to his full height, matching Talin's dragon.

They both nodded their heads to one another, even as Talin kept his eyes locked on Cordelia.

"You're beautiful, too, Talin," she said dreamily, unable to tear her gaze from his. Talin's dragon chuffed softly in return, and she thought it might be the closest he could get to expressing gratitude in this form. Until she heard the next thing.

Thank you, love. I always thought my dragon was pretty impressive.

She startled, rearing back at the sound of Talin's voice in her head.

"What the fuck was that?" Her mouth hung open as she blatantly gawked.

Thane rumbled beneath her as Talin shook with obvious laughter. It sounded like more chuffing in his dragon form, but she knew it was laughter nonetheless. She narrowed her eyes at him.

Cordelia, my love, it's a gift of the shifters. We can communicate with each other with our minds. And with our fateds, conveniently enough.

Thane's voice was the one to fill her head that time, and she shifted her horrified expression to him. She was staring at the side of his face, as he had turned his head as much as he could to look at her from the corner of his eye.

"Well thank you for letting me figure this stuff out as we go, I guess. It would have been nice to have a heads-up before you started reading my mind." Cordelia gave Thane a playful shove as she leaned back on him, letting herself slump over. She was exhausted after this day from hell, and she just wanted to get home, get some sleep, and then maybe try to figure things out.

Sorry. The thought didn't cross my mind until Talin decided to pipe up over there. And to be clear, we can't read your thoughts, just speak into your mind. It's kind of like a phone. We can send and receive messages from you, and hear them as if we were speaking to one another out loud, but we can't hear anything else.

"Wait, you said send *and* receive? So can I do that too?" Well that sounded like a pretty cool ability to have. Especially if one of them was on the ground while the other was in the air in their shifted forms.

Yep! You can practice to get better at it. It's really easy. You just need to kind of push your thought toward us, almost like you need to give it momentum. It might be hard at first, but it'll get easier over time, and soon, it won't take much effort at all, Talin chimed in. He sounded so excited, and it was infectious. She was giddy to try, but right now was not the time. Just the thought of putting energy into mind speaking was draining her even more.

"We have to test this out when I haven't just been kidnapped and semirescued by two giant shifters." She laughed, leaning into Thane. "For now, let's just focus on getting home so I can snuggle Merlin."

Thane rumbled beneath her. *Ready, little witch?*

Cordelia had barely nodded her head in confirmation before Thane took off, forcing her to grip his fur.

They shot through the woods, Thane's giant wolf somehow able to gracefully maneuver the thickly wooded forest. He jumped over fallen trees and rocks, wove through the trees, and ducked under branches as his giant paws thudded against the damp ground. All while making sure Cordelia was safe and sound.

It felt similar to riding on Talin's bike. Everything flew by her, and the wind against her face was so freeing and energizing. Like the sweetest, deepest soul-level cleansing.

It was then that Cordelia heard the boom of wings in flight above her, and she looked to the sky. Talin soared over the tree line, his powerful wings carrying him under the silvery moonlight, casting green, iridescent flashes from his scales.

It was in that moment that Cordelia felt the weight of these two men. Felt the gravity of their relationship, of the fated bond that tied both of them to her. And she couldn't help but feel blessed by the Celestials. She felt so wholly cared for and genuinely loved. And it made her heart soar.

It was so incredibly beautiful, and she let out a deep, rich laugh as she let herself go to the night and her fate.

CHAPTER FORTY-SEVEN

CORDELIA

All-encompassing relief crashed into Cordelia as she walked into her house. Finally, she could feel safe and relaxed. Especially with Thane and Talin with her, so close and so comforting.

They were talking on the porch while she barged into her house, seeking the solace it held. Merlin burst from the hallway, racing to her before pushing himself against her legs, desperately seeking her affection.

"Merlin!" She knelt down and scooped up the black cat, cradling him in her arms as he cuddled into her, loud purrs vibrating through his body.

"Oh, I missed you, my sweet boy," she cooed as she continued to the living room, holding Merlin close to her chest as she nestled herself into the couch. She couldn't help but bury her face in his fur, breathing him in, breathing in the physical reminder of comfort that he represented.

She only vaguely registered the front door opening and the thud of footsteps moving upstairs and then back down before Thane's voice broke her reverie.

"Are you OK, Cordelia?" His voice was raspy, broken. Like he truly wasn't sure she was OK and safe. To be honest, Cordelia could hardly believe it either. Could hardly believe she was back home, not locked away in that cold, dark room in Halloway Manor.

Meeting Thane's eyes as he stood before her, she just nodded. A million emotions passed through them in those seconds their gazes were locked. Like everything she couldn't put into words, she could express through their bond, their link to one another. Thane nodded back, swallowing hard as a shiver ran through his body.

Thankfully, he was clothed now—Talin, too, in clothes she recognized as Thane's. She looked to Talin, standing a few steps behind Thane.

He looked unsure, like he didn't know where he fit into this puzzle. It made Cordelia's heart ache, to see that out-of-place look on his face. Talin was the kind of person who came across as naturally confident, born with a smile on his face. To see him unsteady was unsettling, and she wanted to ease that.

"Talin, can I talk to you alone?" she asked.

His gaze snapped to hers, shock splashed across his features, and a sparkle lighting up his eyes. She glanced back to Thane, who seemed to be feeling much better now that they were home again. Now that he was in close proximity to her.

"I'll head out back, leave you two alone." Thane hitched his thumb toward the kitchen and the back door beyond. Cordelia just gave him a soft smile and nodded.

As Thane retreated to the backyard, Merlin jumped from Cordelia's arms, trailing Thane through the house. She couldn't help but chuckle at that. Merlin had taken so well to Thane already. He was absolutely enamored with the wolven.

Talin took a couple steps forward, drawing Cordelia's attention again.

"You can have a seat, Talin. Make yourself at home." She tried to keep her tone soft and kind, to offer him some comfort. She didn't want him to feel out of place. She wanted him to feel at home because she wanted him to be part of her home. Where he belonged.

Pulling her legs underneath her and crisscrossing them, she grabbed one of the many soft pillows littered across the couch and held it to her chest.

Talin sat on the love seat diagonal to her, his hands resting on his knees as he leaned forward, his head hanging down. He blew out a long breath before lifting his head and meeting her eyes again.

He looked like he was absolutely suffering. There was so much pain in those golden eyes.

"Cordelia, I—" Talin started.

She held her hand up.

"I want to thank you for what you did today. For helping Thane and bringing me home. But most importantly, I want to thank you for coming for *me*." She needed to get this out, needed him to know just how grateful she was.

Because it meant everything to her.

"We haven't known each other long, I know." She paused to collect herself. "But I want to know you, Talin. I want to know you better than anyone else does. I want to keep you close, I want you in my life. I knew that before today, but after everything that's happened, it just solidified my feelings." She was a little breathless, could feel herself melting into the couch as the words left her lips.

Talin seemed to be at a loss for words, his eyes gleaming in the moonlight streaming through the big living room window.

"Talin," Cordelia breathed, "I want you."

That last sentence must have broken him because he tore himself from the couch and was in front of her, kneeling, in a flash. "Goddess, you have no idea what it does to me to hear those words coming from you." His voice cracked, and she felt her throat ache alongside it.

She just smiled, reaching up to cradle his face in her hands. His eyes shone with tears, like little stars in the corners of those sparkling golden irises.

"Tell me," she whispered, unable to bring herself to speak the words any louder. Almost as if her voice could break this little bubble they found themselves in.

"I want you, too, Cordelia." Talin's voice sounded so sure, so strong. "I want to be by your side for as long as you'll let me. I want to know you, all of you. I don't just want to know the you the rest of the world sees. I want to know every facet of you. I want to see you angry, sad, elated, in the throes of pleasure. I want to see you with your hair wet, fresh out of the shower. I want to know the two sides of the sleepy Cordelia, the one before bed and the one waking up. I want to share in your most intimate smiles and laughs. I want to hold you when you need someone there. I want to fight, and be angry, and make up, and feel how exquisite it is to love one another so fucking deeply. I hurt, I ache, and I need you, Cordelia."

She could feel her own tears now, spilling over her cheeks in little cascades. Every word from Talin's lips set more and more of them free, making her feel lighter and lighter as they fell.

She didn't have words, so she threw her arms around him and held him as close as she possibly could. She never wanted to let him go, never wanted to be parted from him.

It felt like the final missing puzzle piece had snapped into place with his declarations. Like the final thread woven into the beautiful tapestry of her life, setting her heart aflame and making the stars of her sky shine.

"Yes, yes, all of it. I want every single piece of you, Talin," she said into his neck, cuddling closer to him still.

His arms were wrapped around her now, his hold on her tightening with her words. It felt like everything was as it should be. It was all just so right. She couldn't see how it was meant to be any different.

"Don't worry, old grumpy ass out there will be alright." Talin chuckled into her hair.

Cordelia laughed at that, her heart soaring at the relief she felt. Thane had told her he was fine, that he wanted her to chase after Talin if that was what she desired. He knew that it didn't change a single thing she felt for Thane. And it didn't change a single thing he felt for her.

"Oh?" she said, pulling back with the biggest smile on her face.

"Yeah, that's why he wanted to wait outside. He wanted me to know that he was OK with this." Talin gestured between himself and Cordelia. "That he wants us both to be happy." He smiled at that, and she could see the pure, joyful relief on his face.

She leaned forward, resting her forehead against his. "So you want to love me, huh?"

Talin's warmth radiated off his body, and she wanted to soak in it. Soak in the beauty that was innately him.

He didn't respond, instead he leaned forward, his lips brushing against hers for just a moment. It sent a shiver down her spine, one that pushed her to lean forward to meet him halfway.

And as their lips met, Cordelia felt like everything around them disappeared. The wind against the trees outside vanished, the quiet hum of the refrigerator in the kitchen silenced itself, and everything was so at peace, yet so electrified.

It was as if her body had been set alight, the magic of Talin seeping into her very bones.

She moaned into the kiss, pressing her whole body to his as she clung to him and opened her mouth, her tongue gently sweeping across his lips.

Talin matched her moan with one of his own, his tongue meeting hers as they melted into the kiss, wrapping themselves up in one another.

It was like being swept into a raging bonfire, out of control and blissful. She never wanted it to end. Never wanted to lose the sense of innate rightness she felt in Talin's arms, in his lips.

He pulled his lips away from hers, peppering kisses across her cheek and jaw as he worked his way down to her neck, licking and kissing as he went.

The rumble in his throat set her blood on fire, her hands gripping onto his arms to keep him close.

He quickly found the sensitive spot below her ear and gave it extra attention as a long groan ripped from her throat.

"That's the spot, huh?" Talin's voice sounded gravelly, wrecked.

Cordelia's only response was to grip his head with one hand, threading her fingers through his silky, coffee-colored hair.

"Alright, you two, no need to get handsy straight out the gate." Thane's voice startled her, forcing an involuntary squeak from her lips as she pulled away from Talin.

Talin just laughed from his spot next to her. "You jealous, Thane? Our honeymoon phase is just getting started. Keep up, pup." Talin's grin was mischievous, and it set a red-hot flush in her cheeks.

"Oh, I can keep up, lizard boy. Don't you worry." Thane winked at Talin, giving a wicked smirk to Cordelia as he stepped farther into the room.

The watery light of the moon cast Thane in a silvery glow, highlighting his body in stark shadows and starlight. He was breathtaking.

In that moment, Cordelia knew just how lucky she was, and she was so grateful for her fateds from the Goddesses.

She settled into the comfort of Talin's arms, closing her eyes and humming, a content smile stretching her lips.

CHAPTER FORTY-EIGHT

CORDELIA

Tension gripped Cordelia as she walked toward Quartz Coffee the next morning. Sure, Talin and Thane were with her. She hadn't been surprised when both of them demanded to escort her on her walk to the coffee shop.

But she still couldn't shake the uneasy feeling that'd riddled her the moment she'd stepped out of her house. She couldn't help but think about that day she'd been followed, those watchful eyes on her outside Quartz Coffee.

The kidnapping in the woods.

Goddess, she hated this. Hated feeling so vulnerable, so out of control. Hated feeling like her life wasn't her own, not with the looming threat of Lydia Halloway ever present.

But she wasn't going to let her mother control her life, wouldn't let Lydia Halloway keep Cordelia from her peace, her comfort, her happiness.

Stepping into the coffee shop felt like slipping into calm routine. The familiar scent of fresh coffee and roses greeted her as soon as she passed the threshold, and she took a deep breath, letting her eyes close.

"I'll grab your table, little witch. Can you get me an iced coffee with cream?" Thane said from beside her.

"Absolutely. Thank you. Talin, do you want anything?" Cordelia turned from Thane to Talin, watching as he took in the coffee shop around them.

It wasn't very busy today, only a few customers scattered around the tables in the front of the shop. The baristas were all chatting behind the counter, their smiles and laughs dancing across the space.

"I'll come with you," Talin said, still engrossed in the menu across the shop. She could see the panic in his eyes at the large menu, could see him desperately trying to make a decision. It brought a small smile to her face.

"Cordelia! Iced lavender latte with oat milk?" Lilith called from behind the counter, her sparkling indigo eyes bright with excitement.

Lilith's straight, moonlit hair was half-up with a few tendrils framing her face where they had fallen down. Cordelia was still amazed at Lilith's beauty, at the magnetic pull she felt toward her. She realized now it wasn't anything romantic, instead an incredible friendship, but Lilith still held so much wonder for her. She was so grateful to have Lilith in her life, and so grateful for the connection they would always share.

"You got it." Cordelia laughed, stepping up to the counter with a tentative Talin in step behind her.

Lilith turned her attention to Talin, amusement dancing in her eyes as she quirked a brow at him. "And who is this mystery man? Is Thane old news now?" Her words snapped Talin's attention to her. He looked to be stuck between whatever thought process had been going through his head and responding to Lilith.

Cordelia rolled her eyes playfully. "This is Talin." She wasn't entirely sure how to explain their situation, so she went with the blunt route. "He's my second fated." Her voice softened, lowering in volume at that last part. Her cheeks heated with a red flush, nervous about Lilith's reaction.

Lilith's eyes widened, her mouth falling open. "Your what?!" she practically shrieked, and she immediately looked around the shop as she realized how loud she'd been. She finally turned back to Cordelia, shock still written all over her face.

"I'm sorry, you have two fateds? What did you do, sacrifice your soul to the Goddesses for that?" The shock was slowly melting from Lilith's features, and a smile grew in its place.

Cordelia was relieved. She knew it was rare to have two fateds, and the idea of actually telling people that had been setting her nerves on edge. Not that she owed anyone an explanation, but she knew it would turn heads when others found out.

She could just picture telling Sage, could imagine the giggles and smiles she would get from her adoptive mother. It made Cordelia warm at the thought, set her at ease. She knew Sage would be understanding.

But she'd been worried about Lilith. The last time she got a fated, things had been a little tense with Lilith. Sure, it'd been a different situation, but still. She hadn't been sure what reaction this update would glean.

"I don't know, but I must have done something right." She blushed further, a smile permanently etched into her face at this point.

She still couldn't believe she had both Thane and Talin, two wonderful men who were kind, soft, and strong. Who believed in her and supported her.

"Anything I can get for you, lover boy number two?" Lilith asked, swinging her attention back to Talin.

He laughed at that, his smile broad and genuine. It made Cordelia's heart melt and warmth spread through her chest.

"I'll have a hot seasonal blend with cream and toasted-vanilla syrup, please."

That fit him, Cordelia thought. Hot and a little sweet—that pretty much described Talin as a whole.

"And can I get an iced coffee with cream for him?" She hitched her thumb toward Thane, who was already waiting at Cordelia's favorite table.

"Sure thing. Coming right up!" Lilith smiled at Cordelia and Talin before grabbing their cups and jotting down their order.

Cordelia paid and then grabbed Lilith's attention again. "Hey, when you have a second, can I talk to you?" She needed to get to the bottom of everything that'd happened with her mother. Starting with how in the world she'd gotten ahold of Cordelia. She still couldn't wrap her mind around how the man who'd grabbed her in the woods just magicked them to the manor so quickly.

"We can talk now, hold on." Lilith passed the order ticket over to another barista before circling around the counter.

Talin touched Cordelia's elbow, giving her an understanding look before turning and heading toward Thane.

Cordelia pulled Lilith to the corner of the coffee bar, away from the other customers. "Do you know much about illusion witches?" she whispered. She knew Lilith was a witch but didn't know whether she possessed enchantment magic like Cordelia, energy manipulation magic like Lydia, illusion magic, or divination magic.

"Yes, I'm actually an illusion witch," Lilith confirmed.

Cordelia relaxed at that, relieved to have someone she could trust that knew intimately what that magic entailed.

"Why do you ask?"

"I had a situation with my mother. We have a terrible relationship, which is a long story. But she's never let me make my own decisions. I've been out of her control for a long time now, but she still tries to manipulate me wherever and whenever she can. I suspect she's had me followed the past couple weeks." Cordelia's heart clenched at the memory of the terror she'd felt being constantly stalked, her every move tracked. "And yesterday, I was out for a walk and someone attacked me on the trail. Before I could do anything, before I could even try to escape, he magicked us away. Right to Halloway Manor."

Cordelia's heart was racing as everything came rushing back to her. The sheer panic, knowing that she was well and truly caught. Waking up in that cold, dark room. The dread she felt seeing her mother.

"Oh fuck. Are you OK? That's so fucked." Lilith's hand was on

Cordelia's arm now, she realized. Reassuring and comforting, and it eased something in her.

"Yeah, I'm feeling better now. Still a little shaken from everything, but Thane and Talin help. I managed to get out on my own, thanks to my magic. But they both came for me and got me back home." Cordelia's mouth tipped up at the corners at that, a small symbol of what she felt for them.

"Good, good." Lilith blew out a breath, running a hand through her hair. "I don't know what I would do if something happened to you, Cor."

Cordelia gave Lilith a reassuring smile before continuing. "Do you know if that's something a witch can do with illusion magic? I've never heard of someone being able to use magic to transport themselves between one place and another."

Lilith paused, and Cordelia could see her turning her thoughts over in her head.

"I think I've read accounts of that happening before, but only with extremely powerful illusion witches. But there haven't been any instances of it in recent history. I'm pretty powerful and skilled in my illusion magic, and I've never been able to do it." Lilith cocked her head to the side. "Are you sure it was an illusion witch?"

"I don't think he was an illusion witch. He kept speaking to me as if he wasn't a witch at all. Which is where my confusion mostly stems from." She still couldn't piece it all together, she just kept drawing blanks. "I know some witches can allow another person to benefit from their magic. Like enchantment witches can cast protection spells on others, to guard against someone else's enchantment magic. But I wonder if someone could cast a spell to allow another to wield their magic, even if it's limited."

"Hm, it's an interesting idea. If he wasn't a magic wielder himself, then there's no way he was able to do it on his own. Transportation like that would take a large amount of power. But transferring that power to another? That might work. I'll do some research and see what I can find."

They could figure this out, they could find a way to discover what

Cordelia's mother was up to, and how she was accomplishing it. And from there, they could stop her.

"Thank you, Lilith. I owe you big time," Cordelia promised, a smile on her lips as she embraced her friend.

Goddess, it still felt so good to call Lilith that. To know they hadn't lost one another.

One of the baristas behind the counter called out their drinks.

"Gotta go make sure those two don't get cranky over coffee. Thank you again, Lilith." Cordelia reached for Lilith again, giving her another big hug before darting off for her coffee, leaving Lilith laughing behind her.

She was amazed she was able to balance all three coffees on her own as she set them down on the table in front of Thane and Talin. She nodded as they gave her their thanks.

"So what was that with Lilith?" Thane asked from his side of the table, taking a drink of his coffee. He closed his eyes, humming and tipping his head back. "This coffee is fucking amazing."

"I'm sure Cordelia tastes even better." Talin winked from beside her, taking a drink from his own cup.

She blushed, shaking her head at the two of them. "I was asking her about illusion magic. I didn't know, but she's an illusion witch. She said she's read cases of illusion witches being able to transport themselves from one place to another, but there hasn't been one powerful enough to do it in a long time." Cordelia took a sip of her own coffee, relishing in the sweet and slightly bitter taste of the lavender and coffee with the silky oat milk. It was absolute heaven and a welcome reprieve from the stress she'd been experiencing.

Thane's body tensed as she talked about what'd happened the day before, when she had so easily been taken away, in a split second.

"I don't think the person who attacked me on the trail was a witch, though. He spoke as if he wasn't one, so I'm wondering if an illusion witch somehow transferred their magic to him so he could take me away like that."

She wasn't sure what type of spell one would need to cast in order to accomplish that, but it wasn't a far stretch from what the enchantment witches could do to protect someone.

"Does Lilith know if that's possible?" Talin chimed in.

"No. She said she's not even strong enough to be able to transport herself like that, let alone someone else. But she's looking into it."

"Good," Thane growled across from Cordelia, drawing her attention again. "Mark my words, we'll track that fucker down, and I won't let them see the light of day again. We will handle this, Cordelia. Your happiness and your freedom are too important."

She reached across the table, grabbing both men's hands. "Thank you. There's no one I'd rather have at my side than you two."

CHAPTER FORTY-NINE

THANE

The past few days had been killing Thane. And it had felt like a hell of a lot more than only a few days.

From Talin and Cordelia finally accepting one another, to Cordelia's attacker and Lydia Halloway, to now, Thane was exhausted. But it wasn't over yet. It wouldn't be for a while.

Since Cordelia broke out of Halloway Manor and Thane and Talin brought her back, safe and sound, Thane had just been grateful that she was home and in his arms. He'd still have to worry about Lydia Halloway and how to take care of her, but that would have to wait.

Currently, he was lying in bed, holding Cordelia as she slept on his chest and he stared at the ceiling. Merlin was also there, curled next to her and fast asleep.

What was keeping him up now was the situation with Talin.

Thane had been pretty possessive and jealous of Talin's bond with Cordelia at first. He grinned at that, remembering the aftermath of discovering their fated bond. How he'd chased Cordelia down and fucked them both hoarse for days.

But now he wasn't jealous and was surprised to find that, no matter how hard he dug for it, he couldn't find it in himself to be upset about it anymore. In fact, he just wanted them to be as happy as he was with Cordelia. And if they found that happiness with each other, that was what he wanted. He hadn't even been the slightest bit upset when he'd seen them kissing the night Cordelia came back home. When he'd walked into the house and seen them together on the couch, his heart had felt like it swelled in his chest.

He liked them together. And he was happy to know that Cordelia would have an added layer of protection.

He trusted Talin, knew Talin better than he knew pretty much anyone. If he was going to be in this with someone, he was glad it was his best friend.

Now he was just worried about them acting weird around him. He didn't want them to feel like they were doing anything wrong, didn't want them to feel like they couldn't be as open with each other as he and Cordelia were together.

In the days since they'd kissed, they'd passed longing glances back and forth, shared brief touches and small affections. But they hadn't ever been outright romantic with one another, hadn't kissed again. It bothered him, that they felt like they had to walk on eggshells.

He was a big boy, and he could handle them together. Hell, he felt like he was more accepting of their relationship than they were. He rolled his eyes at that, snorting softly.

Maybe he should have another conversation with Cordelia? With Talin?

He was tired of having to constantly reassure them, though. He wanted them to relax, to just be with one another and let it come naturally. Goddess knew he didn't hold himself back from her.

Thane rolled onto his side, rolling Cordelia with him so that her back was to his chest. She didn't wake, but she did snuggle into him, making him melt a little bit, his heart clenching at the soft gesture of affection even in sleep.

He resolved to handle things with Talin and Cordelia tomorrow. No matter what it took. It was time to rip the Band-aid off.

Thane stood at the kitchen island the next morning, cup of coffee in front of him on the black marbled-granite countertop. The steam from the mug was rising in great clouds, perfuming the air with the bitter, rich scent of fresh coffee.

Just as he picked up the mug to take another sip, Cordelia's footsteps pattered on the stairs. He just smiled into the lip of the ceramic mug, taking a long drink and letting the hot coffee pleasantly burn down his throat.

"Good morning, sleepyhead," he greeted her as she rounded the corner into the kitchen. She was still in the black lace sleep dress she'd worn to bed the night before, the hem falling high on her luscious thighs.

He couldn't get enough. Of seeing her, being near her, touching her, hearing her laugh, seeing her smile, protecting, and loving her. Life with her was a dream he was happy to never wake from.

"Good morning!" she chirped as she strode into the kitchen. She was always chipper, always alert and ready to go in the morning.

It never ceased to amaze him how quickly she could wake up, how fast she could pull herself from that bleary, sleepy state.

"You didn't wake me when you got up." She pouted, and it was so cute it made him want to catch that lip between his own. He held himself back, forced restraint so he could get to the conversation they needed to have.

"I wanted to let you sleep. Goddess knows you don't get enough, and you're just too cute to wake up."

As she shuffled behind him, preparing her own cup to start the morning, she said, "Yeah, well, that doesn't stop you from waking me up with your cock in the middle of the night when it suits you." She bumped her hip against his as she sidled up next to him at the counter, setting her mug of coffee down.

"Are you saying that's not a good reason to wake you up?" A crooked grin pulled at his lips.

"That's not what I said at all." She blushed, turning away to avoid his gaze. Thane just chuckled.

"So, where's Talin?" He just jumped into it, opting for the blunt route for this conversation.

"What do you mean? He's at his place." She didn't meet his eyes, nursing her coffee with slow, small sips.

"But why? You two are together now, right? Why hasn't he spent more time with you?" He turned, fully facing her. Nowhere for her to run and dodge the subject.

"Well, yes. But it's . . . new. And . . ." She hesitated, not letting go of whatever she was about to say.

"And what?" He wasn't going to back down.

"Nothing. Never mind."

"No, not nothing. Say it, Cordelia." His tone wasn't commanding or angry, but it was insistent. They both knew what she needed to say, what she meant. But she needed to say it out loud so they could get past it.

"And you're here, OK? Not that I don't want you here. But I just feel like it's rude to you if I'm affectionate with him in front of you." She set her mug down, her body now turned fully toward him, though she still wouldn't quite meet his eyes. "I don't want you to get upset. You're important to me. And just because Talin and I are together now, doesn't mean that my relationship with you is any less respected."

Thane took a step forward, resting his hand on top of hers on the counter. "Cordelia, it's OK. I don't want you to hide your relationship with him." His voice was soft, gentle now. "It's not as if I don't know you two are fated. It's not as if I didn't see you kiss the other day. I don't want you to hide. I want you two to be free to be yourselves, in any way that happens."

Her eyes finally met his again, and the expression in them threatened to break him. Those glittering lavender depths held everything. Happiness, relief, comfort, reassurance. And he wanted to crash to his knees at the sight of it. That he'd done that for her.

"Really?" Her voice was broken, cracked in just that one word.

He simply nodded, stepping closer and pulling her into his arms. Her arms immediately wrapped around him, too, crushing herself to his chest.

"Thank you," she mumbled into his shirt.

"Now that we've gotten that over with"—he pulled back and grabbed his coffee, bringing it to his lips for another drink—"when are you two finally going to fuck?"

Her jaw dropped, the hand she had outstretched toward her own mug fell slack on the counter, and he couldn't help but howl with laughter.

"You didn't just ask me that, did you?!"

Thane just laughed harder, his entire body shaking.

He couldn't respond beyond cackling laughter, and through watery eyes, he saw Cordelia regain her composure, turning away from him as she stalked out the back door and to the garden, her cup of coffee in hand as Merlin trailed behind her.

"Well, well, look who's here." Thane grinned at Cordelia from his spot in the backyard.

He could hear crunch of gravel under tires in the driveway out front, and he knew it was Talin.

Cordelia was sitting among the lavender in her garden, enjoying her coffee as Merlin frolicked through the flowers and herbs, pouncing on the bugs and chasing after the butterflies. It was peaceful, and so perfectly normal now. He would never be able to get over the comforting life he had somehow found and settled into.

"You and your freaky wolf senses." She rolled her eyes, tipping her head back toward the sun for a second before letting out a deep sigh, pulling herself from her cozy spot in the flowers, and walking past Thane into the house. "I suppose you'll ask Talin the same questions you asked me this morning?" she asked, her head snapping to him and her eyes narrowing.

"Just the one," he quipped, giving her a wicked grin.

It amazed even himself, how casual he was about Talin and Cordelia. But it felt good to let that jealousy, that anger, go. It felt like a step in the right direction, and he couldn't shake the feeling that it was all meant to be. Not just for Cordelia, but for him too.

Thane got up, following her as she breezed into the house, presumably to greet Talin at the front door. Merlin floated in behind them, taking on his ghost form, as the little cat was fond of from time to time.

He imagined the conversation with Talin would go a little easier considering Cordelia was still in her black lace slip. He wasn't sure he would even need to ask the question if that was what she answered the door in. Talin might just throw her over his shoulder and take her right there.

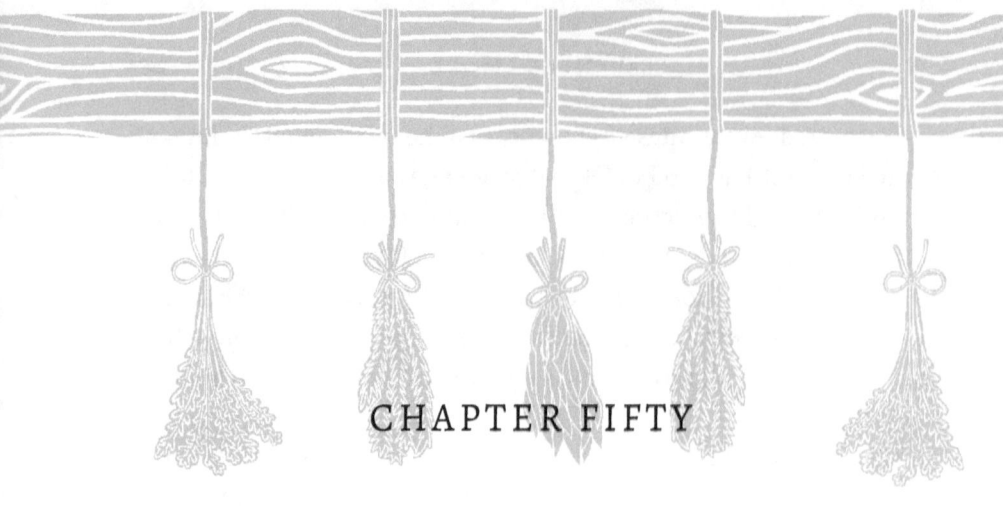

CHAPTER FIFTY

TALIN

Before Talin could even knock on Cordelia's front door, it swung open, startling him.

Cordelia stood before him, her beautiful honey-blond hair pulled back, a few loose strands falling around her face and her usual round, tortoiseshell glasses. She was gorgeous today. Well, she was every day. But she just looked so relaxed, so in her element.

As his eyes traveled farther down her body, he saw that she was only wearing a black satin slip dress trimmed in frothy black lace, and the hem skimmed the tops of her thighs.

His heart raced at the sight—she was so fucking gorgeous. He practically had to use his hand to hold his mouth shut to keep himself from drooling all over her doormat.

"Uh, hey." He couldn't hide the surprise in his voice, his brows raising.

She laughed a little, a bright, beautiful smile lighting up her face, her pale purple eyes sparkling.

Goddess, that laugh. Those eyes, her rounded hips, arms, belly, and thighs. Her rich scent of lavender in a bonfire that wafted around him.

He couldn't believe she was real, couldn't believe how incredibly fucking lucky he was.

"Thane heard you pull in, so I thought I'd meet you at the door." She pulled the door open wider and stepped back, gesturing him inside.

"Always here, that one, isn't he?" Talin teased as he strode into the house.

"You're damn right I am. And you could be too," Thane shot from the threshold of the kitchen. He was lazily leaning against the wall, his hands in his pockets as he gave Talin a mischievous grin.

What was he up to?

"Oh, I think that would be pretty presumptuous, don't you think? Cordelia hasn't even invited me. And besides, why can't she have her space to herself?" Talin shot back.

"She doesn't mind," Thane drawled casually. "I've told her to kick me out if it ever gets to be too much. This is her space, but it's also *our* space."

Talin quirked a brow at that before turning to Cordelia. Her cheeks were flushed, and she was avoiding his eyes. It was so cute, and it made the corner of Talin's lips start to curve up.

"He's right. I don't mind. And I take time for myself when I need it." She smiled before striding past Talin to sit on the couch.

Merlin pranced into the room from the kitchen and jumped up to settle himself in Cordelia's lap, already purring loudly. The little cat was shameless in his need for affection, but he was fiercely protective and attached to Cordelia. Talin loved the little familiar, loved the bond Cordelia shared with him.

"Well, I've got to do my patrols today. You two have fun." Thane winked at them before striding down the hall and up the stairs, out of sight.

Talin had an odd feeling about the way Thane was behaving. Too casual, too OK with Talin being here, in Cordelia's space. Thane's fated's space.

But she was Talin's fated too. He had to keep reminding himself of that. Reminding himself that she wanted him in her life, that she wanted to be with him too. Not just Thane.

"So, what's with him?" Talin rounded the corner of the couch, taking a seat as he hitched his thumb toward where Thane had disappeared.

"In general, or today specifically?" Cordelia laughed, but it came out nervous, and she looked a little on edge, tense.

"Good point. Today, specifically."

"Even if the answer is mildly uncomfortable?" Biting her lip, she gave Talin a wary look, like she was afraid of his reaction.

With a mischievous little smile, he said, "Always. I'm not afraid of the truth."

"Well . . ." She trailed off, squirming in her seat. He could see her fidgeting with her hands and picking at the lace on the hem of her dress.

Thane took that exact moment to make his way back down the stairs, coming out of the hallway with a proud grin on his face. "I think you two need to fuck and finally cut the tension," he announced, not an ounce of shame in his tone.

Talin choked a little. He definitely wasn't expecting that. "What?" he barked out, his eyes snapping between a bright red Cordelia and a wicked-grinned Thane.

"You heard me, Nightveil." Thane crossed his arms, leaning against the hallway wall, still grinning like a fool. In fact, the smile only broadened the longer Talin gawked at him.

"What happened to your growly, possessive attitude from before? The look-at-her-and-die act?" Talin couldn't wrap his mind around this. Around Thane's shift in tone toward him.

They had always been best friends. But when they'd realized Talin and Cordelia were fateds, he'd been pretty sure Thane would have no problem ripping out his throat. Now he was telling them they needed to have sex? Talin's world was turning upside down.

Not that he was complaining, per se. He felt like he was going to jump out of his skin if he didn't touch Cordelia soon. Like his dragon might just rip through his body and claim her for himself. But he was trying to be respectful, damn it. He was trying to respect Cordelia's and Thane's boundaries.

Because even if he and Cordelia were fated to each other, it was both their choice whether or not to honor it. And Thane got a say since he was also fated to her.

"Yeah, well, I got over it." Thane shrugged and Talin rolled his eyes, prompting Thane to continue. "OK, fine. I was still jealous, still wrapping my head around things when Cordelia was taken." Thane winced, glancing toward her to make sure she was OK. She nodded, and Thane pressed on. "And then I saw how fucking out of your mind you were over her. How desperate you were to save her, just as desperate as I was. And then I saw you two together when we finally found her. And, I don't know. I guess it all just clicked for me. Like it all suddenly made sense.

"I'm not going to question it. It feels right to me. To have you two together, and to have Cordelia and me together. And I think it'll work. I want it to work." Thane's eyes shone, and Talin could see the love and deep happiness there.

It took his breath away, lifted a giant weight off his chest that he hadn't known had been holding him down. It felt like everything was going to be alright, truly. Like everything was falling into place perfectly. The way it was supposed to be.

He looked to Cordelia and felt himself melt a little bit at the joy on her face, lighting her up like the brightest star.

"And do you agree?" Talin's voice sounded breathless, rough, like he could hardly get the words out.

Her eyes were shining, filled to the brim with love and affection and pure joy. It was spilling from her in tiny teardrops.

"Absolutely." The word came out choked, like she could hardly contain the emotions flowing from her. "I want you, Talin. In all ways. And I want Thane in those same ways. And I want us to work together. I want us."

Talin didn't have to question it to know what Cordelia meant by *us*. She meant all three of them. Together.

He launched himself off his spot on the couch, closing the small distance between himself and Cordelia. He enveloped her in a giant, crushing hug, her arms flying around his shoulders and pulling him as close as possible.

He pulled back, only to gently cup her cheeks, their lips crashing together in an instant. He groaned into the kiss as she sighed, melting into him.

Talin was vaguely aware of the front door shutting and locking somewhere behind him as Cordelia's hands scrambled over his shoulders and down to his chest. Touching, roaming, desperate. He felt the same.

"Fuck, I need you," he whispered against her lips.

CHAPTER FIFTY-ONE

TALIN

Cordelia nodded enthusiastically, whispering "Yes" before diving back in for Talin's lips.

He gently nudged her down to lie on the couch as he climbed on top, propping himself up with one arm while the other hand cradled her head, his fingers winding their way into her soft, honey hair.

Ripping himself away from her mouth, he trailed kisses down her neck, lower, lower, skimming her collarbone with the gentlest touch of his lips.

A soft mewling sound fell from Cordelia's throat as he teased her, softly and slowly brushing his lips against her skin.

"You like that, pretty girl?"

Nodding vigorously, she pulled him closer.

He hummed against her skin before trailing more kisses up her neck, focusing on the small, sensitive spot under her ear. His hands roamed down her arms, over her waist before settling under the hem of her slip dress, silently asking permission.

She didn't say anything, just reached down to start pulling the black fabric up as he helped her pull it over her head.

Talin's breath caught in his throat at the sight of Cordelia laid out bare before him. Beautiful didn't even begin to cover what she was.

Her body was breathtaking, the dips of her hips, the soft, rolling curves of her tummy, the dimples in her skin. He felt like a starving man at the sight of her. At the sight of his stunning, strong fated before him, desperate for him.

It was like being in the presence of a Goddess.

"You're captivating, Cordelia. Like a star plucked from the burning sky, so fucking beautiful it hurts."

The pretty pink color that rose on her cheeks under his praise was torture. He groaned at the sight, wanting so badly to lean in and lick the color to see what it tasted like.

Everything about her was so soft. In the most ethereal way. Like she was made of actual stardust and materialized in a sweeping wind of magic.

Her skin, her curves, even her clothes were so soft, so gentle, so beautiful. Effortless and just so damn amazing. Because that was what she was. Amazing.

"I don't know if I could ever get used to the sight of you." His voice was deep and gravelly, so different from its usual tone.

It was his desire. It flowed through him like a volcanic river, hot and burning, higher and higher.

She seemed speechless, breathless, as she leaned up and gripped his arms, pulling him in for another searing kiss.

Her hands ripped at his clothes as she pulled him in with her gravity. Like she was the moon and he the tides.

Talin broke the kiss briefly, as much as it pained him, to quickly pull his T-shirt off before smashing their lips together again. It was all chaos, his tongue slipping between her lips, gentle as it coaxed her to open up, to let him in to her magic.

Cordelia sat up to fumble with his belt buckle and the button of his jeans before she finally popped them free. The sigh she let out against his lips sent a shiver through him.

The more layers that were removed between them, the more desperate he felt. To feel her skin against his, to coax the most gorgeous sounds from her mouth.

Once he kicked his pants off, he settled back onto the couch in front of her, running his hands over her moon-kissed legs. He trailed his fingers up, up, up before gripping her thighs and pulling. She fell onto her back with a soft gasp. As he leaned in, he lifted her legs to his waist, his cock pressing against her through his black boxer briefs.

Moaning, she tried desperately to grind against him, seeking friction and more, more, more.

He trailed his fingers up her thighs, over her hips, and across her tummy. He lightly traced her curves, through the dips in her hips, over her stretch marks, mesmerized as he went.

"Goddess, you're absolutely fucking gorgeous, Cor," Talin breathed reverently. "How are you real?"

He dove in, capturing her lips with his as his desire blazed hotter and hotter. He wanted her so bad, needed her like he needed air. More than that.

She pushed against his chest, pushing him up to a kneeling position before pulling back and climbing off the couch. He cocked his eyebrow at her as she arranged him into a seated position on the couch and sank to her knees in front of him.

"Do you feel powerful, Talin? With me on my knees before you?" She grinned wickedly from where she was kneeling, and it sent a shiver racing through his body.

He wanted to bask in her, bathe in her for centuries. "I feel your power."

She hummed, nodding slightly as she leaned into him, closing her eyes and rubbing her cheek against his knee for a moment.

Between one breath and the next, she twisted her head, pressing a kiss to the skin that her cheek had touched not a few seconds earlier. Slowly, lovingly, she trailed kisses farther and farther up his inner thigh.

The press of her lips against his fevered skin was like a gift, a Goddess bestowing favor on an acolyte. And Talin would gladly lay worship at her feet for all eternity. Even for just a glimpse of the glorious power and beauty he beheld in her.

He didn't even notice Cordelia's fingers along his waistband until she started pulling his underwear down. His eyes slowly opened, lazy and heavy as he peered down at her. He hadn't realized he had leaned his head back, giving in to her touch.

"What are you doing, lavender girl?" Talin said, but his words came out much more broken and gravelly than he intended. He was boneless, absolutely made of desire, lust.

That desire was like a river of molten gold, flowing through him and delivering small waves of pleasure everywhere.

"Taking care of my big, strong dragon," she said against his skin as she peppered kisses along his hips, pulling the black fabric farther and farther down his thighs until she ripped them all the way off.

His cock sprang forward, heavy and thick. He didn't think he'd ever been this hard before. Never been this desperate for touch, for another person.

She let out a small sigh, sparkles dancing in her lavender eyes. It made his heart swell, clenching with the endless adoration and love he felt for her.

"Big was right," Cordelia said quietly. "And look how pretty your cock is."

It was long and thick, and flushed red, but it was also ribbed and had a thick knot at the base of it. The blessings of a dragon cock.

He couldn't wait to knot her one day. But only when they were both ready, both for the commitment of it and when Cordelia could physically work her way up to taking it. But Celestials above, did just the thought of it drive him wild.

Her words pulled a grin from the corner of his mouth as he reached forward to brush back a lock of hair that had fallen into her face. "You impressed, pretty girl?"

"Oh shove it, Talin. There's no one else here, no need to be the cockiest boy in the room right now." She shook her head at him, a small smile flashing across her lips.

His laughter quickly turned into a sharp gasp as she gripped him, giving him a very, very small squeeze before letting go, trailing her fingertips along his length softly. It forced him to suck in a breath through his teeth.

She didn't say anything as she continued to explore him, her eyes locked in on his cock, as if she were trying to figure out all of his secrets. Figure out what made him tick, what drove him mad, made him see stars.

He threw his head back as she wrapped her hand around him again and gave him a small pump.

He felt like his skin was going to melt off his bones as her mouth closed over his cock, the warm, delicious heat of her permeating through to his very soul. She very tentatively sucked at him, gentle and slow as she explored, discovered.

"*Fuck*," he groaned.

CHAPTER FIFTY-TWO

CORDELIA

Talin was *whining*, and the sound shot straight to Cordelia's pussy, getting her wetter and wetter by the second.

Working Talin's cock deeper into her mouth, as much as she could handle, she covered the last few inches with her hand and pumped in time with her sucking, bumping against his knot on every downstroke.

His ribbed texture was interesting against her tongue, but she liked it—loved it, in fact. She couldn't wait to feel it elsewhere later.

He gave a little thrust of his hips, one of his hands winding into her hair.

She closed her eyes, loving how she was unraveling him, and slowed her movements. As she pulled back until only the tip was in her mouth, she moaned around his cock, then alternated between sucking his tip and licking short, small strokes up his length.

He groaned, letting out soft, incoherent babbling. "Fuck, just like that, Cor." His voice was wobbly and unstable.

Every sound coming from Talin was like a shot of pleasure to her blood. It set her alight and burned through her body.

She took him in her mouth as far as she could again, sucking slow and hard, while swirling her tongue around his cock. That seemed to break the leash he held on his control.

His hips started stuttering and giving small snaps. Both of his hands were in her hair now, grappling for purchase as he let out a yelp that bled into a whine. "Fuck, Cor, please."

What he was begging for, she wasn't sure. But she didn't stop, didn't let up until he pulled her mouth away.

He was impossibly hard, harder than he had been when she started. The tip of his cock was an angry red, and he was leaking cum. Licking her lips, she savored the taste of him on her tongue, desperate for more.

"Oh, you have no idea what you just started." His voice was low, deep, dangerous, and her heart raced at the sound, pleasure skittering across her skin and sparking like flames.

Quickly, faster than Cordelia could process, Talin changed their positions. Her back was against his chest as he sat her in his lap, his arms wrapped around her. One hand stroked and plucked one of her nipples, the other swirled circles on her thigh.

"Goddess, you're so fucking soft, so fucking sexy. I want to explore every single inch of you. Hands, mouth, tongue, cock—there's nowhere on your body some part of me won't have touched," he said into her neck, his breath ghosting over her sensitive skin and sending a shiver racing through her.

"Yes, yes please." Her pleasure ramped higher and higher as he continued to stroke and touch her.

Settling her legs to bracket his, he adjusted her just where he wanted her with her legs spread wide. "That's my good girl."

His fingers explored her pussy, two circling her clit before dipping down farther, going back and forth over and over, and a beautiful, bone-deep pleasure bloomed deep within her.

"O-oh fuck," she breathed out, her head falling against his shoulder.

"That's right, baby." Talin chuckled as he licked circles against her neck, just under her ear—right in her sweet spot. Whining, she tilted her head to give him even more access to her sensitive skin.

Cordelia melted into a chaotic mess as his fingers continued their slow, decadent circles against her clit and his other hand worked her nipples—the pleasure was astounding. She squeezed her eyes closed, her orgasm a distant glimmering cloud in her vision, building with the delicious tension he was creating in her.

"You like that, pretty girl?"

She couldn't form words, so she just nodded, her eyes still closed as she reveled in the sensations he was pulling from her.

He brought his fingers lower, lower, until he circled her entrance, dipping the tips of his fingers in. The teasing was too much—she just wanted to feel him, feel all of him. But she would start with the two fingers that he was slowly torturing her with.

"Talin, please," she whimpered before capturing his lips with hers.

He breathed his satisfaction into her as he opened his mouth, delicately exploring her lips.

Her tongue met his in a dance, delighting in the sensual moment. He clearly wanted her as much as she wanted him, but he was taking his sweet time savoring her.

"That's my girl," he said against her lips, pushing two fingers in and curling them against her G-spot, pulling stars into her eyes and a gasp from her throat.

He continued to pump in and out, curling his fingers as he plunged in. She was going to explode any minute now—especially as his other hand dipped low to play with her clit.

She wasn't sure which way was up, didn't know anything beyond Talin's name as her orgasm came crashing into her—ripping a moan-laced scream from her lips.

"That's it, baby," Talin cooed, soothing and encouraging, his lips hovering over hers.

As he pulled back, his touch leaving her fevered skin, she opened her eyes and stared into his as he brought his fingers to his mouth and sucked.

Cordelia's jaw dropped as his eyes closed, a moan pulling from his lips. "You taste like heaven, Cor."

She blushed under his praise, and Talin grinned, his hand reverently running up and down her tummy, caressing and teasing.

"Are you ready for me, lavender girl?"

She'd always had sensitive skin, was sensitive everywhere. So it was no surprise to her when the light touch tickled her, forcing a giggle from her lips.

He let out a laugh of his own in response. "Is that a no?"

Cordelia whipped her head around. "No teasing, dragon boy," she said with narrowed eyes, which pulled another deep laugh from him.

Without another word, he pulled her from the couch, holding her bridal-style as he strode for the hallway, making his way up the stairs and into the bedroom where he plopped her down on her soft bed.

She bounced a little, and she felt her body—her tummy and breasts —jiggle with the movement.

"Fuck, just look at you. I can't imagine anyone more perfect than you. Every single inch of you is a revelation, a dream to me. And I want all of you for all eternity. I want to know how you feel under my skin, I want to know every dip and curve on this beautiful, wondrous body of yours." Talin dipped down, pressing a kiss to Cordelia's collarbone. The action sent a shiver racing through her, and she allowed herself to give in to the loving embrace he was offering.

He pulled back, looking into her eyes, searching and making sure she was OK. She smiled in return, which seemed to ease something in him. Reassure him.

"Do we need a condom?" he asked.

"No, I have a contraceptive spell protecting me."

Talin's eyes glittering with promise, he pulled back, wrapping his arms around her and leading her to the floor, in front of the large, full-length mirror that sat against the wall across the room. He gently guided her to her knees before the mirror before settling behind her.

Talin caressed her round tummy, gripped her love-handle hips, skimmed her thighs. His fingers traced the many stretch marks across her body along the way. He moved back up over her tummy and higher to explore her large breasts, holding them in his hands as he ran his fingers lightly over her nipples.

"I love all of this, Cordelia. All of you. You're magnificent, a work of art. And there's no single part of you I don't love—no single part of you I don't find so fucking sexy." His voice was gravelly and sincere, laced with adoration.

She couldn't help but believe him.

"And I'll spend all night proving it if I have to," he growled as he leaned down to nip her ear, one hand dipping down between her legs, immediately finding her clit. "Still so wet for me."

She groaned, turning her head to capture his lips. She was ravenous, in desperate need of him. She wanted to claw her way into his soul and never leave.

He didn't break their kiss as he reached down, lining up his cock and pushing into her slowly. He took his time, making sure she was OK. That he wasn't hurting her or causing any sort of discomfort.

As soon as she started squirming against him, seeking more friction, more of him, he pushed the rest of the way in.

She gasped against his lips, the fit of him so tight, so deep.

He moaned, his hand picking up its place against her clit, swirling and firm as he continued to pump in and out of her, so fucking hard and delicious inside her.

The ribbed texture of his cock was incredible in her pussy. It was absolutely addicting the way it rubbed against her, pulling deep pleasure from her with even the slightest movement. And the bump of his knot against her was fucking delicious.

Talin ripped his mouth from Cordelia's as he used his other hand to turn her chin, forcing her to look in the mirror.

"Look at you, Cor—fucking made for this cock," he growled, his lips so close to her neck as she watched him fucking into her.

"Goddess, you feel so good, Talin."

She could feel every single bump and ridge as he moved in and out of her, could feel them dragging against her, and it made her want to scream, made her feel like she was going to melt into a puddle right then and there.

"That's right, I'm the one making you feel good, pretty girl. You just relax and take that cock. I'll take care of you," he said, his hips giving her a particularly sharp snap before he set a slow, hard pace.

Her head fell back against his shoulder, the pleasure just too much. It was all so fucking good, and she was surprised to find she wasn't sure how long she was going to last—she was already so close.

"Talin, I'm going to come," she practically whispered. She could hardly get the words out, hardly form words at all.

"I know, Cor, I'm close too." He switched to rubbing her clit in an up-and-down motion, giving it a swirl every now and again, making sure to keep up the stimulation. The combination was driving her insane.

Cordelia felt herself cresting that wave again, ready to fall over the edge into her next orgasm.

"That's it—come for me," Talin said into her neck, his hips starting to stutter and lose their rhythm.

One more thrust and swirl on her clit, one last bump of his knot against her pussy, and she let go, a high-pitched whine leaving her lips as she gave in to her orgasm. It flowed out of her like a cascade of glittering moonlight. She could barely tell where her orgasm started and where she ended.

She was vaguely aware of Talin's orgasm crashing into him, spilling into her. He stopped rubbing her clit, and his hand splayed across her abdomen, holding tight to her tummy as he fucked her through his release.

As Cordelia started coming down, she heard Talin chanting "Fuck, fuck, fuck." She reached back, grabbing his neck as she turned and peppered kisses across his cheek, soothing him down from his high.

When they were both spent and slumped, he picked her up again, bringing her into the bathroom and helping both of them clean up before carrying her back to the bed.

He tucked her into him as he pulled the blankets over them, giving her a kiss on her forehead and squeezing her closer to his body.

She drifted to sleep, her eyes heavy as she clung to him, never wanting to let go.

And she wasn't entirely sure she was dreaming as she heard Talin softly whisper, "I think I love you, Cordelia Ashcraft."

CHAPTER FIFTY-THREE

THANE

Thane hadn't been entirely sure what his plan was when he'd stepped out of Cordelia's house. But it surely wasn't to end up at his parents' front door, staring at the weathered wood in front of him and trying to steady his breathing.

Reuniting with his mother recently was something he'd needed, something that had helped steady him and ground him. Before then, he'd been on a chaotic path, wandering aimlessly. Now, he was back on the right track, was where he was meant to be.

That didn't mean it was any less nerve-racking to be faced with his parents. He had the feeling that it would be that way for a little while, at least. Until he got his bearings and a new sense of normalcy about all of it.

He gathered himself, taking a deep breath as he gave the door three heavy knocks.

Inside the house, he could hear footsteps, heavier than his mother's.

The door swung open, Nolen Lycus standing front and center, his brows furrowed together before he realized it was Thane standing on the porch. Once that realization set in, a visible wave of relief and surprise flooded his father's face.

Nolen crossed the threshold quickly, engulfing Thane in a crushing hug and burying him in his chest. Thane was tall, a big wolf. But his father was still larger than him, just a bit taller and wider. It was funny, Thane thought, that his father could still make him feel so small, transport him back to being a helpless five-year-old. He chuckled at that, hugging his father back.

"Alright, Dad, ease up." He laughed as his father gave him one more crushing squeeze before letting go.

"You're home," Nolen Lycus said in that deep, rasping voice of his.

It reverberated through Thane, settled him so instinctively, so quickly. He nodded, overcome with emotion. He was. He was finally home, finally with his family again. Finally had a family to call his own.

Cordelia. Talin.

He was Goddess blessed, and it was all more than he'd ever thought he deserved.

"Well don't just stand there. Get in here, son." His dad turned and walked back into the house.

Thane laughed as he came inside, the soft, familiar click of the door closing behind him a gentle reminder of the comfort of home.

"I assume there's something you want and that you're not just here for the hell of it," Nolen called behind him as he strode into the kitchen.

Thane followed, plopping down at the kitchen table as his father fell into routine and prepared two cups of tea for them.

"You'd guess right." Thane scratched the back of his head, unsure how to approach the subject.

Yes, it was something he needed, to be home again. But he also needed answers, needed someone else to talk to about these kidnappings. He knew his father would have some insight, some sort of theory.

"What do you know about the string of kidnappings in the packs?"

Thane cut right to the chase, not wanting to skirt around it any longer.

His dad was a straight shooter, and he was no different. It was, apparently, a Lycus trait.

"I'd say probably not much more than you do, but I'm glad you brought it up. I've been wanting to talk to you about it. Been wanting to pick your brain." Nolen set down a mug in front of Thane, the teabag string fluttering with the movement as he took his seat across the table, his own mug in hand.

Steam curled up into the air, little wisps dancing in the thin streams of light coming from the window above the sink. The earthy smell of lavender and peppermint floated to Thane in a cloud of warmth. It reminded him of Cordelia, and his heart filled with love. He forced back a smile at the thought of her, needing to stay on subject.

"Well, I think the pattern they're happening in is odd. Whoever it is is only taking males, only taking alphas and betas, and only taking Harmonious wolves. What does that tell you?" Thane raised his eyebrow expectantly, knowing his father would pick up on his train of thought.

Nolen sighed. "I know, Thane. I know exactly what you're thinking. It's either the Artemisian or the Theian wolven. But we haven't been able to pick up any evidence pointing us dead in those directions."

Thane nodded, unsure where to push on it. He knew in his gut that it was one of them. Had to be.

"They don't leave any sort of trail that would indicate who it is, there's no scent left behind, and there's never a calling card, call for ransom, or any sort of taunting aimed at the Harmonious. At least, not anything out of the ordinary. No one is stepping up and taking any kind of anonymous claim to the crimes." Nolen shook his head, eyes cast down. Defeated. Thane knew the feeling.

"But one of them has to fuck up at some point, leave something behind. Something we can go off of." Thane's voice dipped a little lower.

It royally pissed him off that this shit was still happening. That the Harmonious wolven were no closer to figuring it out now than when the kidnappings started so many years ago.

"That's all we can really hope for." Nolen shrugged, his eyes finally meeting Thane's again.

He recognized the look there, the look of hopelessness, of feeling so lost. He felt the same. Ever since everything with his pack had happened, he'd felt like he owed it to them to somehow right the wrongs that had been committed against his fallen pack mates.

"Do we know if any other Magical have been involved? Any sort of sign that points to maybe it not being entirely on the Theians and Artemisians?" Thane asked, staring into the darkening, swirling tea in his mug.

Nolen cocked his head, his eyebrows furrowing. Thane knew he'd caught him off guard with that question. He wasn't even sure anyone had thought to ask it before.

The kidnappings had all taken place deep inside wolven territory, places where other Magical had rarely ever been. If any other Magical had committed the kidnappings, had been that far into their borders, other wolven would have known and sounded the alarm.

The wolven were very territorial, and very private. Turf wars between the different packs had solidified that when the Artemisian, Theian, and Harmonious wolven had finally settled their borders.

But, regardless, the wolven all still lived in the same place—Lunegrove—just divided into three sectors. And Lunegrove was rarely visited by anyone other than the wolven. Had been that way for as long Thane knew.

"Not that I'm aware. Why?" Nolen narrowed his eyes, apparently unsure of where Thane was going.

Thane thought for a second, trying to gather his thoughts, his words. He wasn't sure how exactly to explain this line of logic he was exploring. "I think there might be witches involved. Maybe."

How did it connect? Why would it connect?

"Why would witches be involved?"

"Cordelia went missing the other day," Thane began.

"Your fated, Cordelia?"

Thane nodded. He'd told his mother all about Cordelia when he'd come to visit. Had told her about how much Cordelia meant to him, how absolutely incredible she was. He figured his mother would tell his father, so he wasn't shocked Nolen made the connection.

"She was walking the trails next to her house alone. I went to find her, and when I did, someone was taking her. By force. I tried to run, to grab her before they were gone, but they disappeared instantly." Thane gritted his teeth, anger rising to the surface, bubbling just beneath his skin. "We got her back, but she didn't know how they did it. How they just vanished with her like that. So she asked around and found out that it was a form of illusion magic. Had to be an extremely powerful witch, but it's apparently possible."

"Does Cordelia practice this type of magic? Can she figure it out?"

"No, she's an enchantment witch. But she's trying to learn what she can. She did find out that it takes a very strong illusion witch to cast that sort of spell. She also said that she thinks the one who took her was some other type of Magical. She said they kept talking to her as if they weren't a witch." Thane's eyes narrowed as he took a sip of his tea.

"So what type of Magical would work with witches and want Cordelia? Do you know who took her?" Thane could practically see the gears turning in his father's head, could see him poring over the details Thane had already given him.

"We know it was her mother, Lydia Halloway," he said, an edge to his voice now. Just speaking her name sent a raging fire racing through him.

Nolen froze across the table, his body tensing. "Who did you say?"

Thane had never seen such a look on his father's face. Never seen any sort of fear or anxiety racing through his dark eyes. But he saw it grip his father now.

"Lydia Halloway. Cordelia's mother," he said slowly. "She's fucking awful, and she's the one who orchestrated the entire thing. She had her locked up in a fucking dungeon for Goddess knows what.

Cordelia got out on her own, but she's still worried her mother will come after her."

Thane stopped, waiting for further reaction from his father. But Nolen sat there, staring off, the tension still holding tight to his body. It actually seemed like it heightened the longer they sat there, silent.

"Dad," Thane started, wary. "What's wrong?" He placed his hand on the table beside his mug, bracing himself. For what, he wasn't sure. But this behavior was worrying him.

"Lydia Halloway is a monster, Thane," his father croaked out, his voice rough. "She's up to something. And if I know her, it's not good. For anyone."

A pause.

"She's out for blood," Nolen practically whispered.

Thane froze now, unable to think correctly. Thane had never heard of Lydia until Cordelia, and now this reaction from Nolen?

"Dad, how do you know her?"

A stretch of silence. The tension, the anxiety coursed through the air, pulling it taut as a bowstring between Thane and his father.

"Because Lydia tricked me once. And she tried to kill me."

CHAPTER FIFTY-FOUR

THANE

T hane's entire car ride home was a blur. He could barely remember getting in the car, let alone driving all the way to Cordelia's house, pulling into the driveway, and parking.

But he had. Here he was, sitting in the dark car, the engine turned off.

He was still in shock, he knew. Could barely comprehend what was happening. After his father's revelation, he'd felt himself slipping away. Into himself, into an inner world where he could hide.

He had almost lost his father once. Without even knowing it. He could have lost everything. Everything but his mother. He could barely stand the thought of losing his father—the man who had always been a guiding light in his life.

Nolen had stopped the story there. Hadn't elaborated. Thane had clearly gone into shock, and Nolen wasn't going to discuss it further right now.

But how was he supposed to handle this? How was he supposed to just continue on knowing that Lydia had almost taken his father from him? Then she had almost taken Cordelia from him too.

It was all too much to bear, too much to process. And it filled him with an unending rage.

But he had to calm down, had to cool off and let himself breathe. So he'd left his parents' house and gone out to the meadow where he'd taken Cordelia for their first date.

And he'd run, he'd paced the tree line, he'd lain in the grass—the very spot Cordelia had lain with him—and had counted his breaths.

He could get through this. He could get to the bottom of everything and find a solution. Find a way to make things right. He had to. He needed to. Not only for himself, but for Cordelia, for his family, for his lost pack.

And now he was more sure than ever that Lydia Halloway and the Artemisian and Theian wolven were somehow involved. Somehow connected in the wolven kidnappings. And definitely connected in Cordelia's.

And he would make them pay, one way or another. Make them pay for the suffering Cordelia had been put through, all the victims and their families had been put through, for what his father had been put through, and for what Thane himself had been put through.

Taking a deep breath and blowing out hard, Thane pulled himself out of the car, striding for the house.

He had resolve, purpose, and it felt damn fucking good. For the first time in he didn't know how long, he felt fucking powerful. Like he could take control and fix the shit he'd been stewing in for far too long. To fix the mistakes he'd made, the lives that were lost, the fucking hole in his heart that had been festering for years.

And part of that resolve, that power, was right behind these walls. Safe, sound, and under Talin's protection.

Thane let himself in the front door, closing it hard enough to be heard then locking it with the same loud authority. He wanted Cordelia to know he was home. That she was safe and he was back in charge right now. Because he needed this. Needed her. Needed to know that they were all alright and alive.

"Cordelia," he purred, his deepened voice carrying through the dark house as he kicked off his boots.

They were close to the new moon, so the moonlight was very faint, making everything under it seem that much more shadowed.

Good. It served him well today. He could sneak better this way, hunt better this way. Thane grinned to himself, delighted and wicked.

The lack of response indicated to him that she was upstairs. Still with Talin, since his car was outside.

Must have worn each other out. But they better have a little energy left, because Thane wasn't going to ease up just because there were two of them for his little witch now. Oh no—she was just going to have to keep up with both of them.

He crept up the stairs, taking care not to startle Cordelia as he made his way to her bedroom.

The lights were all off, and no sounds floated to him through the buzzing silence of the house.

Pushing open the bedroom door, Thane found Cordelia and Talin curled into each other, Cordelia's head lying on Talin's chest. Talin's arms wrapped around her, keeping her close as Merlin lay dozing at their feet.

Merlin perked up at Thane's presence in the doorway, getting up to stretch before jumping down silently and rubbing against his legs.

He smiled at the familiar before Merlin pranced off into the hallway. Smart cat.

Making his way toward the bed, Thane took his pants off, kicking them in the general direction of the hamper as he pulled off his shirt too.

He climbed into bed behind Cordelia, pulling her close, breathing her in. He loved her scent, and right now, it was driving him wild. He needed her. Now.

To try to gently wake her, he started peppering kisses against her neck. He whispered, "Cordelia, my darling," and then he nipped her ear.

She slowly woke, yawning as her arm instinctively reached behind her to wrap around him. Her voice was sleepy when she said, "Thane, you're home."

He nodded against her neck as he reached around her, finding her completely naked as he snaked a hand down to toy with her nipples.

Arching back against him and pushing her breasts into his hand, she mewled. She fucking loved having her nipples played with, and Thane intended on indulging that as much as she wanted.

"Oh yes, baby," she breathed out.

"Mmm, you like that?" he mumbled against her ear.

She couldn't do anything but nod, her hips starting to thrust of their own accord.

He grinned to himself. *That's my girl.*

Then Talin started to wake up, rustling against the sheets as he seemed to become aware of his surroundings. "What's going on?" he asked, his voice groggy with sleep.

"Taking care of our girl. You wanna join?" Thane's grin turned mischievous in the dark room.

Talin sat up quickly at that, scooting closer to Cordelia as he whispered an enthusiastic "Fuck yes."

He reached for her, pulling her in for a kiss, and she moaned at the contact, wrapping her arms around him in return. His hands went to her hair and hip, gripping her and keeping her close.

Thane guided them so Cordelia was lying down, with Talin working her nipples and licking her neck. She was a moaning, writhing mess. The two things that witch loved most were neck licking and having her nipples played with.

Thane settled between her legs, pulling them over his shoulders, then slowly kissing and nipping up her thighs.

When he finally made it to her pussy, he gave her a long, slow lick up her vulva and swirled his tongue around her clit before repeating the process. Teasing and testing her, ramping her up. Cordelia moaned, her hips canting up into him.

He held her hips down with one hand, keeping her steady for him. "Be patient, my pretty witch," Thane grumbled against her skin before diving back in.

He teased and licked all along her vulva, running his fingers through her and dipping into her pussy, testing just how wet she was.

The more he worked her, the wetter she got—and she was already a dripping mess.

Teasing his tongue farther and farther into her, he nudged her clit with his nose, pulling the most beautiful sounds from her throat.

"C'mon, baby, be a good girl for Thane."

Cordelia was panting into Talin's mouth, his fingers still plucking and lightly pinching her nipples, working her harder and harder.

Thane could feel the evidence of that, his fingers sliding through her labia and finding her even wetter than before. "You wanna come, baby?" he drawled from between her legs.

Her eyes snapped to his as she nodded hard, desperate for release.

"Oh, baby, you really need to come, don't you?" Thane tsked, continuing to play with her pussy so achingly slowly, so gently.

"Fuck," she said, throwing her head back. "One of you better make me come before I do it for you."

Thane growled as Talin said, "Oh no, Cor. We're the only ones who will be making you come tonight. Otherwise, you won't come at all."

"Then do it," Cordelia challenged.

Thane snorted before diving in at the same time Talin resumed his assault on her nipples and neck.

She let out a squeal, her body writhing under their attention.

Thane's tongue flicked out against her clit playfully, teasingly. Small little flicks, taking her higher and higher as he pushed two fingers into her pussy, maintaining his excruciatingly slow pace.

As he pushed his fingers in, Cordelia let out a long, low groan, her hips trying to take him deeper. He pumped once, twice, before finally curling his fingers, hitting her G-spot at the same time he flicked her clit with his tongue again.

"Fuck!" she called out, losing control of herself.

"That's it, baby, just let go. Let Thane pull that orgasm from you," Talin soothed from above.

Thane was too wrapped up in Cordelia to look up, to do anything but chase her orgasm for all he was worth.

He kept pumping, kept curling his fingers and flicking her clit. He felt her getting closer and closer, her pussy squeezing his fingers so hard he thought *he* might come, just from the feeling alone.

"Thane, baby," Cordelia whined.

And he gave in to her.

Giving her one more pump and curling his fingers, he pulled her clit into his mouth and sucked. As soon as he brushed against her G-spot, Cordelia's orgasm washed over her, her pussy contracting hard against his fingers as she continued to give her slow, shallow pumps and lick her clit in small strokes.

"Such a good girl." Talin was rubbing Cordelia's tummy in small circles, helping her come down from her orgasm.

Thane gave one more suck of her clit, pulling a moan from her before he snuggled her into him, holding her tight.

They both helped her into the bathroom to clean up before Thane carried her back to bed. Cordelia started to reach for him, one hand going for his cock, but he stopped her.

"Tonight was about you, love," he said before kissing her softly.

She smiled against him as he wrapped one arm around her. Talin came in behind her, settling in close and slinging one of his own arms around her and placing a small kiss to her head, whispering into her hair, "Beautiful girl" before closing his eyes.

They all drifted off like that, wrapped up in a lavender haze.

CHAPTER FIFTY-FIVE

CORDELIA

Cordelia stepped across the threshold of Thane's front door the next morning.

They had all decided the night before that they needed to stick together, at least for the time being. With Lydia more unpredictable than ever before, and after the kidnapping, it was best that Thane, Talin, and Cordelia all be under one roof.

So, they were moving into her house. Maybe it was a big leap, but it felt right to her, to the boys too. Plus, she had the larger of their three homes. That and Merlin preferred his own territory, and Celestials knew she wasn't separating from Merlin.

Thane's home was set far back in the woods, with a small yard cleared around the building which was then surrounded by a ring of tall trees of varying species.

It was fitting, she thought, that Thane would live secluded from everyone else.

His light gray ranch home with the wraparound porch was small but felt so much like Thane. It suited him.

Stepping over the threshold, Cordelia felt like she was soaking in the very essence of Thane. His entire home smelled of him, and it settled over her like a warm blanket. She inhaled deeply, briefly fluttering her eyes closed before venturing farther into the house.

It was minimally decorated, which was to be expected of Thane. But it still felt like a home, like it was uniquely his.

Surprisingly, though, he did keep pictures up in his house. They were scattered across the walls, along with beautiful artwork. Like a mosaic of his life.

Pictures of Thane and Talin, Thane alone, Talin alone, and so much more greeted Cordelia as she walked through the house, the groaning of the worn floorboards the only sounds as she looked on in awe.

He had woven such a beautiful life, and she could see the evidence of that in the photos. His smile was something to behold, beautiful and serene. And seeing it plastered everywhere was so refreshing, so unlike the stoic man she knew. But she basked in it, knew she wanted to be the cause of that smile for the rest of her life.

"He's pretty cute when he isn't being an ass, isn't he?" Talin's voice said from behind her. She turned, saw the shit-eating grin on his face, and laughed, giving him a small, playful shove on the shoulder.

"Don't be mean, Talin," she said, but a smile was pulling at her lips, giving her away.

"He can take it," he replied as he walked off toward another room. "And besides, you know I'm right."

Cordelia shook her head, the smile lingering on her face as she continued her tour, unaware of where she was walking as she took in Thane's life captured in photos.

"Enjoying yourself?" It was Thane's voice beside her this time.

She hadn't heard his footsteps, hadn't realized she'd made her way down a hallway until now.

"Sorry, I wasn't paying attention." She blushed as she met Thane's gaze, his eyebrow cocked and lips pulled into a grin.

"Well, it just so happens you're making your way to the room I want you in the most." His voice was low as he gently guided her farther down the hallway.

She was greeted with an airy room, the windows inside opened, light curtains fluttering in the cool breeze.

It was Thane's bedroom, she realized as she scanned the space. The bed was large, fitted with dark gray blankets and a couple pillows. The single nightstand denoted the side Thane preferred to sleep, the surface only carrying a small lamp and a phone charger. A clothes hamper sat half-full in the corner of the room, next to a dresser with a few trinkets and photos on top. A large canvas hung on the wall next to the bed, the painting an abstract piece made of varying shades of gray with splashes of red. It reminded her of Thane's eyes, how they changed color with his shifts. The room was fairly bare beyond that.

"I see we don't share decorating styles." Cordelia laughed, walking farther into the room as she looked around, taking everything in.

"Not particularly." He wrapped his arms around her from behind as he leaned into her neck, breathing her in. His nose ran along her skin. The sensation was so light, so delicious, that she didn't think as her eyes fluttered closed and she opened up to him, exposing more of her neck.

Groaning, he pressed his lips against her, trailing a quick, sloppy line of kisses up and down, finding her most sensitive spots and paying extra attention to them.

"If you two aren't too busy jumping each other, can you help me carry all of this crap out to the cars?" Talin called from behind them.

Cordelia was so startled she jumped, accidentally knocking against Thane and pushing him away from her.

She cleared her throat, straightening herself. "Uh, yeah, sure." Her cheeks heated as she ducked out of the room, leaving a laughing Thane behind her.

They'd gotten most of Thane's things from his house, everything he needed and couldn't leave behind.

Cordelia had taken a walk out to the backyard, wanting to soak in this place, the peace it offered. It was incredible to see Thane's home, to see where he found comfort and solace, and to breathe it in.

She immediately knew she wanted the same of Talin's home. Luckily, they would be making a trip there too. The thought of getting to know her men so intimately and sharing their lives filled her with happiness. It grounded her, brought her so much contentment. Smiling to herself, she made her way through the house. As she wove through the kitchen and out into the living room, she scanned the walls one last time.

Thane had taken a few of his photos and art pieces with him, at Cordelia's insistence. He'd said he didn't want to disrupt her home. But she had taken great pains to remind him that it was now *their* home, all three of them. And she wanted them to contribute however they liked, make it feel as homey as possible for all of them.

She came across a photo she hadn't noticed before. Thane with his arm slung around another man. Thane was much younger in the photo, and within a few seconds of comparing the two, Cordelia could starkly see the similarities between the two men—how closely they resembled one another.

Holy shit.

That was Thane's father. And she recognized him.

Not just because Thane bore a striking resemblance to him, but because she had seen him before. In Halloway Manor.

She didn't realize she'd crashed to the floor, her knees digging in to the wood, until she heard the pounding of footsteps approaching.

"Cordelia. Cordelia, are you OK?" Thane's voice cut through the ringing in her ears, his arms wrapping around her, pulling her into him.

Talin followed closely behind, his voice now cutting through the fog in her brain.

She couldn't come back to reality, couldn't come back into focus. She was off, stuck in her memories now as dark, shadowy flashes came back to her.

"Cordelia, baby, what's wrong? Talk to me," Thane pleaded as Talin's hands roamed her body.

She was vaguely aware of them checking her over to make sure she wasn't hurt, wasn't injured somehow.

Talin took her face in his hands, turning her toward him. Finally, she came back to the present moment, the dark memories scattering for now.

"Cordelia, darling, what's wrong?" Talin's eyes were filled with worry, anxiety. She hated it, she thought. Seeing her sunshine boy filled with sadness, with anything that would trouble him.

She swallowed past the lump in her throat, trying to find the words.

She looked over at Thane, back to Talin, not sure where to start.

"I-I saw the picture of Thane and his father." Her voice croaked out of her, pulling the tension in the small space even tighter.

"What do you mean? What's wrong, Cordelia?" Thane pulled her attention back to him.

"Thane, I recognize your dad," she started, unsure how to say this. "I've seen him before."

Thane's eyebrows furrowed, a puzzled look taking over his face. She could practically see the thoughts swirling in his mind as he tried to piece it together.

"I saw him at Halloway Manor, when I was younger. When I was still trapped there as a girl," she continued. "I-I saw my mother performing spells on him, Thane."

His eyes widened, but he was speechless.

"What do you mean performing spells? What happened?" Talin asked next to her. Cordelia turned, meeting his warm, golden eyes.

"I don't know what spells they were, but I know I saw him there."

"*Fuck*," Thane breathed out.

CHAPTER FIFTY-SIX

CORDELIA

She couldn't register the soft brush of the grass and clovers against her bare skin. Couldn't smell the chilled night breeze or the damp earth around her. All she could do was count the stars above her, trying desperately to seek the comfort of the moon as she sorted through everything in her head.

Her mind was chaos, uncontrollable and quickly derailing as more and more words, feelings, images flooded her. And she gave in to it slowly, let the storm take over and grip her body. Slowly, she drifted away, back into that old, distant memory.

She'd never get the image of that altar out of her head. The altar from the one night that she'd known she should have stayed in her room. But she couldn't, not after she'd heard the screams of terror downstairs. After she'd heard endless rattling and the sharp, splintering crash of wood on the old, scuffed floorboards.

She'd hidden in the shadows, those shadows that seemed to reach out to her with cold, villainous hands. What she'd seen that night was burned in her mind. The blood dripping off that dagger Lydia held, her back to Cordelia as she faced a panting shifter, lying curled on the floor in front of her. The candles lining the salt circle, some knocked over and snuffed out, others standing and stoic.

She would never forget the flicker of those candles against the harsh lines of the scene in front of her. Never forget the pleading and cries she heard her mother wring from that shifter. Never forget the face of the shifter that lay before her mother. She'd darted back to her room, then. Unable to stand the sight in front of her. Unwilling to be a silent participant in whatever scene she'd witnessed.

What Lydia still didn't know all these years later was that her own daughter had witnessed enough of what'd happened to piece together the full story. Or at least enough to know the gravity of what had happened in that sitting room that night. Just another collection of dark secrets for the groaning walls of the cold manor to house. To hold on to forever.

Or at least, what Lydia thought would be forever.

They had gone back home after that, putting off getting Talin's things until tomorrow. They needed to process the shock, try to piece things together.

Like, why would Nolen Lycus be at Halloway Manor, seeking Lydia Halloway's services?

CHAPTER FIFTY-SEVEN

THANE

Thane stood at the back door of Cordelia's house, watching as she lay in her garden, staring up at the dark, endless night above them, the light leeched from the sky in the presence of the new moon.

He was so numb, so lost. Everything was coming to a head, and he didn't know what to do with himself. How to help his father.

Cordelia had recounted to Thane and Talin what she remembered. How she recognized Nolen Lycus. It still made Thane's stomach turn, to think of what Lydia Halloway had done to his father. How she'd tricked him. Almost killed him.

Nolen had gone to Lydia. Thane wasn't sure what exactly he'd wanted, but he could pretty well guess it had something to do with the wolven kidnappings. Cordelia had been an accidental witness to the ordeal. She'd been sneaking through the manor and heard the screams. Upon investigation, she'd seen a man lying on the floor of the sitting room.

Of course, Cordelia hadn't realized who it was at the time, but she knew that she'd seen a man begging for his life, bleeding out on that floor. And she'd run.

Thane felt deep, endless fury at the thought of everything Cordelia had been subjected to in that manor, the things she'd been forced to do, the things she'd seen.

And when Cordelia had seen that picture of Thane and his father, she'd recognized him, put the pieces together, and told Thane.

Now, at least, Thane knew that he was right in his hunch about Lydia. That she was involved with the wolven somehow. He may not have details or specifics, but he knew it couldn't be a coincidence that she'd tried to murder his father, a very prominent alpha in the Harmonious wolven who had almost certainly come to her desperately seeking some sort of help for the terror being wrought upon his pack.

He could have never known that Lydia Halloway had already chosen a side. Had already decided who she would help. And led an unwitting alpha wolf into her home, into her practice. She'd seduced him with promises of help, of being able to rid him of what he thought was a string of random attacks. He could have never known of her ulterior plans, of her motive to assassinate the alpha wolf of Lycus pack.

Thane blew out a breath, leaning back against the house.

He wanted to comfort Cordelia, to offer her some sort of reprieve from the memories flooding her. The memories of Halloway Manor and her mother. He knew she felt some amount of guilt over the entire situation, though he'd done his best to reassure her that there was nothing she could have done. Not when she herself was a prisoner and victim of Lydia Halloway.

He would find a way to avenge both his father and his fated. He wouldn't let anything stop him.

Lydia Halloway may not know who Thane was, may not know that he'd figured out who she was and what she'd done. But she would, in time. And she would come to regret everything. Every action against Cordelia, every second she spent celebrating his father's agony.

She would come to regret the very air she breathed if it was the last thing he did.

EPILOGUE

LYDIA

"She's stronger than I realized," Lydia mumbled to herself as she paced back and forth across the old, creaking floors of Halloway Manor.

Ungrateful, that's what her daughter was. Cordelia never did have the drive Lydia had so desperately hoped to see in her. But that drive could be taught — or incentivized, if need be. But since Cordelia was as hell-bent as ever on defying Lydia's orders, she would need to put a new plan together.

"M-madam? Is there anything I can get for you?" Jane, her assistant, squeaked from the corner of the room.

She couldn't fault the girl, Lydia had been in a blind rage since the incident with Cordelia. She had let her magic fly, taking hold of her emotions and amplifying them. Throwing potion bottles, tomes, and crystals around the manor, using any surface she pleased as target practice for her dagger collection, snapping at anyone who dared cross her path. And if Cordelia were still under this roof, Lydia would have taught her a lesson, ordering her to clean the mess with her enchantment magic, inch by painstaking inch.

"Get the illusionist here as soon as possible. I need them *now*," Lydia barked.

She was grateful for the witch, their illusionist magic incredibly useful for her plans. She had found them upon some recent digging into illusionist magic, discovering just how powerful and clever they were. Lydia had burnt through so many illusionist witches over the last few years, none of them quite up for the task. Once she had this particular one in her employ, though, it didn't take long to discover a way to get Cordelia to the manor quickly and quietly. It just took a little convincing of the wolven to get them to trust the magic, to allow the illusionist to imbue them.

Lydia didn't particularly enjoy working with the wolven, wild and ill-mannered as they were, but she had determined it to be a necessary evil, one that had proven very useful.

Of course, capturing Cordelia was coordinated, but truly it was just a means to get her attention. The true work would have come after, had Cordelia not squirmed her way out of Lydia's grasp.

She resumed her pacing, her hands tightening into fists as she mentally sorted through everything that had happened, trying to find all the cracks so she could never replicate those mistakes.

She hadn't been expecting the display of power Cordelia had shown. She had always known her daughter was strong, yes. It was Lydia's entire intent behind having Cordelia in the first place. But she didn't realize just how much that power of Cordelia's had grown. Which was turning out to be both exactly what she wanted, and a Goddess-damned pain for her to get under control.

She hadn't been particularly fond of Cordelia's father, but had happily matched with him in order to create an heir that would be powerful and cunning enough to take over the Halloway coven. Of course, that was the duty of all Halloway women. To preside over the coven and bless their lineage with even more powerful witches, in turn.

Belmont Halloway had been bland and weak in personality, but powerful and skilled in magic — and the latter is exactly why Lydia wanted him. She wanted his potent enchantment magic woven into her bloodline. And as soon as Cordelia took her first breath, Lydia could feel the strength of the power within her. Could feel how deeply it was threaded through her very blood and bones. As if the Goddess Hecate herself was smiling down upon her heir.

Pleased with herself, she had begun making plans for Cordelia's life. Had grand ideas and aspirations for the Halloways with the help of that enchantment magic. Of course, that meant that she no longer had need for Belmont, dead weight as he was. He was just too soft, had too many wistful dreams in that silly little head of his.

Cordelia, she knew, would have no need for a sire that spent too much time with his head in the clouds. Dreams had no place in Halloway Manor, and Cordelia would need to focus on the path Lydia had carefully constructed for her. Would need to focus on learning the Halloway grimoire, honing her power, and becoming a strong enchantress.

The grimoire. Lydia snapped her head up before taking long, hurried strides to the sitting room on the left side of the manor, their receiving room for clients, and where they performed services. As Lydia passed through the doorway, candles and sconces blazed to life all around the perimeter of the room, greeting her and illuminating a pathway.

After pulling a large, heavy leather tome from the shelf above her main altar, Lydia fell to the floor, the book landing with a loud *thud* as she began flipping pages. As soon as she felt a crackle of magic at her fingertips, she halted — landing on a page for a spell she'd long forgotten.

A wave of seemingly endless ideas crashed into Lydia all at once — all the possibilities for how she could correct course, how she could rein in Cordelia. She knew her daughter would be defiant the whole way, especially after that show of power.

But nothing would hold Lydia back now, not her daughter, not the Hecatean Guild, and certainly not the wolven breathing down her neck. Nothing came before her own needs and wants before, and that wouldn't change now.

It was time she reminded everyone just who she was, just how powerful she was. And if a few heads needed to roll to make that happen, it was a price she was more than happy to pay. Lydia could feel a surge of magic rising within her chest, her heart singing a song of sweet promise, of power yet to be grasped — all soon to be hers.

"You called for me, Madam?" A purring, velvet-like voice called from behind Lydia.

She stood, holding open the old, worn grimoire as she slowly turned, straightening her spine as she felt a wave of excited relief flood her veins. It was all clicking into place in her mind, like locks tumbling open, a pathway flowing like a bright, glittering stream before her. A wicked grin curled across her lips as she took in the white-haired witch before her.

"I have a new plan, Illusionist."

ACKNOWLEDGMENTS

Thank you so much for taking the time to read my debut novel *Lavender Smoke*. This story is so close to my heart and has been a way for me to explore myself, my past trauma, my peace, and my own freedom. Just as Cordelia did the same.

In a lot of ways, Cordelia is a reflection of myself, and being able to write from my own perspective of discovering myself by exploring my mind, my experiences, and my sexuality has been so freeing. It's helped me find a happiness that I never dreamed I would be able to see. And for that, I am forever grateful. I hope that even one person is able to see themselves in Cordelia—or Thane, Talin, Sage, or Lilith—even if in a very small way. And if you do find yourself connecting with any of my characters, know that they would be so honored.

It's funny to look back and see where I started with this story. It came to me in a dream—actually, one specific scene came to me in a dream. That scene ended up changed in so many ways, it didn't even make it into the book! But my very first vision of this story was of Cordelia, Talin, and Thane, and I remember waking up and immediately thinking, "I have to write this." Those three stuck with me and wouldn't leave my memory—instead, they continued to grow, colorize, and flourish in my imagination until I finally immortalized them in writing.

I want to thank so many people who helped me onto the path I find myself on today—without you sweet souls, I wouldn't have a voice, and I wouldn't have a story that rests in my heart and carries my soul. Courtney, you are the one who told me to do the damn thing! You were the very first person who told me to write the book, and you helped me shape and mold my characters and stories into living, breathing entities. Chey—thank you for being the first person to happily read any amount of my book. Your words and encouragement helped me through some of the roughest days of drafting. Marissa and Bex—you have stuck by me and been amazing sources of undying support since the beginning—thank you both and know that you have my gratitude and love. Aspen, you've been with me on this entire journey, and I cannot believe we wrote our debut novels side-by-side! Don't think I've forgotten our promise—we will be having those celebratory drinks together one day! To Amanda and Heather—your undying support throughout the entire writing process is something I hold so close to my heart and treasure endlessly.

To my alpha and beta readers, thank you for all your hard work and the feedback you gave me. My alpha readers, especially, went through a long, arduous journey, getting this manuscript little by little until it was finally completed, and your patience is so valued.

To my incredible, wonderful, genius, astounding editor Anna, thank you from the bottom of my heart. You took a chance on editing my *Lavender Smoke* and have been the most amazing editor and guide through this journey. You helped me see the vision of *Lavender Smoke* at its most basic form and then helped me elevate it to the breathtaking work that is today.

Tay, my dear, sweet, incredible friend, I couldn't have done so much of this without you. You were my rock, my sounding board, the one who kept me sane, and the one who kept me from breaking down so many times. Thank you for your undying, beautiful, easy friendship, and thank you for the special privilege of helping me build Sage and Cordelia's relationship in a way that's so near and dear to both of us.

Let's celebrate with some *Howl's Moving Castle*, Chinese food, and silent couch time together.

Finally, to my kind, reassuring, incredibly supportive partner, Michael. You are my whole heart, my guidepost, and my most treasured being in this world. I couldn't have made it this whole way without you, my love. From helping me talk through world building, watching and encouraging me and my characters, and reading my masturbation scenes for Thane and Talin for believability. I am lucky to have you by my side in this world and this life. Know that my love for you is eternal and unrelenting.

I hope to continue writing and exploring my dreams and imagination for many years to come, and I hope some of you will stick with me along the way. I have so much more in store for the Celestial Bonds universe, and so many more stories to tell.

ABOUT THE AUTHOR

Kayla Darkwood is a goblin masquerading as a human who resides in a hobbit hole somewhere in the Midwest, hunting for rocks and acorns, spotting birds and small creatures of the mud, and escaping into the woods and fictional worlds at every second possible. She lives with her partner, a glittering collection of trinkets, an ever-growing hoard of books, and surrounds herself with the mystical, the magical, and the love of her friends.

You can usually find her on a cold, dreary night staring at the moon and stars or online posting the non-sensical, messy, semi-poetic thoughts that cloud her brain. She loves her crunchy granola music, chaotic cooking, Studio Ghibli movies, and repeatedly watching Over the Garden Wall while constantly quoting and crying.

www.ingramcontent.com/pod-product-compliance
Lightning Source LLC
Chambersburg PA
CBHW030639260626
47157CB00007B/2394